Isle of HOPE

JULIE LESSMAN

D1526332

Published by Julie Lessman, LLC
Copyright © 2015 by Julie Lessman
Cover by The Killion Group
ASIN: B0163HTXLU

DEDICATION

To the late Dr. Roland Winterer—
The man God used to teach me that love—like hope—
never fails.
Daddy, I miss you …

Dear Alli —

May the God of Hope
fill you with peace
and joy all the
days of your life.
— Rom 15:13

Love you, Sweetie!

Julie

ACCLAIM FOR ISLE OF HOPE

"In *Isle of Hope* Lessman tells a poignant tale of first loves reunited and families reconciled. Both emotionally captivating and spiritually challenging, this sweet southern love story deals with issues of forgiveness and restoration. Fans of Lessman will be absolutely delighted with this riveting tale!" **—Denise Hunter, bestselling author of *Falling Like Snowflakes***

"In *Isle of Hope*, award-winning author Julie Lessman weaves a story of how past choices collide with future consequences. Lessman's novel has it all: lush details, dynamic characters, and a storyline that keeps you turning the pages. The characters Lessman created in *Isle of Hope* confront their (in)ability to forgive – and as you fall in love with these characters, be prepared to question your beliefs about forgiveness." **—Beth K. Vogt, author of *Crazy Little Thing Called Love*, and a 2015 RITA® Finalist and a 2015 and 2014 Carol Award finalist**

"Fans of Julie Lessman's historical romances will love this modern day love story! *Isle of Hope* is a heartwarming and inspirational novel about forgiveness sought and restoration found. I'm enamored with the large and wonderful O'Bryen family and I thoroughly enjoyed the romances Julie skillfully crafted for both Jack O'Bryen and his mom Tess. A delight!" **—Becky Wade, award-winning author of *My Stubborn Heart* and The Porter Family series including *A Love Like Ours***

ACCLAIM FOR JULIE LESSMAN

"Truly masterful plot twists ..." —*Romantic Times Book Reviews*

"Readers who like heartwarming novels, such as those written by Debbie Macomber, are sure to enjoy this book." —*Booklist Online*

"Julie is one of the best there is today at writing intensely passionate romance novels. Her ability to thread romance and longing, deception and forgiveness, and lots of humor are unparalleled by anyone else in the Christian market today." —**Rachel McRae of LifeWay Stores**

"Julie Lessman's prose and character development is masterful." —*Church Libraries Magazine*

AUTHOR ACCLAIM FOR JULIE LESSMAN
(authors listed alphabetically)

"With memorable characters and an effervescent plot that's as buoyant as it is entertaining, *Dare to Love Again* is Julie Lessman at her zestful best." —**Tamera Alexander, bestselling author of *A Lasting Impression* and *To Whisper Her Name***

"In a powerful and skillfully written novel, Lessman exposes raw human emotions, proving once again that it's through our greatest pain that God can lead us to our true heart, revealed and restored. Thoroughly enthralling!" —**Maggie Brendan, author of the Heart of the West and The Blue Willow Brides series**

ISLE OF HOPE SERIES CHARACTERS

The Carmichael Family:

Lacey Carmichael: Heroine who returns to Isle of Hope after eight-year absence.

Dr. Ben Carmichael: Lacey's father, estranged from his daughter.

Karen Carmichael: Lacey's deceased mother.

Mamaw Phillips: Lacey's grandmother and Karen's mother.

Nicki Phillips: Lacey's cousin who lives with Mamaw and is engaged to Matt Ball, the hero's cousin.

Spencer Phillips: Lacey's cousin and Nicki's little brother.

Cameron Phillips: Lacey's uncle and Nicki's dad on naval commission in the Mediterranean.

The O'Bryen Family:

Jack O'Bryen: Hero who was once engaged to Lacey before she deserted him eight years prior.

Tess O'Bryen: Jack's mother.

Adam O'Bryen: Jack's pastor father.

Catherine (Cat) O'Bryen: Jack's sister and Lacey's former best friend.

Shannon O'Bryen: Jack's sister and Catherine's twin.

Davey O'Bryen: Jack's little brother.

Matt Ball: Jack's cousin and best friend, engaged to Nicki, Lacey's cousin.

Friends:

Mrs. Myra Penelope Lee: Owner/benefactor of Camp Hope for ill and handicapped orphans.

Mr. Will Hogan: Seasoned cowboy and all-around coach/handyman at Camp Hope.

Deborah (Debbie) Lynne Holbrook: Eight-year-old orphan at Camp Hope with health issues.

Kelly Goshorn and Sarah Baker: Nicki's friends and bridesmaids.

Nate and Justin: Matt's friends and groomsmen.

Jasmine Augustine: A nurse Jack is dating at Memorial Health.

Samuel Cunningham: Jack's friend and coworker, a pediatrician at Memorial Health.

Many are the woes of the wicked,
but the Lord's unfailing love surrounds the one
who trusts in Him.
—Psalm 32:10

CHAPTER ONE
Isle of Hope, Georgia, Early Summer

*W*hen it comes to burning bridges, I am the Queen of Kerosene.

Puffing out a wispy sigh, Lacey Carmichael squinted into the rearview mirror to make sure the coast was clear, then dragged her bulging purse onto the seat with an unladylike grunt. The action caused her dusty blue Honda to swerve on Skidaway Road—along with her stomach.

Oh, crud! She straightened the wheel with a jerk, body rattling more than her 2008 Honda after a cross-country trip. Her gaze flicked to the mirror, and relief coursed like high tide. The road behind revealed nothing but palms and Georgia pines, silent sentinels ushering her home.

Home. Where full moons rose over the marsh and the scent of wisteria embraced summer nights. Where the lazy lull of river grasses swayed in the breeze, soothing a sleepy coastal community that burrowed into one's memory like a long-lost friend. A haven where tidy cottages nestled next to lush antebellum homes, evoking a postcard setting that harkened back to a simpler time.

A simpler time?

Lacey sucked in a deep draw of the rich and humid low-country air that was pungent with the salty smell of the marsh, and instantly zipped back eight years to a time that had been anything but simple. Memories of an eighteen-year-old wild child constricted her throat. A rebel daughter who'd bolted from the hometown that had been anything but a home. Her shoulders slumped as she passed the Piggly Wiggly.

What am I doing here?

She cut loose another gust of ragged air while her eyes focused straight ahead. *Returning to the scene of the crime. The charred debris of all the mistakes that I've made.* One hand welded to the steering wheel, she rifled through her studded leather purse with the other, fingers fumbling on a tube of lip-gloss. With amazing dexterity, she untwirled the screw-on cap and applied "Ooh La La," then puckered her lips. Now if she could only gloss over her past as easily ...

The BP loomed ahead and she slapped on her blinker, veering in to park at the closest empty pump. Her car squealed to a stop at the exact moment the contents of her purse careened to the floor. *Lacey, you lead foot—when are you going to learn?* Mumbling under her breath, she turned the car off and leaned to pick up the spilled items. A woman's high-pitched laughter suddenly riddled the air, desecrating the sacred strains of Justin Timberlake from a radio nearby.

"Jack, you bad boy," a woman's sultry voice said, drifting from the other side of the pump, "what am I going to do with you?"

"Well, I know a few things that come to mind."

Lacey shot up. Her head slammed against the glove compartment. She blinked through a haze of stars at the car on the other side of the pump, too dazed to feel the pain.

That voice. The same voice that had once uttered a proposal of marriage and swore to love her forever. Goose bumps popped as her breathing shallowed. A second onslaught of female laughter grated in her ears, and when she inched up to peer out the window of her Honda, her stomach immediately took a dive.

Whenever she allowed herself to think of Jack O'Bryen—which wasn't often—she convinced herself that memories made people and things far better than they'd actually been.

Yeah, right. Hands propped to the driver's door of a brand-new cherry-red BMW Z4, Jack O'Bryen appeared every bit the hottie he'd been when they'd first started dating over ten years ago. Only now he was taller, his previously lanky frame more filled out, and his physique tighter. Once shaggy chestnut hair, a byproduct of college days, was now trimmed neat and clean at the nape of his neck. He casually scratched the back of his head with a bulge of a bicep that made her mouth go dry, then slacked a narrow hip to the door. "The nozzle leaked, so I'm going in to wash my hands—need anything?" he asked the blonde.

Lacey moaned inwardly. *Yeah. Distance—lots and lots of distance.* She'd expected to run into Jack eventually, but now? Her first two minutes in town? She fought the urge to roll her eyes. *Really?* Heaven knows she wasn't ready. Not even after eight years. She caught a glimpse of his tight, faded jeans and swallowed hard.

God help me, will I ever be?

The blonde shook her head, letting fly with another nauseating giggle that was sheer blasphemy against the strains of *Never Again,* a song that fit perfectly with the theme of Lacey's homecoming.

Never again would she turn her back on the people she loved.

Never again would she seek her will over God's.

Never again would she give her all to Jack O'Bryen.

The man in question disappeared into the station, and Lacey dove for her keys. She cranked the ignition and groaned. The gas needle lay prostrate; so far beyond "E" it was on "F" for fumes. She shot a glance at the Barbie Doll applying hot-pink shimmer to Angelina Jolie lips and then at the station where Jack was nowhere to be seen, and decided to chance it. If memory served, the ladies' room was on the opposite side of the building from the men's—the perfect place to hide.

She could do this.

Jerking the handle, she flung the door wide and slammed it too hard, obviously distracting the blonde from her makeover as she looked up. Lacey offered a nervous smile and made a beeline for the station door, purse clutched to her chest while her gaze darted across the store. Ignoring the curious looks of bystanders, she sprinted to the ladies' room, rib cage heaving as she gripped the knob and turned. *Thank you, Lord, home free!*

"Lacey? Lacey Carmichael?"

Her eyelids sank closed as her stomach contracted, hand now grafted to the door. Warding off a wave of dizziness, she willed herself to turn around, but her smile felt as cardboard as the Timberwolf Chewing Tobacco display over Jack's shoulder.

"Hello, Jack." Her voice was little more than a squeak as she peered up at "Bridge #1," the man whose heart she'd stomped on eight years prior without ever looking back.

He stared in apparent shock, mouth gaping and blue eyes just as wide, a perfect match for a well-muscled pale-blue polo. For a brief moment, his jaw seemed unhinged before he snapped it closed with a nervous bob of his throat. His mouth tamped into a tight smile. "What are you doing here? I mean, I knew you were coming back for the wedding, but that's over two months away."

Ah, yes, her cousin's wedding. Her excuse, God's mandate.

She cleared her throat so she could breathe and attempted a casual stance, cautiously butting against the restroom door. Her purse remained affixed to her bright pink halter top she was pretty sure matched her cheeks. "Well, you know my cousin, Nicki—a little scattered when it comes to details, and with Uncle Cam on naval commission in the Mediterranean, she asked me to come early to help out. And I'm off for the summer, so …" She gulped and forced a megawatt smile. "Here I am!"

He blinked. "Sorry about your mom," he said stiffly, "I heard she passed away a few years back."

Her gaze dropped to the grimy linoleum while she fought the sharp sting of tears that always threatened when she thought of her mother. It had been over six years since depression had stolen her life, but even now, mere mention of her still slashed anew. "Thanks, Jack," she whispered, praying he didn't know her mother committed suicide. They'd kept it quiet, and heaven knows her father would have never let the awful secret out, but small towns had big ears. "It was a difficult time for all of us."

He gave a sympathetic nod before his smile seemed to set like concrete along with his hard-angled jaw, which sported a shadow of dark bristle. "I hear you're a teacher." His words were clipped, matter-of-fact … *cool.* "In San Diego."

Her cheeks warmed, no doubt bypassing "pretty pink" altogether to go straight to "mortified magenta." "Yes, I was … I m-mean I *am* a t-teacher," she stuttered, "but not in San Diego anymore." She fortified for her next statement with a deep draw of air, gripping her purse so tightly she was certain she'd have studs embedded in her chest. "I ... took a job in Savannah ... for the fall."

Silence. A nerve quivered in his cheek as his gaze skimmed from the top of her disheveled blonde ponytail to her lacy pink halter and jean short-shorts that suddenly felt *way* too tight. Without missing a beat, he raked down tan legs to her baby-pink polished toenails, looping her stomach when he scanned back up to settle on her face, the blue eyes thinning considerably. His smile was as flat as his tone. "Really. Alone? Or with your significant other?"

She detected the barest grinding of his teeth, a habit that swooped her back years to countless arguments in his car when she'd tease and tempt, the school flirt dating the pastor's son. His piercing stare unnerved her, unleashing a barrage of babble that always bubbled from her lips whenever she was nervous. "No, alone." She sucked in a deep breath and forged on, anxious to slip past the subject of her wedding debacle. "So I decided to come back here to live ... well, not *here* here ... on Isle of Hope, that is ... uh ... I mean I will this summer, of course, because I'll be staying with Nicki." She swept her bangs out of her eyes with a shaky hand before her fingers slid down to fiddle with renegade strands of hair trailing her bare shoulders. "But come fall, I hope to have an apartment in Savannah or maybe even Wilmington Island because I have a friend who moved there from San Diego, family you know, and she lov—"

"Does your dad know you're home?"

She froze mid-sentence, mouth open and body stiff like when she used to play swinging statues with Jack's sisters on their front lawn, rigid and scared to make a move.

Like now, at mere mention of "Bridge #2."

He shifted, cocking a hip. "He doesn't, does he?"

Lacey felt another blush rise and tossed her ponytail in the air. "Not yet, but to be honest, Daddy's one of the reasons I'm here." She continued coiling the loose strands of hair around her finger, her tone softening as her eyes begged forgiveness. "I hope to make amends," she said quietly, the barest hint of a plea in her words, "to those I hurt in the past."

His lip curled. "Well that should keep you busy." He folded his arms, the motion straining thick muscles against the knit cotton of his sleeves. "Just with my family alone."

"Jack, please …" Her whisper was almost an ache, the memory of Jack's twin sisters—Bridges #3 and 4—twisting her gut. Best friends who'd once been like blood. A quiver of air seeped through her lips, depleting her to the point of exhaustion.

His gaze flicked to her left hand and back. "Not married yet? Or is San Diego littered with broken hearts too?"

Heat blasted her cheeks, and she knew full well she owed him any scorn he chose to lob her way. "Actually, only one—mine." She hiked her chin, ready to take any punishment he sought to mete out. "You'll be happy to know I was soundly dumped by my fiancé, two months prior to the wedding, and good news! It was a double whammy—broken heart, broken bank account."

For the briefest moment, sympathy flickered in those blue eyes as the tight lines eased around his mouth, but Lacey wasn't here for sympathy—she was here to heal and be healed. "So," she said in a rush, anxious to move past the awkwardness of this first encounter. "Nicki tells me you're a big-shot doctor now, working with kids at Memorial." The tension in her face softened along with her eyes. "A pediatrician—very impressive. You always were a sucker for kids."

She spied the barest relaxation of his facial muscles, hinting at a possible smile he probably wouldn't let through. "Yeah, I started in a peds practice at Memorial last week." He threaded a hand through short dark hair streaked with summer sun. "After thirteen years devoted to higher education, it feels good to finally devote myself to kids." One of his dimples winked as he slipped his hands into the back pockets of his jeans, nodding toward the cherry-red Z out the window. "Along with having a little fun for a change, like indulging in a new toy."

Lacey managed a grin. "Very nice, Dr. O'Bryen— fulfillment of a long-held dream, I believe, given all the times you lusted after Todd Raber's cherry Z. Residency must pay well."

He cuffed the back of his neck, a tinge of pink creeping into his summer tan. "Not really. But Mom insisted I live at home till I started in a practice, so other than the token rent I forced her to take and school loans, my residency paychecks mostly went into savings." He gave a small shrug. "So I decided to spend some."

"Well, it's about time, Jack O'Bryen—you've always been way too serious and focused." She glanced out the window where the blonde was buffing her nails while shooting laser looks their way. "And speaking of 'serious,' I think *your* significant other may be getting tired of waiting."

He glanced over his shoulder and grinned, the sound of his husky chuckle bringing back a rush of memories. "Yeah, Jasmine's not the patient type, that's for sure." He turned back, a gleam of trouble in his eyes so foreign to the studious boy she used to know. "Everybody keeps telling me I'm the perfect age and place to settle down, but I'm not buying it." He flashed perfectly white teeth, his manner suddenly bold and edged with a wild streak that hadn't been there before. "Having way too much fun."

She fidgeted with the studs on the front of her purse, uneasy with this new Jack, a man-about-town who seemed light years away from the sweet, intense seminary student with whom she'd fallen in love. Brushing the hair from her eyes, her hand was as shaky as her smile. "Well, it's been great seeing you, Jack. I'm sure our paths'll cross again since we're both in the wedding." With an awkward wave, she turned to manhandle the knob, struggling to open a door that refused to budge.

He reached around and turned it for her, giving it a light shove. It wheeled open as slick as the oil in the pumps. "I'm sure you will," he said quietly, the warmth of his breath against her neck causing her skin to tingle. "If you're home to build bridges, I assume that includes Mom and the twins?"

She peeked over her shoulder. "It does," she whispered, feeling as awkward as if this were the end of a first date. She paused. "How is your mom, by the way—and your sisters?" She rested her hand on the knob to keep her fingers from trembling. "I keep tabs on them through Nick, of course, but I know she hasn't been in touch with your sisters since …" Her words trailed off, not wanting to put voice to the awful tragedy that had befallen them all.

He cleared his throat, hands back in his pockets. "She's good. Praying up a storm, as always. Still hounding me to go to church, which I do for her, but I'm not into that stuff anymore."

Lacey blinked. *Oh, Jack, no* … "B-but that used to be your thing," she whispered.

He studied her through a shuttered gaze. "It used to be my dad's thing, too, remember?"

"Excuse me, please." They both jolted at the presence of an elderly woman who took them by surprise.

"Oh, pardon me," Lacey said as she held the door open for the lady to enter.

"Thank you, young lady." The woman toddled past, and Lacey exhaled slowly when the door closed behind her, her gaze flitting back to Jack. "Well, unless I plan on taking a summer job as BP doorman, I think I better scoot. Take care, Jack, and please tell your mom and sisters I'll be in touch."

The blue eyes all but burned into hers as he nodded, a shadow of a smile grazing his lips. "Will do." Turning, he made his way to the door where the blonde with the perfect nails waited with a pout.

Lacey entered the restroom, numb while the door thudded hard behind her. Eyelids sinking closed, she sagged against the worn and peeling wood while she sucked in a sharp breath, fingers kneading the seeds of a headache in her temple.

"Dearie, are you all right? You look as if you're about to be sick."

Lacey's eyes popped open. She managed a smile at the sweet, gray-haired lady who was blow-drying her hands. "I'm fine, thank you," she said, ducking into the nearest stall. She slid the bolt closed and collapsed against the door, palms flat to the dirty beige steel while her eyes stared straight ahead. She swallowed hard.

Or will be in about two months.

CHAPTER TWO

*S*o *help me, I'm gonna throttle you, Matt!*
Gunning down his driveway to the backyard,
Jack squealed the Z4 to a stop inches away
from his mother's free-standing garage, ready to take
on his cousin and best friend—the same friend who'd
apparently forgotten to mention his fianceé's maid of
honor was back in town. He jerked the emergency
break handle so hard it made a grinding nose that
rivaled the obnoxious squawk of a blue heron nesting in
his mother's massive oak.

Go-go-gos ... frawnk!

"Oh, put a fish in it," Jack hollered, glaring at his
mother's unofficial "pet" who acted like he had more
claim to their backyard than Jack, which galled him
every single time he came home. He slammed the car
door hard, drawing a tinge of satisfaction when the bird
snapped into alert posture with a raise of his head and
wing span flaring wide. Swooping an acorn from the
ground, Jack aimed it just beyond the indignant fowl,
his mood so sour, he was tempted to hit it dead-on.

"Awwwwwwk!" The warning cry rose in volume for
a full two seconds, alerting everybody in the freakin'
neighborhood that the stupid bird was ticked.

"Jackson Alexander O'Bryen! If you continue to
torment Blue, so help me, you'll be sleeping in that tree
and he'll be in your room." His mother's voice carried

from the double kitchen window, and Jack leered at the bird who stood in defiance, staunch and smug in his two-foot-wide nest of pine needles, reeds, and twigs.

"Squealer," Jack muttered, backtracking down the driveway to fetch the trashcans, the faint smell of sun-ripened garbage lingering in the air like his mood— heated and foul.

Sweet Cynthia Marcano sailed past on her bicycle, and he forced a smile and waved, grateful she didn't stop to chat, something he normally enjoyed and even welcomed. Outside of his family and friends, kids were one of the few things that brought joy to his life. As far back as when he was an Eagle Scout working with special-needs children during the summers, he'd known he'd wanted a career devoted to kids. Honest and open and brimming with wonder, they were little people not yet fully tainted by the world, who seemed as drawn to him as he was to them. Which made his career choice a no-brainer and his and Matt's volunteer work at the Big Brother organization as natural as breathing. Whether it was family functions or rounds at Memorial, Jack could always be found smack dab in the middle of a group of munchkins, pulling quarters out of their ears or playing catch and basketball with Nerf balls. He'd even taken to carrying snacks and little toys in his pockets, earning him the nickname Dr. Seuss throughout residency. Blame it on the fact he was big brother to three siblings or defender of underdogs on the school playground. Whatever the reason, Jack preferred a rowdy game of basketball with kids than a poker game with the guys. Undeniable proof, Matt claimed, that Jack had never grown up.

And maybe not. All he knew was he sure got a kick out of lighting up their faces with Donald Duck voices and yogurt-covered raisins or even gummy bears when the pediatric nurses weren't looking. Shy or loud, short or tall, it didn't matter—kids always seemed to bubble with giggles and fun and an innocence he found hard to resist.

Kind of like Lacey before Nicki ruined her. His sour mood instantly returned with a vengeance, complete with the smell of garbage. Sucking in a deep breath of polluted air, he hefted the cans with a little too much force and stalked down the driveway, all but slamming them against the wall inside the garage. Throat constricting, he bowed his head and braced a hand to the jamb, eyes shuttering closed as memories surfaced of the last night he'd seen the girl that he loved.

"Come on, Jack, I dare you."

She'd shot up out of the river like a tow-headed sea nymph, water sluicing down gentle curves of her T-shirt that tempted way more than they should. Her chuckle had been husky and low as she paddled in place off his dock, the sultry sound floating toward him like the mist on the water—hazing his mind, clouding his will. "This is our last night before you leave for that stuffy seminary," she'd said with a toss of her head, "so let's make a memory to keep us warm while you're gone." With a scrunch of her nose, she'd wiggled in the water and shot him a pixie grin that came off devil may care.

Devil may care. Jack grunted. That certainly nailed it to the wall. The edge of his mouth jagged up. *With a freakin' nail gun.* He cocked a hip and sighed, tunneling fingers through his hair as the memory lapped against his mind like the warm, salty waters of the Skidaway River. Against his will, he shook his head, fighting the seed of a smile. Lacey Anne Carmichael had to be the biggest little brat on the Isle of Hope and absolutely everything Jack had ever wanted. Intelligent, warm, and brimming with life and fun and adventure, the perfect complement to his serious and sensible self. Half tomboy, half vamp, she was an adorable little girl in a woman's body whose heart had always beat in time

with his own. A best friend as deep as the rolling river
who sparkled and shined on the surface with a sense of
humor that made him laugh.

Until the summer that everything changed. The
summer of her senior year after her cousin Nicki moved
from California to Isle of Hope, tainting the girl to
whom he was promised. He'd arrived home from
college, and suddenly Lacey was different—wilder,
crazier, as if hungry for a lifestyle forbidden by a strict
father with whom she'd never seen eye-to-eye. From
honor-roll choirgirl to temptress in the blink of a
semester. Sure, Jack knew she'd always had a streak of
the rebel—she'd been his next-door neighbor and
sisters' best friend forever, after all. But he just
assumed graduation and turning eighteen would soften
the edges. Help her settle down and become what he
always hoped she would be—a pastor's wife.

His.

The heron started squawking again, and Jack lasered
the fly-catcher with a dagger look on his way to the
backdoor. "Get over it, duckbill—this was my backyard
before you were even an egg in the nest." He let the
screen door slam behind him as he entered his mother's
large old-fashioned kitchen with its exposed brick and
white-wood-and-glass cabinets. "The heart of the
home," his father would always say when everyone
congregated there for games or homework while his
mother cooked dinner. Then, as now, heavenly smells
of pot roast or apple pie filled the air along with his
sisters' chatter or his mother's laughter, but today Jack
was in no state of mind to join in.

"My-my, aren't we in a 'fowl' mood today," his
sister Cat teased, her strawberry-blonde hair trailing
bronze shoulders. A glint of mischief sparkled in sky-
blue eyes as she chopped carrots at their antique kitchen
table, scarred and scuffed with many a family dinner or
board game.

"Hey, I thought you had a date with Jasmine tonight." Cat's twin sister Shannon paused with a paring knife in one hand and a potato in the other. Two tiny lines puckered at the bridge of her freckled nose, indicating concern. At twenty-five, Shan was the "gentle twin" who worried about everybody including the flippin' heron. *Which* might have brought a smile to Jack's face if he wasn't in such a pond-sucking mood.

"Yeah, Dr. Romeo," Cat piped up. "What's up? Did Miss Loreal #9.5 Pale Blonde discover you're seeing several other shades as well?"

"Catherine Marie, hush," his mother said with a warning scold, always the peacekeeper.

Jack wished he had a nickel every time she'd insisted their home wasn't a warzone, but a haven from all the attacks and pain the world doled out. He scowled as he rifled through the soda cans at the back of fridge. *Too bad Dad never got the memo.* "What the freak happened to the Red Bull I bought last week?" he demanded, rising to give Cat the evil eye. "There were two cans left yesterday."

Cat raised her palms in the air, brows arched high with innocence. "Hey, don't look at me—Matt is *your* best friend, remember?" A slow smile wended its way across her full lips. "He stopped by to borrow that new jacket of yours," she said with a grin, "along with your last two Red Bulls."

Jack stifled a curse, well aware his mother did not allow "language" in her house. He punched the fridge door closed, wishing it were Matt's face instead. Huffing out a tired sigh, he closed his eyes to massage the bridge of his nose. No, that wasn't fair. Matt and he shared everything—*except* news of Lacey Carmichael's return, apparently—and normally Jack'd give him the shirt off his back. He issued a silent grunt. Or the jacket.

His mother wiped her hands on a dishtowel and hurried over to give him a quick kiss on the cheek, hands braced to his arms. "You said you wouldn't be home till late—what's going on?"

He gave her a reassuring hug, the magic of "family" slowly unraveling the knots at the back of his neck. "Nothing's wrong, Mom, I just have a headache, that's all."

"I have Ibuprofen," she volunteered, the tenderness in her tone reminding him just how lucky he was to have her and his family. Loose strands of her shoulder-length blonde hair escaped from a messy ponytail atop her head that made her look more like a big sister in her thirties than a mother halfway through her forties. "A natural beauty," his dad would always say with pride in his eyes, "no need for a stitch of makeup." The memory calcified Jack's jaw. *But apparently not "beautiful" enough, huh, Dad?* He shook the negative thought off to focus on the positive—a mother who had not only been the heart of the home, but was now also the head.

Without question Tess O'Bryen had a glow about her, whether from summer humidity or good genes, Jack wasn't sure. Although if asked, she'd swear it was clean living and deep faith, her pale blue eyes sparkling with tease as she said it. And a clean heart, Jack reflected with a swell of love, turning to retrieve a glass from the cabinet so she wouldn't see the sheen of emotion in his eyes. A kind and gentle heart, so very full of mercy.

Unlike my own.

"I'd rather have a brew," he muttered, hoping to throw her off the scent of his bad mood with a smart-aleck jest, knowing full well she didn't appreciate his occasional beer anymore than she did his salty language.

"Did you and Jasmine have a fight?" she asked, ignoring his comment while she slipped behind to give him a shoulder rub. At six foot three, he towered over her five foot three by a mile, but it never seemed to stop her from babying him with back rubs or hugs. Her voice lowered several octaves as her fingers kneaded the back of his neck. "Goodness, Jack, you're as tight as a two-by-four."

"With just as much charm." Cat plopped carrots into the pot of boiling water and strolled over to pat his cheek. "At least tonight." She ducked out of reach before he could slap her away.

"All right, young man, I want the truth." His mother turned him to face her, eyes thinning into mother mode with a menacing fold of arms. "You were as happy and high as Blue in his tree when you left an hour ago, almost giddy over deserting your family to find a bachelor pad in the city—"

Jack interrupted with a low groan, grinding his temple with the ball of his hand. "Mom, I'm twenty-nine years old, for pity's sake, and fresh out of med school—it's a house, not a bachelor pad." He retrieved a glass from the cabinet and the bottle of Ibuprofen she kept there. "And I am not 'deserting' my family— Savannah's a measly fifteen minutes away."

She snatched both from his hands to fill the glass with tap water and hand him two pills. "Don't change the subject. Something happened in the last hour to bring you home with a headache and a nasty mood, and I want to know what it is."

His jaw tightened. *No you don't, trust me.* He shot the Ibuprofen in his mouth and chugged the entire glass of water.

"Come on, Jack, this isn't like you." Shannon's soft voice was quiet and low, her blue eyes pert near as big as the potato in her hand. "Mom's right—something's wrong, so what gives?"

"Yeah, buddy, out with it," Cat said, all jest fading away as she washed her hands at the sink, her voice conveying a thread of worry that matched her sister's. "It's not like you to be a crab for no reason."

Jack patted her arm and shuffled over to the table, sliding a chair out next to Shannon. He sat and straddled it, arms folded over the back and chin resting on top. His gaze wandered into a faraway stare. They would find out eventually anyway, and they needed to know. His eyelids lumbered closed, and instantly he was barraged with memories that took the ache in his head straight to his heart. Noisy games of Scrabble or "spoons" in their large, homey kitchen where family, friends, and neighbors all seemed to thrive. He could almost hear Lacey's giggles bouncing off the sunny cream-colored walls alongside his sisters' or see peas in flight across the supper table when his parents' backs were turned. Pinochle games and laughter between Lacey's parents and his while the kids played Twister on a black-and-white linoleum floor that smelled of Clorox and Mop & Glo.

"Jack, you're starting to scare me," his mother said quietly. "What on earth is wrong?"

Everything. A nerve twittered in his cheek. *The ghost of families past returning to haunt.* He peered up at his mother who watched him over her shoulder while stirring something on the stove with a crimp in her brow. Her lavender tank and blue jean shorts revealed a slim and toned body, compliments of Pilates. Sucking in a deep draw of air, he pushed the words off his tongue, their taste as bitter as his memories. "Lacey's back."

Silence reigned except for a soft gasp from Shannon and the rolling boil of carrots. His mother blinked and then laid the spoon aside in slow motion, gaze lost in a pan of gravy that bubbled before her. Head bowed, her back seemed to sag as her question drifted up with the steam that misted her face, as heavy as the humidity in the marsh-scented air. "How do you know?"

"Yeah, did you see her fly in on her broom or something?" Cat's tone had a bite to it, but then it would. Lacey had been the person she'd idolized, the best friend who'd turned her back on them all. And the sister-in-law that was never to be.

His gaze veered her way. "I ran into her at the BP."

His sisters exchanged glances, their faces as pale as their mother's as she slowly moved toward the table. Easing into her chair, she wore the same look of shock Jack had felt when he'd first seen Lacey's face. A girl full of life and love so like one of their own.

A sister. A daughter.

And almost a wife.

"She's back for good. Took a teaching job in Savannah."

"But why?" Cat's eyes darkened to slits of midnight blue. "I knew she'd be back for the wedding, but for the love of all that's decent, why move back where she's not wanted?"

"Catherine …" His mother's soft warning was as gentle as the hand she laid on her daughter's arm.

His sister jerked away. "No, Mom, it's true, and we all know it. For years she belonged more to our family than hers and then all hell breaks loose, and what does she do? She bolts at the first sign of trouble, turning her back on the people who really cared to take the side of a home wrecker—"

"Enough!" His mother's voice rose with a deadly calm that never failed to silence her children. Steam continued to boil into the air along with the bitterness that hovered whenever the Carmichael family was mentioned. Squaring her shoulders, his mother lifted her chin in a show of authority no one dared to defy. "Karen was Lacey's mother and my friend," she said quietly, the steel in her tone belying the tender touch of her hand over Cat's. "And I would hope you would have done the same for me."

"You wouldn't do what she did," Cat bit out, the blue eyes bristling with anger.

His mother scooted close to wrap Cat in a hug. "One never knows what one will do given the weight of circumstances beyond our control, darling, which is why the grace of God—and His forgiveness—is as vital as air."

"Where is she staying?" Shannon asked, her eyes too warm with empathy for Jack's taste, especially for the likes of Lacey Carmichael.

Cat grunted, sliding her nail back and forth in a groove gouged by a quartz rock Jack and she played catch with when he was ten. "Not with her old man, that's for sure."

. Jack exhaled and gouged a thumb at the sinus pain above his eye, hoping to ease the ache. "With Nicki for the summer, then an apartment in Savannah or maybe Wilmington Island."

"Oh, Wilmington Island, please—the farther, the better." Sarcasm coated Cat's words, almost tugging a smile to Jack's lips. No question Mom and Shan were the softhearted ones in the family while Cat and he were the keepers of the grudge.

A tiny frown popped at the bridge of his mother's nose. "Matt never mentioned Lacey was coming home early for the wedding, much less moving back, did he?"

"Nope, which is why he's dead meat when I get my hands on him," Jack said in a near growl. "He could have at least cushioned the blow."

"Humph, nothing would cushion that blow," Cat groused, "but a double dose of anesthesia—"

"Did she happen to say why she's moving back?" his mother interrupted, proceeding to massage Cat's shoulders. His sister emitted a soft moan as she closed her eyes, some of the tension fading from her face.

His mouth took a slant. "To make amends, she says."

Cat grunted. "Thus the move because it will take the rest of her frickin' life."

A heavy sigh parted from his mother's lips. "It's about time. Heaven knows we all need closure, and none more than Lacey's father." She gave Cat's shoulders two brief taps with her palms and stood, hurrying to stir the gravy. "We've forgiven your father and moved on, and now it's time to do the same with the Carmichaels."

"Uh, you, Shan, and Davey have forgiven Dad, Mom," Cat said with a pointed look, rising to help her sister set the table. She grabbed a fistful of knives from the utensil drawer and wagged them in the air as if she had a target in mind. "Not Jack or me."

Her mother arched a brow, spoon in hand like a threat. "You will if my prayers and Shan's have anything to say about it."

"Ha! It'll be a cold day in—"

"Jack, you're home!" A blur of blue and yellow streaked into the kitchen to scramble onto Jack's back as he straddled his chair, bringing a grin to his face as only a little kid could.

"Hey, squirt," Jack said with a chuckle, tousling his little brother Davey's hair. His gaze hardened on his cousin Matt Ball who followed behind, the best friend who'd failed to warn him about the bomb that had just shattered his good mood. He locked on his little brother's wrists as he stood up, searing Matt with a glare while Davey dangled off his back. "Thanks for the heads-up, Ball," he said in a cool tone.

Matt halted mid-step, a football tucked under one arm and blue eyes in a blink, his muscled Duck Dynasty T-shirt spotted with sweat. "What?"

"Don't play dumb, Matt—Lacey moves back for good two freakin' months before the wedding, and you fail to mention it?"

The dark tan on Matt's face suddenly paled while he shoveled fingers through spiky blonde hair, his look sheepish at best. Best friends since they were babies, his cousin Matt had moved in with them when his dad was transferred during Matt and Jack's senior year. Not wanting to disrupt her son's schooling, Aunt Olivia had reluctantly allowed Matt to stay with her sister Tess through college and then after when he landed a coaching job at the high school. Together through every trial and trauma of their lives, Jack and Matt had forged a close bond that went deeper than blood. Even so, Jack's jaw began to grind. Blood that was about to be spilled if his cousin didn't have a good reason for keeping Lacey's homecoming to himself.

With quick recovery, Matt plopped the football on the table and strolled toward the sink, shooting Jack a flash of white teeth in a face burnished by the sun from coaching sports year-round. "Sorry, bro—planned to tell you after our game tomorrow night." He looped an arm around Jack's mother at the stove. "So, how'd you find out?"

"Oh, no you don't—you two can hash it out later," Jack's mother said in a tone sharp with warning, obviously hoping to derail any further unpleasantness in her kitchen. Her nose wrinkled when she caught a whiff of her nephew. "Good heavens, Matt—you reek. I suggest you and Davey take a quick shower before dinner if you plan to eat."

"What's 'reek' mean?" Davey pretended to fall off of Jack's shoulder with a flail of arms.

"He stinks," Cat and Shan said in stereo.

Matt sauntered over to the icebox, probably intending to poach another Red Bull. "Because that's how a man who excels in sports is supposed to smell, ladies, which of course you wouldn't know since your brother always smells like a girl." He ducked to peer in the fridge. "Hey—who took the last Red Bull?"

"You did," the girls said in perfect sync.

A lazy smile tilted on Matt's face as he flipped the door shut, delivering a smirk in Jack's direction. "Oh, yeah, that's right."

"Do I stink like a man?" Davey offered Jack a whiff of his scrawny underarm, and Jack sniffed with great drama, scrunching his nose. "P-U, I'll say—almost as bad as your cousin."

"*Yesssss!*" Matt said with a fist bump to Davey.

"Hey, Jack, wanna play a quick game of hoops with Matt and me?"

"Sure, squirt." Jack latched on to the little guy's dirty T-shirt with a chuckle, twirling him around to the front before tossing him over his shoulder. Slight for eight, Davey was born after their father left, leaving Jack to step into the role of man of the house, which suited him just fine. As crazy as he was about kids, he was hoping for a passel himself some day. Davey's laughter and squeals bounced off the kitchen walls as Jack tickled his waist. "As long as Matt doesn't cry when I beat him."

"Oh, dream on," Matt said with a smirk. "When it comes to athletic prowess, I'm light years older than you."

Jack slid his cousin a paper-thin stare. "Older? You're six months younger than me."

Matt moseyed on over to ruffle Davey's hair, delivering a wink in Cat and Shan's direction. "True, but *I've* been living and working in the *real* world making men out of boys on field and court while *you've* had your nose in a book." He snatched a grape tomato from the salad Cat was making, then quickly dodged the warning wave of her knife. Shooting a grin Jack's way, he popped the tomato in his mouth. "Which means maturity and expertise are on my side, bro. So you may be older chronologically, but when it comes to sports, you're barely out of the womb."

"What's a womb?" Davey asked, squirming on Jack's shoulder like a night crawler.

"A mama's tummy," his mother said in a rush, neatly side-stepping the issue as she pressed a kiss to Davey's cheek. "And no hoops, young man—we're eating early tonight, so showers only." She swooped Davey off Jack's shoulder with another kiss before aiming him for the door via a pop on his butt, then turned to Matt with lift of her chin. "And that means the both of you—*now,* please."

"I'm going, I'm going," Matt said with the same disgruntled look as Davey while the two of them plodded from the room. He turned midway to peer at Jack, eyes in a squint. "Hey, wait a minute, I thought you had a date tonight. And I know Jasmine couldn't have dumped you for somebody better looking 'cause I'm still here." He draped an arm over Davey's shoulder. "So what's the story?"

"A horror story," Cat muttered, and Jack's mom sent her a warning look.

Matt's white-blonde brows shot high as his gaze darted to his cousins and back. "Uh-oh, something stinks, and it sure ain't me or Davey. What gives?"

"A cold shoulder, if I have anything to say about it," Cat mumbled while she pulled a loaf of their mother's butter-twist bread hot from the oven. "Talk about something that stinks worse than you."

"Catherine Marie—one more negative word, and the dishes will be yours for the rest of the week." Tess shot a mock scowl in Matt and Davey's direction. "Off with you to the showers, boys, or you'll be eating outside with Blue by the fishpond. You have exactly fifteen minutes before dinner's on the table, so scoot."

"Ohhhhh, no—not before I get the scoop." Matt snatched the football from the table and bobbled it hand-to-hand as he stared at Jack with a stubborn gleam in his eyes.

Despite the mouthwatering smell of homemade bread, Jack's stomach soured. "I'll fill you in at dinner, so hurry up—I'm starved."

"Okay, okay." Matt ruffled Davey's hair with a curious smile, but the intent look he gave Jack was considerably more sober. Some of the sparkle dimmed in his eyes as he steered his cousin toward the hall with a hand to the back of his neck. "Come on, sport, let's unload this grime, and I'll even let you use some of my great-smelling stuff that drives the girls wild."

"Ewww ... I don't wanna drive girls wild," Davey said.

"Good, then we'll let you borrow your brother's instead—the *real* expensive stuff." A smile inched across Matt's face as he tossed Jack a grin over his shoulder. "Because we'll need to smell real good since your brother's got news that apparently stinks to high heaven."

Jack grunted. His gaze locked with Cat's, lips pinched as tight as his.

Yeah. Right guess, wrong direction.

CHAPTER THREE

*E*dging the Honda to the curb in front of her grandmother's house, Lacey parked and switched off the ignition, hand limp on her keys while her eyes glazed into a zombie stare over the dash. Sucking in a shaky breath, she could still see Jack's bitterness in her mind—the rock jaw, the stony lips, the pale blue eyes as cold and hard as blue quartz. A reedy breath withered on her lips. *This is gonna be harder than I thought ...*

"Mamaw, she's here!"

Lacey glanced over the white picket fence of her grandmother's front yard to where her cousin Nicki did a little jig at the screen door of the wraparound porch. Darting out of the house in pink and red Flintstone scrubs she wore as a pediatric oncology nurse, she let the screen slam hard, the resounding crack making Lacey both smile and wince. Mamaw would have her head for sure with a mantra that Southern ladies do not charge in or out of a house like hooligans. Her cousin's loud squeal brought a grin to Lacey's face as Nicki Phillips—the only girl cousin on her mother's side— barreled down the red-brick steps and sidewalk at warp speed.

"*Squeeeeeee!*" Nicki waved her arms in the air as if poor Fred and Barney were on fire, flung the pretty white gate aside, and darted around to Lacey's side of the car. "Oh. My. Gosh! I cannot believe you're finally *here—and* moving back for good!" She let fly with another giggly squeal that made Lacey laugh out loud.

"Moving back to *Georgia*," Lacey emphasized with a chuckle, hopping out to crush her favorite relative in her arms. "Not Isle of Hope. I doubt many here would welcome me back with open arms other than you, Mamaw, Spencer, and Uncle Cam."

"Oh, poo! There are lots of people who can't wait to see you, silly." She retrieved two suitcases from the backseat and handed one off to Lacey before hooking her free arm through her cousin's. "*Including* the new associate pastor at Hope Church who's marrying Matt and me." She wiggled her brows. "Who just happens to be both single *and* a hunk."

"Ohhhhhh no you don't ..." Lacey skidded to a stop at the gate, a clear warning in her tone. "I just got dumped, remember? And *you* promised you'd let me grieve in peace, without sinking to Mamaw's level of matchmaking."

Nicki arched a russet brow, her short, spiky red hair and blast of freckles making her look more like an imp than a twenty-six-year-old pediatric nurse about to get married. "I beg your pardon—I do not 'sink.'" She bumped tan shoulders with Lacey, all but dragging her to the front door while her pert, speckled nose jutted high in the air. "I stoop gracefully, I'll have you know, a talent proudly acquired from our very own Southern belle grandmother."

"Sweet tea in Georgia, as I live and breathe—Lacey Anne Carmichael is alive and well." Her grandmother Mildred "Mamaw" Phillips stood holding the door, the twinkle in her rheumy blue eyes betraying rose-colored lips pursed in a mock scowl.

Lacey laughed. "Well, 'alive' anyway, although just barely." She dropped her suitcase with a thump on the oval Persian rug of Mamaw's high-ceiling foyer to

swallow her tiny grandmother in a ferocious hug. Eyes
drifting closed, Lacey immediately felt the sting of tears
at the familiar scent of oranges and herbs from
Mamaw's Breck shampoo combined with the heavenly
aroma of pot roast from the kitchen, a Sunday staple in
Mamaw's house. Although she towered over her
grandmother's petite five-foot frame by four inches or
more, Lacey felt all of six years old in her silky
embrace. Tucking her head into Mamaw's neck, she
breathed in her childhood with hints of White Shoulders
perfume and the clean scent of starch, the comfort of
"home" surrounding her like Mamaw's loving arms.

Eyelids lifting, she scanned the curved maple
staircase lined with oil paintings and family pictures,
and memories flooded of PJ parties with popcorn and
old movies. Games of "spades" and "pass the trash."
Melancholy struck hard over all the times she and Nicki
had snuggled with Mamaw in her double bed when
Gramps was out of town, giggling the night away with
secrets and spook stories and little-girl laughter.
Emotion clogged in her throat, and with a powerful
squeeze, she clung with all of her might, gratitude
spilling from both her heart and her eyes over the
blessing of this precious woman in her life. A woman
whose very prayers, she had no doubt whatsoever, had
set her upon the path to faith, no matter how long the
journey. With an awkward swipe of her eyes, she pulled
away to press a tender kiss to her grandmother's soft
cheek. "Oh, Mamaw, I've missed you so much."

A soft and throaty chuckle rose like a caress as her
grandmother hooked arms with Lacey to usher her
down a wide amber hallway embellished by white
molding and warm maple floors. Her standard white
Keds were replaced by the leopard house slippers Nicki
had given her for Christmas last year, and Lacey
couldn't help but grin when Mamaw teased with an
affectionate smirk. "Well, now, if that were true, young

lady," she said with a toss of silver curls set and dried every Friday at the kitchen table with an old-fashioned bonnet hair dryer, "we would have seen you on Isle of Hope more than once or twice a year, sneaking in and out so fast, no one even knew you were here."

A chuckle rolled from Nicki's lips as she set the second suitcase on the foyer floor and hurried to catch up. "Uh, I think that was the plan, Mamaw."

Lacey cringed. *Ah, yes, the plan.* In and out. Down and dirty. Like a Band-Aid on a festering sore—yank the sucker off so fast you never feel the pain.

"A plan that slurps marsh water if you ask me," Mamaw said with a wry twist of lips, modifying one of Nicki's favorite expressions to make it more palatable. She and Nicki bantered back and forth while Lacey soaked it all in like a woman coming out of a coma after too many years asleep, reveling in her family as if seeing them for the very first time.

With her stylish silver white coiffure, Mamaw looked more like sixty than almost seventy-five. Sleek and slim in white linen slacks, she wore a cotton top splashed with a hodge-podge of ladybugs that clashed with her leopard slippers. Uncle Cam always said she was as cute as a bug's ear, and the memory tilted Lacey's lips into a smile because it was so very true. Mamaw was one of those cute, little old ladies that dogs liked to sniff and lick, and everybody else wanted to hug. A bunko-playing dynamo, who could be as sweet and deadly as her famous peach crumble pie.

"Spencer, look who's here," Mamaw said. She led them into her sunny kitchen overlooking a lavish serpentine brick patio flanked by mulched gardens of roses and boxwoods. Spacious yet cozy, the state-of-the-art country French kitchen and garden were a gift from Uncle Cam, who insisted on "nothing but the best" for the woman who cooked and cleaned and cared for his children. Here amid the wonderful smells of pot roasts and peach pies, Mamaw reigned supreme, providing a haven of hope and home for family and friends. Sunlight was at home here as well, glinting off a golden oak floor and cottage glass cabinets, each complemented by pristine white granite counters that sported every kitchen convenience known to man.

Lacey's eight-year-old cousin Spencer sat at an antique provincial kitchen table in a nook area backdropped by a lush yard of towering oaks dressed in Spanish moss. Shafts of sunlight spilled through the oversized bay window, illuminating the intricacies of his Snap Circuits, Jr. building project, which sat in a shallow wooden box his dad had probably built for ease of transport. On the edge of the box perched two of Spencer's favorite action figures that pretty much went everywhere he did, according to Nicki. At the base of his chair lay a snoring Sherlock Holmes—Spencer's beloved sheep dog—who hadn't a "clue" anyone else had even entered the room. Spread-eagle on his back, Sherlock looked more like a mop than a watchdog, gray wisps of hair fluttering with every growl of a snore.

"Hey, Lace," Spencer said in a shy voice that held no hint of the stutter that appeared when he was nervous or excited. Tiny for his age, Spencer possessed an innate gentleness in hazel eyes the exact color of his sister's, black-rimmed glasses magnifying them all the more. When he blinked, the thick lenses imparted the effect of a baby owl, giving credence to his studious nature and keen intellect. A thatch of brown hair as unruly as his rumpled dinosaur T-shirt barely covered protruding ears while a timid but sweet smile inched across his freckled face.

"Hi, buddy—how's my favorite cousin?" she asked with a tight squeeze, noting his impressive electrical display.

"Hey—I thought I was your favorite cousin?" Nicki shot a playful scowl over her shoulder, giving Spencer a wink in the process. She pulled a tray of cookies from the oven, and the sweet smell of cinnamon instantly trumped the pot roast, watering Lacey's mouth. Snickerdoodles … her favorite!

Lacey ruffled Spence's hair even more than it was. "Nope, you're too much of a girly-girl who can be a pain at times while this sweet boy here is no trouble at all. Plus *he* watches sports with me." She pressed a kiss to Spencer's head, skimming a finger across his intricate circuit board. "So what's this, Einstein—circuitry to zap your sister when she gets out of line?"

"Naw." He gave a bashful duck of his head, offering Nicki and Mamaw a sheepish grin. "This is a burglar alarm."

"Ohhhhh, I see," Lacey said, jutting a brow as she watched Nicki sample a cookie before transferring them from the sheet to a plate. "To keep your sister out of the cookie stash so she won't pork up before the wedding?"

He giggled, a soft and gentle sound that made her wanna hug him all over again. Painfully shy with strangers, Spencer was diagnosed as borderline Asperger's Syndrome, resulting in behaviors other children considered odd such as finger twisting or the slight fluttering of his fingers when he turned a page in a book. According to Mamaw's letters, kids called him "oddball" or "Dense Spence" at school, making it difficult for him to make friends, an ongoing worry for both Mamaw and Nicki. *Especially* with his father on naval commission halfway across the world, an officer on the *USS George H. W. Bush.* The poor little guy never really knew his mother since Aunt Susan passed away from cancer when he was small, which was when Mamaw stepped in to help Uncle Cam.

"Hey, I'll have you know I baked these especially for you, you little brat." Nicki sauntered over with the plate of cookies and a pursed smile. She plopped them on the clear end of the table with a thud and patted a chair, chin pointed at Lacey. "Sit. I have exactly fifteen minutes till I have to drive Spencer to his first baseball practice before clocking in for my shift, so I want the *Reader's Digest* version of a Cliff Note update, please."

Lacey's smile took a slant. *Easy.*

Saved by faith.

Dumped by fiancé.

Strong-armed by God.

She inhaled deeply, the sweet smell of cinnamon and sugar filling her senses like God's love had filled her heart. Where to begin? How to tell them that she hadn't lost a fiancé, but gained a life? That the old Lacey with the salty tongue and sexy ways had traded in profanity for purity, and sex for sanctity? She stalled by rifling through the cookies, nudging past the darker ones burned to a crisp like Nicki preferred, to inspect the lighter ones she favored. Extra cinnamon crackles on pale-yellow dough, slightly underdone. Night and day. Her smile went wry. Just like her life now that God had intervened. She scrunched her nose as she flicked a particularly dark cookie aside. "Uh, not exactly sure where to begin ..."

"Excuse me, young lady, are you going to finger every cookie on that plate?" Mamaw clunked three blue ceramic saucers on the table with a familiar scold that sparkled with tease. "Are your hands clean, I hope, or will I have to make you eat each cookie you mauled?"

Lacey laughed, jumping up to wash her hands at the sink. "Nope, sorry. The pump at the BP leaked, so they're pretty grimy, I'm afraid." *As my life used to be.* The thought poured peace through her body like the tap water into the sink.

Nicki leaned a hip to the counter and gave the Keurig caddy a spin. "So what's your pleasure? We have cinnamon roll, macadamia nut cookie, hazelnut, and crème brulee."

"Oooo—macadamia nut cookie, please," Lacey said. She retrieved Half & Half from the fridge and hurried back to the table where Mamaw was admiring Spencer's burglar alarm.

Circling Spencer from behind in a tight hug, Mamaw kissed his head. "Okay, mister—you need to head up and put your uniform on, all right?"

"Yes, ma'am," Spencer said, shooting Lacey a shy smile before removing his circuit box from the table, carefully placing the action figures safely inside. He roused Sherlock from the dead in the process, who shook a windstorm of floating hair before he followed him upstairs with a yawn.

Lacey waited till she heard the squeak of the steps before turning to Mamaw. "How's he doing?" she said quietly, her grandmother's last letter about Spencer's bout of depression still weighing on her mind.

Mamaw sighed, the sound too heavy for such a tiny woman. "Better, I think, especially now that we signed him up for Little League." She offered Nicki a smile as her granddaughter plunked two steaming cups of coffee on the table for her and Lacey. "I think he's excited about the prospect of making new friends."

Nicki cut loose with a grunt as she settled into her chair with a cup of her own. "Or any friends at all," she said with a sad crook of her mouth. "The poor little guy has had a pretty rough year."

"True," Mamaw said, "but we're hoping that will turn around, especially since this is not the parish league with all of his classmates." A sigh feathered her lips. "I'm praying he can get a fresh start, maybe build some self-confidence before the next school year." She took a sip of her coffee then set it aside, hands folded in her lap as she homed in on Lacey with laser precision. The sharp blue eyes that had missed nothing when Lacey was growing up now narrowed into serious grandma mode. "Spencer will be fine, I think, but what I want to know now, darling girl—will you?"

"Sure she will," Nicki said with a defiant thrust of her chin, eyes stormy. "She doesn't need that loser to be happy—it's his loss, not hers."

Lacey couldn't stop the grin that tickled her lips. "I'd hardly call the valedictorian of UC Berkeley School of Law a loser, Nick, but thanks for the support."

"So what happened, sweetheart?" Her grandmother laid a frail hand on Lacey's arm, the concern in her eyes bringing moisture to Lacey's own.

"We just grew apart," Lacey whispered, well aware that the fissure between her and Tim had probably begun long before she'd started attending Joy's church. Although she'd known Joy for almost eight years now, it hadn't been until Lacey's engagement to Tim, when she needed a church for the wedding, that Lacey found her curiosity about Joy's faith growing. Her friend had always persisted in talking to her about God, sure, but Lacey had never really seen the point. God had let her down years ago. Besides, she'd achieved everything she'd ever wanted on her own—a job she loved, a hunky fiancé, a gorgeous townhouse in the best part of town, and a cozy six-figure income between the two. But somehow six months out from the wedding of her dreams, she sensed deep down that something was missing. And it hadn't been until she started attending church with Joy—to Tim's utter dismay—that she finally understood what it was.

Peace.

She looked up at Mamaw now and realized it had been her grandmother's unflappable faith that had gotten Lacey through every heartbreak of her life. From years of loneliness as an only child, to years of teenage rebellion that set her at odds with her father, Mamaw had been relentless in prayer, becoming Lacey's anchor. Through a volatile divorce between her parents, a bitter estrangement from her father, and finally the heart-wrenching pain of losing her mother—it had been Mamaw she'd turned to, not God. Tears sprang to Lacey's eyes as she placed her palm over her grandmother's, suddenly aware that God had never left her as she supposed, but His love had been alive and well through the powerful faith of both her grandmother and her friend Joy.

"What do you mean, you grew apart?" Nicki wanted to know. She glanced at her watch with a frown. "He wasn't cheating on you, was he?"

Lacey laughed, not sure when Tim would have had time to "cheat" with his grueling, make-partner-or-die hours at San Diego's top law firm. "No, nothing like that, I promise. I guess you might say it was more like me cheating on him." Her teeth tugged at the edge of her lip. "With God."

"Come again?" Her cousin's brows shot straight up.

The shock on her face was so comical that Lacey battled a grin with a gruff clear of her throat. "Uh, I turned over a new leaf and became a good girl, Nick, just like you did when you met Matt. You know—going back to church?" She gave a little shrug, a sad smile lining her lips. "And I guess Tim couldn't see himself married to a—and I quote—'professional prude.'"

Her cousin blinked, eyes as round as the snickerdoodles on her plate. "You mean you two stopped having—"

"The same viewpoint on life, *yes*," Lacey said quickly, heat warming her cheeks as she shot Nicki a pointed look, mere mention of her former lifestyle embarrassing her in front of her grandmother. She released a tentative sigh, laden with both relief and regret, wishing she had come to her senses long before she'd depleted a good chunk of her savings on wedding deposits. "So we parted ways, and that was that."

"Wow." Nicki slumped back in her chair. "When you do something, Lace, you go for broke, kiddo."

"I know," Lacey said with quiet quiver of air, "literally." She took a bite of her cookie, her spirits rebounding. "But the truth is, I may be lonelier and broker than before, but in a strange way, I'm also happier." She popped the rest of the snickerdoodle in her mouth and chewed while she slipped Mamaw a sheepish smile. "I'm just kicking myself I didn't listen all those years you tried so hard to drum faith into my head."

"You listened more than you know, sweetheart." She squeezed Lacey's hand.

"I'm ready." Glove in hand, Spencer clomped into the kitchen wearing a short-sleeved blue "Hurricane" jersey so big it came to his elbows.

"Wow, cleats and everything," Lacey said with a low whistle. "Looking pretty sharp, Spence."

"Yeah." Spencer grinned, pushing his glasses back up his nose. He adjusted the rim of his blue baseball cap, then pounded a tiny fist into a brand-new baseball glove that was almost bigger than him.

Nicki hopped up and carried her cup and saucer to the sink. "Okay, sport, we're outta here in two shakes and a shimmy." She tucked both dishes into the dishwasher.

"Don't forget his water bottle in the fridge," Mamaw reminded.

"What's a shimmy?" Spencer asked with an adorable owl blink of eyes.

"It means we need to hustle if I'm going to get you to practice and then me to work on time, capiche?" Nicki grabbed a water bottle and ambled over to kiss Mamaw's head and squash Lacey in a bear hug. "Soooo glad you're home, Lace, and can't wait to catch up tomorrow." Her brows danced with mischief. "It's my day off, you know, and I have a surprise planned."

"Uh-oh." Lacey eyed her with suspicion. "If it includes any male other than Matt or Spence, your name is mud, Phillips, you got that?"

"Mmm ... Mrs. Nicki Mud Ball." She flashed a grin. "I like it, although Matt's mom, Mrs. Ball of the Hamptons, may not."

Mamaw chuckled while Spencer scrunched his nose. "What's 'capiche' mean?"

Lacey pinched Nicki's waist before jumping up to give Spencer a quick squeeze. "It means give your cousin a hug before you leave," she said, tugging on his baseball cap. "You may not know this, kiddo, but I was top pitcher on my softball team, so you and I are gonna have to play catch, and I'll even hit you some grounders."

"Gosh, you mean it?"

"You bet, slugger. How 'bout tonight after you get home?"

"Cool!" He flashed her a smile that melted her heart and spun on his heels to follow his sister to the door.

"Oh, and Lace?" Nicki paused to hook her purse over her shoulder. "I was supposed to be off tonight so I was going to pick Spence up from his practice at six, but I'm filling in for a friend at work." She fluttered her eyelashes in a pitiful plea. "So would you mind saving Mamaw the trip? It's at the Paulson Complex."

"No problem." Lacey gave Spencer a wink. "Of course we may have to detour for some Oreo ice cream at Coldstone on the way home."

"Yes!" Spencer fist-punched his glove, luring huge grins to all of their faces.

"It's good to have you home, sweetheart—for *all* of us." Mamaw's soft words punctuated the slam of the front door.

Expelling a loud sigh, Lacey slumped back in her chair. "Thanks, Mamaw, I wish everybody felt the way you do."

Her grandmother leaned in to fold her arms on the table, her pensive gaze assuring Lacey that she understood all too well. "You haven't talked to him yet?"

"Yet?" Lacey grunted. "More like 'since.'" She rubbed her arms and expelled a shuddering breath heavily tainted with guilt and remorse. "I was so angry when Mom died that I barely spoke to him at the funeral, remember? It was so convenient to just blame him for the way it all turned out, for the total destruction of our family. I mean he was the one who turned his back on me long before Mom ever left him."

Her gaze lagged into a cold stare while a shiver skated her spine. "It's only been the last few months that I finally realized how wrong I was to do the same. To turn my back on him after Mom died—not returning his calls, his letters, his emails." Regret constricted the muscles in her throat as her voice trailed into a whisper. "Until they stopped coming altogether ..." Her eyelids fluttered closed briefly as feelings of grief and hurt tiptoed in at the corners of her mind, reminding her just how much she had wished him dead back then instead of her mother.

God, forgive me, please ...

She opened her eyes to her grandmother's tender gaze, which reflected the same grief Lacey still bore in her soul. Laying a veined hand over Lacey's, she gave her a gentle squeeze. "I know you came back to help Nicki with the wedding, darling, but we both know the real reason you're here."

A knot of fear convulsed in Lacey's throat. "I know," she whispered, "but there's been so much time and bitterness between us, Mamaw, that I worry it's too late."

Mamaw's chuckle was soft. "It's never too late to love, darling."

Lacey expelled a tremulous breath. "I know that, too," she said with a skittery smile. "I just don't know how …" —she chewed at a piece of skin on her lip— "to do it, you know?"

Mamaw smiled and patted her hand. "It's not difficult, darling—you show up on his doorstop one evening with one of my peach pies he so adores and say, 'Dad, we need to talk.'"

Lacey unloaded another grunt. "Yeah, right, and I have peach on my face after he slams the door." She peered up at Mamaw, eyes in a squint. "Do you ever talk to him anymore?"

"Oh, heavens no—he's far too bitter for that. You're not the only one he cut out of his life when your mother betrayed him, you know." She rose from the table, cup in hand. "Not that I didn't try, mind you. I called and wrote letters till I thought he'd get a restraining order, even after he asked me to leave him alone. I finally let it go a few years back except for the standard cards— you know, Christmas, birthday …" She paused, a definite twinkle in her eye. "Father's Day."

"No ..." A slow grin traveled Lacey's lips. "You don't." She chuckled. "Ouch. I'll bet that burns."

Mamaw jutted her chin, lips pursed in a stubborn smile. "I certainly hope so. Somebody needs to light a fire under that bull-headed pup." She rose to fetch more coffee, glancing over her shoulder with an imp of a grin. "And it's better than a propane torch." She nodded toward Lacey's half-empty cup. "Need a refill or warm-up before I serve up our dinner? Pot roast and vegetables, just as you like it, and it's all ours since Nicki and Spence already ate."

Lacey's mouth watered at the mere mention of Mamaw's signature Sunday dish. "No on the coffee, but the pot roast sounds heavenly," she said, a giggle slipping from her lips. "And as far as Daddy's concerned, Mamaw, I'd hardly call forty-six a 'pup.'"

"It is when you act like a child. Humph—and him one of the top cardiac surgeons in the country—*ha!*"

Lacey's smile faded as she wandered into a faraway stare. "I feel sorry for him," she whispered. And for herself too—a virtual orphan at twenty-six. She snapped out of it with a loud huff, mouth canting into a dry smile. "Which just goes to show how much I've changed. Up until six months ago, I wanted to see the man take a long walk off a short pier. *After* I filed a suit for emotional malpractice."

Mamaw chuckled. "Well, it's a suit you would win, that's for sure." Placing her cup on the table, she settled back in her chair, the smell of hazelnut wafting through the air. She took a sip while giving Lacey a wink over the rim. "And trust me, darlin'—all lawyer fees would be on me."

CHAPTER FOUR

*L*acey nosed her Honda into the last spot in the parking lot of the Paulson Complex, eyes scanning the various fields for any sign of Spence. Slinging her purse over her shoulder, she got out and shielded her eyes, a smile skimming her lips when she spotted him playing in the dirt with some other kid. With a quick glance at her watch, she made her way to his field where it looked like practice had just ended, kids and parents milling about.

"Lacey!" Spencer hopped up and bolted toward her, grabbing her hand to tug her over to his friend who was still playing on the dusty field. Although his smile remained shy, Spence's hazel eyes sparkled like topaz. "Meet my new friend, Mack Hartford," he said, voice breathless.

"Why, hello, Mack—I'm Lacey, and it's so very nice to meet you." Lacey bent to offer her hand to a little boy who sported more freckles than Spencer. Sitting cross-legged in the dirt with an action figure in hand, Mack grinned, his sky-blue eyes a perfect complement to red hair spiky with sweat. "Hi, Lacey."

"And guess what?" Spence said to Mack, his rush of excitement so rare, emotion thickened in Lacey's throat. "Lacey was a champion pitcher, and she's gonna hit me some grounders tonight." Pride gleamed in his eyes, giving Lacey a warm glow. Plopping down in the dirt next to Mack, he swooped up his own action figure, settling in as if he and Mack intended to camp out.

"You bet, bud, but first things first." Lacey shot a quick glance at the field to make sure practice was actually over, satisfied when she spotted several men packing bats and other gear in an equipment bag. She squatted down, a smile teasing the edge of her lips. "First we have to buy you an Oreo Overload at Coldstone, right?"

"Yeah!" Spencer shouted, vaulting into the air like a fly ball. "Can Mack come, Lace, please, please?"

"Well, sure," she said with a scan of several scattered groups on the field. "But we'll need to check with his mom or dad first, then we can take him home after, okay?" She tousled Mack's hair. "That all right with you, sport?"

"Yes, ma'am!" Mack said with equal enthusiasm, flashing Spencer a crooked grin.

"Sounds like a plan." She peered up at the few remaining people standing around. "So, Mack—where are your parents?"

"They're not here," he said in a matter-of-fact tone, swooping his action figure through the air as he jumped to his feet. "Coach Mehl always takes me to practice 'cause I'm on his way home, so I'll just ask him if it's okay." He darted toward two men chatting by the bleachers, one of them with the equipment bag strung over his shoulder.

Lacey grinned as she watched Mack hop up and down in apparent excitement, hands folded in a plea while the coach glanced Lacey's way. She rose and tugged on her short-shorts in an effort to lengthen then, then hurried over just as the other man left.

"Can I, Coach, please, please?" Dancing foot to foot, Mack twitched with anticipation, giving Lacey second thoughts about pumping sugar into his bloodstream.

She extended a hand and a warm smile. "Hi—Coach Mehl, I presume? I'm Spencer's cousin, Lacey Carmichael."

Smile lines appeared in the tan face of a stocky man she guessed to be in his forties, his return grip as strong as the muscles cording his arms. "Lee Mehl, Miss Carmichael." He shifted the bag on his shoulder while his gaze flicked to Spencer and back, his eyes softening enough for her to notice. "We're glad to have Spence on our team—he's a great kid." He tweaked the back of Mack's neck with a broad grin. "And I've never seen any kids hit it off faster than these two Power Ranger pals, that's for sure, eh Ranger Mack?"

"Yes, sir," Mack said. "So can I, Mr. Mehl, please?"

"I don't see why not," he said with a wink at Mack before the boy dashed off to rejoin Spence.

Lacey exhaled a silent sigh of relief. "Thanks, Mr. Mehl. I can't tell you how much this means to Spence—and to his grandmother, sister, and me." She shot a glance over her shoulder, battling the sudden prick of tears in her eyes. "He's had some difficulty making friends."

"Call me Lee, please, and Spence's grandmother already filled me in on the problems he's been having, so I'm thrilled to see the boys get along." He glanced at his watch. "How 'bout I tell 'Ranger Mack's' mom you'll bring him home after ice cream, all right? He lives on Bluff Drive."

Bluff Drive? Lacey gulped, the mention of her old street shrinking her rib cage. She deflected her sudden unease with a bright smile. "Absolutely, Lee, and please—call me Lacey. We're just going to Coldstone, so you can tell her forty-five minutes tops, okay?"

"Sounds good, Lacey. Have fun." Hoisting the bag higher on his shoulder, Lee offered a wave on his way to his car.

Fun? Yeah, well maybe at Coldstone, but after? A chill slithered Lacey's spine, icier than the ice cream in Coldstone's freezer. She ushered the boys to the car, oblivious to their nonstop chatter as her thoughts returned to the street she'd grown up on. Hands pinched on the steering wheel of her car, she peered up at a pastel sky just edging toward dusk. *Uh, I've been in town all of three hours—don't you think it's a liiiiittle too soon for a stroll down memory lane?*

Apparently not because here she was forty-five minutes later—inching her way down her father's street, heart racing while her breathing skidded to a stop. Memories rushed in like the tide on the shore, swelling her throat over forgotten games of hopscotch and foursquare and sardine's ghost after dark. Stately oaks bowed over a meandering drive in a gracious canopy dance, gnarled limbs casting shadows of lace on faded asphalt while Spanish moss swayed in the breeze. Two pig-tailed little girls sped by on pink Barbie bikes. Their giggles merged with the summer sounds of whispering pines and rustling palms, all laced with the squawk of seabirds and the buzz of boat engines from the shore on the other side of the street.

"Which house, Mack?" she said with a frog in her throat, silently praying he lived on the other end of Bluff Drive rather than where her father lived. *And* the best friend and ex-boyfriend she'd dumped without so much as a goodbye …

"Next block," he said, wrestling in the backseat with Spence like they'd been best friends forever. She swallowed the frog. *Like Cat and I used to be …*

"What's the address?" she asked, voice hoarse.

"Thirty Bluff Drive. It's the house with pink roses in front of the white fence."

Of course it is. Lacey gulped, fighting the rise of Oreo Overload. Apparently the Hartfords bought Jack and Cat's old house—her home away from home. Her eyelids flickered as a wave of dizziness hit hard. Right next to her father's. Sucking in a sharp breath, she slowly pulled up to Mack's curb. Her gaze instantly darted to her father's house on the other side of an eight-foot Japanese privet hedge that hadn't been there when she'd left.

"Wait—I want Spence to meet my brother," Mack said, already out of the car and sprinting down the red paver driveway toward the back of the house where laughter and the clunk of a basketball could be heard.

Lacey slipped Spence a wary smile over her shoulder, dead-set on hiding out in the car. "Hey bud, why don't you run and meet Mack's brother real quick, then hurry back so we can get going, okay?"

"Uh … sure," he said quietly, obviously not anymore eager to meet someone new than Lacey. She heard his heavy exhale before he grappled with the door, taking his sweet time to get out of the car.

Lacey's knuckles whitened on the steering wheel. *Come on, Spence, move it before somebody—*

A low groan scraped past her lips when Mack came barreling around the corner with an entourage in tow. *Whoops … too late.* Straightening her halter top, Lacey eased out of the car, giving the ol' cutoffs another firm modesty tug as she flashed a smile toward Mack and his family. "Hello, I'm—"

Gonna keel over right here, right now. Lacey gasped, an interesting mix of shock and nausea snatching all air—and sound—from her throat as she stared at Jack and his family, who apparently were as speechless as she. Warding off the urge to hyperventilate, she pried the words from her tongue, voice cracking in the process. "Uh … uh … I d-don't understand … M-Mack lives *here*?"

"Mack?" Jack was the first to speak, eyes narrowing considerably.

"Yeah, Mack Hartford," Spence said with a nod at his new friend, the crunch of his brows indicating this was something everybody should already know. "You know, Davey's Power Ranger name?"

A sliver of a smile tipped Mrs. O'Bryen's lips once the daze left her eyes. "Ah ... I see, and Spencer here is the butler, I presume?" she said slowly, hooking an arm around Spencer's shoulder. Her soft gaze met Lacey's, the sparkle of humor unable to mask the depth of emotion in her eyes. "Operation Overdrive," she explained with a dip of her head, "Davey's current obsession with Power Rangers. His favorite happens to be the red Overdrive Power Ranger, you know— otherwise known as 'Mack Hartford.'"

Of course it is. Lacey's smile compressed to restrain the silent groan climbing her throat.

"Yeah, and Spence is my loyal butler Spencer who gives me advice," Davey said, head in a tilt that said anybody with half a brain should know that.

Heat crawled up Lacey's neck. *Well, that pretty much describes me ...*

Spade in hand, Mrs. O'Bryen wiped her free hand against her gardening jeans before giving Lacey an awkward hug while Spence and Mack swooped action figures over each post of the white picket fence. "How are you, Lacey? It's been a long time," she said softly, her warm smile like the sun compared to the scowls on Jack's and Cat's faces.

"Yes, ma'am, it has," she whispered, terrified to take her eyes off of Jack's mother.

A lump shifted in her throat as Shannon approached, the gentleness in her eyes a balm to Lacey's soul. "We've missed you, Lace," she said quietly, hesitating for only a moment before offering a hug that immediately produced a sting of tears in Lacey's eyes.

With halting arms, Lacey returned her embrace, squeezing her lids shut in a sad attempt to ward off the moisture that pooled beneath. "I've missed you too," she whispered, her frail words breaking on a heave.

Lacey jolted when Mrs. O'Bryen's arm cradled her waist. "Come in for a cup of coffee," she said, her words as tender as her touch. "As luck would have it, I just happen to have a fresh batch of monster cookies— your favorite, as I recall."

Shannon's giggle brushed against Lacey's hair before the twin pulled from their embrace. "And trust me—'luck' doesn't have it very often in this house, so you best take advantage."

Take advantage. Lacey silently cringed as she stole a peek out of the corner of her eye at Jack and Cat, the two people whose friendship she'd certainly taken advantage of … right before she turned her back on them both. But this was what she'd hoped for—prayed for—wasn't it? Restoration of relationship with the people she loved. Unfortunately the stony looks of two of them shrank her rib cage considerably, depleting her air. "Uh … actually, Mrs. O'Bryen, I just arrived today, so my grandmother is expecting Spence and me home any moment. Maybe another time?"

"Let's hope not," Cat mumbled, whirling on her heel to stalk back into the house before her mother could correct her.

Mrs. O'Bryen gently cupped Lacey's waist. "Don't let Catherine's sour attitude put you off, Lacey—she's just hurt inside, which is all the more reason we need to get together soon, to talk … and to heal."

"Come on, Davey," Jack said, "we're playing horse, and I've got HORS." His gaze shifted to Spence with a crooked smile, ignoring Lacey altogether as he lowered to a squat. "Nice to meet you, Spence. Maybe you can play with us next time, okay?" Jack raised his hand to give him a high-five.

"Cool." Spence's wide smile was in total contrast to his usual shy personality, reminding Lacey just how much of a magnet Jack had always been with kids, making them feel special. He slapped Jack's palm, and then Davey's too, eyes aglow with the much-needed attention of an older male. "Maybe after next practice," he volunteered, shooting a hopeful look Lacey's way.

"Maybe," Lacey said with a slow nod, following Jack's lead in avoiding his gaze.

"Sweet." Jack gave Spence a wink before smiling at Davey. He turned to amble down the driveway, ignoring Lacey without another word.

Her heart cramped as she watched him walk away.

A delicate sigh drifted from Mrs. O'Bryen's lips before she squeezed Lacey in another hug. "I know it looks scary, Lacey, but promise you'll come back. We all need to forgive and forget." She pulled away with a tender gaze, hands still braced to Lacey's arms. "We need you in our lives again, sweetheart, and I think you need us too."

Emotion crowded Lacey's throat, Mrs. O'Bryen's words echoing deep in her heart.

If you do not forgive others, then your Father will not forgive your transgressions.

Her eyes flickered closed with the point-blank reminder that *this* was the real reason she was in Isle of Hope.

She needed their forgiveness. And from the knowing look in Mrs. O'Bryen's gaze, apparently her son and daughter needed it too.

With a shaky nod, she managed a weak smile. "I promise," she whispered, drawing strength from the compassion that radiated from Jack's mother and sister. "Soon."

"Good girl." Mrs. O'Bryen patted her arms and stepped away, casting a glance at her son and his new friend as they rolled and wrestled on the lawn. "David Montgomery O'Bryen—introducing your new friend to fleas and chiggers is not proper hospitality." She clapped her hands, voice raised an octave. "Spencer needs to head home, young man, and you need to head into the shower after one game of horse."

Davey froze on the lawn like a dead June bug, legs bent in the air. "But I just took a shower before practice," he moaned, the pain in his voice tipping Lacey's lips into a smile.

"Yes, but all the dirt and bugs crawling on you did not."

Lacey opened her car door and lifted her chin. "Come on, Spence—Mamaw's probably wondering where we are."

Spencer sat up on the grass, a crease between his brows. "But we can come back another time, right, Lacey? Or Mack can come to our house soon?"

"You bet, bud—next practice, okay?"

"Okay." Popping to his feet, he shot a shy grin at Davey over his shoulder as he trudged to the car. "Bye, Mack—see you at practice."

Mrs. O'Bryen and Shannon joined Davey at the curb, each with a hand on his shoulder as they stood on either side. "Next week after practice would be good, Lacey, if it works for you," Jack's mother called, a gentle authority in her tone.

Lacey paused to stare over the roof of the Honda, one foot in the car. "We'll be here, Mrs. O'Bryen, God willing." Sliding in, she closed the door and clutched the steering wheel with clammy hands.

A slow smile eased across Jack's mother's face, a bookend reflection of Shannon's. "He does, sweetheart," she said, her face practically aglow with hope. "And it's Tess now—we're both grown women, destined to be good friends, you hear?" A sudden sheen of tears glimmered in her eyes. "Because it's time, sweetheart."

With a jerky nod, Lacey turned the ignition key, glancing at Spence in the next seat to make sure he was buckled. A slow, reedy breath escaped when she pulled away while Spence waved wildly out the window of the car.

No question about it—it was time, indeed.

Time to deal with the past.

Time to face her demons.

And God help her, she thought with a queasy roll of her stomach.

Time to face her father again.

CHAPTER FIVE

Woof-Woof-Woof.

Tess O'Bryen glanced up from her laptop to peer through the thick hedge between Ben Carmichael's patio and hers. Her heart thumped at the sound of a screen door sliding closed as Ben's black lab Beau streaked into his backyard.

Saving her patient's call history in the Hope Hospice & Healthcare file, Tess closed the computer and rose from her comfy patio chaise, never more grateful that she could work from home as an RN. Not only did it give her the opportunity to arrange her schedule to be home for her children, but it offered the chance to catch her elusive neighbor on his day off before he and Beau left to go fishing. Her lips quirked. A neighbor who'd taken great pains to avoid her for almost eight years despite her attempts to restore the friendship. Well, no more. The time had come for Dr. Ben Carmichael—chief cardiac surgeon at Memorial Health—to have a little heart surgery of his own. She carried both her computer and her cell phone inside and placed them on the kitchen table with a heavy sigh. No, it was beyond time, she decided. Not only for her children to forgive and forget regarding Lacey and her family, but for Lacey's father to forgive and forget regarding Tess's family as well.

Not to mention his daughter.

Peeking at the pretty painted-wood blue heron clock the kids gave her for Christmas, Tess retrieved the Tupperware container of monster cookies she'd hidden in the pantry. Three fifteen—good heavens, she could set her watch by the man! She ducked into the fridge to retrieve two pieces of fried bacon, silently blessing Jack for taking Davey fishing on his day off. Since Matt had baseball practice with his summer league and Shan and Cat had a teacher's meeting at the school where they taught, she was home free.

Because *that* meant nobody was home to question her sanity as to why she was carrying a container of cookies, two pieces of bacon, and a UPS package to "Dr. Doom" next door. She nibbled on the edge of her smile. A nickname coined by her children after Ben Carmichael turned his back on her family, erecting a wall—and a hedge barrier—between his former neighbors and friends. *The apple sure doesn't fall far from the tree*, she thought when Lacey came to mind, but it was far past time the fruit was washed and dewormed to make it healthy again.

Container in hand, Tess plopped it on the UPS box with the bacon on top, a stiff smile on her face as she pushed through the screen door of the plantation-style house that had been in her family for years. Ben Carmichael received packages from UPS all the time, but when the UPS man had knocked on Tess's door today, requiring a signature—a rarity in itself—she'd known it was a sign. The one she'd prayed for since Lacey had brought Davey home three days ago.

Careful to close the screen door quietly behind her, she bolstered her confidence with a deep draw of air. The sweet scent of honeysuckle wrapped around her like the pillared front porch wrapped around the charming two-story house, its white wood planking and Cape Cod blue shutters desperately in need of a coat of paint. Stained tarps and cans of paint were neatly stacked between the peeling porch swing and pretty stone urns spilling ivy and purple petunias, all lying in wait for Jack to work his magic. Shoulders square, Tess carefully made her way down her cobblestone drive to skirt the hedge Ben had paid big bucks for after his divorce. Her mouth pressed into a tight smile as she said a quick prayer.

Okay, God, now to work a little magic of Your own ...

Apparently Beau could sniff her—or the bacon—a mile away. His low-throated growls morphed into pathetic squeals through Ben's wood-slatted fence, the chocolate eyes following her every move while his tale tick-tocked like the metronome on Shannon's piano. Tess grinned—beautiful music, indeed, the sweet and welcome whine of an oversized Labrador puppy, who used to nudge her screen door whenever she'd fried bacon for breakfast. Of course, that was *before* the hedge of Jericho went up. Lips pursed in an "o," she gave him little fish kisses. Together with the bacon, the soft popping sounds caused strands of slobber to dangle from Beau's mouth.

"You don't fool me for a moment, Beauregard Carmichael—I know it's the bacon you're excited to see, not me, but I'll take it." She plucked the bacon off the Tupperware lid and waved it in the air, causing sweet Beau to squeal, bark, and dance in circles on his hind legs. Tess's laughter countered Beau's hungry howls, unleashing a familiar ruckus that had once been as common as the shrieks of children in her back yard. Unwrapping the plastic wrap, she tossed a piece of bacon high so he had to leap in the air, giggling like a little girl as always when Beau performed his Underdog tricks.

"It's nice to know *somebody* will be glad to see me," she said with a crooked smile. Plastic wrap tucked in her pocket, she waved the second piece of bacon for several moments to coerce the pup into howling loud enough to draw the bear from his cave.

"What the—" Ben Carmichael stormed around the corner of the house and froze, the bronze tan he'd obviously picked up on a Caribbean medical convention leeching from his chiseled face. Hazel eyes the color of Colombian coffee with a touch of cream stared back, so wide she swore she could see the ring of striking green around his irises. Dark hair sifted with gray at the temples gave him the distinguished look of a man who was aging well. Although her husband had been no slouch in the looks department, Tess couldn't deny that Ben Carmichael was a true looker. So much so that she had almost pitied her best friend Karen for being married to a man who obviously caught every woman's eye. Too good-looking to be trusted, or so Tess had believed, even though Ben had never given any cause for suspicion. No lingering looks, no second glances at other women, no husky comments—nothing in the over twenty years the two couples had been best friends and neighbors. A sudden malaise tempered Tess's smile. No, instead it had been her husband—a devoted pastor—who had stolen Ben's wife away, robbing them all of the close family ties and friendship they'd once taken for granted.

"The UPS man delivered a package for you, so I thought I'd bring it over as well as bacon for Beau."

The man didn't move, didn't speak, didn't blink. Just stared like she'd dropped in from the next galaxy rather than merely next door.

Despite the smile on her face, her chin rose along with the plate in her hands. "And I have monster cookies," she said in a sing-song tone usually reserved for her children.

Silence. Except, of course, for Beau's whimpering lament. Her smile compressed. *Okay, buster, have it your way.* Eyes never straying from Ben's, she sailed the bacon far into the yard, grit girding her smile as Beau bolted away with whines of euphoria. *Because when it comes to the evil eye, Doc, I can outlast a dirty eight-year-old Power Ranger who bucks a bath, so bring it on ...*

"Why." It sounded more like a grunt than a question ... and still nothing moved on the man's body.

Tess hiked a brow, a challenge in her smile. "Why? Because they're your favorite, silly ... or at least they used to be."

"No," he bit out, the hard planes of his face calcifying even more. "*Why* are you *here—now?*"

Tess blinked, a wee bit worried for his patients if he couldn't figure this one out. She tapped the package with her fingers, head dipped as if talking to Davey. "Uh, your package?" She paused, expectant. "You know—it needed a signature?" She battled a full-fledge grin over stormy eyes shadowed by beetled brows. *Come on, Ben, you can do this.*

The fog cleared from his eyes, but the snark remained. With a grunt of thanks, he extended a muscular arm over the fence, his large palm surprisingly calloused for one of the country's top heart surgeons.

She angled a brow, stealing a page from Dr. Doom's playbook when her body didn't budge.

The scowl on his stone face slashed even deeper, revealing a hint of the "gargoyle glare" Lacey had always feared—hard, searing, and more than a little bit scary. *And* a glare that didn't faze Tess in the least. If she learned one thing from being best friends with the Carmichaels for almost a quarter of a century, it was that Ben Carmichael was all bluff, not all that different from her son Jack, really, which was one of the reasons Tess had always liked him so much. Serious, moody, yet a depth of passion and integrity that told her he was a bottomless well of emotion roiling beneath a mirror-lake he worked so hard to convey.

Ah, yes ... still waters run deep.

Her smile tipped. And, turbulently it seemed, given the forbidding glower on his face.

He slacked a hip, a motion that coincided with a noisy blast of air to reveal his frustration. "Beau will give you a drool bath, Tess, so just give me the stupid package," he said in a near growl. He flexed impatient fingers while Beau obliged with a mile-long strand of drool that quivered and swayed like Spanish moss in a breeze.

"Drool I can handle, Ben—I raised three grown children, a bulldog, a basset, and am still wiping up after a hyperactive eight-year-old." Her chin engaged for battle. "It's rudeness I can't abide."

He had the grace to blush, a ruddy color that blotched its way up his neck, just shy of a well-defined chin that sported a shadow of beard. His lips thinned as he unlatched the lock. "It's kept you away till now," he muttered, jerking the gate ajar enough to slide through, blocking Beau in ... and Tess out. A tic flickered in his angular jaw as he reached out again, palm up. "Thank you for the cookies and the bacon. Now, may I please have my package?"

"Sure." She secured her hold on the box with a blazing smile. "After we talk."

His mouth flat-lined, deader than a corpse in the hospital morgue. "I don't need this," he mumbled, jerking the gate open to retreat into his yard before slamming it closed again. "Keep it." He stormed away in a huff, Beau in his wake.

Well, that went well. She stood her ground for several moments, pretty sure that any package that required a signature had to be important enough for him to relent. *And* she was equally certain he expected her to park the package inside the gate or on his front porch as she had in the past.

Poor deluded man. Did he not know she was a veteran in the trenches when it came to children demanding their own way? Apparently not. Mouth skewed, she shimmied a finger beneath the Tupperware lid to steal a cookie and leaned against a towering pine tree, humming the *Jeopardy* song with a waggle of her head. "Doo-doo-doo-doo, doo-doo-doo …"

A mild curse sizzled the air on the third stanza as he reappeared. "What are you still *doing* here?"

She studied him while she chewed, her manner matter-of-fact. "Enjoying one of the best monster cookies I've ever made, if I must say so myself." Popping the remainder into her mouth, she swallowed before bobbling the package in one hand. "The secret is extra peanut butter *and* extra chocolate chips, you know, and uh … looking for this?"

He scowled, the hazel eyes as thin as the dead pine needles beneath her feet. "No, I'm looking for the 'secret' to get rid of an obnoxious neighbor."

"Easy as monster cookies, my friend—just open the gate and let me in."

He continued to glare, but the barest crook of his lip told her she had breached his defenses. "What do you want, Tess?" he whispered, almost as if he didn't really want to know.

Her look was open and honest, and her voice gentled, suddenly void of all tease. "I need closure, Ben," she said quietly, "and so do you. And heaven knows we both could use a friend who understands the pain of betrayal."

A heavy sigh escaped him as he hung his head to knead the bridge of his nose. Without a word, he opened the gate and walked away, obviously expecting her to follow as he rounded the corner of the house.

"Okay, Dr. Doom," she said to herself, almost giddy at the prospect of finally clearing the air. "It's no gabfest, but it's a start ..." Closing the gate with a backward kick, she headed to his patio, barricading a silent grunt with a clamp of her smile. Clear the air? Ha! Only after bulldozing a mountain of garbage.

"This is a mistake," he said quietly, hunched on the edge of one of the British green Adirondack chairs they'd sat in around his stone fire pit so many years ago. Hands loosely clasped and head bowed, his mind seemed to wander somewhere faraway, his lifeless stare locked on the slate patio mortared with moss.

"Why?" she asked, strolling over to the door to let a whining Beau back in the yard before she took the seat on the opposite side of the pit, placing both cookies and package on a side table. The perennial pup instantly darted past in pursuit of a rabbit at the far end of the yard, where a privacy fence was overrun by what had once been Karen's prized climbing roses. Knees angled to the side, Tess settled in like old times with her feet tucked beneath her and palms flat on the arms of the chair. She strove for an air of calm, but inside her heart thundered against her ribcage, her desire for reconciliation a fragile dream hanging by a slender thread of hope.

He glanced up beneath hooded eyes, moody and morose. "Why? Because I'm of no mind to dredge up the vile pain from the worst time of my life, that's why."

"Maybe you need to," she said softly, eyes in a squint. "You know, face it once and for all to find the peace and healing you need?" Her voice faded to a bare whisper as her eyes searched his. "And the forgiveness."

Vaulting to his feet, he bludgeoned a tight-fisted finger in her direction. "Look, Tess, if you came over here to peddle your sanctimonious mumbo-jumbo, I don't want to hear it. I'm fine just the way I am."

She pinned him with a level gaze. "Sure you are, Ben. That's why you're known as the Terror of the fifth floor at Memorial, Dr. Snark to your nurses, and Dr. Doom to every kid on the street. The girl scouts won't darken your door, you haven't spoken to your neighbors on either side for almost eight years, and your daughter is a virtual stranger." Her lips thinned into a tight smile as she arched her brows. "Other than that, sounds 'fine' to me."

He slammed his chair out of the way as he stalked to the back door. "Leave the package or not, I don't care."

Tess's body tensed in the chair, her voice firm. "Lacey's back, Ben—for good. You care about that?"

He froze on the threshold, fist knotted on the knob. Hard muscles flinched in a broad back as stiff as the frame of the door beneath his white-knuckled hand.

Seconds ticked by like the lethal pulse of a bomb, every one echoing her own heartbeat as it thudded hollow in her chest. And then, the angry bluster seemed to slowly seep from his body like a balloon with a slow bleed of air, massive shoulders shrinking into surrender with the drop of his head. Her heart squeezed at how difficult this was for him. "Please talk to me, Ben," she whispered, her voice a low ache. "Don't close me out again."

Still framed in the door, he gouged his temples with forefinger and thumb, all fight appearing to leak out along with the air-conditioning from his house. With a cumbersome sigh that slumped his shoulders, he closed the slider and made his way back to his chair, sinking into the slatted seat with eyes closed as he rested his head against the back. "When?"

"Over the weekend. She's staying with Karen's mother and her cousins."

Generous lips normally full in repose now pinched in a downward curve as he kneaded his temple with the ball of his hand. "How did you find out?"

"Jack ran into her at the BP on Sunday, then she dropped Davey off from his first baseball practice that evening."

Mouth cemented into a hard line, he peered up beneath dark lashes the same color as thick ebony hair edged with silver "How is she?"

"Nervous." Tess studied him with gentle eyes. "She told Jack she was back to make amends."

He grunted, the sound bringing a trace of a smile to her lips as she reflected on the hard-nosed surgeon who had a knack for making people nervous with his testy manner. A belligerence Tess suspected was more to keep people away rather than a nasty personality or out-in-out meanness. She'd seen the real Ben too many times in the past, before his wife had cut out his heart. A serious man with strength of character and a dry wit. *And* a wall of steel around his emotions that would make the impassable hedge look like air.

One side of his mouth crooked. "Nervous, huh? Yeah, well, I tend to bring that out in people apparently. It's a gift."

A smile twitched on her lips as Beau made an appearance with a half-chewed Atlanta Braves baseball cap, sliding into a comfortable spot next to Ben. "Only if you're an ostrich, turtle, or a mole looking to shut everybody out. Now me? I'd rather be at peace with the world, you know?" She wriggled a cookie from the container, then extended it across the fire pit with a wriggle of brows. "More nice surprises that way, like monster cookies from a really nice neighbor."

He stared at the cookies proffered, then at her before he finally took one, the barest trace of a smile on his face. "I've actually dreamed of these."

"Well then, see? Dreams come true when one is at peace with the world and nice to their neighbors."

That formidable jaw chewed slowly, deliberately, while those hazel eyes nailed her to the chair. "You at peace with the world, Tess?" he asked quietly.

She broke eye contact to scrub Beau on the head, his question catching her off-guard because she knew what he was asking. Had she forgiven Adam? The very question she asked herself almost every single day of her life when she prayed for the father of her children. The popular seminary student with the Dennis Quaid smile who had wooed her relentlessly until she said, "Yes." The same man who swore to love her till death do us part. Only it wasn't death that had ended their marriage. It was adultery with her neighbor and friend.

A death all the same.

She forced a casual tone, avoiding his stare. "Not for a long time I wasn't, but I think so now, at least with Adam, although it's been far more difficult for Jack and Cat, both with their father and ..." She glanced up to meet his gaze. "Your daughter."

His jaw shifted as he looked away, a grinding motion she'd always noticed whenever they'd played board games. He'd been a fierce competitor back then, Mr. Do-or-Die, no matter how much they'd tried to laugh and tease him out of it. A fighter to the bitter end, bent on winning.

Just like now.

Tess fortified with a deep draw of air as she slipped her feet to the ground and leaned forward, arms crossed on her knees. "It's time for the bitterness to end, Ben," she whispered, her solemn tone coaxing his gaze to hers. "Between our children, between our families, and between you and me."

For the first time in almost eight years she saw a glimmer of the gentleness she knew Ben Carmichael possessed, despite all the stories to the contrary. "I don't have a beef with you, Tess," he said softly.

She hiked a brow. "You could have fooled me."

Eyes in a squint, he stared aimlessly into the backyard. "It wasn't you," he whispered, grief threading his tone. His Adam's apple ducked hard in his throat. "I just couldn't see you without seeing ... Adam and ..."

"I understand, Ben, but unto everything there is a season—a time to weep and a time to laugh, and don't you think both of us are due a little laughter after the heartbreak we've endured?"

He peered up at her with a ghost of a smile. "You don't seem to have any problem—I hear laughter over there all the time."

Her smile took a swerve toward dry. "Yes, well, I'd rather be laughing *with* you rather than *at* you, Dr. Doom, if you don't mind."

Her response prompted a trace of a twinkle in his eyes before it faded once again. "Your faith certainly doesn't seem any worse for the wear."

"Actually it's stronger," she said slowly, struck for the very first time just how much more she depended on it than ever before. "When I was a pastor's wife, I thought my faith was strong, but I had no idea how weak it really was. It was almost as if I was going through the motions for Adam and our church back then. More of a long-distance relationship with God than intimate and personal like I have now." A sense of awe floated over her like a summer breeze kissed by the scent of the sea—calming her, uplifting her, buoying her with hope. She tilted her head, a faint smile of wonder skimming her lips at the revelation that suddenly flooded her soul.

"God is my husband now," she said quietly, reverently, "and more faithful than any lover could ever hope to be. True testimony to the fact He causes all

things to work together for good to those who love
Him." She glanced up, unable to thwart the tears that
stung in her eyes. "Even divorce due to adultery."

Ben sat back with a stiff fold of his arms, his smile
hard. "Yeah, well, I'm afraid it had the opposite effect
on me. I have as much use for God now as I do your ex-
husband."

"Doesn't surprise me in the least," Tess said with a
slow nod. "Jack's the same way, both about his father
and God. Flat-out refused to join the others when Adam
flew them out to Colorado three times a year before he
went overseas, or even to speak to him on the phone."
She couldn't help a devious smile. "Although I may not
be able to coerce him into making amends with his
father, trust me, I still have my ways of getting his butt
into a church pew every now and then."

A semblance of a grin slipped across his face.
"Come now, blackmail, Mrs. O'Bryen? Hard to believe
of a pastor's ex-wife who's now tight with God."

Her chin rose in defense, in total contrast to the tease
in her eyes. "Good news, Dr. Carmichael—perfection is
not a requirement for being 'tight with God,' so you're
good to go."

"No, thanks—been there, done that." He glanced at
his watch and stood with a gruff clear of his throat.
"Well, Beau and I have a fishing date, so I need to head
out, but thanks for the cookies, Tess, and the package."

"Sure." She stretched her arms high in the air,
hoping to unkink both her muscles and her
disappointment over his obvious escape. "Keep the
Tupperware—I'll pick it up next time."

He paused, assessing her through a half-lidded gaze.
"Next time," he said, his tone as flat as the press of his
lips. "There's no need for a 'next time,' Tess. We've
talked, we've cleared the air, we're good."

She squared her shoulders, her will engaging as taut
as a finely tuned bow. "No, Ben, 'good' is an amiable

friendship like we used to have." She plucked the package up and tossed it at him. "You know— humorous banter when moles invade my yard, then move to yours? Meaningful chats with cookies and coffee over the best grass seed to buy? Pleasant camaraderie when one needs advice, help, or maybe just a shoulder to cry on?" Picking up the cookies, she strolled around the fire pit to plop them on top of the package he held, giving him a firm jut of her chin tempered by a stubborn smile. "Honest-to-goodness friendship, Dr. Carmichael, guaranteed to help cure what ails you. Like an apple a day to keep the grouch away." She snatched a cookie from beneath the lid, then whirled to make a beeline for the gate. "You should try it sometime."

"Apparently I'm slated to whether I want to or not," he said in a gruff voice, the bite of his words dangerously close to a growl. "Look, Tess, I want to be left alone, all right? And it's an apple a day keeps the *doctor* away, which is exactly what I prefer to do."

She spun around, cheeks chunky with cookie as she swallowed, totally ignoring the warning muscle that flickered in his cheek. "Sorry, Doc, doesn't work with annoying neighbors." She waved the remains of her cookie in the air before disappearing around the house, her cheerful voice trailing after her. "Bon appétit!"

"Tess!"

She backtracked to pop her head around the corner. "Yes, Ben?"

He had that grinding thing going on, so much so she wondered how the poor man had any teeth left. His eyes narrowed to slits of amber, dark brows digging low. "Why is this so all-fire important to you?"

She paused, studying the man who needed a friend more than anyone she'd met in a long, long time. A veritable gem buried beneath a trash heap of bitterness and blame. She could still see glimpses of the good and caring guy he used to be, and her heart ached over the damage that had been done to them both. Her exhale was shaky and tenuous, like their path back to friendship was likely to be. But she stared him down nonetheless, never surer that this was exactly what God had called her to do. Her solemn words carried the weight of her prayers, her voice lowering to help cushion the sober truth. "Because my family and I need peace and closure, Ben, and so do you and yours." As if to underscore the importance of her goal, words from her morning devotional drifted through her mind. A gentle reminder that souls were at stake if she just walked away and never looked back, just like Ben wanted her to do.

For the Lord disciplines those He loves.

With a scrunch of her nose, she tilted her head, lips curling into a full-fledged grin. "But if you must know, Dr. *Garbo*, the real reason I'm doing this is as foreboding as the nasty look on your face." She nodded to the blue of the sky, unblemished by any clouds of concern—like her faith at the moment. "Somebody up there'll kick my butt if I don't."

CHAPTER SIX

"Yeah? And how do you know I won't kick your butt if you do?" Ben muttered under his breath, staring long after Tess disappeared around the house. He blasted out a noisy sigh and headed for the door, bobbling both package and cookies with a scowl. The last thing he needed—or wanted—was to open up communication with his next-door neighbor. His hedges and gates were there for a reason—to keep people, peddlers, and neighbors out of his life. *And* out of his heart. Not to mention memories too painful to remember.

He whistled, and Beau came running with ears flopping and that goofy doggy grin that always helped disarm Ben's sour moods. "Good boy," he said with a genuine smile, closing the door behind Beau before setting the package and cookies down on the polished stone and teak sofa table his decorator picked out. Squatting, he swallowed his best friend in a fierce hug, crooning his praises as he scratched the animal's neck.

Dogs were so easy to trust. Loyal and true, Beau loved him no matter what, be it testy or tired, and most importantly, he would never leave him or run away, never abandon him like everyone else.

His father.

His mother.

His wife and his daughter.

Head buried against Beau's, Ben clung to his animal, the dog's warm tongue lathering his face. God help him, he had no desire to let another human being get too close ever again.

God help him?

Ruffling Beau's shiny coat, Ben paused mid-scrub, lips taking a hard slant. Not likely given that God hadn't been there for him before, even after Tess and Adam had badgered him into going back to church on a regular basis. He couldn't deny there were times when belief in God had felt almost good, almost possible to believe there was a heavenly Father who loved him. But that fairy-tale had been neatly lanced when his best friend and pastor had slept with his wife, destroying any further faith in God.

Or any human being He'd created.

Except maybe my kids. He issued a silent grunt. The ones who *weren't* blood-related, and the only "family" he cared to have. Exhaling a weary sigh, he rose and made his way to the kitchen, fingers feathering Beau's head as the lab trotted by his side. His mind reflected on the special children whose lives he saved every year. Special because like him, they had no family who cared. Orphaned, abused, or lost in the foster-care shuffle, they were his chance to redeem himself as a father without all the messy and painful involvement that had plagued him all of his life. Kids like Juan Diaz, one of his favorites who brought a smile to Ben's face every time he saw the boy for follow-up. All of seven years old, the kid was bright, witty, and a real pistol, claiming he wanted to grow up to be just like Ben. A second grunt made it past Ben's lips. *No you don't, bud.* His mouth sloped off-center as he dug a Milk-Bone biscuit out of the pantry. *You'll end up a crabby, old hermit like me ...*

"Old" he wasn't so crazy about, but "crabby" and "hermit" suited Ben just fine, keeping his emotional commitment to a level he could handle. Safe. Casual. Social when necessary. And focused on the people who mattered the most—the kids that needed him. Of course his partners thought he was crazy for doing so many pro bono surgeries a year, but in a way, the Children's Miracle Network had been his salvation. His chance to give back, to bring a smile to some little kid's face. And to save lives—lots and lots of lives. He exhaled. Along with a boatload of guilt.

"I think somebody needs a treat," he said with a warmth he reserved for Beau, his drill-sergeant secretary Martha, a few select friends, and his pro bono family. "Sit …"

Beau jumped up and down, front paws jiggling in excitement as he shimmied into a perfect pose, back straight and head high. "Good boy." Carefully balancing the Milk-Bone biscuit on the animal's nose, Ben waited several seconds, a smile squirming over both the dog's life-and-death intensity and a quivering strand of drool. "Release!"

With a flawless flip in the air, Beau locked enormous jaws on the bone and crunched it to oblivion before nuzzling his nose into Ben's hand, obviously looking for more.

"Okay, okay, you're darn lucky I love you, you know that?" With a grin and an affectionate tousle of Beau's ears, Ben awarded him two additional Milk-Bones before they both traipsed into what most people referred to as "the family room"—a misnomer if ever there was. His smile went south. He hadn't had a "family" since the day his father died when Ben was only five. The one parent he'd adored, stolen away by a fatal car accident on one of many business trips, plunging his mother into a depression so debilitating, she barely knew Ben was alive.

The depression finally lifted when she married his stepfather two years later, a sanctimonious physician and taskmaster who shoved religion down Ben's throat but didn't live it himself. Before long, the man put a stranglehold on Ben's mother and him, intent on controlling and bullying them both. Looking back, Ben could almost understand why his mother took her own life, living under the thumb of a pious dictator whom neither of them could ever please. But the scar of abandonment left on her son cut deep, festering through his teens and into his so-called marriage. An all-too-familiar ache throbbed as his thoughts strayed to Karen, and for the thousandth time he wished it had been different. Wished he'd tried harder in their marriage, wished he hadn't shut her and Lacey out. But his heart was apparently toxic to anyone who even got close, proving once and for all he had no business opening up to anyone ever again. Tears burned the back of his lids, but he fought them off with a hard clamp of his mouth, wondering why, after all of these years, it still mattered at all.

Forcing his thoughts to the present, he rifled through the mail he'd tossed on his teak serpentine side table, sifting through envelopes for things that *did* matter. Like The Children's Heart Foundation or The Coastal Pet Rescue—people and things that gave him a place to channel his love. Causes and surgeries that restored a child's life, a family's hope, and his own confidence that he was a man who possessed a heart, even if he never let anyone in.

Stacking the envelopes in a neat pile, he set them aside and sank into his bomber-jacket leather recliner—an overstuffed lounger his decorator had indelicately referred to as a "monstrosity." He flipped the footrest up and snatched the TV remote to turn on the 60-inch LED, all interest in fishing suddenly sapped. All he wanted to do right now was relax after a day of back-to-back surgeries. His den—he refused to call it a family room—was comfortable despite high-ticket teak furniture and flooring that lent a sophisticated, almost stark ambiance. A white leather sectional his decorator said he just had to have spanned the length of an ultra-modern room that was as different from Karen's taste as he could possibly get. Wall-to-wall windows overlooked a manicured back lawn with a smattering of powerful oaks that created a sanctuary surrounded by the tallest, thickest hedges money could buy, utterly and completely private. His lips compressed as he flicked through the channels.

Or used to be.

Settling on an NCIS rerun he'd seen a half dozen times, his mind roamed to Tess O'Bryen, the next-door neighbor he'd worked so hard to avoid. Against his will, the pinch of his mouth softened the slightest bit, almost giving way to a smile. As much as he hated to admit it, Tess had always been one of his favorite people. Warm, funny, a little bit ditzy, but always able to lighten a mood whenever the four of them got together, even when Karen and he were fighting. A great gal, really, with only a few flaming flaws.

Too pushy, too perky, and Adam's ex-wife.

A constant reminder of all Ben had lost and all he had failed.

Not the least of which was Lacey.

Jaw steeling, he squinted hard at the TV. Nope, best to nip it in the bud right now and avoid the woman like the plague. His gaze flicked to the Tupperware container of cookies that taunted on the table by the door, and a colorful word hissed from his lips. With a hard jerk of the footrest lever, his feet hit the floor and he jumped up to retrieve the container, ticked off when he started salivating like Beau with his bone. Returning to his chair, he plopped back down and took out a cookie, mouth watering worse than Pavlov's stupid dog. Against his will, a groan of pleasure rumbled in his throat at first bite, a deadly reminder of just what a great cook Tess had always been. *And* how bribery with sweets had always been her favorite way to handle Adam and the kids. Ben shook his head, cookie ecstasy warring with annoyance over exactly what the woman was trying to do.

Monster cookies ... to tame the monster, no doubt.

Polishing off his fifth one, he snapped the lid back on and tossed them on the table with a grunt, determined to return the others when the woman wasn't home. Because whether Tess O'Bryen liked it or not, this was one monster with a nasty bite and a penchant for chewing. Aiming the remote, he jacked the volume up with a hard grind of his jaw.

And he sure wasn't talking cookies ...

CHAPTER SEVEN

"See? This is exactly why I didn't tell you in the first place—you get all moody on me, Jack, and start drinking more than you should."

Jack peered up at Matt with a half-lidded glare, the near-empty Blue Moon in his hand suddenly as acidic as his mood despite the usual revelry going on at Clancy's Pub. Their mainstay watering hole following most baseball games, Clancy's was particularly wild tonight, strains of Coldplay filtering through raucous laughter punctuated by the crack of ivory from the pool table at the back of the bar. For once, the noise got on Jack's nerves, darkening his disposition even more. His favorite hangout was just too freakin' joyous tonight to suit, especially with his teammates celebrating another victory that secured their first-place lead in the Savannah's Men's League. A lead that called for beers all around, giving Jack the perfect excuse to drown his troubles despite his cousin's disapproval. A cousin who now studied him from the next barstool with concern in his eyes.

Returning his gaze straight ahead to the hodge-podge of framed jerseys over the bar, Jack gulped another drink to douse the burn of Matt's silent rebuke, a best friend who'd found faith about the same time Jack had lost his. Matt's barstool finally squealed when he angled Jack's way, indicating he had come to the end of his silence. "Come on, Jack—snap out of it. Lacey's back, so get over it. She's Nicki's maid of honor and you're my best man, so you may as well make the best of it."

"The 'best of it,'" Jack said in a tone as lifeless as his body, fingers limp on the bar while they circled his glass. "And what would that be, Matt? The fact I won't ever have to talk to her again after you and Nicki are married?"

Matt upended his Red Bull and banged it down on the bar with a hard crack that told Jack he was ruining Matt's evening as well as his own. His cousin whirled to confront him with a tight press of lips, his usual happy-go-lucky manner dwindling as fast as Jack's sobriety. "Come on, Jack, you're my best friend and this is supposed to be the happiest time of my life, so get a grip and lighten up. Do it for me if not for yourself, will ya?"

Jack blasted out a noisy sigh and gouged his temple with the pads of his fingers, not anxious to pile guilt on top of an already black mood. "Okay, Matt. I'm sorry. I'm not trying to ruin your wedding, man, really. It's just that—"

"You're still carrying a torch for her," Matt said, his voice cautious as if trying to wheedle the truth out of him.

The very thought shot fury through Jack's veins like adrenalin, and he slammed the rest of his beer to the back of his throat. "No way, man—the chick leaves me cold, trust me."

One hand flat on the bar, Matt studied him through pensive eyes that reflected more doubt than trust. "I'd like to, Jack, but something tells me you don't even trust yourself when it comes to Lacey."

His grunt was harsh. "You got that right. It's going to take everything in me not to chew her up and spit her out, which doesn't bode well for a happy and cozy bridal party." Holding his empty glass up with one hand and Matt's Red Bull with the other, he signaled the bartender for refills, his bitterness toward Lacey and her family rekindling his ire.

"Which is all the more reason you need to get past it," Matt said, expelling a heavy blast of air. "You've been carrying a grudge against Lacey and her family forever now, and it's time to bury the hatchet."

Jack glanced up through wary eyes. "Don't tempt me, Matt. I'm willing to hold my tongue and be civil for your sake during the wedding, but don't ask me to cozy up to her before that because it ain't gonna happen."

"Yeah ... well about that ..." Matt scratched the back of his head, avoiding Jack's gaze.

Jack homed in, all but cauterizing Matt with a look. "A-bout *what?*" he ground out, each syllable a near hiss.

The bartender returned with their drinks, and Matt jumped up, wasting no time digging in his wallet to pay for the tab. "Thanks, Pete," he said, quickly pushing Jack's beer closer before he squinted at the menu on the wall. "Hey, Jack, you want nachos with that beer?"

A tic throbbed in Jack's cheek over Matt picking up the bill since it was Jack's turn to pay, sending prickles of alarm through his body. *Guilt money*, he thought, biting back a curse. He spun to face his cousin dead-on, clamping his arm like a vise when Matt refused to look his way. "A-bout what, Matt?"

The giant red "B" on Matt's Savannah Bombers baseball jersey rose and fell as Matt took a deep draw of humid air, thick with the smell of grilled burgers and brats, before he slumped back on the stool. Venting with an exaggerated sigh, he finally faced his cousin, sympathy dark in his eyes. "Sorry, Jack, but there's a lot to do for the wedding, so I can't leave it all to Nicki, you know? And you said you'd help me with anything I need, right?" He paused, the weight of his words steeling his facial muscles despite the regret in his tone. "Which means sooner or later, you're going to have to work with Lacey because that's why she's here too."

Jack's jaw began to ache. "*How* much 'sooner'?" he bit out, every nerve on alert even through the haze of two beers.

Face in a scrunch, Matt yanked on his left ear, an absent-minded habit that only occurred when he was on the hot seat with teachers, parents, or the best friend he was about to burn.

"Hey, babe." Both of them whirled around to see Nicki plant a kiss on the back of Matt's neck before she slid onto the barstool on his other side, leaning forward with a forced smile. "Hey, Jack, haven't seen you in a blue moon."

Blue Moon. Good idea. "Hey," he said in a clipped tone, draining half of his Blue Moon in three hard gulps. He swiped the side of his mouth with his hand when he came up for air, jaw tight because they weren't exactly the best of friends. Not since she'd merked him by ruining the girl he'd hoped to marry. "I've been busy with the new job," he said with a stiff smile, well aware he avoided her as much as she did him despite their mutual love for Matt.

"Yeah, Matt told me. Congrats on scoring a spot on Augustine's team, by the way. That peds experience should come in handy with this one here." She bumped her fiancé's shoulder with an impish grin, earning a sweep of Matt's arm to tickle her into a kiss.

"So, where is everybody?" Matt glanced over his shoulder while he held her close, scanning the bar with a crimp in his brow.

Everybody? The beer pooled in Jack's mouth right before it went down the wrong pipe.

Following Matt's gaze, Nicki grinned and waved her arm like a wild woman. "The girls headed over to the pool table first to round up the other groomsmen."

The girls? Jack began to hack.

"Hey, buddy, pace yourself, will ya?" Matt pounded on Jack's back, ducking his head to peer up with a hint of humor in blue eyes crinkled with apology. He leaned in to whisper in Jack's ear. "Uh, I guess I forgot to tell you, man—this is sort of a bridal-party planning meeting."

Jack snatched the napkin coaster beneath his glass and wiped his mouth, his eyes hot enough to weld his cousin to the wall. "Planning meeting?" he croaked, throat hoarse from hacking and spewing beer all over the counter. "The only 'planning' I've got in mind right now, Goof Ball, is tearing you limb to limb."

A grin slid across his cousin's face as he gripped an arm over Jack's shoulder. "Ah-ah-ah … you took the Hippocratic Oath, remember? You have to put people back together, not tear 'em apart."

Teeth grinding to near nubs, Jack shoved Matt's arm off his shoulder with no little force. "Sorry, pal, but the *Hypocritical* Oath cancels it out," he hissed, suddenly bone-dry for about six more beers—three to pour over Matt and three to numb his brain. "Which means I can make hamburger out of any hypocrite who says he's a friend, then pulls a stunt like this."

"Oooo … a hamburger sounds good." Nicki squirmed onto her own barstool, eyeing the overhead menu like a Survivor contestant at a Vegas buffet.

"Well, if it isn't the long-lost doctor!" Kelly Goshorn sidled up to slip a bare arm around Jack's waist, the scent of Juicy Couture reminding him what a flirt Nicki's best friend was. "I thought I heard something about you rejoining the human race."

Broiling Matt with a final tight-lipped glare, Jack swiveled to face the girl who'd tried to pick up where

Lacey left off so many years ago, offering Jack a sympathetic ear, a shoulder to cry on, and anything else he wanted. "Hey, Kelly, you're looking good." He forced a nonchalant tone, his smile as flat as his interest in the long-legged lawyer who looked like a Gen Y version of *The Good Wife*. "How've you been?"

"Better than ever," she said with a sultry sweep of chestnut shoulder-length hair, a gleam in sable eyes that implied she was talking about far more than her state of mind. "And you're looking good, too, Dr. O'Bryen." Arms crossed over a well-fitting tank top, she angled her head to study him, the almond shape of her eyes thinning in apparent assessment. "Although I'm not sure just *which* is more attractive—those brawny arms or the brawny title."

"Oooo, I'll take the arms," Sarah Baker said with a wink, nudging Kelly out of the way to give Jack a warm hug he had no trouble returning. Sarah had always been his favorite of Nicki's friends at the get-togethers Matt had managed to drag him to. She pulled back with an easy smile and a tip of her head, the auburn streaks in her shaggy blonde bob a testament to her successful beauty-salon business. "Congratulations on your hard-earned degree, Doc—maybe *now* you can hang out with us a little more and have some fun?"

"Maybe." A half smile played on his lips as he tugged on a loose auburn strand of her hair, the generous spray of freckles across an upturned nose suddenly reminding him of his sisters.

"Hey, we *are* going to move this party to the big booth in the back, right? Where we can finally eat?" Matt's friend Nate slid his empty mug onto the bar and rubbed his hands together, gaze darting from face to face. "Matt says he's picking up the tab, so I'm hungrier than usual."

Matt groaned. "Which means I probably have to duck out and hit the ATM before the night is over." He gave both Nate and his other friend Justin a friendly shove toward the back of the bar where a reserved sign sat on the table of their favorite booth. "Come on, you jokers, we've got some planning to do before I feed you."

"Mmm … well, I call dibs on the doctor," Kelly said with a slip of her arm through Jack's. "Nate and Justin are all yours, Sarah and Lacey."

Lacey.

In the space of one ragged heartbeat, the crowd thinned like clouds drifting apart to allow a single ray of sunshine through as Lacey came into view. The sight of her in a short melon-colored sundress with spaghetti straps and that adorably messy ponytail all but sucked the air from his lungs. Their gazes locked, and his heart seized still for a full three seconds while she offered a shy smile that made his mouth go dry. "Hey, Jack," she said softly, her voice almost breathless while she chewed on the edge of those luscious pink lips that had once been his for the taking. "Good to see you again."

Good? His skin flashed hot and then cold, like a brain freeze that traveled to every nerve in his body, ticking him off something fierce. She had no right to make him feel this way, to mess with his mind, to screw with his pulse. As far as he was concerned, she was sheer poison—then and now—and there was only one antidote for that kind of poison.

Anger.

Offering a tight smile that was barely civil, he slipped a hand around Kelly's waist and whispered in her ear, making her laugh as he led her to their table at the back. He allowed Kelly to ease into the booth next to Matt and Nicki while Nate, Sarah, and Justin made room for Lacey on the other side. His smile evaporated. Directly across from him, of course, looking every bit as uncomfortable as he.

Their favorite waitress appeared to hand out menus, and Jack was grateful for the interruption, shooting Wanda an easy smile that earned him a sassy wink. "Well, well, I see the gang's all here," she said with a butt of her hip against his arm, "including Isle of Hope's most eligible bachelor." She teased him with a sexy look while she played with the hair at the back of his head. "So, what's your poison tonight, doc?"

Without meaning to, Jack's eyes flicked to Lacey's and held, giving him a modicum of satisfaction when a blush stole into her cheeks before she looked away.

"Bring him a Red Bull, Wanda," Matt said from the other end of the booth, "I need him sober since this is a working meeting, and he's already had two."

Sarah angled a brow. "Whoa, since when do you tip more than one, Dr. Jack? Don't tell me med school drove you to drink?"

He shot a tight smile in Matt's direction. "No, that honor belongs to Ball tonight, I'm afraid." Draining the last of his glass, he pushed it away. "*Blue Moon*, Wanda," he emphasized with a narrow look in Matt's direction, figuring Matt deserved it for not warning him about tonight. Ignoring the scowl on his cousin's face, he draped an arm over Kelly's shoulder. "Who else? My treat."

"Sounds good to me." Kelly inched closer while everyone else opted for D.P. and Coke.

When Wanda finished taking all the orders, Matt got down to business. "Nicki and I have been talking, and we've both decided to have the wedding and reception in Nicki's backyard."

Sarah bounced in her seat with a clap of hands. "Oh, I'm so glad—Nick's backyard is absolutely perfect, especially as private as it is with Mamaw's gardens overlooking the river." She folded her arms on the table. "You are going to have a tent in case it rains, right?"

"You bet," Nicki said with a gleam in her eye, "the whole nine yards. I got Mamaw to agree by telling her she'd get that gazebo and rock walkway she's been wanting all these years, complete with landscaping."

"Which is why we're all here tonight, as a matter of fact." Matt glanced around the table. "Nicki and I thought instead of you guys popping for a wedding present, renting tuxes, or buying bridesmaid dresses— which we'll take care of—we'd see if you wanted to help build the gazebo and landscape Mamaw's yard instead. We figure it shouldn't take more than three or four get-togethers to get it all done, and Nicki's dad's paying for all materials."

A silent groan clogged in Jack's throat. *Three or four get-togethers?*

"Not to mention that Mamaw will be providing all food and refreshments," Nicki added with a waggle of brows.

"Oh, man, count me in," Nate said. He cast a hopeful look at Nicki. "You will tell her to make those red-velvet balls, right? And that seven-layer dip?"

Matt laughed. "If that's what it takes to get you there, Sherman, you bet."

"Then count me in too." Justin draped an arm over Sarah's shoulder. "Especially if Sarah agrees to make her famous cannolis."

"Done!" Sarah said with a quick brush of her hands.

"Well, I'm certainly game." Kelly cocked her head to peer up at Jack, her smile an invitation. "This sounds like a lot of fun if Jack's involved."

"Well, that's the plan all around." Matt snaked an arm around Nicki to pull her close while Wanda delivered their drinks. He zeroed in on Jack with a crooked smile. "And of course Jack's involved—he's the only one here besides me who knows how to use a hammer and saw—not to mention he owes me big time."

Jack smiled his thanks at Wanda, then passed the various sodas around the table, eyes in a squint. "Yeah? How you figure, Ball?"

A twinkle lit Matt's eyes. "Because I've covered your sorry butt on house chores for four years of med school and three years of residency, O'Bryen, so it's payback."

"Payback?" Jack slowly took a drink of his beer, his eyes narrowed over the rim of his glass as his gaze flicked from Lacey to Matt, his voice laden with threat. "Count on it."

But Matt only grinned while Nicki pulled out a notebook and pen, poised to take notes. By the time the food arrived, she and Matt had a workable plan and schedule in place and appetites were high. Both for the food and the prospect of Matt and Nicki's "dream wedding," which according to Sarah, "each of them would always remember."

Jack tore into his burger. Yeah, that was the problem. He didn't *want* to remember this wedding or anything to do with. Not when it meant spending time with a woman who left him cold. He popped a couple of fries while Kelly offered him the catsup. *Correction.* Left his heart cold. But his body? He pounded back a hefty swig of beer while Lacey laughed with Nate and Sarah. The sight of her tan and toned in a skimpy sundress—even if it was worlds more modest than what the other girls wore—pumped heat through his veins like lava, slow and hot.

Man, I need another drink bad. He snatched his glass from the table and downed it in one long glug, caught off-guard when the room began to spin. Clutching the edge of the booth, he jerked his eyes wide open, blinking to clear the glaze from his vision. Heat crawled up the back of his neck when he saw Lacey watching him with a sad look in her eyes, like she felt sorry for him. *Yeah? Well, a little late for that, Carmichael.*

"So, everybody okay with that?" Nicki's voice broke into his stupor as she scanned the table with a lift of brows. "Good, then let's meet at church next Saturday at seven, okay?"

Jack blinked, his hearing apparently as impaired as his vision. *Church?* "Uh, sorry—I missed that, Nicki. What'd you say?"

"Our next planning meeting will be at Hope Church next Saturday at seven. There's a wedding Pastor Chase thinks would be simple and inexpensive to copy, so he invited us to check it out, followed by volleyball in the gym after."

Jack nailed Matt with a narrow gaze. "I don't *do* church," he muttered, upending his empty glass only to scowl when nothing but dregs dribbled down his throat.

"It's a wedding, Jack." Matt's tone was even with a slight edge of challenge.

"Followed by volleyball in a gym," Nicki emphasized, head dipped as if daring him to defy the man she loved.

"Might do you good, Jack, you never know." Lacey raised her Coke in a toast that was more of a tease.

He charred her with a look. "And what would *you* know about 'doing me good,' Carmichael?"

"*Allllllll righty now,*" Nicki said with a roll of her eyes, "moving right along ... "

Matt shook his head, a low chuckle rumbling from his chest. "Yeah, Lace, it might do our boy some good, but I doubt the same for the church." He hefted his glass with a wink. "The way Lover Boy's been burning the candle at both ends lately, the place might just go up in flames if he darkened the door."

French-tip fingernails latched onto Jack's arm as Kelly moved closer. "Oooo, I'm a fan of fire myself, so you can darken my door any day, Lover Boy."

Matt leaned back in the booth, one arm loosely draped over Nicki's shoulder as he guzzled his DP, gaze sharpening on Jack. "Now don't go all cray on us, dude—nobody's forcing you to go to church, but you just may have a good time, Jack. Chase has some pretty cool friends joining us for volleyball, and a couple of them are real lookers."

"Boy, I'll say." Justin offered Jack a thumbs-up before he devoured a handful of fries. "I got my eye on one, I can tell you that, so you should go, Jack."

"And they're *nice* girls," Nicki stressed, her way of letting Jack know she didn't approve of the wilder women he'd been dating. "With good heads on their shoulders."

"I don't like nice girls," Jack muttered, signaling Wanda for another beer. "They're only interested in marriage."

"Mmm … well, this could be your lucky day then, Dr. O'Bryen." Kelly peered up at him with a secret smile, French tips skimming through the dark hairs on his arm.

Matt slid Lacey a smile of apology, nodding his head toward Jack. "Sorry, Lace. This joker's not the same boy scout you used to know, so sometimes you just have to ignore all his sulky moods and crass comments like I do."

"Too bad," Lacey said softly, those sober hazel eyes tinged with regret. "I was rather partial to that boy scout."

"But not enough to stay, eh, Mike?" He bit out the former nickname without affection, his words clipped with a bitterness that all but swallowed him whole.

"*Ooooooookay now …*" Nicki said with a stab of her salad. "This appears to be an appropriate time to decide who will be paired up with whom." She slid Matt a sideways glance, her voice lowering as if she didn't want anyone else to hear. "I know you want Jack as your best man, but maybe he and Kelly are better suited—"

"Oh, I second that." Kelly nibbled a fry while giving Jack a coy smile.

Matt shook his head. "No, Jack's my best man no matter how much of a derp he's being." His blue eyes narrowed in threat. "He'll shape up, I promise, even if I have to do it with a fist."

Shooting Nicki an unspoken plea, Lacey laid her sandwich aside. "Look, Nick, I don't have to be your maid of hon—"

"No!" Nicki's tone stopped Lacey cold and everyone else at the table. She slanted in, eyes snapping like dry twigs in a hot fire. "You are the closest thing I have to a sister, Lace, and I am not going to let some Hatfield and McCoy feud ruin my wedding, so *you're* my maid of honor, case closed." Eyes hard as topaz, she turned on Jack, gaze glowing hotter than a welder's torch. "The best man *will* behave, won't you, Jack?"

Glaring Nicki down, Jack balked at her tone, lips as thin as his patience as he belted back a healthy swig of fresh beer delivered by Wanda.

Nicki slammed a fist on the table, rattling the dishes. "*Won't you,* Jack?" she repeated, revealing a touch of that red-headed temper Matt had always warned him about.

He cast a sullen look Matt's way before drilling both Nicki and Lacey with a pointed gaze. "As long as she doesn't get any hare-brained ideas that she and I'll be friends."

Lacey shot to her feet. "Oh, *puh-leez*, give me a little credit, will you? I have no interest in banging my head against a brick wall, bucko—I'm not that stupid." She hurled her napkin on the table, all prior softness in her eyes erupting into bronze fire. She jutted her chin to the level of intimidation he recognized from the fights they used to have. "Or at least I haven't been for the last eight years." She slapped the strap of her purse over her shoulder while her gaze darted to Nicki. "I'll be back, Nick—right now I need some air bad."

She stalked off, leaving an awkward silence that Matt finally broke with a low warning aimed right at Jack. "Hey, lay off, man. The poor kid just got dumped by some other guy, so cut her some slack, will ya?" Stress lines ridged his brow as he pushed his plate away, mouth leveled in a tight line. "She doesn't deserve your grief, Jack, and neither do I."

Jack mauled his face with his hands, feeling like a royal jerk for doing this to Matt and everyone else. "Sorry, man," he whispered, kneading the bridge of his nose. "Too much brew, I guess." He pushed the nearly full beer away and lumbered to his feet, offering Matt a look of regret. Taking his wallet out, he tossed a wad of twenties down, then scanned the table with an apology in his eyes. "'Sorry' doesn't cut it, I know, but at least I can cover the tab." He nodded toward the door. "I'm gonna go, Matt, but I'll be there next Saturday."

The tension in his cousin's face eased. "Thanks, man—appreciate it."

Jack gave a short nod. "So long, everybody," he muttered, barely hearing the goodbyes that followed him to the door.

"Jack, wait!"

He turned, not overly thrilled to see Kelly hurrying to catch up. "Why don't you let me drive you home? I'd hate to see you get a DUI or put a dent in that pretty new car."

"Thanks, Kelly, but three beers is well within my legal limit, so I'm good." He gave her a half smile, the dizziness in his brain feeling anything but legal.

She moved in close, her arms slipping around his waist. "I know you're good, silly, but you *could* be even better," she whispered, lifting on tiptoe to nuzzle at his earlobe.

He closed his eyes, uncomfortable with the flash of heat her touch produced. Matt would skin him alive if he got physically involved with one of Nicki's converts, no matter how luke-warm that convert may be. With a slow skim of his hands down her arms, he held her at bay, wishing he could just take advantage of the blatant invitation in her eyes. *Anything* to rid himself of the freakin' fire Lacey had stirred in his gut. "Look, Kelly, you don't want to get involved with a guy like me— you'll just regret it. Then I'll regret it, and Nicki will string me up for leading you astray."

"I'm a big girl, Jack—I think I can handle it."

He sucked in a deep inhale of air, grazing her cheek with the pad of his thumb. "Yeah, but I can't. I'm not looking for anything but a good time right now, Kelly, and that's not what you're looking for."

"Says who?" She moved in close, her body flush against his, spiking his pulse.

He nodded behind her, one side of his mouth tipping up. "Says them."

She spun around and groaned as Nicki and Sarah approached, causing his lips to quirk when he spied the mama-bear glint in Nicki's eyes.

Nicki latched on to Kelly's wrist, tugging her toward the ladies room with a stiff arch of her brow. "We need to talk."

"About what?" Kelly said, heels all but skidding across the slatted floor as Nicki and Sarah dragged her to the restroom.

Jack couldn't help but grin as Sarah waggled her fingers in a goodbye before the trio disappeared into the hall, admiring their loyalty and common sense, if not their religion. Shaking his head, he waved to a number of his teammates before stepping out the door, a clean wash of sea air helping to cool the heat of both the bar and Kelly's tease. He unlocked his car and opened the door, sliding in to grab one of the Tootsie Roll miniatures he kept in his cup holder, the need for his sweet obsession all the stronger after such a sour evening. With a toss of the paper into the ashtray, he popped the candy in his mouth and started to close the door. His fingers froze on the handle when he spotted a female shadow on Butterbean Beach. Moonlight shimmered behind her on the Skidaway Narrows, and he instantly frowned, wondering what female was stupid enough to walk at night by herself outside of a bar on the Redneck Riviera.

A breeze fluttered the woman's dress, and the moment Jack saw a ponytail sway in the wind, he didn't have to wonder anymore. He swore under his breath and got out of his car, slamming his door hard. Eyelids flickering, he lurched to a stop for several dizzy seconds to clear the haze of booze from his brain. Despite his bravado with Kelly, he was as close to hammered as a traditionally one-beer guy could be, which only fed his fury toward his ex all the more.

Muscles bunched in his jaw, he wove his way through the parking lot toward the Intracoastal, determined to give her a piece of his mind—or what was left of it—about strolling a beach by herself at night.

Because Lacey Carmichael may have played him, tempted him, and left him for dead, but she didn't deserve some half-drunk cowboy or ballplayer giving her trouble.

He gritted his teeth, looking both ways before he strode toward the beach.

Not unless it was him.

CHAPTER EIGHT

*R*eleasing a weary sigh, Lacey plopped down on the sandy shore of Butterbean Beach and tented her legs, hands clasped around them as she peered up at the blue-black sky. Her anger at Jack suddenly seemed as scattered and far away as the stars winking overhead.

Okay, God, I blew it. Her eyelids weighted closed. *Again.*

Chin on her knees, she breathed in the earthy scent of the marsh and seawater, her guilt mingling with melancholy over the once-familiar sights, sounds, and smells of one of Jack's and her favorite haunts.

A man-made beach just off the boat ramp at Skidaway Narrows, Butterbean was where locals went to launch their boats, swim and sail on rope swings, or have a private picnic far from the crowds on Hilton Head or Tybee. She could hear the gentle lapping of the water against both the shore and the towering wooden tide pillars that jutted out of the Intracoastal, where seagulls perched during the day. The salty breeze shifted and she wrinkled her nose at the pungent smell of dead fish, reminding her of the rich life cycle of low-country marshes and tides. Death, giving way to new life, making it richer, deeper, stronger than ever before. A rebirth that set the heart and soul free.

Just like You did for me ...

Except for tonight. Tears stung at the thought and Lacey inhaled sharply, grateful that no matter how many times she screwed up, God had her back with His strength, His healing, His unfailing love. That no matter what, He would make good from her mistakes. *For my power is made perfect in weakness* ... Her lip quirked. Heaven knows she could certainly keep the Almighty busy, that was for darn sure. She remembered just how weak and shallow her life had been without Him a few short months ago. Empty and haunting in spite of endless pursuits, plans, and pleasures that brought no peace, no hope, no real happiness at all.

Her thoughts drifted to Jack, and a heaviness settled on her shoulders like the cloying press of humid air when the sea breezes refused to blow. He and her father were the main reasons God had sent her back, to show them His unconditional love just like God had shown her. Not only to bring healing to them and herself, but a renewal of hope and faith to the people she loved. Through grace, patience, and hard-earned humility.

Not temper.

A low groan ground from her lips as she buried her head in her arms, voice raised in frustration. "Ooooooh ... I screwed up, and I'm *so* sorry." With a harsh grunt, she gouged up two fistfuls of sand and pelted them toward the water, emitting a growl. "Talk about epic fail."

"A talent of yours, apparently."

Lacey's head jerked up and spun around, heart thumping like a flat-bottom gigging boat on the water at full speed. "Jack," she rasped, a brain-freeze chill blasting full body at the shock of seeing him standing not five feet away, hands slung low on his grass-stained pants. "W-what are you doing h-here?"

He slacked a hip, moonlight revealing a scowl on his handsome face. "No, a better question is *why* a girl who's supposed to have a brain in her head is walking the Redneck Riviera at night by herself?" The scowl thinned into a smirk as his gaze trailed from her sandy feet up her bare legs to the short hem of her sundress, now bunched to her thighs. "Unless, of course," he said with a nasty smile, "you're *looking* for that kind of trouble."

She bristled. *Nope, but apparently I found it.* Hopping up, she yanked her dress in place and brushed off the sand, fully aware that sniping back at a bitter ex-boyfriend was no way to make amends. With a silent prayer, she tamped down the old temper by counting to ten. Taking her time to pick up her purse, she finally looked up with as much humility as she could scrape together. "I appreciate your concern, Jack," she said in a careful voice, slinging her purse over her shoulder. "I suppose it was stupid to wander off like that."

A muscle twitched in his cheek. "Yeah, well, I guess it can't be helped."

She blinked, brows crimped in confusion. "Pardon me?"

Those wide lips that once had devoured hers pinched flat, as narrow as his cobalt-blue eyes, which now morphed to black. "It's in the DNA, apparently—both 'wandering' and 'stupid.'"

Her mouth fell open ... right before she slammed it shut again, afraid of what might come out. *One. Two. Three. Four ...*

He shifted with a casual fold of arms, muscles corded as hard and tight as the flex of his jaw. "Both clearly talents of yours ..."

A snappy comeback all but rammed against her teeth. *Five. Six. Seven. Eight.*

His eyes raked her head to toe. "Along with teasing and tempting the locals, I guess," he drawled, his mouth hooking into a cold smile that told her he was baiting her, pure and simple.

It worked.

She slanted in. "Okay, I've had about enough of your snide remarks, Jack O'Bryen," she said with a step forward, all but spraining her finger when she poked him hard in the chest. "I came back to make amends, not butt heads with some hotshot Romeo who's not man enough to let bygones be bygones."

He grabbed her wrist, fusing her to the spot. "Real easy when they're not *your* bygones, Mike," he hissed, all but spitting the words in her face.

She stared at him in the moonlight, his grip as stiff and smarting as her neck, now painfully craned to confront his towering six-foot-three. Anger throbbed in his eyes as wildly as her heart throbbed in her chest, and the smell of beer on his breath was a painful reminder of just how much she and her family had altered his life.

And then in one fractured beat of her pulse, the years suddenly washed away like the tide from the shore, revealing the godly boy she'd once pledged to marry. A kind and good man meant for far better things before tragedy had befallen them all. Fingers quivering, she slowly placed her palm over the hand that shackled her wrist, her tears blurring the features of this man who still claimed a piece of her heart. "Oh, Jack, I still grieve over the pain my family and I caused, and I hope someday you'll find it in your heart to forgive me because I so desperately want to be your friend."

"My friend," he said in a slow, menacing drawl, hand dropping listlessly to his side while his gaze bore into hers. "The last time I saw you, Mike, you wanted way more than that, as I recall."

Her heart stuttered when he slowly skimmed the side of her face with his thumb, sending once-familiar shivers through her body while he caressed the shape of her mouth. Warm, dangerous shivers that collided with pinpricks of warning when his gaze drifted to her lips.

*No, Jack, please—not now, not like this. Not while
beer and bitterness poison your mind ...*

"I wasn't willing then," he whispered, slowly
tugging her close with a slide of his hand to her waist.
He tightened his hold, and alarm rolled in her belly as
paralysis struck. "But trust me, sweetheart, I'm more
than willing now ..."

All protest seized in her throat when his mouth took
hers with a vengeance, as if he were paying her back for
every kiss he'd denied himself so many years ago when
virtue trumped attraction. She shivered at the taste of
beer and bitterness in his mouth, tinged with a touch of
Tootsie Roll, his trademark candy that instantly swept
her years back to his kisses on the dock. Only this
wasn't that kind and tender boy anymore who'd once
treasured and taken care of her. No, this one jerked her
close, hands wandering at will, and she suddenly knew
he was punishing her, not only for breaking his heart,
but for all the times she'd punished him with
temptation, testing him to the max.

Just like he was testing her right now.

"Jack, stop!" She shoved him away, stumbling back
when she broke his grip.

His eyes glinted with anger. "What's the matter,
Lace? You begged for it once, remember?" His mouth
curved in a hard smile. "I'll just bet you give out more
samples than the little old ladies at Sam's."

Needles of shock stabbed over the cruel intent of his
taunt. To make her feel small and cheap like her dad
always had, his painful barbs sending her sobbing into
Jack's arms, the one person who'd always understood
just how much Daddy had hurt her.

*"Don't think you're anything special. Any whore
can get 'em excited."*

Against her will, the hot sting of water welled in her
eyes, familiar tears over a father she could never please
no matter how hard she tried. And, apparently, an ex-

boyfriend with no qualms about turning the knife. Fingers quivering, she adjusted the purse on her shoulder and turned away, salty wetness slicking her face as she stalked across the beach.

"Lacey!"

She heard the regret in his voice, but she dare not stop, not with sobs rising in her chest over the wound he obviously meant to inflict. A sharp and slicing stab straight to the heart, meant to make her bleed. She broke into a run. *Well, good for you, Jack—you met your mark.*

"Lacey, wait!"

But she couldn't because distance was the only thing she wanted from Jack O'Bryen right now. A hurt, little girl bolting away from rejection like she had so many years ago. Vision bleary, she stumbled on until a buried piece of driftwood hooked the strap of her sandal. It flung her headlong into the sand, breaking both her pride and her spirit as she lay there and wept.

The moment he touched her, she flailed and bucked like a catfish on the shore, wanting no part of Jack O'Bryen ever again. "Leave me alone," she hissed, eyes swollen and body gritty with sand. "I don't want you to touch me."

Ignoring her, he knelt on the beach and bundled her in his arms, immobilizing her completely from any further thrashing about. "Lacey, I'm sorry," he whispered against her head, tucking her body to his as he knelt beside her, his steel hold gentle but firm. Her heart drummed like that of a baby bird with a broken wing while his thumb slowly caressed her arm, his voice husky and low. "I didn't mean it, I swear. I'm just …" She felt the hard shift of his Adam's apple against her hair, the ache in his tone revealing the caring and tender boy who long ago had stolen her heart. "Angry inside, you know? And … still pretty hurt, I guess … over what might have been."

Her body stilled in his arms. "I know," she whispered, "me too." Pulling away, she swiped at her eyes. "I never meant to hurt you, Jack, I swear." She looked away, gaze fixed on the black waters rippling in the moonlight, remembering with painful clarity the awful row she and her father had the night he kicked her out of the house.

"Well, well—a whore for a pastor's wife. That ought to put a pretty good dent in his career."

"Why did you do it, Lace?" Jack said quietly. "Why did you leave without a word?"

She pulled back to look at him then, wishing with all of her heart that things could have been different. That her parents' marriage had been better than it was. That her mother hadn't cheated on her father, and that her family hadn't destroyed Jack's. Her eyes shuttered closed. *And that I hadn't been so hell-bent on living life my way.* She drew in a deep breath. "I ... wasn't ready for that kind of commitment, Jack," she whispered, "and I didn't know ... didn't know how else to say goodbye."

"So you took the coward's way out." The words came out sharp and clipped, making her wince.

She swallowed hard, desperate to make him understand. "We weren't right for each other—"

"That's bull, Lacey, and you know it." A muscle throbbed in his temple as he leaned in, his gaze piercing hers. "We were crazy about each other. For crying out loud, you couldn't keep your hands off me, and you were everything I ever wanted."

"But not everything you needed," she whispered, aching inside that the decision she'd made for his "good" back then had only backfired, driving him to the "bad" instead. She reached for his hand, clinging to it like a tether of hope, her eyes pleading with his. "The past is over and done, Jack, but we can start over again if you'll let us—as friends."

He stared at the hand that clutched his, gaze slowly lifting to hers. "Friends," he said quietly, his eyes deep pools of hurt and pride and more than a little longing. "That's how we started out before." Her stomach flipped when his glance lowered to her lips. "What makes you think we won't end up there again?"

Heat swamped her face, and she looked away lest he see the regret in her eyes. "We won't," she whispered. "We were oil and water back then, Jack, and we're oil and water still." She looked away then, knowing beyond a shadow of a doubt that the same thing that had separated them then, still separated them now. Her eyes flickered closed as she felt a wrench in her chest.

Faith.

Avoiding his gaze, she slipped her sandals off and slowly rose to her feet. "I need to go."

"Lace." He stood and shoved his hands in his pockets like an awkward little boy.

She forced herself to look up, her smile half-hearted at best. "Yes?"

His gaze locked with hers, the sobriety in his face so reminiscent of the serious young boy who had been her whole world. "I'm not sure I can be your friend." He shifted, glancing away at the moonlit waters. "Too much past, you know? And too much hurt." Exhaling a wavering sigh, he turned to face her head on, the faint pulse of a nerve in his cheek. "And way, *way* too much chemistry," he whispered.

She nodded, stomach looping as she studied her bare feet in the sand for several seconds. "Okay. Well then, how about just friendly wedding partners?" Tipping her head, she glanced up with a faint smile, determined to forge a truce for Nicki's sake, if not her own. "And I promise not to step on your toes this time," she said, bringing a ghost of a smile to his lips over the first time they'd danced at her junior prom. "Deal?"

That slow smile with which she'd fallen in love eased across his lips, causing the faintest of quivers in her belly. "Deal." His grin took a slant. "As long as I get to lead."

"Sure, why not?" She released a slow and silent sigh, peace settling for the first time all night. Sandals dangling from one hand, she offered a handshake with the other, ignoring the jolt of electricity that sparked when his palm met hers. With a sassy flip of her ponytail, she turned on her heel and marched toward the highway, tossing one final smirk over her shoulder. "Just don't expect me to follow."

ISLE OF HOPE   97

CHAPTER NINE

*J*ack plucked the basketball from Matt's hands
and bounded in the air, his jump shot skimming
the net with nary a sound, effectively trouncing
his cousin without mercy. Fetching the ball, he tucked it
under his arm while he swiped the sweat from his face
with the sleeve of his T-shirt, searing Matt with a
menacing look. "You could've warned me."

"Seriously?" Matt perched hands low on his hips, his
breathing labored as he peered up. "Give me a break—
you would've bailed."

A scowl tainted Jack's face as he upended his
Dasani, throat glugging while he watched Matt over the
upturned bottle. "You know me better than that."

"Yeah, Jack, I do," Matt said with a heavy sigh,
gouging his fingers through his water-spiked hair. "You
didn't talk to me for a solid month when I started dating
Nicki, remember? Then when I told you I asked her to
marry me, you stormed out of here like I just insulted
your mother." He rubbed the side of his jaw. "Not to
mention the swing you took at me when I refused to tell
her she couldn't have her cousin in the wedding."

"I was drunk," Jack said with a loud crunch of the
empty water bottle, sailing it into the recycle can as
easily as a ball through the net. "And I apologized,
didn't I?"

Matt grunted, one edge of his lip zagging into an off-centered smile. "Only after Aunt Tess threatened to throw your butt out if you didn't."

A predatory grin eased across Jack's face as he bobbled the ball in his hand. "Two out of three?"

"Why not?" Matt rolled his neck, his faded Third Day T-shirt soaked with sweat. He positioned himself close to the net, hands on his knees and grin going head-to-head with Jack's. "Maybe it'll help vent some of that deep-seated anger and jealousy you have."

Arms poised for a throw, Jack paused to fry Matt with a razor-thin stare. "What deep-seated anger and jealousy?"

Matt grinned. "Over the fact that in two short months, I'll be waking up next to the love of my life, enjoying all the bells and whistles of a marriage with the girl of my dreams."

Jack grunted, eye on the basket as he rose up on the balls of well-worn Nikes to sail a three-pointer that clipped the back of the board. "Don't need marriage for that," he said, lips curling in a satisfied smile when the ball ricocheted into the net. He snatched it on rebound and slid Matt a smirk. "Right now I've got more bells and whistles than Amtrak."

With a low-throated chuckle, Matt slapped the ball from Jack's hand and spun to launch it into the air, making Jack wince when it dropped in with a neat, clean swish. He swooped it away with a lazy grin that told Jack exactly what his cousin thought of his love life. "Oh, that's right—with the 'loves' of your life— one for every day of the week, just like underwear." He squinted and took aim, arcing the ball into the basket with an annoying whoosh. Rushing to retrieve it, he scored with a hook shot, obviously indifferent to Jack's searing gaze. "So, tell me, Jack," he said with an arch of his brow, eyes intense despite the humor lacing his tone, "which one is the *number-one* 'love of your life'?"

Thoughts of Lacey burned in his brain, torching his temper. "Shut up, Matt," he said with a sneer, slamming his cousin out of the way to steal the ball. A groan erupted when it bounced off the backboard, right into Matt's hands.

With a quick flick of his wrist, Matt skimmed the rim with a backhanded toss, laughing out loud when the ball spiraled in with a near soundless thrum. He palmed it with a cheeky grin, giving Jack a wink. "Kinda looks like I'm in the lead."

Sweat rolling down his face, Jack slacked a hip, hands planted low on his thighs. "You can be a real horse's butt, you know that, Ball?"

He grinned, passing the ball hand-to-hand with a cocky air. "Yep, learned all I know from my older cousin." A glint of trouble sparked in his eyes. "What d'ya say we make this more interesting, O'Bryen? Say, a little wager?"

A broad smile spanned Jack's lips while he wiped the sweat from his face with the front of his shirt. "I thought gambling was a sin to you straight-and-narrow types."

Matt chuckled, spinning the ball on his finger. "Not when it gets a heathen's butt into a church pew, Pagan Boy."

It was Jack's turn to laugh. "As if *that's* gonna happen."

"Oh, yeah?" Matt bandied the basketball back and forth. "This ball says it will." He paused, his voice a dare as his chin dipped low. "Unless, of course … you're chicken?" He began to flap his arms. "Balk-balk-balk …"

Jack flashed some teeth, egging Matt on with a wave of his fingers. "Bring it on, Choir Boy—I'd kind of like to see you spend your summer painting the house for Mom instead of me, so name your terms."

Matt's gaze flicked to the side of the high two-story house with its steep pitch and peeling shutters, including a blistered wraparound porch with endless pickets to sand. A muscle ducked in his throat before his shoulders finally squared, facing Jack with a smile considerably more sober than before. "If you lose, you attend every event at Hope Church I ask you to without complaint."

Jack sized his cousin up, the challenge more than tempting. Since Matt had asked him to be best man, he'd been hounding Jack to go to church, and to be honest, Jack was getting tired of it. He pinned him with a narrow gaze. "Wedding-related events only," he said with a slow grind of his jaw, uneasy that he could be roped into setting a foot in a church more than he liked.

"Wedding *party*-related events only, Jack, which means anytime the wedding party does anything at the church, you're there on time—a mime in his Sunday best."

Jack's lips canted into a dry smile. "My Sunday best is a sheet and a pillow, Ball, but you have my word I'll dress appropriately, complete with a piece of duct tape on my mouth." He swiped the ball from Matt's hands and let it fly, grinning when it spun into the net with a satisfying swoosh. "*If* you win, which is a pretty big 'if' given I've whipped you five games out of six just last week."

"*And* ..." Matt continued, "you have to shine up that Boy Scout badge of yours till it dazzles both Lacey and Nicki blind with your charm, got it?"

"Piece of cake." Jack strolled away from the net with a swagger meant to assure his cousin he intended to win, cutting loose with a three-pointer that shot through the basket like a net-seeking missile. "I was an Eagle Scout, remember? But if I win," Jack threatened, nailing Matt with a pointed look, "I don't want to hear one whiney word out of you about me and church ever again, you got it? Your wedding and rehearsal will be the last time I darken a church door for you until they baptize your babies or wheel you out in a box, understood?"

Matt's teeth gleamed white. "Or you … after I annihilate you."

"Ha!" Jack strolled toward the half-court line with a shake of his head. "Dream on, buddy boy, and I'll even let you have the ball first."

"Deal. Except for two more conditions." Matt halted him with the ball under his arm, eyeing Jack with the same bull-headed look he wore when his team at school battled on the field. "If you lose, I don't want to see a hint of temper, sulk, moodiness, sarcasm, or complaint out of you until this wedding is over, Jack, because if I do …" He inhaled slowly, his six-foot-two frame expanding as his eyes narrowed in threat. "Not only will you be painting this house, dude, but you'll be attending church with Nicki and me for a solid year after the wedding, got that?"

Jack stared, sleet slithering his veins at the notion of going to Matt's church at all, much less for a year. The very thought churned his supper like a garbage disposal chewing up chicken bones, and he had to suck in some air to steady his nerves. For one solitary moment, he toyed with the idea of telling Matt to take a flying leap, but the deadly dare in his cousin's eyes stopped him cold. All he could think of was in all the years he and Matt had challenged and dared each other—be it eating worms or racking up shots in a bar before Matt got religion—neither of them had ever backed down. He rotated his neck to unkink any hesitation that stiffened his bones. "I got it, bro, but six months, not a year."

Matt grinned. "Why, afraid you'll lose?"

He skewered his cousin with a pointed look, his smile grinding along with his jaw. "I don't plan to lose."

"Neither do I, so the year stands," Matt said with a secret smile that held way too much confidence.

Jack offered a tight smile to deflect the jitters inside. "And the last condition?"

Matt's good humor dissolved, giving way to a serious look that underscored his cousin's deep affection and concern. "Lacey's home to stay, Jack," he said quietly, "so you're just gonna have to accept it and move on, for your peace of mind and hers." A trace of a smile shadowed his lips as he tossed the ball to Jack. "And mine."

With a short nod, Jack ambled over to half court and lined up, his hands sweaty beneath the ball. *Home to stay? Yeah, he could accept that.* Eyes on the basket, his killer instinct kicked in, jaw and will as steeled as the post that held up the net. *In Georgia, maybe.* His soles lifted off the pavement as he let the ball fly, watching as it spun into the net with a stony clamp of his mouth.

Not in my heart.

CHAPTER TEN

*S*houlders square and body taut, Lacey stared straight ahead with a cement smile, not daring to blink. Lips pinched to restrain a giggle, it was everything she could do not to laugh out loud as Jack sat in the pew next to her in Hope Church, as rigid and unmovable as the polished wood beams overhead. Her lips squirmed. And just as "trussed" up in an Armani charcoal suit with silk tie that matched the stormy blue of his eyes. A veritable mannequin with an expression more starched than his shirt.

"I, Sydney Anderson, take you, Calvin Robert Ryan, to be my lawfully wedded husband, to have and to hold, from this day forward, for better, for worse ..."

For better, for worse ...

Lacey couldn't help it—her cheeks puffed with a renegade snicker just aching to break free. Poor old Jack certainly got the "worse" according to Nicki, who said the only reason he was even in a church tonight—and would be innumerable times between now and the wedding—was he had lost a bet to Matt.

"Till death do us part ..." Mouth compressed, her face tightened into chipmunk cheeks, as if she were holding her breath to stop hiccups. Ah, yes, "death"—an appropriate word, indeed—at least for Jack O'Bryen, who swore he wouldn't be caught dead in a church before Matt's wedding. A tiny grunt broke free through

her nose, and she quickly lifted her chin to thwart impending laughter. Especially since he sat stiff as a corpse without a casket, hands deathly still and folded on his lap. Not unlike a trap about to spring. She could almost hear the tic in his hard-angled jaw—tick, tick, tick—like a bomb about to explode ...

The snort she'd been holding erupted from her lips mere seconds before the pastor pronounced ol' Syd and Cal husband and wife, so at least she was saved by a swell of applause and whistles. But ... not before Jack gave her the stink-eye from the corner of his, completely unhinging any control she may have had with a snorting fit of giggles.

"This-isn't-funny," he ground out, the same lethal tone as when Cat and she used to play practical jokes on him as kids, or when she'd tempt and tease him when they were going together. So studiously serious, she practically had to beat a sense of humor into the man. But she had—*slowly*, over time—and it meant the world to her when he'd told her once that was one of the things he loved most about her.

Or used to.

"Sure it is," she whispered close to his ear, "I'm pretty sure I heard God snickering too. 'Hey, Pete, looky here—got that ol' heathen Jack O'Bryen on a technicality.'"

He slid her a sideways glare, but she grinned when she saw the bare twitch of a smile. "You are such a brat, Lacey Carmichael, and you haven't changed a bit."

"Wanna bet?" She wiggled her brows, rising when the wedding march ushered the happy couple out of the church. "I've finally taken the high road, Brye, while you ..." She scrunched her nose, a touch of tease in her smile. "Well, let's just say we're swinging on different pendulums now, Doc."

"I guess we always were," he said quietly, a hint of melancholy in his smile that plucked at her heart.

"So, what'd ya think?" Seated to Lacey's left, Nicki prodded her while the crowd filed out. "I loved the trellis idea with pearls and hydrangeas. But, yikes, those dresses looked like something from a 70's ragbag, didn't they? Oh, but the photo collage video of their history together was pretty cool, although that would take extra time we don't have."

"Agreed," Lacey said, not a fan of technology ruining the natural beauty of a garden wedding. "Besides, a screen would be so crass and not at all intimate, so I'd nix the video."

"I guess you're right." Mouth puckering in a reflective pout, Nicki whirled around to badger Matt instead, leaving Lacey to scoot out of the pew. She nodded at Jack with an impish smile while he waited beside their row like a Mafia usher, hands clasped low in a funeral-director wrist cross. The moment she stepped foot in the aisle, he hooked her arm and all but dragged her down a runner scattered with rose petals.

"Whoa, where's the fire, big boy?" She peered up with a sideways grin, a bit of the devil tickling her tone. "Trust me, from what I hear, you'll get there soon enough."

"Cute." Smile flat, he tugged her down a corridor of classrooms, not stopping until they rounded a corner where they were completely alone.

Lacey's pulse stuttered along with her mischievous mood, causing her words to do the same. "Uh, J-Jack, I'm s-sorry—I d-didn't mean to laugh, honest—"

"Shut up, Lacey, and let me get this out." He pressed her to the wall with one hand and took a step back, fists sinking into his pockets as he studied the shine on his Cole Haan shoes. Her heart thudded slow and hard while she waited, grateful she could study him unaware, without those blue eyes probing hers like some hypnotic spell, making her want to do things she didn't want to do. At least not anymore. Sinfully dark lashes longer than hers—a playful bone of contention in the past—fanned his bronzed cheeks while a crimp appeared between thick brows angled low in thought. His lips were parted, emitting shallow breaths, triggering memories of those same lips fondling hers. She quickly averted her gaze, no desire to go there whatsoever.

Liar.

Her mouth tamped down. Okay, yes, judging from the acceleration of her pulse and ragged breathing that now matched his own, she obviously still harbored some deep-seated attraction to Jack O'Bryen. But ... there was *no* way she could act on it. Not with a man who no longer embraced the same faith as she, and especially one who'd always held too much sway over her emotions. The annoying swirl of heat in her belly was clear indication of that, as well as the sudden dampness of her palms, which she attempted to casually rub down her silk floral sundress. *Come on, Jack, spit it out, before me and my dress melt into a puddle ...*

"Lacey, I'm ..." A heavy blast of air escaped his lips as he slashed fingers through the hair at the back of his head, a habit of his whenever he'd been frustrated or embarrassed or both. His chest expanded with a heavy inhale before his gaze finally lifted to meet hers. What she saw revealed a humility and softness she hadn't seen before today, an unsettling glimpse past all the bitterness and bravado into the real Jack O'Bryen. She swallowed hard. The one she'd fallen desperately in love with. His groan disrupted her thoughts. "Look, I'm a first-class jerk, and you should have slapped me silly."

She blinked several times. "What?"

He gestured in the direction of the front doors. "At the beach last week, when I ..." A lump jogged in his throat as he stared at her, eyes naked with shame. "Insulted you. Made a pass. It was stupid and it was wrong, and I'm really sorry, especially for making you feel ..." He expelled a wavering breath, his expression suddenly tender. "Well, just like your dad used to make you feel." The flicker of a smile teased at the edge of his lips. "So I'm hoping you can forgive me and we can, you know, be—"

"Wedding partners?" she said with a stern arch of her brow, lips pursed to keep from smiling.

The slow grin that had always melted her insides eased across his lips, raising her body temperature to way beyond sweaty hands. "I was going to say friends, but yeah, that too, although partners in crime might be more apt." He grimaced and shook his head, looking down at impeccably shined calfskin leather brogues. "Because it's a crime the damage you could do to my brand-new shoes when you and I have to dance."

"Well, well," she said with a jut of her chin, giving him a proud smile of approval, "what do you know? The boy has grown a sense of humor."

"Had to." He grabbed her hand to lead her back down the hall, glancing at her out of the corner of his eyes. His smile tilted toward cocky. "Had a clown for a girlfriend years ago, and I guess it rubbed off."

She tossed him a smirk. "Well then, I guess my work here is done, now isn't it?"

"Not quite, kiddo." He tweaked the back of her neck, causing her shoulders to hunch with a giggle. "If you have any hope of beating my team in volleyball tonight, *friend*, I'd say your work's just beginning."

"Wait." She slid to a stop and faced him, eyeing him with a taut fold of arms. Her gaze narrowed. "This whole apology and 'friend' thing isn't because you lost the bet and Matt made you do it, is it?"

He placed his hands over his heart, his wounded look shadowed with tease. "Come on, Lace, how shallow do you think I am anyway?" He prodded her with a palm to the small of her back, staring straight ahead with a smile on his face. "Of course it is."

She threw her head back and laughed, the sound echoing in the long hallway as she gave him a sassy smirk. "Good."

CHAPTER ELEVEN

*V*olleyball under his arm, Jack battled a scowl by swiping the sweat on his face with the sleeve of his shirt, his mood as damp as his body over an unexpected loss. Not the volleyball game, which his team was winning handily because of him, Matt, and the preacher guy. But the loss of his cool, which he was losing by the moment due to one major flaw in this newfound friendship with Lacey.

Pretty boy pastor Chase Griffin.

The preacher boy who could spike like nobody's business—on the court and off, apparently, given the moony smiles on half of the girls, spiking both balls and hearts with the serve of a smile.

Not that Jack wasn't drawing his fair share of attention from the female sector, because they'd welcomed him with open arms. Especially Kelly—flirting and teasing and trying to make him feel at home. But he would never feel "at home" in a church building ever again, nor with a woman shackled by so-called morality. His mouth went flat. Hypocrisy wasn't his thing.

"Come on, Jack, let's send 'em packin'," Chase called from the front of the net, getting on Jack's last nerve when he commenced to sparring with Lacey on the other side. *Again.* Jaw grinding, Jack took four paces back and tossed the ball high, vaulting it in the air to execute a perfect jump shot left over from championship volleyball days in college. His extreme competitive streak surfaced, and he slammed the ball through the air like he wanted to slam ol' Pastor Chase, sending *him* packin' along with the other team. The bullet found its mark—a curveball rocket that plummeted between Lacey and another guy like a comet in a statuary, eliciting groans and gaping mouths when both of them missed it standing still. Cheers exploded on his side of the net while everyone slapped him on the back.

"Great shot," Preacher Boy said with a pump of Jack's hand, making him feel like a heel for hating him. He actually was a pretty solid guy according to Matt, a former Navy Seal who had a "Come-to-Jesus" meeting with a piece of shrapnel in Afghanistan. Somebody Jack would actually be friends with if the guy wasn't ogling Lacey all night. Lips clamped in a tight smile, Jack exhaled his frustration through his nose, well aware he was being a jerk and hating himself for it. "Thanks, Rev," he said, coining his own nickname for a guy he had no intention of getting to know better. "You've got a pretty mean arm yourself."

"Hey, Chase, where d'ya want the chow?" one of the guys called from across the gym, pizza boxes stacked high in his hands. Chase turned to wave him toward the back door, and Jack suddenly felt like a real jerk. Closing his eyes, he gouged the bridge of his nose, wondering where in the world the nice guy went. The one he used to be—a lover of family, kids, and senior citizens—who had purposely chosen a career path to help others, not harangue them. Matt had told him what a great guy Chase was, even funding the food for these gatherings out of his own pocket, and yet here he was, unwilling to cut the guy a break. A deflated sigh trickled out as he became painfully aware that the guy he used to be had gone AWOL for a long while now.

Especially since graduation, it seemed—drinking more, losing his temper more, acting like a snot-nosed punk instead of a physician who'd graduated with top honors and a spot on the Memorial peds team. A "Romeo hotshot," Lacey had called him, and she was right, playing the field hard when all he ever really wanted was to be married to one woman.

The one who'd left him high and dry.

He jolted when the rev slapped him on the back. "I hope you're planning to come back because it sure is nice to have an ace in the hole," Chase said, strolling to the sideline to grab a bottled water from a cooler.

"Oh, he'll be back," Matt said, hooking an arm to Jack's shoulder. "Won't you, buddy?"

Jack slid him a narrow gaze. "Wedding-related events only, I believe the fine print said," he muttered under his breath, "until after the wedding." He grabbed the Dasani that Chase threw his way before nodding his thanks.

Matt upended his water, eyes glittering with that annoying twinkle whenever he thought he had the upper hand. "Wedding-*party*-related events, Jack my boy, and since most everybody here is involved in the wedding in some way, these weekly games more than qualify."

Shrugging Matt's hand off his shoulder, Jack grilled him with a mock glare. "My, my—first gambling, now blackmail. What's next, Matt—carousing on River Street?"

"Naw, did that last week after the volleyball game." Matt raised his water bottle in a smug toast. "To-go cups of Red Bull and a record number of tracts handed out for those who've gone astray." He winked. "Saved one for you, just in case."

Jack bit back a snide remark and stretched his arms high, twisting side to side to loosen both his muscles and his mood. "Rather have the Red Bull, man," he said with a lazy grin, determined to clean up his act on his own, *without* any lame religion or tracts. "My butt's draggin' from patching and painting."

"Oh, yeah, that's right—the job you tried to pawn off on me." Matt glugged his water several seconds before swiping his mouth with the back of his hand, shooting him an evil grin. "Good practice for the gazebo and landscaping, bro."

Two fingers to his teeth, Chase silenced the gym with an ear-splitting whistle and a nod toward the back door. "Okay, everybody—save the jawin' for the pizza out on the picnic tables, and a big thanks to the ladies for pitching in with home-baked cookies." Hefting the cooler with an impressive swell of biceps, he ambled toward the playground like the Pied Piper, fawning females and sweaty guys following in his wake.

Determined to make the best of the evening for Matt's sake, Jack followed his cousin, reveling in the crisp sea air that cooled the sweat on his skin the moment he stepped outside. The scent of honeysuckle from a tangle of bushes by the door gave way to the mouthwatering smell of cheese and pepperoni spiced with garlic and oregano, and for the first time all night, he actually sort of enjoyed being here.

With a rumble of his stomach, Jack clambered onto the bench of the table Nicki saved for her wedding party, grateful Preacher Boy was seated at the other end. Chase said grace, but at the sound of "amen," appreciative groans and laughter circled along with the pizza. Snatching two pieces from a box piled high with every vegetable known to man, Jack flinched when somebody kicked his leg. A grin eased across his face at the sight of Lacey on the other side, eyes scanning the sky with great drama while she nibbled on a ridiculously flat piece of cheese pizza—her favorite. "Hey, what was that for, Carmichael?" he said, aiming a crumb of bacon that bounced off her nose.

"For being such an annoying jock and making us lose." Chin high, she sailed the bacon right back, landing it in his hair. "And don't play with your food, O'Bryen. Don't you know there are people starving in China?"

Bolting down his first piece, Matt reached for another two, tossing one on Jack's plate before he popped a pepperoni in his mouth. "Hey, there's starving people here too, Lace, and victory always makes winners ravenous, right, Doc?"

"You bet," Jack said with an easy smile, eyes crinkling with humor as he slowly bit into his pizza, his gaze pinned to Lacey's. "It's hard work harnessing all that natural athletic power to avoid debilitating the other side."

"Yeah, and in a church no less," Matt piped up, wolfing his pizza down in mere seconds.

"It's a school gym, sweetheart, not a church," Nicki said with a patient smile, her tone as thin as her hazel eyes. She fluttered her lashes. "And I don't believe you've *seen* debilitation yet, darling."

"Uh-oh, I smell a Scrabble game coming," Lacey said with a bob of her head, licking sauce off her finger.

Dual groans rose from Matt and Jack's side of the table while everybody entered the fray, guys against girls over a noisy discussion of the best and worst games to play. When the boxes were empty and the cookies all gone, somebody challenged the group with a wiffle ball and bat, and in no time, both teams were flying the bases, expending what energy remained from a night of challenge and chatter, laughter and fun.

Much as Jack hated to admit it, he'd had a pretty good time and even promised Kelly and several of the other girls that he'd try and come back. *Try?* He issued a silent grunt as he helped pick up trash and close the windows in the gym. *Like I have a choice.*

"So who's coming over for Speed Scrabble?" Nicki asked with a devious rub of her hands, sizing up those who hadn't yet left.

"I'm game," Sarah said with a yawn, "but I warn you—I turn into a pumpkin at midnight."

"Great, that's a fourteen-point word," Nate said with a tweak of her neck.

"Sure wish I could." Kelly shot Nicki a look of regret before her gaze flicked to Jack. "But I've got some prep work to do for a meeting tomorrow, so I need to scoot."

"I've got a grueling day tomorrow, too, so I'll pass." Justin draped an arm around Kelly's shoulders. "Come on, Kel, I'll walk you to your car."

"Oh, bummer, you guys!" Nicki wrapped her in a hug. "Well, don't stay up all night, all right?" She pinched Justin's cheek before spinning around to Jack. "So ... how 'bout you, Jack? Although my competitive nature warns against inviting a medical doctor with a high-powered vocabulary, I think I can give you a run for your money."

Gaze flicking to where Lacey was clowning around with Matt and Chase, Jack had a sudden urge to say yes. After all, this friendship with Lacey could only be a good thing, right? He reached for his gym bag, eyes meeting Nicki's once again. "Sure, why not?" He teased her with a slow smile. "I'll try not to use any big words."

"Since I'm in the medical field as well, Doctor, don't forget I know some too," she said with a cocky wag of her head, but the warmth in her eyes told him he was making inroads with Lacey's cousin as well as Lacey. He winced when she put two fingers to her mouth in a shrill whistle that rivaled the Rev's. "Okay, people— my house in ten, and first one there gets to go first."

"I'm riding with him," Sarah called, racing after Nate while he darted for the door. She saluted Matt and

Chase on her way out as they stored the volleyball equipment in the closet.

Lacey strolled over with her purse and gym bag, head tilted at Jack with a dare in her eyes. "So, O'Bryen, you heading home … or to humiliation?"

He laughed, gym bag draped over his shoulder. "I might remind you, Carmichael, I know enough high-dollar words to incur stroke in a hypochondriac, so it remains to be seen over whose downfall this will be."

"Ooooooh, so the doctor's a little full of himself, is he?" She shifted her bag to her other hand to adjust the purse on her shoulder. "Well … let's just see who burns whom when you take on an English teacher with a degree in communications. Who, I might add, aced every vocabulary test from grades one through eight."

A lazy grin slid across his lips. "Bring it on, Teach," he said, reaching to take the gym bag from her hand. "And I'll even drive you to your demise."

The grin stiffened on her face as she glanced over her shoulder at Matt and Chase, her good humor fading into an awkward chew of her lip. "Uh … Chase already volunteered to give me a lift, so you're off the hook, Brye." She faced him again with a bright smile that came off forced, giving a tiny shrug. "What can I say? He lured me with Oreo Overloads for the troops, and we both know I can't say no to temptation like that."

The pizza in his stomach felt like a volleyball made of lead. Shaking his head, he "tsked" to deflect the jealousy that suddenly coated his throat like bile. "Imagine that." His smile was casual as he handed the bag back. "Bald-faced temptation, and from a pastor at that." He glanced at his watch and frowned, schooling his voice to convey disappointment he didn't feel at all. "Oh man …" he said with a ridge in his brow, well aware Lacey could probably see right through him. She always had. "I just remembered I promised Davey bass fishing at daybreak, so I probably should call it a night." Rubbing the back of his neck, he looked up with a lop-sided smile that held a hint of an apology. "The little guy gave me a chug-bug lure for my birthday that he wants to try, and the top-water bite is especially good early in the morning, so ..."

Her eyes softened, socking him in the gut when he caught a glimpse of hurt before she gave him a perky smile. "Sure. Besides, it's kind of tough to compete with a little boy and a bass, *especially* with a Scrabble game where you get your butt kicked by an ex-girlfriend."

He laughed, head bowed while he scratched the back of his neck. "Yeah, I thought about that." He peered up, the tender look on her face twisting him inside out. "Look, I'm gonna run, but will you let Matt and Nicki know?"

"Absolutely," she said, her ponytail swinging to and fro when she whirled to join the others on the far side of the gym. "Probably just as well," she called over her shoulder, hand to her mouth. "First Oreo Overload, then trouncing Dr. Jock 'take it to the mat' O'Bryen in a game he can't win?" She gave him a salute with a mischievous gleam in her eye. "Not sure I can handle the temptation, you know?"

Yeah, I know. He returned her wave with a sick feeling as he made his way to the door.

Neither can I.

CHAPTER TWELVE

"So ... now that you've spent some time with him, what do you think of Chase?"

Lacey's smile skewed as she lay on Mamaw's patio lounger, eyes closed while she soaked up the summer sun next to her cousin, both in their swimsuits. A gentle breeze cooled the sweat on her skin, the scent of honeysuckle mingling with the coconut of Coppertone, taking her back to summers squealing over high school crushes while they worked on their tans. *Until* she fell hard for a senior, that is, her best friend's older brother, whom she'd grown up with as a neighbor and friend.

Friend. The smile faded from Lacey's lips as she recalled the almost imperceptible look of hurt in Jack's eyes when she'd told him Chase was driving her home last night. She expelled a withering sigh at the memory, quite certain navigating the waters of friendship with an ex-boyfriend she'd once planned to marry would be no easy matter. Heaven knows she had already wounded him enough in the past; she sure didn't want to do it again, which was why friendship was undoubtedly the best course. Or at least she'd thought so when they struck their truce. Chill bumps pebbled her skin despite the heat of the day. A truce that reintroduced them to the same easy fun and flirting friendship they'd enjoyed years ago ... before their feelings had ripened into love.

A wave of melancholy struck hard, and she sighed again.

"*Please* tell me that lovesick sigh is for Chase, because I gotta tell you, Lace, he's only seen you a handful of times at church, but the guy is already smitten, according to Matt."

"Uh ... no ... but I think he's a really great guy," she managed, tone nonchalant.

Even with her eyes closed, she could feel the heat of Nicki's stare, punctuated by her impatient tone. "But ...?"

She squinted at her cousin out of the corner of her eye. "But what? He's loaded with smarts, looks, personality, and faith—a poster boy for every church-going girl."

"*But ...?*" Nicki popped up. Her look torched a hole in Lacey's composure.

Venting with a noisy exhale, Lacey sat up and snatched her mug of ice water, glugging a few swallows before she poured some in her hand to pat on her face and neck. "Come on, Nick, what's with all the 'buts'?" She set her water aside to tilt her face to the sun, arms braced behind her as if she hadn't a care in the world. "I like Chase, I do—he's a lot of fun."

"*Ohhhhhhh* no you don't, kiddo," Nicki said. "You're not going to sidetrack me that easily, so let me be perfectly clear in case you're hoping to weasel out with some lame response." Swinging her legs to the patio, she perched on the edge of her chaise, head ducked as she peered up at Lacey with a gaze so potent, it made Lacey squirm. "Do-you-like Chase?"

"Yes, of course ..." Lacey's words tumbled out in a rush, her mind desperate to derail a conversation she did *not* want to have. "Didn't you hear what I just—"

"*Enough-to-date-him?*" Nicki interrupted, each syllable clipped like a threat.

Lacey rolled her eyes, lips thinning to wry. "Has anyone ever told you you're a *really* pushy person?"

"Matt. Daily. Don't change the subject." She flicked a fly off her shoulder, eyes welded to Lacey's with soldering precision. "Enough to date him?"

"Well ... sure ..." she said slowly, barely able to get the words out for the gulp in her throat. She flopped back on the chaise and shut her eyes, wishing she could shut out her cousin as well. She swallowed hard, her voice barely audible. "Someday."

"*Some*day ...?" Nicki's tone rose several octaves, continuing the climb to near-shriek. "What the heck is that supposed to mean, Lace—'*someday*'? What's wrong with '*now*'?"

Eyelids barely lifting, Lacey snuck a peek Nicki's way, quite sure her cousin would give her nothing but grief over what she was about to say. "I'm just not sure it's such a good idea to date him right *now*, that's all."

Nicki's jaw dropped like it'd been greased with 10W40. "Oh. My. Gosh." She slumped back on the chaise. "It's O'Bryen, isn't it? You still have feelings for him."

A groan slipped from Lacey's lips. "Oh, for crying out loud, Nick, of course I have feelings for Jack!" She shimmied further into the chaise, burrowing in like it was a bunker, ready to hold her ground. "We were closer than air, and I was going to marry the man, for heaven's sake. But that's all in the past now, and all I want is to maintain an amiable friendship, for both my sake *and* yours." Her mood drooped at the unlikely notion of mere friendship with a man who still stirred her, both body and soul.

She inhaled deeply, hoping to fill her lungs with confidence as well as with air. After all, she could do anything for two months, right? Her eyelids flipped up. Couldn't she? She chewed on the edge of her lip, eyes begging Nicki to understand. "Come on, Nick, the way

I hurt him when I left years ago, it almost feels as if …
well, as if dating Chase right now would be rubbing salt
in the wound, you know?"

"Are you kidding me?" Nicki gaped in protest. "Matt
says Jack's out with a different woman every other
night, and we're talking *way* more than a kiss at the
door. And *you're* worried about dating a pastor who'll
help get you over that loser ex in San Diego?"

Lacey winced, the thought of Jack involved with
other women finding its mark. Unbidden, she felt the
sting of moisture at the back of her eyes. *Hate to tell
you this, Nick, but it's not the ex in San Diego I need to
get over …*

Scooting to the edge of her seat, Nicki reached to
give Lacey's hand a gentle squeeze. "Look, Lace, I
know you want to move on with your life, and I thought
we agreed that dating a decent guy would help you do
that?"

Lacey opened one eye to a slit. "You agreed, not me,
until you badgered me nonstop the first week I arrived."

"Yes I did," Nicki conceded with a sharp nod, "but
only because I love you and as a nurse, I know what's
best for you."

The edge of Lacey's mouth quirked. "Oh, so now
I'm a medical problem?"

Nicki wrinkled her nose, teasing with a rasp of air
through clenched teeth. "Actually, it's more of a mental
problem, Lace, but don't worry—I did a rotation in
psych, so we're good."

"Oh, real funny, Nurse Ratchet." Lacey flicked
water from her mug at her cousin before her grin
tapered off into a sad smile. "But to be honest, I'd say
it's more of a heart problem," she said quietly, thinking
of all the hearts she'd broken and needed to mend.

Nicki pushed a toe against Lacey's hip, rocking the
chaise as well as her cousin's body. "Well, cheer up,
kiddo—I just happen to have the name of a great

cardiologist who might even give you a family discount …"

"Ouch," Lacey said with a scrunch of shoulders. "Low blow, Phillips."

"Sorry, cuz, but now that we're on the subject …" Nicki adjusted her chaise to sitting position and plopped back, sympathy softening her gaze. "Have you given any thought as to when or where you're going to approach your dad, otherwise known as Memorial's Dr. Snark?"

A harsh chuckle erupted from Lacey's throat. "Only every day," she said, clicking her chaise into position to sit up like Nicki. "And then my stomach gets nauseous and I break out in a cold sweat." She released a heavy sigh. "So I pop a couple of Tums, take a shower, and pray like crazy that I can buck up and face the fear."

Nicki tipped her head, confusion reigning over her sea of freckles. "You know, Lace, I remember all the blow-outs you had with your dad in high school and the night he kicked you out of the house, of course, before you left Isle of Hope. And there's no question he changed for the worse after you and your mom left, but … to be honest, growing up, Uncle Ben always struck me as a pretty decent guy."

"Ha!" Lacey shifted on the chaise. "That's because he wouldn't dare give the cold shoulder to relatives or friends—he was a 'pillar of the community,' you know. But Mom and me?" She wrinkled her nose. "Most of the time it was like living in an ice palace with occasional thaws until Mom and he would go at it again, and then he was a 'pillar' all right, with a heart of stone to match."

"That's so odd," Nicki said, nose scrunched as her eyes narrowed in thought. "All I ever remember are things like Uncle Ben cuddling you whenever we watched movies on vacation or you sitting on his lap in the boat with that goofy grin whenever he'd let you

steer. I mean, I know you two got into some awful
rows, but you always seemed fine at family get-
togethers and vacations, you know?"

Yes, she knew. Those wonderful pinpricks of light
and love when she actually thought her dad had cared,
only to be snuffed out when Mom or she had triggered
his ire. And then gone altogether when she started
dating boys, his disappointment in her becoming more
real than his love, as if she had betrayed him by
growing up into a woman.

"I thought so too," she said quietly, "which is why it
hurt all the more when he shut me and Mom out of his
life, like we weren't worth the trouble to love." Her
laugh was bitter. "Our relationship pretty much sank
into the bottom of the river after that, especially when
he called me a whore and kicked me out of the house."

Her shoulders slumped at just how impossibly
difficult reconciliation with her father would be,
especially since *she'd* been the one who rejected *him*
after her mother died, too poisoned by bitterness to give
him another chance.

"Although he's never come out and said it, deep
down I think he blames me for the way our lives turned
out," she whispered, unable to keep the quiver from her
voice. Moisture smarted in her eyes when the familiar
ache of rejection reared its head, a specter that had
followed her around since she'd been small, when
Daddy was never around. Medical school, residency,
and a new practice saw to that, leaving Mom and her
the dregs of a man they only wanted to love.

"Everything?" Disbelief coated Nicki's tone.

Lacey expelled a weary sigh. "That's the feeling I've
always had—from the arguments he had with Mom
while I was growing up, to her affair with Jack's dad,
and then finally Mom's death." She looked over at
Nicki with a sheen of moisture. "It's all the culmination

of something I've felt from little on, Nick—my dad just didn't like me."

Nicki shook her head. "I'm sorry, Lace, I just don't believe that, at least not growing up. I wasn't around much in the early years when we lived in California, I know, but whenever our families vacationed together, Uncle Ben seemed to fawn over you. It wasn't until we moved back to Isle of Hope when Mom was sick that I noticed the strain between you two."

Head cocked, Lacey gave it some thought. "The vacations were wonderful, as I recall, but it always seemed like once Daddy got back home, work consumed all of his time, and we seldom saw that loving side of him." Her gaze trailed into Mamaw's yard while her mind trailed into the past, heart weighted with so much grief and guilt over a father she didn't fully understand. "And then the moment boys started noticing me—*whoa!*—he morphed into this browbeating tyrant, lecturing me on morality so much that all I wanted to do was defy, defy, defy!"

Nicki grunted her agreement. "And then I moved back—the she-devil from California—and all hell broke loose."

A grin surfaced on Lacey's face. "Yeah, but it was *you* who saved my life by master-minding the seduction of one Jackson Alexander O'Bryen, remember? A California makeover that helped open the eyes of the hottest senior in high school so he would know I was alive."

"Oh, I'm pretty sure he always knew you were alive, Lace—you were his sisters' best friend, after all, always underfoot." She winked. "I just made sure his *hormones* knew you were alive."

Lacey laughed, helping to dispel the malaise that had settled inside. "You were a freakin' miracle worker, Nurse Phillips, turning my lost and lonely teen years into endless summers I will never forget."

"Yeah, I know," she said with a droll smile. "*That's* the problem, Ms. Carmichael—you need to forget those summers, or at least the guy who made them endless." She cocked a russet brow. "Trust me, Jack certainly has. I'm pretty sure he's not thinking about *you* when he wines, dines, and heaven knows what else half the nurses at Memorial, so why should you?"

Lacey blinked, Nicki's reminder of Jack's current lifestyle jabbing deeper than she liked. There was no question Jack had moved on with his life, and maybe Nicki was right. Maybe it was time for her to do the same.

"I guess you have a point," Lacey said, expelling an unsteady breath that deflated her good mood.

"You bet I do, and it's not on my head like yours when it comes to Jack O'Bryen."

"Okay, okay, 'point' taken, and no pun intended." She secured a loose strand of hair with a bobby pin and sat back with eyes closed, allowing the sun to work its magic in melting some of her concerns away. "So, yes, I will go out with Chase if he asks me, but *only* when Jack's not around and *only* if Chase cools it in group settings when he is." Her chin notched up to signify her mind was made up. "I refuse to flaunt another guy in front of my old boyfriend, at least until after the wedding. By then I'm praying our friendship will be comfortably casual and remote."

"I suppose that's fair enough," Nicki said with approval. "So … that's one of two problems resolved."

Lacey lifted her head to stare at her cousin, face in a bunch. "And what's the other?"

The edge of Nicki's lip crooked. "Duh, Einstein— your dad?"

A slow grind of a groan rattled from Lacey's throat as her head plunked back. "Don't remind me."

"Well, somebody has to before Mamaw sets you down for '*the talk.*'"

The talk. Lacey couldn't help the squirm of a smile, quite sure she and Nick had heard "the talk" dozens of times over the years.

"My lands, girls, grudges hurt you more than the person you refuse to forgive, so you may as well get it over with so we can enjoy our popcorn and a movie. Remember, the devil is just a spit away, looking to ruin your life and our evening, so what's it gonna be?"

"I know," Lacey said with a sigh, "I've been waiting for her to say something since it's been two weeks already, and I haven't made a move yet."

"Well, she's getting ready to, I promise. She's already asked me twice now if you've said anything about contacting your dad, and she had that hell-or-high-water look she gets, you know when she gums her lips till they disappear and her eyes burn like a laser?"

Lacey smiled. "Oh, yeah, I've actually had nightmares about that look, not to mention the heaping-coals talk, so I suppose I'll need to do something soon. Although at the moment, Mamaw's burning look sounds a whole lot better than frostbite, which is what I'm up against with Daddy when he freezes me out."

"Ah, yes, the good old 'heaping-coals concept,'" Nicki said with a sage nod of her head, "killing them with kindness." She shot Lacey a wicked grin. "I always did like that Biblical principle, especially envisioning my enemy's hair on fire."

Lacey chuckled. "Yep, I've charred a few heads myself when I was younger, but I doubt that was what Mamaw had in mind."

"You know, Lace," Nicki said, her gaze suddenly pensive, "maybe your dad won't freeze you out. I mean, eight years *is* a long time for a man to mellow, so maybe he's ready to make amends too."

"Ha! When you-know-what freezes over," she said with a twist of her lips. "'Freeze' being the operative word. Especially since I did the same to him after

Mom's funeral, refusing to answer his calls, emails, and letters, even being snotty enough to return all envelopes unopened, just for spite." She shook her head. "No, Nick, this confrontation with Daddy will be the hardest thing I've ever done and chillier than taking a dip in an Antarctica ice pond." An involuntary shiver iced her spine. "Brrr ... turns me blue just to think about it."

A low-throated chuckle rumbled from Nicki's mouth as she angled toward the sun, a smug look on her face. "Well, then I guess it's a real good thing you're into the Bible these days, Alycia Anne, isn't it?" She opened one eye to give Lacey a smirk, making her laugh when she attempted a wink. "Lots of lovely coals to keep you nice and warm."

CHAPTER THIRTEEN

"*H*ey, wait a minute …" Jack paused with great drama, head angled as he placed the stethoscope below five-year-old Tyler Foster's chest, eyes squeezed tight while listening to the little boy's lungs. "Did you have animal crackers for lunch, because I hear a lion growling in there."

Tyler giggled and shook his head, glancing at his mom who sat in a chair across the room, his little sister Sophie tucked on her lap with a thumb in her mouth.

Jack tousled his hair. "Well, okay then. I think you'll be good as new in a few days, Ty, as long as Mom feeds you plenty of popsicles, Jell-O, yogurt, and ice cream to soothe that sore throat, okay?"

A mischievous grin skimmed across Tyler's lips while Jack rolled back on his stool, arms folded across his white jacket to address his last patient for the day. "Just one thing left to take care of, then, sport—you want a dinosaur, teddy bear, or giraffe?"

The little boy stared wide-eyed, the flush in his face deepening from something other than fever. "What do you mean?" he asked, hope in his eyes coaxing a soft smile to Jack's lips.

Sending a wink Sophie's way, Jack fished two balloons out of his coat pocket and held them up. "I mean that not only do I have a degree in medicine, Mister Ty," he said in his deepest doctor voice, "but I

have a degree in balloon animals as well, so you and
little sis over there each get to pick one."

Sophie—all of three maybe—grinned up at her
mother before she offered Jack a shy smile, confirming
for the one hundredth time that day that he had chosen
the right profession. Even after thirty patients, he felt
more energized now than he had with his first exam of
the day, handling everything from well visits and
immunizations, to pinkeye and the flu.

"Okay, Ty, how 'bout you pick first, then I'll give
Sophie a turn, all right?"

"Cool! Can I have a dinosaur?" Tyler said, jiggling
his legs while they dangled over the edge of the
examination table.

"You bet." Jack went to work, fingers flying until a
purple dinosaur appeared, eliciting a gasp from the little
girl's mouth.

"Wow, that's way cool!" Tyler held it up, examining
the dinosaur from every angle.

"What do you say to Dr. Jack, Tyler?" Mrs. Foster
prodded her son with a kind smile.

"Thank you, Dr. Jack," he promptly said, never
taking his eyes off the dinosaur.

"You're more than welcome, Tyler. And how 'bout
you, Soph?" Jack rolled over to Sophie, stretching a
pink balloon while he assessed her with a quizzical
smile. "You know, I think you *may* just be a teddy bear
kind of girl, what do you think?"

Laying her head on her mom's chest, she nodded
slowly, a trace of a smile blooming behind the thumb in
her mouth.

"All righty, then ..." Jack twisted and turned the
balloon in record time, creating a pink teddy bear that
coaxed a grin to her face. Reaching back in his pocket,
he pulled out a pink ribbon with hearts and tied a tiny
bow around the bear's neck, giving Tyler a wink over
his shoulder. "Gotta have a bow, of course, since this is

a girl bear, you know." He handed the bear to Sophie and grinned outright when she dropped the thumb from her mouth to grasp the bear with both hands, a look of wonder lighting her face.

"Sophie …? What do you say?"

"Thank you," the little angel whispered, and Jack swallowed a lump of emotion, almost feeling guilty for taking a paycheck.

"You're welcome, Sophie." He lightly tapped her nose before retrieving his prescription pad to write Mrs. Foster a scrip for Tyler. He handed it to her along with two small packets of yogurt raisins. "To feed the balloon animals, of course, when they get hungry."

"Of course," she said with a broad smile. "Thank you so much." She rose with Sophie in her arms, latching a good-sized sack purse over her shoulder. "You know, I'm almost ashamed to admit this, but I was a bit worried when they told me Tyler's regular pediatrician was out sick." She shook her head, a smile breaking free. "But I have to say, Doctor, you're wonderful!"

Embarrassed by her praise, Jack spun around to whisk Tyler off the table in an airplane whirl, eliciting a chuckle from his mother's lips. "Goodness, I hope you plan to have a slew of kids of your own someday, Dr. O'Bryen," she said with a look of approval, "because you're a natural."

Heat singed Jack's collar as he led them to the door. "Well, that's my plan someday, Mrs. Foster, but till then, I get a kick out of taking care of great kids like yours." He tweaked Tyler's neck, causing the little guy to giggle and squirm. "Do what your mom says, Ty, and you'll be good as new in no time, okay? And remember—lots of popsicles, Jell-O, yogurt and ice cream till you're all better, got it?"

"Got it," Tyler said with a nod, following his mom and sister out the door.

Jack returned the little boy's wave as they traipsed down the hall, grinning when little Sophie gave him a tiny wiggle of fingers over her mother's shoulder. Contentment swelled in his chest as he strolled back to his office, rolling his shoulders to dislodge a kink. Pausing at his door, his euphoria popped faster than an overblown balloon animal at the mountain of paperwork piled high on his desk.

He scrubbed his face with his hands, then dropped into the leather chair of his cherry-wood desk in front of the window, grateful for this office that would become a second home. Overlooking a parking lot with a lush park beyond, the ample-sized room was cozy and comfortable, thanks to Shannon, the creative twin with an eye for decorating. Framed watercolors of Isle of Hope—painted by Shannon herself in high school— graced warm, buff-colored walls, the muted blues and greens offsetting the sterile look of framed university and post-graduate degrees. His smile tipped as he eyed a picture of his family on his desk, prominently overshadowed by a separate photo of Cat vamping it up for the camera—her sole contribution to his decor. "Keep this here for any cute single doctors who come in," she'd instructed, never really intending for him to comply. But he did, nonetheless, because it always made him smile.

"Okay, that settles it—I guess you're going to have to teach me how to make those stupid balloon animals." Jack's friend and rival from residency, Samuel Cunningham, strolled into his office and plopped into one of two chairs in front of Jack's desk. His white doctor's jacket hung wide open to reveal a navy polo rather than the crisp tie and button-down shirt that Jack and most of the other doctors wore. He promptly flopped his feet on Jack's desk with a lengthy groan, head resting on the back of the chair while he peered through shuttered eyes. "I'm working way too hard to get these little rug rats to like me, while all 'Dr. Jack' has to do," he said, infusing a bit of attitude into Jack's name, "is twist a little latex and he's a superhero."

Jack grinned, not even bothering to look up from the notes he was jotting. "Come on, Ham," he said invoking the nickname that fit Sam Cunningham to a T, "we both know it's my good looks and dazzling personality that wins them over."

Sam grunted. "Wins the moms over, you mean." He sifted a hand through dark curly hair. There was more than a little jest in brown eyes the nursing staff had once labeled as "deadlier than melted chocolate laced with liqueur." He sighed a dramatic sigh, a totally unwarranted reaction given that Sam Cunningham had been the heartthrob of Memorial the first two years of residency. *Until* their schedules eased up in third year, that is, when Jack decided to focus more on women than books, a pursuit that solidified their friendship. One edge of Sam's full lips quirked up. "Actually heard the mom of your last patient bragging to old man Augustine about your 'gift' with children."

Signing his name to the last patient's record with a flourish, Jack finally glanced up, his grin easing toward a false bravado that had been the mainstay of their three-year friendship and rivalry. "I know—crazy, isn't it?" He plucked a miniature Tootsie Roll Pop from a crystal candy dish on his desk—his mother's contribution based on his obsession with Tootsie Rolls—and sat back in his chair to peel the wrapper. "You'd think it'd be the immature one in the group, the one who acts most like a kid that they'd relate to, you know?" He popped the sucker in his mouth and crumpled the paper into a ball, thumb-shooting it at Sam in a bull's-eye that hit dead on. It bounced off Sam's "classic" nose just as Jack nudged the candy bowl his way. "Sucker?"

"Apparently," his friend said with snatch of a pop. "I volunteer to assist Augustine on some of his worst cases ever, getting spit and sneezed at and thrown up on in the process, while you're chalking up points dazzling pretty moms with animal balloons and candy." He slapped the sucker in his mouth and rolled the wrapper into a perfect spiral before tossing it on Jack's desk. "And you call *me* the kid." The stick rolled around in his mouth as he sank back in his chair. "I think I may need to revisit my bedside manner."

"Nothing wrong with your bedside manner, Sam," Jack said. He slashed notes and signatures across patient records with the same speed with which he devoured the sucker rotating in his mouth, gone in a matter of crunches. "At least according to Jasmine. She says you've got one of the best at Memorial." He tossed several files into an outbox on the corner of his desk and pitched the stick into his wastebasket with a smile, pumping his brows in jest. "Of course a paycheck doesn't come with *those* types of house calls, Doctor Love."

"Sure it does," Sam said with lazy smile, his brown eyes twinkling with humor. "You should know that better than anyone, O'Bryen." He paused, head tipping to the side in an obvious goad. "Or is the luscious Jasmine Augustine cutting into *your* house calls?"

Jack's gaze darted to the door and back, his voice lowering considerably. "Keep your voice down, Sam, will you? Old man Augustine doesn't even know we're dating, and that's the way I want to keep it."

"I don't know why. If Jasmine ever gave me a second chance, I'd shout it from the rooftops." He stood, sailing his stick into the waste can with absolute precision before sitting back down, palms flat on the arms of the chair. "But it appears the lady's got it bad for you, Dr. Jack, although I'll be hamstrung if I know why." He grinned. "Must be the balloon animals."

Jack's smile took a slant. "Or the fact you blew it with her in second year by dating other women behind her back." He punched his schedule up on his laptop.

"Now, see?" Sam sat up. "Explain to me how that's *any* different from what you're doing right now, O'Bryen, because I don't get it."

Focusing on his screen, Jack made several entries on his calendar, then saved it and shut his computer. He absently cleared his desk before he finally gave Sam his full attention, lounging back in his chair with hands braced to the back of his neck. "Honesty, man, pure and simple. Which separates the players like *you* from the straight-shooters like *me*. I make sure every woman I ask out understands from the start exactly where I stand. After burying myself in books and studies for the last decade, I'm just looking to enjoy life for a while without anything serious, and they all know that. The decision is theirs if they want to go out with me or not. The bottom line? Women appreciate knowing the bottom line." Jack's smile tipped off-center. "You should try it sometime, Ham—honesty's good for the soul."

Sam cut loose with a grunt. "And bad for the social life. No, thanks, Doc, the last time I opened up and got honest with a woman, I got my heart ripped out and stomped on by a two-timing coed in college, so I think I'll pass."

Jack shrugged, thoughts of Lacey suddenly dimming his good mood as he wandered into a cold stare. "Sorry to hear that, Sam, but sometimes that's the chance we take, and the same for the women we choose to see. But so far, this casual arrangement seems to suit me and everyone I've dated just fine."

"Except for Kathy Watkins." Sam pierced him with a knowing look, reminding Jack of the sweet peds nurse Jack had broken it off with after she got too serious.

Rising to his feet, Jack expelled a heavy sigh. "Yeah, except for Kathy, which probably ate at me way more than it did her."

"I doubt that." Sam followed suit, stretching with arms high over his head. "Well, one thing's for sure, Jasmine doesn't seem too worried about the risk. She stopped in to see her dad during your last appointment, but we both know he wasn't the reason she came by."

"Jasmine was here?" Jack felt a twinge in his chest over the way he'd been avoiding her.

"Yeah. Told me to tell you she missed you."

A low groan scraped past Jack's lips as he gouged the bridge of his nose, wishing he'd taken it slower with her like he had with the others. But the truth was, Jasmine was his favorite. The one whose company he enjoyed the most. The one who, like Lacey, had a knack for making him laugh and have fun. He put a hand to his eyes. *And* the one who teased and tempted him the most.

Until Lacey.

"You know, Jack, something tells me Jasmine's in way over her head here, so if you don't plan to take it anywhere, maybe you should just cut her loose, you know?"

Jack peered up beneath his hand, knowing full well that Sam was right. And yet for some reason, he stalled, not exactly sure that's what he wanted to do. He cared about Jasmine, he knew that, but since Lacey ...

"Chase ... lured me with Oreo Overloads for the troops, and we both know I can't say no to temptation like that."

Yeah, temptation like that. A nerve pulsed in his cheek as jealousy tightened his gut.

A good-looking pastor whose faith matched her own.

Glancing at his watch, Jack rose too quickly. Sam was a good friend, but not close enough that Jack had ever mentioned Lacey. Up until a few weeks ago, she'd been nothing more than a part of his distant past, and that's how he intended to keep it, at least as far as his workplace was concerned. "Sorry, bro—gotta run. Got a Big Brother fundraiser tonight."

Sam followed suit, but curiosity sharpened his features as he slowly slipped off his jacket. "So … about Jasmine …"

"Look, Sam, I know you and Jasmine are still good friends and that you care about her a lot, but the truth is, I do too, and I've been thinking lately that maybe …" He scrubbed the back of his neck, knowing he needed to fish or cut bait.

"Maybe what?"

Jack expelled a heavy sigh, glancing up at Sam beneath hooded eyes. "Well, that maybe it's time Jasmine and I are exclusive, you know? Just to see where it goes."

Sam nodded, his smile tinged with the slightest bit of regret. "Good. I'd like to see Jasmine happy, and right now as much as I hate to admit it, you're the one she wants." His gaze zeroed in on the frames at the edge of Jack's desk, and he absently picked one up, letting loose with a low whistle while interest sparked in his eyes. "Wow, does Jasmine know about this little dish?"

Jack's mouth swagged to the right. "That 'little dish' is my little sister Cat, so I suggest you back off because she's off limits."

"Now there's something to make a grown man weep." He cocked his head. "How old—twenty-one, twenty-two?"

Jack snatched the frame from Sam's hand. "Twenty-five and off your radar, Cunningham, so keep the drool in your mouth." He carefully set it back down next to the picture of his family. "Trust me, you'll see a grown man weep if you ever mess with my sister, and it won't be me shedding the tears."

"Too bad," he muttered while he picked up the next one, his eyes suddenly flaring wide. "Wait a minute— there's *two* of them that look like that?" He slammed a palm to the right side of his chest, his forlorn expression downright comical and true to his name. "Be still my heart."

Jack chuckled and hung his jacket on a hanger in the closet, delivering a warning grin over his shoulder. "That can be arranged, Ham—along with your pulse and your breathing—if you ever even flirt with my sisters."

Chuckling, Sam followed Jack out the door. "A little bit of a double standard, Jack, don't you think?" Hands in his pockets, he trailed him down the hall. "Taking your pick of the pool while you lock your sisters away in an ivory tower?"

"Yep." Jack nodded at several techs as he gripped the exit knob at the back of suite, cuffing Sam's shoulder while he led him out the door. "And that, Dr. Love, is how it's gonna stay."

CHAPTER FOURTEEN

*H*eat from the oven rippled the sunlight shafting into Tess's cozy old-fashioned kitchen, her freshly laundered white eyelet curtains rustling with the hint of a marshy breeze. Dishtowel draped over her shoulder, she hummed while she peeked into the oven, the aroma of garlic, basil, and oregano making her mouth water. With Papa John's less than a mile away, it had been too long since she'd made her family's favorite—her famous homemade pizza from scratch—but today she would surprise them all. Both Jack and Davey had been begging for it for weeks, and even sweet, undemanding Shannon had hinted at a craving for those rare personalized pizzas that took hours of kneading, rolling, and chopping every ingredient known to man.

Jack and Matt always shared a meat-lover's special, pure heartburn heaven with jalapenos galore while her girls preferred pineapple and bacon—Cat with onions and green pepper and Shan without, opting for black olives and mushrooms instead. Davey was the easy one with plain cheese, although Tess had no earthly idea how anyone could settle for something so flat and tasteless when one could have mountains of chopped veggies smothered in provolone.

With a quick glance at the clock, she removed Davey's pizza and her own mile-high version from the oven, hers loaded with every vegetable she could find and more than her fair share of bacon and pepperoni. She popped Jack and Matt's meat-lover's pizza in next, figuring the girls wouldn't be home from work until well after the guys had their showers following a sweaty hour of basketball. Closing her eyes, she paused to savor the sweet promise of a homemade dinner with *all* of her family, as rare as it may be with adult children who buzzed in and out as quickly as the honeybees that hovered over her garden.

"Okay, we're off." Jack barreled into the kitchen and skidded to a stop, Matt and Davey colliding behind him like stacked-up rail cars. All three stared, eyes gaping as wide as their mouths. "You made your homemade pizza?" Jack said, the pout in his tone sounding younger than Davey. "You didn't tell us you were making pizza."

Glancing up, she grinned at the look of shock on their faces. "It's a surprise, silly, although I don't know why with all the badgering you and Davey have been doing to bully me into it." She retrieved a stack of plates from the cabinet and slid them on the kitchen table with a smile. "Here—make yourself useful, boys, and set the table."

"But ... but ..." Matt wandered over to stare at her pizza, both a groan and Davey trailing after him. "I can't believe you fixed our favorite, Aunt Tess, and now we have to leave."

"What?" Rifling through the utensil drawer, Tess dropped a fork as she spun around, eyes bugging while she scrambled to pick it up. "What do you mean you have to leave?" she said, clunking the utensils on the table with a little too much force.

Jack ambled over to her pizza and filched a pepperoni. "We told you we have the Big Brother basketball fundraiser tonight at Matt's school, Mom, which is why we just spent the last hour practicing."

"You most certainly did not," Tess said with a stern heft of her chin, her Irish heating up more than the kitchen from the pizzas, *which* she'd just labored hours over for a special family dinner. Key word, "family." She dashed to the pantry to study the calendar, then slapped today's date box with the back of her hand, completely void of any red-ink entry. "And there's nothing written here either unless it's written in that invisible ink Davey is so fond of using for his homework."

Jack glanced at Matt. "Didn't you tell her about tonight?"

"No, I thought you did," Matt said with a crinkle of brows. He plucked an olive from Tess's pizza and tossed it in his mouth, frowning as if it were the olive's fault.

"It's *your* fundraiser, Coach." Jack pilfered another pepperoni while Davey picked at the cheese on his pizza.

"Yeah, but she's *your* mother, bro." Matt absconded with a jalapeno.

"Whoa, these are hot!" Davey exclaimed after snitching a jalapeno that left a hole in Tess's pizza.

Tess gritted her teeth. "Ohhhhh, you haven't *seen* 'hot' till you try walking out that door without eating dinner." She slapped Jack's hand as he went for another pepperoni, her gaze burning hotter than the 400-degree oven. "I can't believe you have the nerve to waltz in here and ruin my family dinner, and *then* you pick my pepperonis off my pizza?" She prodded and pushed him toward the table, pummeling him once or twice for good measure. "I suggest you park your butt in that chair, mister, or I'll park it with my foot."

"Ouch," Jack said with a grin, disarming his mother with a wraparound hug from behind while he chuckle-kissed her cheek. "I haven't seen you this riled since I tossed my red jersey into your load of white underwear."

Squirming out of his hold, she refused to give in to the smile that tickled her lips, unwilling to let them off the hook so easily. She seared all three with a maternal glare, underscoring it with a stiff fold of arms. "Yes, well a rare home-cooked meal with my entire family, *whom* I love and slaved over pizza for, is far more important than any pink underwear, young man." Brow arched, she tapped the back of the chair. "Sit, eat, and *then* you can desert your mother."

"Dessert?" Davey said with a squeak in his voice, pizza sauce ringing his mouth.

Jack chuckled and swooped his brother onto his shoulders, groaning when Davey got sauce on his neck. "Wrong 'desert,' champ. This one will only make you guilty. Here, clean your hands," he said after wiping sauce from his neck, "then give our angel mother a smooch." Sidling up to Tess, he hooked an arm to her waist to deposit a noisy kiss to her cheek that Davey duplicated perfectly. "Sorry, Mom, can't—we're late as it is, but I promise to make it up to you soon." He waggled his brows. "Maybe next week with my famous ribs?"

"Yeah, and Jack and I will even go crabbing and shrimping one night to add to the grill," Matt said, flipping a final olive into his mouth.

"Ooooh-ooooh … can I go too, please, please?" Davey hopped up and down on Jack's back like a top-water lure.

"You bet, sport." Matt gave his aunt a side hug on his way to the door, sliding his hand up and down her arm with remorse in his tone. "Don't be mad, Aunt Tess—it's for a good cause. And we'll snarf your pizza down tomorrow, I promise. Jack and I are treating Davey and our little brothers to burgers after, along with the coaches, so we won't be home till later, but we

can't leave till you forgive us because I gotta tell you—
I feel like a real dog."

"Not to mention looking like one," Jack said with a
crooked grin, eliciting a husky chuckle from Davey.

Shoulders drooping, Tess gave up the ghost and
tossed in the towel—literally. Unleashing a sigh that
came out more as a groan, she vented by pitching the
dishrag onto the table before dropping into a chair. "I
forgive you," she muttered, deciding that surprises were
best saved for little children rather than the grown-up
kind, especially ones whose schedules sported more red
ink than their mother's.

"We'll make it up to you, Aunt Tess, we promise,"
Matt said with a sheepish wave, slipping out ahead of
Jack and Davey as fast as his guilt could carry him.

"You're the best, Mom—love you to pieces." Jack's
voice trailed out the back door, increasing her gloom
when she realized his departure from her house would
soon be permanent.

"Love you, Mommy!" Davey called, his little hand
flailing goodbye before the screen door slammed
behind them, effectively sealing Tess in a funk.

Folding her arms on the table, she laid her head on
top, lower lip jutting forth in a rare sulk while she
stared out the oversized kitchen window. There Blue
sat, perched on his favorite limb, which bobbed in the
breeze as if he were giving her a soulful nod,
commiserating with her plight as a mother deprived of
her children.

"Why do things have to change, Blue?" she
whispered, lost in a moment of malaise that harkened
back to when Adam had abandoned her to run away
with her neighbor and friend. After he'd left, God and
her children had been her saving grace back then, the
glue that held her together during the most painful time
of her life. "And soon they will all leave," she said
sadly, heart aching that both Jack and Matt would be

gone by summer's end, living their own lives outside of
the haven she'd tried to create for them all. "First the
older boys, and then my girls." A sheen of tears glazed
her vision as her gaze lagged into a faraway stare, quite
sure she would blink one day and Davey would be gone
too. "All alone," she whispered, the sound as
melancholy as the distant hoot of an owl seeking a
mate.

No, never alone.

The thought bolted her upright, piercing her heart
with the truth from the One Who *was* the Truth, the
Light, and the Way. A peace purled through her as
always when she needed it most. *His peace.* A smile
wended its way across her lips. "Okay, Lord ... it's You
and me." Her gaze flicked toward the hall where the
tromp of footsteps could be heard on the front porch.
"*And* my girls," she said with a sudden grin.

The squeal and slam of the front door signaled Cat
and Shan were home right on time, sending Tess
scurrying for napkins and glasses to finish the table.
Her heart did a little flip as she chewed on the edge of
her smile, the idea of a girl's pizza night recharging her
mood.

"Oh, wow, something smells to die for," Cat said
with a noticeable moan as the twins stood in the
doorway of the kitchen like bookends, the deep pucker
of brows a mirror reflection of each other. "Oh, Mom,
you made your famous pizza? On a night we're not
home?"

Tess whirled around with the salad bowl in her
hands, her mouth slacking open like her daughters'.
"What? What do you mean on a night when you're not
home?"

"We have a planning meeting for the fundraiser at
Camp Hope tonight, remember?" Shan side-stepped her
sister to hook an arm to her mother's waist. She pressed

a kiss to Tess's cheek, then plucked a grape tomato from the bowl and popped it into her mouth.

"No ... no, that's tomorrow night." She hurried over to the calendar hanging in the pantry and tapped a finger to the day. "See? It says so right here—your meeting is Wednesday, not tonight."

Cat sauntered over to the calendar, giving her mom's neck an affectionate squeeze. "Uh, hate to break it to you, Mom, but I think you lost a day. Today *is* Wednesday."

"Oh, no!" Tess plunked the salad bowl on the table and kneaded the bridge of her nose, shoulders slumping in disappointment. "I knew I shouldn't have taken Monday off—my days have been off-kilter ever since. Showed up a day early for my appointment with Mrs. Tucker and threw the poor woman into a tizzy." She glanced up with a weighty sigh. "I am so sorry, girls."

"Not as sorry as we are," Cat said, strolling over to the oven to take a peek inside, a look of longing on her face. "Oh, well, at least I love cold pizza for breakfast."

Tess shot a look at the clock on her way to the oven. "Oh, no you don't—I can put your pizzas in right now, and they'll be ready in no time. So just sit down, and I'll get you something to drink."

"Wish we could, Mom," Shan said, eyes soft with regret, "but we're already late. We just came home because we forgot our notes from the first meeting."

"Because *somebody* rushed us out the door this morning." Cat draped an arm around Tess's shoulder, drawing her close with a side hug.

"Oh, crud ... I just didn't want you to be late," Tess said with a grimace, making a mental note to purchase a bottle of the Ginkgo Biloba she'd read about for improved memory and focus. Good mood deflated, her hopes for a lovely family meal puffed out with a weary sigh. "Well, at least you can eat a piece on the way ..." She snatched two paper towels and bustled over to retrieve Jack and Matt's pizza, the blast of heat from the oven wilting her as much as her keen disappointment.

Shan moved to the door, her tone contrite. "Sorry, Mom, but Miss Myra's ordering pizza for everyone, and there's no way I'd be able to stomach that after tasting yours. I'd rather save it for tomorrow when I can really give it my all."

Cat kissed her mother's cheek. "Me, too, Mom—cold pizza for breakfast is one of my faves, so wrap that puppy up." She darted to the door in her sister's wake, the two of them blowing kisses. "Oh, and it's okay if I take your car, isn't it? I'm meeting friends downtown after, and Shan has some errands to run."

"Sure, sure, have a good time." *Don't worry about your lonely mother—I have plenty of pizza to keep me company.* Tess offered a half-hearted wave—her evening and her pizza growing colder by the moment.

Cold pizza. Cold dinner.

Cold, lonely life without family or friends.

"No!" Palm slapping the table, Tess shot to her feet, determined she wouldn't give self-pity a chance. After all, it wasn't like she was really alone. She was a blessed woman with four beautiful children, two best friends who were also her prayer partners, tons of good friends at work with whom she played bunko and what not, and a Bible study of great ladies at church, many of whom were very dear friends. What more could she want?

Perhaps a crotchety but formally wonderful neighbor with a penchant for pizza?

A slow grin slid across Tess's lips as her gaze flicked to the Great Wall of Privet, where she'd heard Beau barking and whining earlier. Just last week she'd noticed the beginning of a hole beneath the hedge, and she was pretty sure it wasn't the work of a rabbit. Stifling a giggle, Tess tiptoed out the screen door, taking great care to close it without a sound. With all the stealth of a nosy neighbor, she knelt close to the near hole on her side of the hedge and peeked through. Her grin grew when she spied Ben relaxing in his Adirondack chair, head back and eyes closed while his hand rested at the base of a soda can on the arm of his chair.

Tess scrunched her nose. Soda. Not her drink of choice, but then fresh-brewed peach tea was her addiction, whether pizza or steak. Her gaze drifted to sweet, ol' Beau sprawled out at the base of Ben's chair, and when the lab lifted his head to sniff the air, an idea struck. One night last week when she'd fixed BLTs for dinner, she remembered hearing Beau's whines from the other side of the hedge, right before Ben had called him inside.

Feeling delightfully devious, Tess carefully rose to her feet and went inside to fry several pieces of bacon. When they were nice and crispy, she carried the hot pan outside to her wrought-iron table and fanned the fumes Beau's way with a magazine. In no time, Beau was sniffing at the hedge, which immediately escalated to whimpers after Tess placed a piece of bacon by the hole on her side. As suspected, sweet ol' Beau commenced to digging, the volume of his whines rising as fast as the chuckles in her throat, which she worked hard to restrain while ol' Ben lounged lazily in his chair.

"Oh, knock it off, you big baby," Ben called, causing Tess to jump back when her neighbor lifted his head to glare at his dog. "You have absolutely no reason to whine."

A giggle escaped Tess's lips as she perched hands on her hips and stared at the top of the hedge. "Oh, yeah? Well, you'd be a baby too, mister," she called loudly, "especially if you spent all afternoon making homemade pizza for your family and then had to eat all alone." Tess held her breath, the silence on the other side of the hedge deafening despite Beau's woofs and whines.

––––––––

Tess? Ben stared at the privet hedge, jaw gaping before he snapped it closed again to silence a groan. *Come on, lady, why can't you leave me alone?* He exhaled slowly and opted to just wait her out, hoping she'd take her bacon and pizza smells back inside and forget he was even around.

Silence reigned except for the pound of his pulse in his ears, and then ... "I can hear you breath-ing ..." she said in a sing-song tone that drawled out the last word.

He found himself holding his breath, the absurdity of it actually making him smile.

"Cheesy-gooey, hot, and straight out of the oven." She continued on as if talking to herself, and he'd lay odds her cadence punctuated each word with a back-and-forth bobble of her head. "Mounds and mounds of Italian sausage ... and bacon ... and hamburger ..." She paused, no doubt for effect, and he swore he could almost see the twinkle in her eyes through the hedge. "Oh, and pepperoni! You know the real thin, crispy kind that all but melts in your mouth? And, of course, lots and lots of veggies—mushrooms and Vidalia onions and broccoli and ..." She droned on and on until he figured the stupid pizza had barely fit in her oven. "All smothered with the yummiest cheeses ever, like Mozzarella, Provolone, Parmesan ... and just wait till you hear what's in the salad ..."

He couldn't take it anymore—he had more drool on him than Beau. "Stop!" he shouted, pretty sure she could hear the rumble of his stomach. "*Why* are you tormenting me, Tess?"

She hesitated while he imagined her smiling. "Because I slaved over this gourmet pizza half the afternoon, Dr. Doom, and I have no one to eat it with." There was a lull where Beau stood on his hind legs to paw at the privet before Tess's voice bled through the hedge as a near whisper, lancing his heart. "And because I really, really hate to eat dinner alone."

"You get used to it," he called, hoping to tamp down any sympathy she might arouse.

"Oh, Ben ..." Her tone faded to soft, although its intensity did not, "I don't ever want to get used to it because ..." The sound of her wispy sigh wreaked havoc with his defenses. "Sustenance nourishes so much more when it's shared."

Head bowed, he slipped his hands in his pockets and slowly exhaled his dissent, wondering how in the world Tess always managed to disarm him, be it foul mood or temper. It had always been something she'd been particularly gifted at, even when the couples had been friends. His jaw stiffened. *But not this time.* "Tess, I have dinner plans later," he lied, a last-ditch effort to put her off. It was drinks at Rocks on the Roof with friends who had bulldozed him into meeting a "lovely doctor," but she didn't need to know that.

"Come on, Ben, please? Appetizers, then ..." There was a plaintive, little-girl quality in her soulful tone that totally undid him, like when Lacey was little and used to beg him to come home from overnight shifts.

His eyelids shuttered closed at the memory, and gouging his temple with the ball of his hand, he unleashed a noisy exhale that smacked of surrender. "Deep dish or thin?" he said in a near groan.

"Thin. But deep, *deep* on the veggies, cheese, and meats, I promise."

His sigh could have ruffled the hedge. "Okay, pushy neighbor, where will we nourish then—your place or mine?"

Her little squeal crooked his mouth into a grin, even as he stood there kneading the bridge of his nose.

"My house, please," she said, the hurry-scurry of wrought iron scraping stone nearly drowning her out.

"My ruffians are gone for the night, and my patio is calling."

"Yeah, well I'm pretty sure I could have ignored the stupid patio," he muttered, lifting his chin to project his voice through the hedge. "So, what can I bring ...?" His mouth shifted sideways. "Besides a court injunction?"

Her giggle made him smile despite himself. "Just your crabby self and whatever you want to drink."

He snatched his soda off the table and paused, suddenly craving something a lot stronger. "You want a beer?" he said, squinting at the hedge.

"Oh, heavens no—bite your tongue." Several seconds passed while he imagined her chewing her lip like she used to whenever she'd said something she wished she hadn't. "Uh ... but thank you."

The grin came more naturally this time, making it a record for the most grins in a day, at least lately. "Yeah, well keep in mind, Mrs. O'Bryen, that *none* of this would be happening if I had."

Ambling to his slider, he ducked inside to grab one of the Blue Moons his fishing buddy Mort had left, then headed toward the gate. He patted the thigh of his Dockers to signal Beau to come, eyes narrowing when he spotted a hole beneath the hedge. His smile went flat. A hole considerably deeper than the rabbit hollow he'd noticed when he'd mowed last week. He halted to cock a hip. "So *you're* the culprit, are you? Trying to dig your way to the bacon lady, huh? And all this time I've been blaming the poor rabbits."

Beau woofed his response, jumping and dancing in circles all the way to the gate, obviously as excited about bacon as Ben was about pizza. The thought stopped him cold at the front edge of the border. *Excited—him?* About stepping foot into enemy territory for the first time in almost eight years? His eyes lumbered closed, the very notion depleting his air. He absently scruffed Beau's head while the dog attempted to nudge him along. But Tess wasn't the "enemy," he reminded himself, only one betrayed by him just like Ben. An innocent who—unlike himself—hadn't deserved such pain. He expelled a weary breath and continued his trek down Tess's driveway to her back patio, where a woman who had once been a good friend waited, armed with pizza to assuage his hungry stomach.

And maybe—just maybe—her own hungry soul.

Beau bounded toward her with a humiliating squeal, drooling like he hadn't been fed in a week, while Ben followed behind, shaking his head. *What am I, buster, chopped anchovies?*

She fawned shamelessly over his dog with bacon brandished in the air, her laughter filling the summer night with the lure of it and oregano, lightly seasoned with just a hint of honeysuckle from the bushes that lined her garage. "Ah, the power of pizza," she said with a hand splayed to her chest, her blue eyes sparkling more than the glimmer of river on the shore across the street. "Enough to entice the crabbiest of hermits to a neighbor's table."

"But not enough to tempt the kids to stay home, eh?" He regretted the barb the moment it left his mouth, but she only laughed, her smile as lively and bright as the candle that flickered and danced on a blue woven placemat.

"Oooo ... low blow, Dr. Doom." She tapped one of the wrought iron chairs they all used to sit in on summer nights. Only these were newly painted a pristine white with heron blue striped pillows that matched the shutters. "I can see my pizza and I have our work cut out for us. Sit, and I will administer the cure for the snarkiest of moods."

He slid into the chair and watched as she flitted around her garden patio lighting torches, reminding him of Tinker Bell on octane, her air of excitement bubbling

more than the cascading fountain edged with hostas.
She tossed a grin over her shoulder as she lit the final
torch, and if he didn't know better, he'd swear she
wasn't a day over thirty, her sloppy ponytail bouncing
as she hurried about. A smile flickered at the edge of
his lips when her eyebrows did a Groucho Marx.
"Mosquito repellent so we're the only ones doing the
nibbling," she explained with a playful innocence that
incriminated the direction of his mind.

'Nibbling,' indeed. The random thought took him by
surprise as did the stutter of his pulse when his eyes
scanned from loose curls that fluttered a graceful neck
to a baggy tank top that couldn't obscure the curves
beneath. Heat crawled up his throat, and he doused it
with a long swig of beer as she reentered the house,
forcing his gaze from the back of shapely legs framed
by jean shorts and sequined flip-flops.

For crying out loud, Carmichael, grow up, will you?
He was a respected middle-age physician, not some
pimple-faced pup OD-ing on hormones. He sat up stiff
in his chair, girding himself for an eat-and-run. After
all, this was an old neighbor and friend, not some fix-up
with a friend of a friend in a bar.

"Hey, I didn't even ask you what you like on your
pizza." The screen door slammed behind her as she
toted a humongous cooking stone laden with a thin-
crust pizza that would put any deep-dish to shame.
From a distance it could've been a bloomin' Bundt cake
streuseled with icing, for all he knew, except for that
heavenly garlic and onion smell that gurgled his
stomach. With a look of impish pride, she plunked it
down next to an amazing-looking salad with a satisfied
smile. "Hope you like a pizza with everything," she
quipped, and his smile veered dry as he snapped a
nautical-style napkin onto his lap. *Yep, everything but
perky neighbors.*

His mouth watered while she disappeared inside for fresh grated Parmesan and those little dried pepper flakes he'd had at Pizza Hut once, plopping them and sea salt down next to a stack of paper napkins. "This looks incredible, Tess," he said, mouth full of drool as he ignored the salad to heft a giant piece of pizza with both hands.

Mere inches from his mouth, the pizza froze like every limb on his body when she bowed her head and whispered a prayer that put him to shame. "Thank you, Lord, for this willing—" The blue eyes peeked up beneath a sweep of the longest natural lashes he'd ever seen, twinkling with mischief. "*Or* unwilling, whatever the case may be—person to share my pizza tonight at a time when I was feeling just a tad lonely. I pray that you bless our food and our conversation and especially our friendship. Amen." She proceeded to pile a dark leafy salad on her plate and drizzle it with vinegar and oil.

"Amen," he mumbled around a huge bite of the pizza, shoving it in before any saliva could escape. Reaching for a stash of paper napkins, he eyed her while he chewed and swallowed, glomming onto the part of her prayer that surprised him. "I can't imagine anybody who cooks like this being lonely, Tess, especially not with four kids. This is great."

She poked at a cherry tomato that glistened with oil, chewing slowly while she studied him with a pensive look. "I'm not usually lonely, but lately—with Jack and Matt and the girls growing up and going their own ways—well, it just seems like my time with them is dwindling away, and I guess that makes me sad."

"There's always Davey," he said with a smile, anxious to restore that light and fun air of hers that seemed to be a balm to his own empty mood. "Should be lots of basketball and bath-time battles left in your life, I would think."

That did the trick. He sat back and devoured his pizza while she chattered on and on about what a total shock and "blessing" her final pregnancy had been, sharing laughter and stories that relaxed him far more than the beer he'd consumed. She was a woman fiercely in love with her family and it showed, loosening more and more of his laughter with every Davey debacle disclosed.

When they'd been close as couples, he'd always known her to be fun and full of life, which at times like tonight gave her an almost innocent, little-girl air. But the moment she spoke about her children, she became the consummate mother, it seemed, still fun-loving, but somehow steeled by a quiet authority and confidence that surprised him, impressed him. By the time she'd finished her salad and pounced on her second piece of pizza, he knew more about her life than anyone who was a part of his and strangely enough, he felt the beginning of a bond he hadn't expected. A comfortable silence ensued as she closed her eyes to chew a piece of pizza that barely fit in her mouth, and he tried to remember the last time he'd felt this relaxed. Body mellow, great food, his gopher dog sprawled out by his side, and the easy company of one of the few women in the world he actually trusted.

And then in one swallow of rosemary-seasoned crust, he suddenly craved to hear that bubbly quality in her voice once again, each and every word shimmering with the potential to laugh whenever she spoke of her family. He cleared his throat and reached for more pizza, hoping to bait the sudden silence with another topic to make her smile, teasing her with a lazy smile of his own. "And then, of course," he said when she opened her eyes, pizza slice poised mid-air, "one can't have grandkids until the older ones leave the nest."

She grinned, and the dusky garden patio suddenly lit up like it was strung with a million twinkle lights. "Oh, yessss," she drawled, cheeks bulging when she took another chomp, practically swallowing it whole behind a smug smile. "Trust me, I *live* to be a grandmother—spoil 'em rotten and send 'em on home."

He smiled, trying not to notice the way her tongue swept away a glob of pizza sauce from the corner of her mouth. "Just compensation, I'd say, for all the gray hairs and wrinkles kids dole out to their parents." He took a long draw of his beer, assessing her over the rim of his bottle. "Although I can't see where you've gotten your fair share of either, Tess. You've aged well."

The muted pinks of dusk seemed to settle and glow in her cheeks. "Why, thank you, Dr. Carmichael. I credit eight glasses of water a day, lots of vegetables, SPF 50, and clean living."

He chuckled, the sound almost foreign to his own ears. "I'll vouch for the last one—a veritable Scrabble Gestapo as I recall, who refused to let the rest of us fudge."

"You mean 'cheat,'" she said with a righteous jut of her chin, a gleam of tease in her eyes that underscored the squirm of her smile.

Cheat. The very word sucked all oxygen from the air, paralyzing his lungs. Ah, yes, not all that uncommon, apparently. Cheating in Scrabble. Cheating in cards.

Cheating in marriage.

The pizza seemed to congeal in the pit of his stomach, and glancing at his watch, he pushed away from the table and rose, tossing his napkin on the chair. He was suddenly anxious to be gone—somewhere, *anywhere* but here—where his failure as a husband and father swelled in his throat like the pizza swelled in his gut. "I need to go, Tess, but thank you—the pizza was wonderful."

She wobbled to her feet as if his abrupt announcement had sideswiped her, leaving her in a daze while her napkin slithered from her lap to the floor. "B-but I have dessert, Ben, warm apple pie with vanilla bean ice cream."

He pushed in his chair, regret bleeding into his tone. "I'd love to, really, but I still have to shower and shave if I'm going to make Rocks on the Roof by nine." He passed a hand over his bristled jaw as if to validate his need to go. Eyeing Beau spread-eagle under the table, he squatted to rub his rump, giving a couple of firm pats. "Come on, Sleeping Beauty, time to go home."

Beau yawned and lumbered up, rattling the dishes on the table when he shook hard as if he were soaking wet. One hand massaging Beau's head, Ben extended the other to Tess, hoping she couldn't read the guilt in his eyes. "You're a good person, Tess, and I'm glad we're friends again."

She took his hand, holding on when he tried to let go. "Are you, Ben? Glad to be friends again?" She studied him intently, head tipped in serious question, all of that beautiful tease suddenly nowhere to be found. "Because deep down I get the feeling you're not."

Heat braised the back of his neck while he eased his hand from hers and slipped both in his pockets, staring at his Sperrys while he tried to think of what to say. "It's ... still hard, Tess, I won't lie to you, this ... this friendship between us." Expelling a shaky sigh, he looked up, the gentle look in her eyes reminding him just how badly he had failed and how very much he had lost. "Still too close to home, you know?"

A smile played at the corners of her mouth. "Yes, well that tends to happen when one lives right next door, Dr. Carmichael. Of course ... I could move, I suppose, but you'd probably never talk to me then."

He dropped his head and smiled, finally peering up with affection in his eyes. "Like I'd have a choice?"

The adorable grin surfaced. "Well, probably not because believe it or not, I do have a tenacious streak, or so I've been told."

He shook his head, unable to thwart a smile. "Absolutely shocking."

"So ..." she said, staying him with a hand to his arm, "the least you can do is let me wrap you a piece of my pie if you won't stay and eat it with me."

He acquiesced with a slow exhale and a patient smile. "Sure, that would be great."

"Good boy—wait right here." She led him over to the screen door and scurried inside, exuding so much energy he wondered if she existed on caffeine or just possessed some natural God-given high. His lips canted into a dry smile. *God-given being the operative word.*

He watched as she paused to answer her phone, but when the knife dropped from her hand with a faint cry, he opened the screen door and stepped inside, only to be slammed with memories so powerful he actually swayed on his feet. Gripping the doorframe, he forced himself to focus on Tess rather than the emotional tide whirling within, raging waters that wanted to suck him under.

"I'll be right there," Tess said, her voice cracking on what might have been a half sob, her fingers trembling as she ended the call and clutched the phone to her chest. "Davey's hurt," she whispered, a glaze of terror coating both her eyes and her words. "Fell off the third tier of the bleachers at Hope High School. Jack rushed him to the ER with a possible broken leg, so I have to go."

"What can I do?" he asked, his throat hoarse as he watched her rifle through her purse like a madwoman, far too upset, in his opinion, to drive herself to the hospital.

She glanced up with a hollow look in her eyes, body quivering while she continued to rummage through her bag. "Pray." It was only a whisper, but it shouted her fear loud and clear before she assaulted her purse once again. "Where-are-my-keys?" she bit out.

"How 'bout we pray together … on the way to the hospital?"

"No, you have plans—" She dumped everything onto the table, frantic as she turned her purse inside out. "Oh, no!" A painful groan parted from her throat. "Cat took my car."

"Doesn't matter—I'm taking you," he said with a clamp of his jaw, striding to the oven to turn it off before he hooked her arm to lead her to the door. "What needs to be done before we go—doors locked? Candles blown out?"

"Just those on the patio, then the front and back doors."

Without a break in his stride, he bolted the front, then the back, dousing the candles after shoving the remaining pizza and salad in the fridge. Hand clutched firmly to hers, he led her around the hedge to his driveway, helping her into the passenger side of his Range Rover before sliding in on the other side. He started the car and backed out with a squeal, pausing to shoot her a reassuring look. "It's probably just a minor fracture, if that."

She nodded, hands welded to the purse on her lap. Biting her lip, she looked at him out of the corner of her eye, brows tented in worry. "You really think so?"

"Absolutely." He slipped into physician role with a practiced smile, prickles of alarm over the sudden compulsion to comfort her in his arms. She ingested a deep draw of air before she expelled it in one long, bumpy sigh, and he wondered just how and when she'd breached his defenses. "I have a gut feeling he's going to be fine," he reaffirmed, forcing his gaze straight ahead where his emotions retained some element of control.

Now, me? He swallowed hard while she started to pray.

All bets are off.

CHAPTER FIFTEEN

"Jack!"

At the sound of his mother's voice, he turned in the tunnel hall that led to the ER waiting room, his senses assaulted by vending-machine coffee, rubbing alcohol, and 80-proof vomit from some drunk who'd puked at the door. Unfortunately, his normally calm and in-control mother looked like she was ready to do the same thing—saucer eyes in a pale face and an off-center ponytail that appeared to have seen better days.

As have I. Venting with a weary sigh, Jack strode to meet her, determined to cut off any worries at the pass. "He's fine, Mom. A little bruised, a little sore, but I don't think his leg is broken." He pushed the cup of machine coffee into her hands with the patient smile of authority he'd mastered as a third-year resident. "Here—decaf—you need this more than I do."

"B-but ... but ... if he fell from the top of the bleachers, how can you be sure?"

He arched a brow, one edge of his smile veering high. "Third row, not the top, Mom, and we can't be sure till he comes back from X-ray, but after eleven years of school and a real nice picture frame that clears me for pediatrics, I'd say we're looking at a mild fracture, if that."

"Oh, Jack …" She wrapped her arms around his middle, coffee and all, squeezing a grin out of him. "I was so worried!"

"I know, but he's going to be all right, I prom—" Jack halted mid-sentence, his gaze meeting Ben Carmichael's over his mother's shoulder, standing there mute not ten feet away. Lacey's father stared back with his hands in his pockets, wearing that same cold look he'd always reserved for Lacey's boyfriends.

Especially me.

Jack stiffened, the gentleness of his hug fading as he stepped back from his mother. "What's he doing here?"

His mother glanced over her shoulder and back before her chin elevated several degrees. "Ben was kind enough to drive me here since Cat took my car, Jack, so I'll thank you to temper your tone."

Ben cleared his throat. "Tess, I'm going to take off now—"

"Yeah, that would be real good," Jack said, voice curt.

His mother cauterized him with the same fiery glare as when she'd caught him smoking behind the garage the summer he was ten. "That's quite enough."

"Jack?"

He and his mother whipped around to see the resident physician—a year behind Jack in residency—striding forward with a file in his hand. "Looks clean, but I'd feel a whole lot better if you took a look, if you don't mind, since he's your kid brother."

Jack held the X-ray up to the light, squinting hard. "Looks good to me, Steve, but I'd like to check it out under the view box." He shoved the X-ray into the folder and handed it back. "I'll be right in."

"Sure, Jack."

"Hairline fractures can be tricky to diagnose," Ben said quietly from behind, a mere foot away. "I'll be happy to offer a second opinion if you like."

Jack spun on his heel, eyes itching hot. "Might I remind you you're not a specialist, *Dr.* Carmichael," he snapped, shocked at just how much anger he still carried for Lacey's father, the man he blamed for Lacey running away. The same man who had always treated him like dirt, from the moment he'd answered the front door on his first date with Lacey.

A nerve twittered in Lacey's father's jaw, hazel eyes burning like a brushfire spark about to flash out of control. "Neither are you ... *Jack*," he said in a lethal tone, the tight clip of his name a loaded gun aimed right at Jack's heart, letting him know what he really meant to say. The name he'd reserved for Jack alone from the first moment he'd caught him making out with Lacey in the hammock on his front porch.

Punk.

Jack's mom pushed him aside to face Carmichael head-on, making Jack flinch when she grasped the jerk's hand, her tone soft and soothing like the idiot was somebody who deserved respect. "Thanks again, Ben, for the lift, but Jack can take it from here. You have plans to keep."

Carmichael's gaze flicked to Jack, as hard and cold as a tiger-eye stone before it lighted on his mother, softening enough to squeeze Jack's ribs in a vise. "Anytime, Tess. If there's any question at all as to a hairline fracture, don't hesitate to ask for a CT scan, okay?"

Jack bristled. He walked toward the ER double doors, hoping his mom would take the hint when he glanced at her over his shoulder.

"Thanks, Ben," she whispered, dropping Jack's jaw when she gave the moron a hug.

"Let me know how the little guy fares, okay?" Carmichael slipped his hands in his pockets.

"Jack!" Lacey rounded the corner at the end of the hall with Spencer, obviously returning from the cafeteria with soda cups in hand.

A silent groan grated his throat when she took off in a run. With Spencer in tow, she dragged the poor guy down the polished linoleum hall, which sparkled more than the lenses in the kid's Coke-bottle glasses. Every nerve in Jack's body strung tight as his gaze darted from Lacey to her father and back, spiraling around his chest until he thought he couldn't breathe.

"How's Davey?" she called, huffing to a stop in front of Jack, apparently oblivious to the frozen stance of her father all of ten feet away.

"He's f-fine," he stuttered, wishing she and Spence had never insisted on following them to the hospital. "I'm heading in to double-check the X-rays now, but we think it's clear, so you two should go on home." In a split-second reflex, he glanced at her father before he hooked her arm to lead her back to the waiting room entrance, but it was more than enough.

Lacey peeked over her shoulder, a smile blooming when she spotted his mother. "Mrs. O'Bryen, hello—" Voice tapering off, her body went to stone the moment she saw her father, like the statue game they used to play on his front lawn, smile frozen and face marble white.

"Lacey, it's so good to see you again," his mother said, gathering her in a warm hug, "and Spence too." She skimmed the boy's cheek with a gentle stroke before she looped Lacey's arm with her own, as if shoring her up when she faced her father for the first time in years.

"D-daddy," Lacey whispered, her tone as tense and taut as every limb on Jack's body, the slight falter of her voice clear indication of just how much she still feared her father.

The fool had the gall to stand there and stare as if she were some awful apparition, a tic twitching in his cheek faster than the sprint of Jack's pulse. He gave a curt nod, his voice gruff and low. "Lacey." Without another word, he turned and strode silently down the hall. The sliding doors swallowed him up, spewing him out on the other side of a glass wall as thick and cold at the one he'd erected around his so-called heart.

"He'll come around, Lacey," his mother said with a gentle pat of her waist, smoothing a palm down Lacey's ponytail. "You'll see. All it takes is a little patience and a lot of prayer, honey, and you'll both be on your way to a new start."

"Thanks, Mrs. O'Bryen," Lacey whispered.

"It's Tess, remember? And you're more than welcome, sweetheart—always." His mom pressed a kiss to Lacey's hair like she used to when Lacey was small.

Body shuddering with a heavy exhale, Lacey turned to Jack with a tremulous smile, the sheen of moisture in her eyes reigniting his fury at her father. He ground his jaw tight in an effort to keep from pulling her into his arms and comforting her like he used to, kissing all the hurt away. His temple twitched. But that was no longer his right or responsibility, he reminded himself, squaring his shoulders as she curled an arm around Spencer's shoulder. "I think Spence and I might go back to the cafeteria," she said with a shaky smile, "for that piece of French silk pie I resisted before. You or Tess want anything?"

"No, sweetheart," Tess said, "but thank you."

Jack sighed and raked a hand through his hair. "Nope, we're almost through here, Lace, so you and Spence can head on home."

Her chin jutted up in a familiar show of pluck, her trademark twinkle returning to her eyes. "I think not, Dr. O'Bryen," she said with great drama, "Spence and I plan to stick it out to the bitter end if it takes every piece of pie in that cafeteria to do it."

Bitter end. A prophecy if ever there was. He forced a smile, latching an arm to his mother's shoulder. "You always were a sucker for pie, I guess."

"Ooooo, suckers! I think they had some of those too, didn't they, Spence?" She tickled her cousin's side, coaxing a giggle as they made a U-turn for the cafeteria.

His mother laughed. "My kind of girl," she called over her shoulder, shooting a grin while Jack ushered her toward the ER, "and definitely headed in the right direction, Lace, both with the pie *and* with your father."

Jack's mouth wrenched tight, memories of all the grief her father had given Lacey causing a sudden ache in his jaw. Yeah, he'd like to head in the right direction with her old man too, a direction his fist had been itching to take for a long, long time.

A hard right.

CHAPTER SIXTEEN

*W*ith a look of longing at the Mercedes, Lexus, and BMW lined up for valet parking, Lacey nosed her Honda past the posh Bohemian Hotel, opting to park a block away at the underground garage instead. Eyelids pencil thin, she cast an evil eye at the four-inch, gold-glitter stiletto sandals on the passenger seat—the ones Nicki had talked her into buying along with a way-too-short gold silk skater dress. Her feet would be hamburger by the time she walked back to the hotel, making her wish she'd come with Nicki and Matt to this "wedding party dinner" rather than driving herself. But she'd been so freaked out after running into her dad at the hospital last night that she'd barely slept a wink, at least not well. And the forty miles she'd biked this afternoon hadn't helped either, diffusing some of her tension, certainly, but leaving her zapped in the process. A sigh drifted out as she turned into the garage and yanked a ticket from the turn-style. So what could she do?

She crashed and overslept.

"Uh-oh, busy night," she muttered, circling her car four times to the top level where a scant few spots still remained, wondering what the odds were that she'd run into her dad again tonight. Probably pretty good, given her rotten luck lately and the fact that Rocks on the Roof—one of Savannah's newest hotspots—was a haunt of the higher-ups at Memorial, at least according to Nicki.

Heaven knows other than her faith, everything else in Lacey's life had gone south—her new car totaled, necessitating a clunker, and then loss of most of her savings to wedding deposits and pricey rent after Tim left. Not to mention that the only teaching position she'd been able to get in Savannah was subbing until a waitlist cleared for the next fulltime slot. With a calculating grate of her lip, she carefully shoehorned the Honda into a spot the size of a postage stamp and shifted into "Park." Ah … clearly one of the perks of owning a junker. She killed the ignition with a wry smile. Yep, things were definitely looking up.

Oh sure, she still had to work up the nerve to confront her father, but at least her relationship—correction, *friendship*—with Jack was on solid ground once again, and that alone brought Lacey a great measure of peace. They were well on their way to "comfortably casual and remote" as she'd mentioned to Nicki, and Lacey had every intention of keeping it that way. She eyed the stilettos in the next seat with trepidation, no earthly intention of putting them on until she absolutely had to. With a tight grimace, she snatched those suckers up and opened the door, thinking how much easier it would have been if Chase had picked her up—and dropped her off at the entrance—like Nicki suggested. But Lacey had put the kibosh on that before Nicki had even finished her sentence, begging her not to invite Chase tonight. No way would she risk upsetting the tenuous balance between Jack and her.

"Take your wedding party to that snazzy new hotspot on me," Uncle Cam had written in his latest letter to Nicki, and Nicki had been more than eager to oblige, promptly booking a reservation for dinner and dancing at Rocks on the Roof.

Lacey slipped out of the car in her trusty flats and humidity slammed, as thick and cloying as the guilt she felt over excluding Chase in a dinner he had every right to attend. She almost wished Jack could have brought a date so Lacey could do the same, but a wedding party evenly matched in couples made it rather awkward to do.

Marching toward the elevator, Lacey slowed as she spied a cherry red BMW up ahead, the "KIDS ROCK" personalized plates giving it dead away. Her mouth quirked into a smile. "What's this, Dr. O'Bryen?" she said under her breath, "car payments too steep to pop for valet pa—" The jest caught in her throat as she squinted through the convertible's back window, which apparently was up tonight, and it was a good thing. She stared hard at a movement that caught her eye before she realized there was a blonde all over Jack, glomming onto him like warm honey, gooey sweet, and molded curve for curve.

She blinked, heat rising into her cheeks that had absolutely nothing to do with the humidity. So much for "comfortably casual and remote," she fumed, noting there was nothing "comfortable, casual *or* remote" about the blonde bimbo kissing Jack in the front seat of his car. "Sit on his freakin' lap, why don't ya?" she hissed under her breath, shocked at the vehemence within. Her fingers suddenly itched for a hank full of bleached blonde hair. A flippin' dental hygienist, no doubt, paying a house call on Jack's molars.

"Get a room," she shouted as she passed, royally ticked off as she bolted for the safety of the stairwell before either of them could untangle their limbs in a timely manner, if they even could. With a grinding grit of her teeth, she flew down four flights of stairs and flung the exit door open, the merciless bang of the door to the wall matching her mood perfectly.

"And to think I was worried about flaunting a guy in front of *him*," she said, thumping the stilettos against her chest, quite sure those four-inch heels would come in handy if Dr. Love asked her to dance. "Ha! So much for shying away from flaunting, Jack Carmichael, not when you and Miss Blonde Bombshell have already perfected it to an art form."

By the time Lacey entered the lobby of the Bohemian Hotel, her composure was as frazzled as her hair. Shoving the door of the ladies' room open, she strode in and hurled both her purse and her heels onto the marble counter, grateful the restroom was empty. "What exactly is your problem?" she hissed in the mirror. "You are acting like a jealous shrew, and you have absolutely no right to do so. Jack is a single man who can date any floozy he wants, just like I can date any man I want. Chest pumping she glared in the mirror, knuckles clenched whiter than the marble beneath her grip. "Although I sure in the heck wouldn't crawl all over him."

You did once.

Lacey blinked, the truth of that quiet reminder pooling moisture in her eyes. Palms to the counter, she slumped forward, unable to face herself as she hung her head over the sink, her reedy expulsion of air tainted with more than a little shame. "God, forgive me. I have no room to talk, not with the way I've acted all these years before You opened my eyes." Sucking in a deep breath, she slowly looked up and exhaled her anger. "I can do this," she said to herself, "I can be the friend Jack needs me to be. *And* the example of God's love that he and that bim—" Her lips tightened to choke back the word before she expelled a loud bluster of air. "He and that *blonde* need me to be."

Closing her eyes, she shored her confidence up with a much-needed prayer, then proceeded to touch up her lips with her tube of Pink Envy lipstick—the irony of the name not lost on her at all. With a quick comb through her hair, she assessed the loose curls as they spilled over her bare shoulders onto her halter-top dress, satisfied with the way Nicki's oversized gold hoops shimmered in her ears. Her gaze dropped to the stiletto sandals Nicki had badgered her to buy, and venting with a reluctant sigh, she tucked her flats into her gold lamé sack purse and slipped on the stilts. Shoulders back, she was surprised at how confident those four extra inches made her feel, and with a shake of her head, she silently thanked her cousin. Because heaven knows if ever there were a night she needed an extra lift, it was tonight when she was stag while her ex was playing kissy-face with a blonde goddess.

"Okay, Carmichael, buck up and get through this evening," she muttered, heading back to the lobby to take the elevator to Rocks on the Roof. The doors opened and Lacey slipped in and pressed the Rocks on the Roof button, sagging against the wall with eyes closed to muster her strength.

"Hold the elevator, please ..."

"Uh-oh ..." Eyelids popping open, she tried to slam a finger to the "open door" button, but pressed the "close door" one by mistake, just as a muscular arm thrust into the crack, parting them once again. "I am so sor—" Lacey halted when she met Jack's humorous gaze, which promptly heated her cheeks. *And then again, maybe not ...*

He grinned, his lips sporting a shimmery gloss that did nothing for Lacey's resolve to be nice. "Close call." He pushed the button for the roof.

"I'll say," she said with an awkward smile. *Too close.*

The heat in her face bumped up to a small brushfire when his gaze traveled the length of her in frank perusal, a low whistle parting from his lips. "Wow, Lace, you look great." He slid an easy arm to the blonde's waist, taking the concept of "looking great" to a whole new level with a stylish single-breasted blazer over a pale-blue T-shirt the exact color of his eyes. "Lucky Chase." The bridge of his nose crimped in an inverted V. "Where is Preacher Boy anyway? Did he drop you off at the door?"

"Oh, I wish." She lifted one of the stilettos to divert his attention from her face, her tone a lot dryer than her sweaty hands. "These things turn a city block into a mile, trust me." Forcing a bright smile, she turned her attention to the blonde who was nothing short of stunning, even with Jack's whisker burn pinking her chin. She extended her hand. "Hi, I'm Lacey Carmichael, Jack's partner in the wedding," she said, suddenly aware that Jack's compliment of "looking great" was no competition for a goddess with pale-gold hair and almond-shaped eyes.

"Jasmine Augustine," the goddess said with a stiff smile, shaking Lacey's hand before she casually fondled Jack's arm in an apparent show of possession. "It's good to finally meet. Jack's told me so much about you."

"Uh-oh, badmouthing the ex, eh?" Lacey offered Jack a teasing smile as the doors opened onto Rocks on the Roof. The mouthwatering smell of roasted chicken and beef sliders lured them in while live music beckoned couples onto an open-air dance floor. Lacey immediately relaxed, soaking in the urban-chic setting that boasted a warm array of wood, granite, and river rock.

"You're late!" Nicki appeared out of nowhere, snagging Lacey's arm after greeting Jack and his date. She ushered them toward a cozy table at the back of the restaurant, allowing Jack to go on ahead while he led Jasmine to where Matt was waving them down. "You look fabulous, by the way," she whispered in Lacey's

ear, screeching to a halt by the bar when Lacey's
fingernails pinched into her skin. "Hey—that hurts."

"It's nothing compared to my feet, Nicolette
Phillips," Lacey hissed, "and for mercy's sake, *why*
didn't you tell me Jack was bringing a date?"

Eyebrows peaking high, Nicki offered a repentant
scuff of her lip. "I'm sorry, Lace, but I just found out
myself when Matt asked the waitress for two extra
chairs. Apparently there was a breakdown in
communication between my fiancé and me because *he*
thought Chase was invited, even though I could have
sworn I mentioned he wasn't." She snuck a peek in the
direction of their table, a definite apology in her tone.
"So when Jack asked if he could bring a friend, Matt
said yes."

"Friend? Ha!" Lacey's tone climbed several octaves.
"With benefits and then some, I'd say, judging from the
way they were making out in the parking lot."

"Oh, Lace." Nicki turned to brace her hands on
Lacey's arms, her eyes soft with sympathy. "I told you
Jack's moved on, so you need to do the same, which is
why I've been begging you to say yes to Chase, and not
in secret either."

Lacey's chest rose and fell with a weighty sigh.
"Yeah, well, it's too late to do that tonight."

Nicki cocked her head, hazel eyes narrowing in
thought. "Maybe not ..."

"Oh, no you don't! I do not want you calling Chase
this late, Nick, as if he's some ... some afterthought."
Lacey squared her shoulders and stood tall—
considerably easier with the stupid stilettos—and
decided to make the best of what promised to be a very
long evening.

"You sure? I don't want you feeling like odd man
out." Nicki's look was timid beneath sooty lashes, the
tender affection in her cousin's eyes shifting Lacey's
attention to where it belonged—on Nicki and Matt.

Lacey swallowed her up in a hug. "Absolutely! And it's odd woman out, Cuz, but that's okay because you're the only reason I'm here in the first place, right?" She pulled away to hook her arm through Nicki's, steering her toward the table with a bright smile. "That and a juicy medium-rare steak."

At the table, Lacey could have kissed Nicki for bumping Nate to the other end so Lacey could sit next to her, as far away from Jack and his date as possible. It wasn't hard to see why Rocks on the Roof was considered Savannah's new "it club," and Lacey actually found herself easing into its relaxing atmosphere with little to no trouble. Laughing and chatting with Nicki, Matt, and Sarah throughout dinner allowed her to unwind and enjoy all the action and ambiance of a rooftop lounge overlooking Savannah's historic riverfront.

"So, Jasmine, how'd you meet Jack anyway?" Kelly twirled her swizzle stick in her drink before taking a sip, her voice cool.

All chatter ceased while everyone stilled to hear Jasmine's answer.

"In the storeroom at Memorial," she said shyly, giving Jack an adoring look beneath heavy lashes. "He was looking for something, so I helped him find it."

"I'll just bet you did," Nicki muttered under her breath, and Lacey kicked her under the table.

"You see I'm a nurse on peds," she continued, "and all the nurses voted Jack the resident they most wanted to be stuck in a storeroom with, Dr. McDreamy, so to speak." She gave a shrug of tan shoulders before she stroked Jack's cheek, his face shadowed with beard and sporting a sheepish grin. "So I guess you could say I won."

"You could, but I wouldn't count on it," Nicki whispered to Lacey, muffling her voice with a pat of her napkin.

"Hey, how come Chase didn't come tonight?" Sarah asked, taking a sip of her mango Shirley Temple while her brown eyes blinked wide over the sugared rim of her glass.

Jack's eyes homed in on Lacey, curiosity thinning his gaze. "Yeah, I asked you in the elevator where he was, Lace, but you didn't answer."

Lacey sank deeper into the leather and teak chair as she and Nicki exchanged glances.

"I'll tell you where he is—at home—because *someone* forgot to invite him," Matt said with a tweak of Nicki's neck, his knowing wink at Lacey ensuring her that her secret was safe with him. He stood, offering Nicki his hand. "Come on, Someone, you can redeem yourself on the dance floor."

Nicki paused, her eyes following Jack as he rose and led Jasmine out for a slow song, causing Justin and Nate to follow suit with Sarah and Kelly. "Why don't you dance with Lacey first, Matt—I need to visit the little-girls' room, okay?" She rose to brush a kiss to his lips before giving Lacey's shoulder a squeeze.

"Sure," Matt said with a crooked grin, "as long as the dancing queen doesn't step on my brand-new shoes." He offered her his hand with a wink while Nicki made her way to the restroom. "I've heard stories of your dancing skill, Lace, or lack thereof."

"I beg your pardon, Matthew Ball," she said in a pretend huff, "but your cousin over there did some damage as well. Nearly put me in a foot cast, as I recall."

Matt grinned. "Well, he *was* a bit of a nerd back then, nose in the books all the time, so what d'ya expect?"

Lacey took Matt's hand, eyeing Jasmine plastered against Jack so tight, they could have been one. "Well, I'd say he's certainly picked up a thing or two since then," she muttered as Matt led her onto the floor.

Relief expanded in her chest when he chose a spot on the other side, his hold loose and comfortable. She exhaled slowly, enjoying the airy feel of glass garage-style doors that opened onto a balcony with cozy couches, umbrellas, and fire pit, all overlooking a beautiful river view. "I can see why Rocks on the Roof is so popular," she said. "The atmosphere up here is wonderful."

Matt smiled, but she didn't miss the sobriety in his eyes. "Usually, although not as much tonight, I guess."

Head tipped, she gave him a curious gaze. "Why's that?" she asked, although from his tender expression, she had a suspicion.

He nodded in Jack's direction, his tone gentle. "About tonight, Lace, I'm really sorry. If I'd known Chase wasn't coming, I would have never said yes when Jack asked to bring a date."

"It's okay, Matt," she said quickly, striving for a casual air. "I'm fine, really."

He focused hard, as if searching for the truth behind her forced smile. "Are you?" The soft concern in his voice caused a sting of moisture at the back of her lids. When it came to Jack, she and Matt had always shared a camaraderie over the years—the wild cousin who felt a kinship with the wild girlfriend. And like Jack and her, it seemed Matt and his cousin had traded places too, Matt's wild ways mellowing into a solid faith while Jack threw caution—and any prior beliefs—to the wind. As Matt studied her now, he probed with a knowing look that dismantled any desire to pretend she was all right. "Nicki says you still have feelings for him …"

She gave a little shrug, her tone suddenly more somber than before. "Sure I do, Matt, why wouldn't I? I was in love with the man—those feelings don't just go away completely. So of course I still care about him."

"And he cares about you, Lace, more than he's willing to admit."

She sighed, her smile tinged with sadness. "I know. Which is exactly why I asked Nicki not to invite Chase tonight. No reason to cause Jack anymore hurt, you know?"

Matt's smile tipped on one side. "Yeah, I do. It's too bad he didn't feel the same way." He glanced across the dance floor where Jasmine was nuzzling Jack's neck. "But I got the distinct feeling that he can't handle the idea of you and Chase, which is why he brought Jasmine tonight. She's his buffer against the feelings he doesn't want to have for you."

She shook her head. "I know. It's a mess, isn't it? Two people whose love was torn apart at the seams, still tethered by slender threads of caring way too much." The song came to an end, and she sighed, lifting on tiptoe to press a kiss to Matt's cheek. "Thanks, Matt, for being such a good friend to us both."

He paused, his hands on her arms while his face dipped in question. "I've been wondering, Lace, do you think …" A sigh blustered from his lips as he tunneled his fingers through the hair at the back of his neck. "Well, I've seen the pull between the two of you, you know, and I can't help but wonder …" He hesitated, the love for them both shining in his eyes as he pinned her with a hopeful look. "It's just that you and your faith would be so good for Jack," he whispered.

"I agree." The very notion of loving Jack again ushered a warm shiver through Lacey's body, but reality quickly doused all romantic notions. "But as a friend, Matt, nothing more, which is what I'm praying for. As far as a man I can marry someday?" She shook her head as she hugged her arms to her waist, her tone laced with regret. "He seems to have this vendetta against God and faith that scares me and puts me on guard. And you and I both know, Matt, I can't afford to give my heart to a man who not only doesn't share my faith, but is downright hostile to it as well."

"Yeah," he said quietly, slipping his hands in his pockets. He peered up with a half smile, concern deep in his eyes. "I'm just not sure Jack can be friends with you, Lace, and not want to take it further, you know?"

A knot ducked in her throat. "I know." She managed a wobbly smile. "But it doesn't look like either of us has a choice right now, not with the wedding."

"Nope." Matt slipped an arm to her waist to guide her back to the table. "But for what it's worth? I'm hoping that somehow, someway, you'll be the one to finally break through that wall of bitterness Jack's erected against God. A wall that his mom, Shan, nor I have been able to scale, so my prayers are on you, Lacey Carmichael, as the love of his life."

"*Ex* love of his life," she said with a shaky smile, Matt's words unleashing an unsettling mix of both fear and hope.

Chuckling, he pressed a palm to the small of her back, the jest in his tone at odds with the serious look in his eyes. "For you, maybe, Carmichael, but something deep down inside is telling me loud and clear that it's not the same for our boy."

CHAPTER SEVENTEEN

I am such an idiot. Jack seated Jasmine after their sixth dance, the floor finally clear while the band took a break. His gaze strayed to where Lacey wandered slowly to the open glass doors by herself with a swizzle drink in her hand, obviously with the intent to check out the view. Or to grab a moment alone, he suspected, away from being the only single in the group. Sure, each of the guys had asked her to dance—all but him because of Jasmine's stranglehold—and she certainly seemed to be having a good time. But he sensed her awkwardness, even from across the room, or maybe it was his own unease at being stupid enough to bring a date. Either way, he couldn't help the clamp of his jaw at the realization that Lacey Carmichael was the only woman he knew who could make him feel like a heel.

"Jack?"

Jasmine's hand on his arm jolted him from his reverie. *Make that one of two women.* The anxious look in her eyes ensured him she was worried about his feelings for Lacey. She'd made that perfectly clear in the parking lot after they arrived, letting him know as always that she was ready to give him her all, something he'd been dodging since he'd first asked her out six months ago.

Back when Lacey had left, she'd taken his heart with him, leaving him no stomach to ever get close to a woman again. And then his father had left, all but destroying any faith Jack may have had, and suddenly he'd found himself trading in one Savior for another. Medical school became his new salvation, his only focus other than family until he coasted into his first year of residency, when his grueling schedule had him sleeping more hours at the hospital than at home.

Only he'd done way more than sleep in that call room in his early heyday as an intern. A cold slither of "what-ifs" iced his skin at how reckless he'd been. Heyday? More like "play day," when any morals he had left were more exhausted than he. There had been no shortage of nurses, then, willing to usher him back into the world of dating, and he quickly earned a reputation as a player, which suited him just fine.

Until a "player" broke his sister's heart. Jack's stomach cramped. Shannon, his shy and gentle sister, had fallen for the wrong guy, a womanizer just like Jack had been. Far too gentle of a soul for this world, she'd had a breakdown when all was said and done, and that was when Jack called it quits on playing it loose. He made a pact with his sisters right then and there, pledging to wait until marriage if they did too.

A pact honed to iron after a trauma of Jack's own. Sweet Dawn Janis had helped seal the deal, apparently "head over heels" and pregnant to boot, even with the protection both she and Jack had used. He had expected to be relieved when she miscarried early on, but the whole situation had just hollowed him out. Made him sick inside. Children were far too important to risk on pleasure or lust, he'd decided, and certainly too valuable to be branded an accident.

Of course, everybody thought he slept with every nurse he dated, including Matt, but Jack always stopped short of making love to a woman, refusing to give that part of himself away to anybody but a wife ever again. He fought a quirk of his lip. A mindset that seemed to entice the various women he dated all the more, and none more so than the green-eyed beauty who waited before him now. Forcing his attention back to Jasmine, he rubbed her arms with his palms. "Sorry, Jazz, what did you say?"

She glanced at her watch. "I said I have a friend who works downstairs, so I promised I'd pop in to say hi when her shift begins at eight." She leaned in to slowly brush her lips against his. "Wanna come? We won't be long."

He reeled her close to finish off her kiss with one of his own, luring a soft moan from her lips. "No, you go—I should stay here, and I need to hit the head anyway."

Her full lips pushed into a tiny pout. "But it's *you* she wants to meet, Jack, Dr. McDreamy in the flesh."

He shook his head and chuckled, doubting he'd ever get used to all the attention women doled out, not after so many years with his head in the sand. He deposited a kiss on her nose. "If she's just starting her shift, then she'll be there when we leave, so how 'bout I meet her then?"

She sighed, her pout easing into a sulky smile. "I guess. But I promised I'd come by at eight and she's probably waiting at the door, so I'll go tell her we'll be by later, okay?"

Leaning in, he skimmed her mouth with his own before he rose to his feet, pulling her up along with him. "Sounds like a plan, Nurse Augustine. Now hurry back, because I'll be waiting."

He watched her leave, grinning when she blew a kiss at the door. The elevator closed behind her, and his gaze immediately flicked outside. Taking advantage of Matt entertaining the table with one of his wild coaching stories, Jack zeroed in on the terrace, determined to make things right with Lacey.

Any other night, the balcony would be teeming with people, every loveseat and table occupied and standing room only, but Nicki had been smart enough to plan this get-together on a Thursday, so Jack had no trouble spotting Lacey. She was leaning against the brick balcony wall at the far end of the building, arms folded on the steel crisscross railing beneath a towering palm. His pulse picked up as he made his way to where she stood alone, those silky blonde curls fluttering in the breeze. In natural reflex, his gaze slowly roamed down her very short dress, affording him a generous view of her beautiful legs.

Whether entranced by Savannah Bridge at twilight— a watercolor wash of purples or pinks spilling into the water—or the sounds of foghorns muffling his footsteps, she didn't seem to hear his approach. Careful not to startle her, he slowly eased a hip against the brick wall, her profile dusky pink in the waning light. "I owe you an apology, Lace," he whispered, so low he wasn't sure she even heard it.

Her gaze remained fixed on the sail-like, cable-stayed bridge that was so much a part of Savannah's historic riverfront, and she never moved a muscle. Except, of course, for the barest curve of her lips as the sea breeze toyed with her hair. "Don't be silly, Jack, we've both moved on with our lives, I know that. Besides," she said with a glimmer of a grin, "a hottie like you with a medical degree? I'm surprised you don't carry a stick."

He laughed, turning to lean over the railing like her, hands casually clasped over the steel grid. "I leave it in my car."

The tease in her eyes nailed him as she tilted her head. "Needed it in the parking garage, did you?" She finally angled his way, the dry slant of her lips telling him loud and clear what she'd seen in his car.

He winced, his gaze trained on the swirling waters below. "So that was you, huh?" Hoping to distract her from the heat crawling up his neck, he slid her a sideways grin while the breeze drifted the familiar scent of peach shampoo his way. "I didn't think good Christian girls advocated hotel rooms for unmarried couples."

It was her turn to blush apparently, the shadows of a fuchsia sky unable to hide the deepening tint of her cheeks. "I make it a practice to stay out of the personal lives of ex-boyfriends, Jack, so your secret is safe with me."

"There are no secrets, Lace," he said with a casual drawl. "I'm just a nose-to-the-grindstone medical-school graduate who finally decided to play the field, that's all."

She peered up at him out of the corner of her eye. "Pretty crowded field the way I hear it, Dr. McDreamy." Her face crinkled in a scrunch. "And Jasmine's okay with that?"

He shrugged, choosing to stare out at the meandering river current rather than Lacey's face. "I've made it perfectly clear to Jazz and every other woman I've dated that after spending the last seven years killing myself, I just want to have a little fun for a while." His gaze veered up to the moon, a slice of tangerine dribbling a mango ribbon across rolling waters. "I've always figured honesty is the best policy, and they always have the option of saying no, right?"

"But few do, it seems," she said, her soft chuckle almost accusatory.

Sucking in a sharp breath, he faced her with a hip to the wall, his voice painfully serious. "You did."

A glimmer of pain streaked across her face as she hugged her arms to her waist. "Come on, Jack," she said softly, "I told you before—it was me, not you. I just realized I wasn't the right girl for you nor was I ready for a commitment back then, so I ran away. And now everything's changed, and the tables are turned because I want things that you don't want anymore." She reached out to place a hand on his arm, her tone issuing a plea. "I care about you, Jack, more than I can ever express, but please … can't we just move on and be friends like we decided at that wedding last week? For Matt and Nicki's sake as well as ours?"

He studied her face in the moonlight, a face he'd kissed and adored so many times on summer-scented nights just like this, and he ached to hold her like he used to. To return to a time when she longed for his touch as much as he longed for hers right now. To make love to her on a blanket on the dock like she'd begged him to do so long ago on so many moonless nights. But God had stood in their way back then through Jack's misguided devotion, and now it was God Who still stood in their way today through hers. Sliding his hands in his pockets, he filled his lungs with a deep draw of sea air and slowly released it again, almost wishing she had never come home. "I don't know if I can do that, Lace," he said quietly. "Every time I see you, I almost feel like we belong together, so when guys like Chase flirt with you, I get …"

"Jealous?" She cocked her head, lips in a slant. "Talk to me when you see Chase and me playing Twister in the front seat of his car."

He couldn't help but grin. "You know what? I think I liked it better when I hated you."

A dark brow angled high. "That can be arranged, Dr. McDreamy, just give me the word."

His smile faded into soft affection as he expelled a slow and surrendering sigh. "I guess the 'word' is going to have to be friendship then, Lace, although I have no earthly idea how I'm going to do it."

Her smile was as tender as his. "Well, I suspect there's a drop-dead gorgeous nurse inside who's more than ready to make house calls, Jack, so I'd take advantage, my friend."

He couldn't resist the tease in his tone. "Already have."

"Oooo-kay," she said with great exaggeration, giving him a playful roll of eyes. "Then I think you're going to be just fine."

"Yeah, until I see you with Chase." His smile leveled off.

Every line in her beautiful face softened. "Right now Chase and I are just friends, Jack, just like you and me."

He glanced up with a half-lidded smile, a bit of the devil in his eyes. "Only he has kissing rights and I don't," he countered.

She shook her head, her grin traveling wide. "No, you most definitely do *not*, Jack O'Bryen. Your kisses are way too deadly as I've learned all too well in the past."

His gaze traced every feature of her face, every dimple, every faded freckle, every twinkle in hazel eyes that still haunted his dreams. "I love you, Lacey. Always have, always will."

A sheen of tears glazed in her eyes. "I love you, too, Jack. Forever and ever, amen."

His heart cramped at the reference to the Randy Travis song they used to ham up together fishing on the dock or just floating in the dory. *Their* song, Lacey had called it.

Once.

"Ah ... so *this* is where you two are hiding."

Both Jack and Lacey whirled around to find Chase striding forward, a crooked smile on his face. "Hey, Jack, good to see you again," he said, offering a handshake before turning to Lacey with a sheepish smile. "It seems my invitation got lost in the mail, but

Nicki threatened me with my life if I didn't come anyway."

Lacey managed a chuckle, the sound as awkward as Jack felt. "I knew she was a bully, but I didn't realize she'd stoop to badgering the clergy as well."

Chase laughed, his interest in Lacey as obvious as the twinge in Jack's gut. "I think the band just started a new set," he said, nodding toward the dance floor through the mile-wide doors. "You up for it?"

"Uh … sure …" She shot Jack a glance steeped in apology before her hesitant gaze returned to Chase. "Jack and I were just finishing up, so how 'bout I meet you back at the table?"

Jack cleared his throat. "No, really, Lace, go on—we're done here."

Palms in the air, Chase took a quick step back, concern crimping the bridge of his nose. "Hey, man, I'm sorry—I didn't mean to interrupt, it's just that Nicki said Lacey was out here and that your girlfriend was looking for you too."

"Yeah, I need to get back." Jack clapped him on the shoulder before reaching to gently squeeze Lacey's hand. "And no worries, Chase, we're done," he said with a stiff smile.

"You sure?" Chase paused, gaze flicking from Lacey to Jack, "because I can wait if you're not."

Chest in a vise, it took everything Jack had to eke out a casual tone. "Nope, we're through, I promise, so she's all yours." He shot them both the mask of a smile on his way to the doors.

Whether I like it or not.

CHAPTER EIGHTEEN

*L*acey sniffed the air as she entered Mamaw's kitchen, salivary glands going crazy. "Oh, wow, Nick, our favorite—peach crumble pie!" She made a mad dash across Mamaw's kitchen to pick a sugar-dough crumb off one of five pies cooling on trivets at the end of the whitewashed kitchen table. She popped it in her mouth and moaned. "Oh, Mamaw, I love you!"

"Not after I slap your fingers with a wooden spoon, you won't." Her grandmother arched a silver brow, the stern purse of her lips betrayed by the twinkle in her blue eyes. She paused at her cutting board on the cream granite island, knife poised over a stalk of celery. "And *please* tell me those fingers are clean, young lady," she said with a kink in her smile.

Nicki ducked around from behind to pinch some sugar crumbs of her own, her deep chuckle reverberating in Lacey's ear. "Oh, yes, ma'am, clean as a whistle—I watched her lick 'em myself after the dip cones we ate."

"You had dip cones?" Spence looked up from his Minecraft Lego village, which occupied the other half of the table. His long lashes blinked several times behind thick lenses.

"Uh-oh, now you've done it," Lacey said with a nudge of her elbow into Nicki's side. She scuttled over to where Spence knelt on the floral seat cushion and hugged him from behind, sidestepping Sherlock Holmes, who snored loudly beneath the rungs of Spence's spindle-back chair. "Hey, buddy, I promise I'll buy you ice cream the very next time we're out, okay?"

"I guess ..." His little voice was so draggy, Lacey could have sworn she saw a scowl on the Power Ranger's face who stood guard over his village.

"*Which,* young lady," Mamaw said while she scrubbed at the sink, her obsession with cleanliness second to none, "will be very shortly." She glanced at the clock before she sent Lacey an impish smile, drying her hands with a perfectly bleached-white dishtowel. "I need you to deliver pies."

Nicki froze, her finger stuck in the pie like Little Jack Horner. "Wait—you're not giving them *all* away, are you?"

The alarm in Nicki's tone echoed in Lacey's mind as well. Panic ping-ponged in her chest as she gaped at her grandmother. "You *did* bake one for us, right?"

Mamaw's chuckle sounded devious, an ideal match for the bit of dickens that usually gleamed in her eyes. Her face scrunched in thought as she counted on her fingers. "Now let's see ... five pies. Two for my card club luncheon, two for shut-ins, and one to give away ..."

The girls' groans rose in perfect sync, causing Mamaw to giggle all the more as she plopped a cooked chicken on her cutting board. "I suggest you girls start praying right now that Lulu got a babysitter for her hooligan grandsons or I'm thinking one pie for card club may not be enough ..."

"Mamaw, you are nothing but a scamp," Lacey said with a pinch of her waist, stealing a piece of chopped chicken in the process. "*Now* I know where Nicki gets it."

Nicki tossed a sugar crumb in the air and chomped it before following Lacey over to Mamaw's cutting board for chicken larceny. "You betcha, and it happens to be one of my finest qualities, right, Mamaw?"

"Mmm ..." Mamaw absently patted Nicki's arm while her focus remained on Lacey, obviously more intent on issuing errands than tease. "If you say so, dear," she said in her distracted grandmother tone, eyes on Lacey like a mother eagle scoping its prey. "I'll need you to deliver a pie to Mrs. Hedgewood right away, Lacey, because her favorite soaps start soon, and she won't answer the door or the phone once they do."

Lacey froze, mid-chew. "No, Mamaw, please—not Mrs. Hedgehog! She chewed on me for over an hour the last time you sent me over there, dressing me down for leaving both you and Isle of Hope high and dry." She cast a frantic look at Nicki. "Can't Nick do it this time?"

"Ohhhhh, no you don't," Nicki said with a nervous glance at the gleaming white clock on the wall. "Matt and I have appointments across town with the tuxedo place and the florist, remember? And I'm already late." Snatching a final piece of cooked chicken, she bussed both Mamaw's and Lacey's cheek before hefting a large, flat box with two of the pies. "I'll be happy to carry these two pies out to your car though, Lace," she said with a wink, tossing a smirk over her shoulder. "But let me know how Mrs. H's surgery went, okay? Oh, and be sure to have her show you her scar." Nicki scrunched her nose at the door. "It's epic."

A guttural groan scratched from Lacey's throat, her desire for tender pieces of chicken suddenly as flat as Mrs. Hedgehog's incision. "You really know how to make somebody pay through the nose for peach pie, Mamaw, you know that?"

"Oh, you have no idea, sweet girl," her grandmother said with a sympathetic pat of her cheek, before quickly returning to her chicken with a few more whacks. After the final chop, she tossed it into a huge bowl along with her chopped celery and onion, then bustled to the sink. She proceeded to wash and sanitize her hands with a gargantuan bottle of Purell, a close second in size to her ceramic iced tea dispenser.

Expelling a weary sigh, Lacey sagged onto the cream leather cushion of a white-limed wooden stool, elbow slanted to prop her chin in hand. "So who are the other pies for?" she said in a glum tone that failed miserably at a half-hearted attempt to be perky.

"Well, Davey invited Spence for dinner tonight, and when Tess heard I had a luncheon tomorrow, she offered to keep Spence overnight as well. So, naturally I have to send one with Spence too."

Lacey sighed again. "Naturally."

"Is it time, Mamaw?" Spence glanced up, owl eyes blinking wide as Minecraft village pieces dropped from his fingers, plunking onto the table. Apparently his village now ranked as a garbage dump of plastic compared to Davey's house.

Mamaw's gaze darted to the clock. "Yes, dear, so go get—" Spence was halfway up the stairs before his grandmother could even finish her sentence. She chuckled and shook her head while brewing a K-cup. "The poor thing has hounded me no less than four times an hour since lunch about when he could leave," she said, dousing the coffee with cream. She set it—in a to-go mug, no less—before Lacey with a smile. "This is the highlight of his week, you know—an overnight with Davey, complete with basketball and fishing with Jack and Matt."

"Jack and Matt?" Lacey's mouth crooked while the smell of macadamia nut taunted her senses. Breathing in an appreciative sniff, she took a slow sip, savoring the nutty flavor of her favorite coffee. "Sure one pie is enough?"

Chuckling, Mamaw joined her at the bar with her own cup, apparently settling in for a break. "No, but it'll have to do because the last pie is for a lonely shut-in who lives on the way to Davey's house, so it should be a slam dunk, as Spence likes to say."

"Anybody I know?" Lacey asked. She took another drink.

"No, or not well, anyway." Mamaw blew on her coffee, eyes somber despite the bare curve of a smile. "Just a widower who's pretty much alone in the world." She paused, eyes closed while translucent hands held the cup to her mouth. "The poor man is such a grouch, I understand the children in the neighborhood call him Dr. Doom, if you can imagine that."

Hot coffee pooled in Lacey's mouth. She gulped it down, eyes burning more than the liquid scalding her tongue. *Dr. Doom?* There was only one man who fit that description as far as Lacey knew. Her cup sank along with her jaw as she shook her head in slow motion. "Oh, no, Mamaw … you wouldn't."

"Wouldn't what, dear?" Her grandmother asked with an innocent lift of brows, the tender look in her eyes confirmation that Mamaw would, indeed, do anything to nudge her grandchildren along the path she believed they should take.

Lacey pushed the to-go cup away, her tongue suddenly parched. "I have no problem dropping Spence off or even checking out Mrs. Hedgehog's scar—"

"Hedgewood," Mamaw corrected.

"Hedgewood, Hedgehog, whatever, but you cannot expect me to deliver anything to my father." She hopped off the stool and went to the sink to pour a glass of water, gulping half of it before she clunked the glass down with attitude. She turned, butting against the sink with a tight fold of her arms. "Sorry, Mamaw, but I'm just not ready."

Her grandmother tilted her head, gaze far more tender than the set of her jaw. "And when might that be, dear?" she said, the intensity in her eyes searing straight through to Lacey's soul. "When your heart turns back to stone?"

"No, of course not." Lacey upended the water, hands shaking when she set the empty glass back down. "I'll do it, Mamaw, I promise, but at the right time." Hands clenched on the counter in desperation, Lacey appealed to her grandmother in terms of faith. "Honestly, Mamaw, you better than anyone should understand the importance of God's timing, the need to follow His leading instead of our own."

Mamaw's eyes softened. "Of course, darling girl," she said quietly. Her tender smile was gilded with patience. "As long as it's Him doing the leading ... and not fear."

"Laaaaacey ... I'm readdddy ..." Spence ran into the kitchen, skidding to a stop with cheeks flushed and eyes bright. He looked like a pack mule with a stuffed gym bag in one hand and ball glove in the other while a Power Ranger backpack bulged on his back.

Mamaw held out her arm. "Spence sweetheart, why don't you wait for Lacey on the front swing for just a few moments, but first come here and give Mamaw a smooch."

Gym bag and glove clunking to the floor, Spence flew into Mamaw's arms, eyes pinched closed as he squeezed with all his might. "I love you, Mamaw, thanks for letting me go."

"You're welcome, darling boy, but make sure you mind your manners," she said with a tap of his nose, "and don't stay up all night, you hear?"

"Yes, ma'am. See you outside, Lace." And with that he streaked out of the kitchen and down the hall, the slam of the front door deafening against the silence of the kitchen.

Mamaw turned back to the sink to face Lacey, sympathy warming her eyes as she patted the stool beside her. "Come sit, Alycia Anne, just for a moment, sweetheart."

Feeling way younger than her twenty-six years, Lacey huffed out a noisy sigh and plodded over to sit on the stool next to Mamaw, shoulders in a slump. "I need more time, Mamaw," she whispered, "I just know it."

Without a word, Mamaw slid the to-go cup toward her before skimming Lacey's hair over her shoulder, gnarled fingers lingering to gently massage. "That may be, darling, but it's been this old woman's experience that when God changes our heart of stone to a heart of flesh, it's a wee bit like laying a new foundation." Issuing a delicate sigh, her grandmother shifted to face her on the stool. "Remember when your grandpa laid that foundation for my gardening shed at the side of the house? The one you and Nicki embedded your handprints in and hearts with the initials of the boys you liked? And on the entrance ramp, no less, for all the world to see?"

Lacey nodded, a sliver of a smile forming at the memory of the summer Nicki came to stay with Mamaw when they were thirteen. Lacey had been so starry-eyed over Jack even then, when she was nothing more than his little sisters' best friend. "J.O. loves L.C. forever," she'd written, and oh! How Grandpa had chewed them both out for ruining his perfect concrete.

Mamaw's soft chuckle broke Lacey's reverie. "I thought Grandpa was going to skin you two alive, he was so upset, bemoaning the fact that the concrete had set by the time he'd seen it." She absently tipped her cup to her lips and for several moments, her gaze wandered faraway while melancholy stole over her features.

Sensing her grandmother's malaise, Lacey gently massaged her arm. "He refused to give us jawbreakers the rest of the summer, as I recall, and I don't think he ever did forgive us."

"Oh, he forgave you all right," she said quietly, the memory tugging a sad smile to her lips. "He told me later, when you girls weren't around so much anymore, just how he cherished those finger scribblings—lasting reminders of two little girls we both loved so much."

Expelling a gentle sigh, she placed her cup back on the table and angled to regard Lacey with the same doting look she'd reserved for every skinned knee and heartbreak in their past. Then as now, the love in her eyes was better than any balm she'd always applied. "You know, darling, in the beginning of our faith, our hearts are a wee bit like that fresh concrete that you and Nicki so enjoyed. A clean slate that's soft and pliable, ready for God to impress His will and His ways. His Word speaks of a covenant He's made with us—'I will put My laws in their minds and write it on their hearts' so that they may 'walk in My statutes and observe My ordinances.'" A fragile sigh drifted from Mamaw's lips as she absently caressed the hand Lacey had laid on her arm. "Unfortunately, the longer we wait to heed His call, darling, the more we run the risk of our new heart calcifying just like that concrete. Seasoned yes, but with our will instead of His." With a final pat of Lacey's arm, she returned to her coffee, palming the cup with both hands as she took a sip. "And you can't risk that, Lacey, because if we want the blessings of God in our lives, we have to make sure we have a clean heart."

Who may stand in His holy place? The one who has clean hands and a pure heart.

Lacey's eyelids shuttered closed with a silent groan, Mamaw's words piercing her with the painful truth. And if there was anybody who knew about clean, it was Mamaw. In fact, Lacey was pretty sure she was a distant relative of Mr. Clean, neatly pinpointing the growing grime in Lacey's attitude.

When she'd first arrived in Isle of Hope, she'd been committed to making amends with her father, almost eager to get on with what she'd felt certain God had called her to do. But every day since, the initial excitement to do the right thing had somehow faded, especially after her father's cold reception at the hospital when Davey was hurt. With each passing day, she found herself a little further away from being ready to face a man who not only scared her half to death, but one who had made her feel worthless and rejected. Truth be told, she wanted nothing to do with Ben Carmichael, but that was no longer an option.

If anyone turns a deaf ear to My instruction, even their prayers are detestable.

A ragged sigh left her lips as she put a hand to her eyes. "All right, Mamaw, we'll do this your way," she whispered.

"No, darling girl, not my way—*His*—the only way you will ever truly be happy."

Lacey nodded and slowly rose, reaching for her coffee before facing the door.

Mamaw's frail hand lighted on her wrist, her tone gentle. "Now remember, darling—'the Lord will take your hand and help you—Isaiah 41:13."

Lacey's lip quirked. "Sure, easy for Isaiah to say— he doesn't have to face both my father *and* Mrs. Hedgehog," she muttered, bussing her grandmother's cheek with a hasty kiss. "I hope you have a piece of pie cut and ready to go when I get home, Mamaw, because I'm going to need a little pampering after Daddy chews me up and spits me out." She retrieved the final pie from the counter before plodding to the door with a limp wave, not even bothering to turn around. "Or maybe I'll luck out and he won't want the pie, then I can polish it off by myself at Wormsloe."

Mamaw's chuckle followed her down the hall. "Oh, he'll want it all right—the man's addicted to my peach pie. How do you think I'd get him to open the door when I used to visit?"

"I don't know, a bullhorn and a stick of dynamite?" Lacey mumbled to herself, thinking she'd never met a more stubborn man than her father.

She was grateful Spence chattered all the way to Davey's—a completely rare occurrence, which only underscored just how excited the little guy was. He ended up being a godsend at Mrs. Hedgewood's, saving Lacey a trip inside for a peek at her scar when he hung out the passenger window of her car, begging her to hurry. She'd no more pulled into Davey's driveway before Spence was flying across the lawn to their front porch as quickly as he could with enough baggage for a month rather than just a day. "Bye, Lacey," he shouted without so much as a glance back.

Lacey sighed. "Okay, God, it's You, me and the peach pie, I guess." Easing her car out of the driveway, she pulled into her father's drive, heart slowing along with the car as she put it into "Park." She sat there and stared, stomach churning more than the deer weather vane spinning atop the three-dormer roof, a birthday gift from Mom since Daddy liked to hunt. Lacey's mouth took a twist. Certainly appropriate since he'd look like a deer in headlights when he saw her on his stoop. *Not unlike his daughter.* Heaving a weighty sigh, Lacey got out of the car with a pie in hand, wishing Daddy would stay true to form and not even answer. *Maybe he's not home ...*

With a slam of the car door, she turned toward the house and stopped, scanning her childhood home from the new serpentine rock walkway, up two stories to a brand-new and very expensive gray slate roof. Other than the basic bones of the house, she almost didn't recognize it anymore, its presence that of a stranger.

Like the man who occupied it.

Every single one of her mom's flower berms in the
yard had been replaced with lush grass except in front
of the spindled wraparound porch, which was now
flanked by meticulously manicured boxwoods instead
of her mother's beloved roses. The delicate pink
dogwood that Daddy had given Mom for Mother's Day
was gone, replaced by a sturdy trimmed oak to offer a
clean, shaded view of the house. Even the color of the
siding was different—stark white instead of the pastel
blue Mom had loved, black shutters instead of white, as
if Daddy had hoped to erase any semblance of Mom's
feminine touch. Her eyes flicked to the far corner of the
porch, now bereft of the offensive hammock that had
ignited her father's temper when he'd found Jack and
her kissing in it the night before he left for seminary.
The memory now tainted her tongue just like it had
tainted her life back then. Nausea rolled in her stomach.
The hammock had obviously been kicked to the curb,
no doubt, along with the trash.

Just like his daughter.

She paused on the first step of the porch, eyelids
shuttering closed when her conscience pricked,
reminding her once again that it had been *her* decision
to turn her father away after her mother's funeral, not
his. Fortifying with a massive draw of air, she slowly
mounted the stairs to the porch, hands damp beneath the
pie, which had long since cooled from the oven. Finger
quivering, she pressed the doorbell like it was a
detonator switch, back-stepping several feet when she
heard the familiar *bong-bong-bong* of the doorbell, a
sinister sound that had always reminded her of a horror
movie. Seconds ticked by like eons, a surreal passage of
time where her mind and body moved in slow motion.
Only her sweat glands seemed to be working overtime,
glazing her with a trickle of moisture between her
breasts. She tried the doorbell again, but its ghostly

sound was met only by silence, making the pounding of her pulse in her ears all the more deafening.

"He's not home, sweetheart," a voice called from the street.

Lacey spun around, almost dropping the pie. Her heart took off in a sprint as she blinked at Jack's mother, who peeked around the hedge. "Oh, Mrs. O'Bryen, hello! My grandmother asked me to drop a pie off for my father, but I have one for you, too, that I planned to deliver next, when I came to say hello."

"Yes, Spence told me, so I thought I'd let you know that Ben seems to roll in after eight on Fridays, so why don't you come over here to wait," she said, hurrying forward with a welcoming smile. Her face was aglow and void of makeup except for a touch of gloss and a fine sheen of moisture, no doubt from the high humidity. Wispy strands of honey-colored hair fluttered loose from a messy ponytail that made her look more like a fresh-scrubbed teenager than a mom in her forties. Scampering up the porch steps like a girl half her age, she promptly relieved Lacey of the pie. "Here, let me take that for you, and you can pull your car on the other side of the Wall of Jericho," she said with a wink. "Then join me on the patio in the back."

Lacey grinned, suddenly remembering one of the main reasons she'd always loved spending time at the O'Bryen's. Jack's mom had been a dynamo of smiles and fun, joining in on games of Twister and wiffle ball with the kids while Lacey's parents and Pastor O'Bryen watched from the sidelines. Mrs. O'Bryen trotted off, and Lacey felt the vise around her ribs slowly loosen, Jack's mom's reference to the "Wall of Jericho" luring a chuckle from her lips.

Favorite memories came rushing back of her, Cat, and Shan cuddled together on the O'Bryen's couch watching musicals and old movies, especially one of Lacey's favorites, *It Happened One Night*. The reference to the infamous "Wall of Jericho"—when Clark Gable divided the twin-bedded motel room he shared with Claudette Colbert into two parts by stringing up a wire and a blanket—certainly fit for the gargantuan hedge her father had put in. Strolling back to the car, Lacey supposed if anyone might succeed at dismantling her father's walls, it would be Tess O'Bryen. She started the car and backed out, her smile slipping away into a silent sigh. Heaven knows she and her mother certainly hadn't.

Parked in front of the O'Bryen's house, Lacey left her purse in the car and grabbed the second pie before locking the door and pocketing the key. A wealth of memories flooded as she made her way down the cobblestone drive to the back of the house. A squawk from above drew her attention, and she glanced up at the towering oak that shaded the back patio as she rounded the corner.

Go-go-gos ... Frawnk! The sound brought a grin to her lips at the sight of a particularly noisy blue heron standing over her nest.

"Oh, Blue, hush—that's no way to greet company." Mrs. O'Bryen took the pie from Lacey's hands and sniffed, rolling her eyes in a grand show of ecstasy while she nodded to one of the white wrought-iron chairs. "Spence mentioned you brought us a pie, so bless you because there just happens to be a tub and a half of my best homemade vanilla bean ice cream in the freezer, just waiting to be scooped alongside. Sit, young lady, while I get you a drink. Sweet tea, lemonade, or water?"

"Sweet tea would be great, thank you, Mrs. O'Bryen." Lacey gladly sank into the blue and white striped cushion, the pie she'd brought for her father almost taunting her from the center of the table where Tess had placed it. Quickly averting her gaze, she breathed in the heady mix of marsh and honeysuckle that instantly took her back to better times. The gurgle of a fountain happily melded with Mrs. O'Bryen's off-key humming, warming Lacey as much as the summer sun peeking through leafy branches that swayed in the salty breeze.

"Here you go, sweetheart," Mrs. O'Bryen said with a bright smile, placing a tall glass of iced tea before her, beautifully garnished with a sprig of mint and a fresh peach wedge. She reached up to pull the chain on the woven ceiling fan overhead before plopping into her chair with a languorous sigh. "Oh, that feels so good, doesn't it? And it's Tess, remember?"

Lacey nearly moaned at her first sip of tea, wondering how she could have forgotten that Jack's mother made the best peach tea she'd ever tasted. "Oh my, how I've missed your tea, Mrs. ... uh, Tess," Lacey quickly amended, unable to stop herself from gulping half of it down. A smile wrapped around her sigh. "Nectar of the gods, bar none."

"Why, thank you, Lacey Anne!" Reaching for her *Better Homes & Garden* magazine off the table, Jack's mother shimmied back in her chair with legs tucked beneath, head resting on the back of her chair. She slowly fanned herself while studying Lacey with a gentle gaze. "But goodness, I'm hoping you missed more than the tea, because I certainly have."

Lacey blinked, unable to thwart an unexpected sting of tears. She nodded, her throat suddenly closing up.

"Oh, honey ..." Tess hopped up and rounded the large, rectangular table, squatting to embrace her in a tight hug. "You were like one of my own, sweetheart," she whispered. "If ever two people were meant to be together, I had so hoped it would be you and Jack."

"Me too," Lacey said with a soggy sniff, pulling away to swipe at her eyes with an embarrassed chuckle. "But I guess it wasn't meant to be."

Tess stroked several fingers down the curve of Lacey's cheek, searching her face with a wistful smile. "Are you sure, sweetheart? Sometimes God throws us off with a detour that's meant to make us grow before it leads us back to what He intended all along ..."

A ball of emotion ducked in Lacey's throat. "Well, it certainly took *me* long enough to do some growing, Tess, especially in my faith, but ..." She inhaled shaky air before expelling it once again, praying that Jack's mother would understand what she was about to say. "It appears that Jack and I have ..." She locked gazes with his mother, regret damp in her eyes. "Grown in different directions."

Understanding flickered across Tess's face as she nodded and rose, padding back to her chair with a heavy sigh. "Ah, yes, my son's rapid decline in faith and extreme bitterness toward his father." Her mouth quirked into a sad smile as she nodded heavenward. "Both of them."

"Nicki tells me Jack has little or no faith anymore," Lacey said quietly, brows sloped in pain to match the thread of disbelief in her tone. "She says he has no use for church or God, opting for a lifestyle that flies in the face of every belief he once held dear."

Tess nodded, the sheen of moisture in her look confirmation of just how much she grieved for her son. "I kept hoping it was just a phase after his father left," she whispered, but it seems the hate and unforgiveness toward Adam has hardened his heart to stone, and Cat's too, no matter how much Matt, Shan, or I try to talk to them."

"I'm so very sorry, Tess ..." The ache in Lacey's heart bled into her tone.

The barest of smiles shaded Tess's mouth. "Me too, sweetheart, but hope is a byproduct of faith, so my money's on the God of Hope to do His thing with my son."

A sigh quivered from Lacey's lips. "That's certainly my hope as well."

"*Which* ..." Tess reached across the table to graze Lacey's fingertips with her own. "Is one of the reasons I'm so very glad you're home. I believe you could be the answer to my prayers, the key to unlocking my son's heart and rekindling his faith."

The air swirled still in Lacey's lungs. "I ... I don't know how, Tess. I've only just begun living my faith, so I'm little more than a baby at all this." She lowered her eyes when her cheeks grew hot. "You probably weren't aware, but back when Jack and I were promised, my faith was pretty nil, and my morals even worse. I'm ashamed to say that it was Jack who actually kept us above board, his faith that carried us through, not mine." The muscles in her throat convulsed as she slowly looked up. "I'm not sure how someone as new and inexperienced as me could ever reach someone as bitter about religion as Jack."

A gentle smile softened the worry lines in Tess's face. "Out of the mouth of babes hast Thou ordained strength," she whispered. "Besides Jack still cares about you, Lacey, so as his friend, you have more power than you know."

"Maybe, but I care about him, too, Tess—more than I realized—so I'm not sure I'd have the strength to keep the friendship from straying into something deeper."

"And would that be such a bad thing?" Tess asked softly.

Lacey buffed her arms, a chill taking her by surprise as she avoided Tess's eyes. "My heart's still reeling from a broken engagement," she said quietly, "and my faith is so new and fragile right now, I'm not sure I can handle a bitter ex-boyfriend whose beliefs run counter to mine." She lapsed into a melancholy stare. "My mom told me once she believed that was the main reason she and Daddy fought so much. She said her faith was

strong when they got married, but Daddy's wasn't, and
after a while, it took a toll, and hers suffered too."
Lacey finally glanced up, arms in a nervous clutch at
her waist. "I just want to marry a man whose faith
matches mine, Tess, because after seeing what my mom
and dad went through, I need all the stability I can get,
you know?"

"Yes, I do." Tess expelled a weary sigh. "It's our
loss, sweetheart, but I have to say, you're a wise
woman, Lacey Carmichael."

No, ma'am, just a very wounded one. Her eyelids
fluttered closed as she sucked in a shallow breath,
remembering those awful fights between her mother
and father over Daddy's disdain for the church, even
with a pastor as a close friend. It wasn't until faith had
become an important part of her own life that the strain
between her and Tim suddenly appeared, finally
escalating out of control. *Just like Mom and Daddy.*
Since her breakup with Tim, she'd vowed to only marry
a man of deep faith. She frowned. But then, Tess had
married a man of deep faith, hadn't she?

Throat suddenly parched, she quickly reached for
her tea, taking another sip before she managed a wry
smile. "Not so wise, Tess, just pretty gun-shy. I saw
what being unevenly yoked did to my parents'
marriage, and I have no desire for more of the same."
Her lips skewed into a wry smile while she raised her
tea in a toast, giving a sharp nod toward the sky.
"Which is why from now on, it's His way or the
highway for me, you know? Hopefully to up my odds
for success."

"Success, yes …" Tess nodded, her eyes trailing into
a backyard sanctuary canopied by trees. "Well, we both
know I learned the hard way there are no guarantees
whether one is evenly yoked or not. But the four of us
always had such a great time together, I just assumed
any fights we had with our spouses were a natural part

of marriage." The line of her throat shifted as she continued to stare, voice faraway and gaze unblinking. "Like Adam and me." She finally glanced up, her reverie broken. "And it is to a degree, I suppose, but also a symptom of something deeper that couples need to explore, and pray about, and heal. But even so, sweetheart, I believe your parents loved each other no matter how much they butted heads."

"I suppose," Lacey said quietly, not sure at all that her father had harbored much love for either her mother or her.

As if reading her mind, Tess leaned in, the intensity in her tone drawing Lacey's gaze. "I truly believe your father has mellowed, Lacey, and although he may give you a fight over your desire to make amends, I pray you don't let his gruffness push you away. Ben Carmichael may not know it yet, but he needs you desperately, honey, and you need him."

Lacey slowly twirled the empty glass in her hands, her stomach suddenly rolling along with it. "I know," she whispered, "but what if he keeps turning me away? I'm not sure how much more rejection I can take."

"He won't, not if you hang in there and show him you're as tough as he is." A smile squirmed on Tess's lips. "He fought me, too, when I started going over there after that night you brought Davey home, but I wore him down with persistence, pizza, and monster cookies. And if I recall, your father has an unnatural fascination with both your mother's chocolate chip pie and my monster cookies, so maybe that's the next bribe you bring."

A grunt rolled from Lacey's mouth. "The next one? You're assuming my grandmother's peach pie will work this time."

Tess winked. "Oh, it will, trust me. Because you, Lacey Carmichael, are staying for dinner tonight, and as soon as we hear Beau in the backyard, that's my cue to pray while you deliver the pie."

Lacey froze for a split second, the thought of having dinner with Cat as frightening as seeing her father. "Oh, no, not dinner, Tess, I don't want to impose. I can come back later, really—"

"Nope." Tess shoved to her feet with a firm jut of her chin. "Trust me, it's nothing fancy—Davey's requested sloppy Joes, chips, and marshmallow fruit salad—so it's no imposition at all, truly. And the girls won't be home for dinner, so there's plenty of room."

Relief flooded Lacey's veins. "Well then, what can I do? Set the table, take drink orders?"

"Drink orders would be lovely." Glancing at her watch, Tess nodded toward the O'Bryen's fishing dock across the street on the Skidaway River. "Tell the boys they have thirty minutes to fish or cut bait before I ring the dinner bell."

"Will do." Ponytail bouncing, Lacey rose and pushed in her chair, the lure of the fishing dock calling her home to countless memories she still cherished in her heart. Magical summer nights spent with Jack, Cat and Shannon—fishing, talking, swimming, what have you. Her heart picked up pace along with her feet, reminders of the "what have you" suddenly warming her cheeks. Shaking off the thought, she pulled out her cell phone to let Mamaw know she wouldn't be home for dinner.

"Oh, and Lacey ..."

She whirled around on the driveway, finger poised on the keypad. "Yes?"

Affection skimmed across Jack's mother's face. "It's been eight long years, sweetheart, and I suspect you haven't cast a line since, so I'll bet Jack will still bait the hook if you ask him real nice."

Lacey grinned and waved to deflect a gulp. Quickly leaving a message for Mamaw, she disappeared around the corner and shuffled down their driveway. "He already has," she muttered before screeching to a dead stop at the curb on Bluff Drive while a car sped by. She shaded her eyes to peer across the street where Jack, Matt, and the boys laughed and fished on the O'Bryen's cozy dock with its long, weathered ramp and cedar-shake, cabana-style roof. Little more than miniatures in the distance, they were far enough away to ensure the privacy she and Jack had always sought on summer nights. Jack cast a line wearing nothing more than cutoffs and Sperrys, and Lacey's stomach tumbled along with her composure when his tan shoulders rippled with the motion. His broad back tapered into a narrow waist while sweat gleamed on muscles molded to perfection, causing a second gulp to rise in her throat. Swallowing hard, she glanced up at the sky, a plea in her eyes. "All I'm asking is *please* don't let it be me who swallows the bait," she said, her tone veering toward dry, "or it'll be hook, line, and sink *her*.

CHAPTER NINETEEN

"*H*ey, Jack, look what Spence caught!" Davey's excited words ricocheted across the water from the grassy shore where he'd wandered while fishing with Matt and Spence.

A grin slid across Jack's face as he spied the piece of driftwood dangling from Spence's rod, the boy's wide smile matching the pride in Davey's voice. "Good job, Spence. That'll make a nice souvenir after we sand and polish it, won't it, Davey?"

"That's what I told him, so can we do it after supper?"

"You bet." Jack's line jerked with a flash of a sea trout, and he casually reeled it in while he glanced in the boys' direction, both waist deep in a gentle sway of marsh grass. "Any bait left on that hook, Spence, or do you need another worm?"

"Nope, still have some, but thanks." Spence dislodged the driftwood and carefully set it aside before sailing his bobber back into the water.

"If you boys get tired of catching wood with Matt's worms, just let me know, and I'll fix you up with a shrimp and popping cork like I'm using." Jack taunted them with a wave of his good-sized trout before hooking it onto a stringer rigged to the side of the dock.

"God's just throwing you a bone, O'Bryen," Matt called. "Apparently He feels sorry for you 'cause I've caught three fish to every one of yours." He tossed a grin Jack's way as he ambled further down the shore.

Jack shook his head and re-baited his hook with a jag of a smile. "He's throwing me a bone all right," he mumbled under his breath, thoughts straying to Rocks on the Roof a few nights ago when he and Lacey had talked. "A flippin' T-Rex femur, right in the head."

"I love you, Lacey. Always have, always will."

"I love you, too, Jack. Forever and ever amen."

Muscles taut, he all but hurled his line into the river along with a colorful word that hissed from his lips. *And yet we're only friends.*

"Battling fish and talking to them is one thing, Dr. O'Bryen, but swearing at them too?"

Jack's head jerked around, pulse pounding hard in his throat.

Lacey strolled to the edge of the dock, hands clasped behind like a little girl with mischief on her mind. She scrunched her nose as she peered up with an impish smile. "Not sure, but I'm thinkin' that might be overkill."

He grinned when his line suddenly tugged, and setting the hook hard, he focused on reeling in another fish. "Oh, I don't know, seems to work fine for me." Grabbing the lower lip of the bass, he held it up and cupped a hand to his mouth. "Hey, Matt, you got another stringer I can borrow? Mine's a *little* full."

Lacey laughed, waving at the boys when they spotted her on the dock. "Mmm … that's not the only thing that's full, apparently," she said with a tilt of her head, her grin just shy of a smirk. "Still the hotshot when it comes to fishing, I see."

"No brag, just fact, Miss Carmichael," he said with a chuckle. He squatted at the edge of the dock to hook his fish on the stringer, then rinsed his hands in the water. "Taking potshot at me on my own dock, are you?" He dared her with a half-lidded grin. "Why don't you put your money where your mouth is, Carmichael, and wet a line. Maybe you can teach me a thing or two."

She studied him with a narrow gaze. "All right, bucko, you're on." Tongue rolling inside her cheek, she strolled over to where several rods were propped against a white, weathered Adirondack chair, and making her selection, she marched over to Jack. "First one to land a fish wins, all right? What bait are we using?"

Leg cocked, he placed hands low on his hips, studying her with a twitch of humor. "Live shrimp on a cork, but I suppose I'll have to bait your hook too, won't I?"

"Come on, Jack, you know I can't stand to touch slimy things." She wrinkled her nose. "Unless they're boiled and served with cocktail sauce, so man up and bait my hook, 'cause your hands are already smelly."

He reached for the bait bucket with an exaggerated roll of eyes. "I swear, you're the only tomboy I've ever met who won't bait her own hook, you big sissy."

"I'm a girl, Jack, and we like to smell nice, so sue me." She perched on tiptoe to watch him closely while he fished his hand in the bucket. "Just make sure you don't give me a shrimp shrimp, O'Bryen, one that's tinier than yours."

He arched a brow. "First you mock me, then you boss me around?" He rose and tossed her the rod, laughing when she caught it with a squeal. "Some things never change, I guess."

"Nope. On your mark, get set, go!" Before he could blink, she stepped away and arced the fishing line up in a clean sweep across the water, squinting in concentration as she drifted the line downwind.

"Hey, I'm not even ready yet, you little brat." Slashing a hand into the bait bucket, he rigged his line in record time, then whipped it high in a perfect cast that rippled over the water. "But that's okay, Mike," he said with a lazy grin. "You'll need all the time you can get."

Her gaze never strayed from her line while her jaw notched up, a flicker of a smile flitting across her lips. "Your mother said you have twenty minutes tops, O'Bryen, till dinner is on, so that may hurt you, but me?" Her profile sported a grin. "I won't need that long."

The dock thundered with the clomping of little-boy sneakers that sounded anything but sneaky. "Lacey, Lacey, you fishing too?" Spence and Davey screeched across the dock, thumping and rattling the wooden planks so much, Jack was pretty sure any fish had hightailed it to the other side of the river. "What are you using?" Davey skidded to a stop with a pole and stringer in hand. Behind him, Spence carried his piece of driftwood like a priceless treasure.

"Same as Mr. Cocky here—shrimp on a cork," Lacey replied, a gleam of trouble in the side glance she slid Jack's way. "In a contest for first fish landed before dinner because *somebody* here has to teach this guy a little humility."

"Good luck with that," Matt said, moseying onto the dock with a string of decent fish. "I've been trying since the boy was knee-high to a crawdad, but for all his book smarts, he's a *liiiiiittle* slow."

Jack chuckled. With an expert snap of his wrist, he patiently popped his cork, producing a chugging sound that resulted in a splash of water eight inches high. "That's because 'slow' is key, my man, especially when fishing with a popping cork, as Miss Twitchy Fingers here is about to learn when I win."

"What do you win?" Spence asked with a scrunch of freckles, the driftwood clutched to his chest.

Jack's gaze converged with Lacey's. "Well, I don't believe we set the terms yet, now did we, Miss Carmichael?" he said with an evil grin, enjoying the competitive camaraderie he and Lacey had once shared. "But I think it should be something really good, don't you, Spence?"

"Yeah!" Davey vaulted and fist-pumped the air. "Ice cream at Coldstone after supper."

"Uh-oh." With a grate of her lip, Lacey offered a penitent glance, shoulders hunched in apology. "Sorry, guys, but Mamaw sent a peach pie that Davey's mom plans to serve with vanilla bean ice cream."

"Awesome," Matt said with a tickle of Davey's neck. "I've had Mamaw's peach pie, and it's killer, Dave, trust me. Especially with your mom's homemade ice cream."

"Cool!" Davey high-fived Spence, then spun around to face Lacey. "But what else would be a good prize?"

"Well ..." Lacey's lips pursed in thought as she skipped her cork across the water. "How about the loser takes drink orders and serves them?" she suggested, bobbling her cork way too often to Jack's way of thinking. "That's the job Davey's mom gave me when she invited me to dinner."

"Wow, you're staying for dinner?" Spence's eyes blinked even wider than usual as a shy grin eased across his lips. "Way cool!"

"I'll second that," Jack said with a much slower, steadier pop of his cork, grinning when he felt a slight tug on his line, "but let's up the ante to both drink service *and* loser waits on the winner all night."

"Deal!" Lacey jerked her rod up hard, her line as taut as the smile on her face while she strained to reel in a definite flash of silver at the exact moment Jack set his hook.

Screeches blistered Jack's ears as the boys bounded into the air with hoops and hollers when a beauty of a trout leapt from the water at the end of his line. Adrenaline coursed as he fought to reel him in, his muscles tense and slick with sweat. "Come on, baby," he whispered, determined that Lacey Carmichael would—for tonight at least—do his bidding.

"Holy cow, it's a tie!" Davey shouted, rattling the dock with wild stomping while cheers and whistles sounded from behind.

Matt moved to the edge of the dock, his laughter ringing as Lacey and Jack battled it out, grunt for grunt. "Then biggest fish wins," he called, and Jack had no time to compare. All he knew was he hadn't had a fighter like this all summer, and it was a flippin' monster. He prayed—likely for the first time in years—that his line wouldn't break. He'd be bushed after landing this one for sure, but that was okay because tonight he could rest on his laurels. Reeling it in, he quickly squatted to hook his fingers into the massive jaws of a truly beautiful spottail bass, lifting it from the water with a satisfied grin. Oh yes, indeedy. Lacey Carmichael would be waiting on him tonight.

Hand, foot, and finger.

CHAPTER TWENTY

"*B*oy, I sure could go for another piece of pie—is there any left?" Matt pushed his chair back as if to rise, scanning the table with a crooked smile. "Anybody else want some?"

"No thanks, I'm stuffed," Lacey said, tugging on Matt's sleeve to make him stay put, "but Jack'll be happy to get you another piece, won't you, Jackson?" Smile smug, she fluttered her lashes, savoring the tight press of Jack's smile as he seared her with a narrow look.

"The deal was I'd wait on *you* all night, Your Highness, not some overgrown driftwood angler," Jack said over the rim of his coffee mug, the twinkle in his eyes belying his gruff tone.

"Sorry, Jeeves, but 'waiting on me' entails doing whatever my little heart desires, right, guys?"

"Right!" A chorus of shouts and giggles circled a table laden with dirty dishes that flickered in the soft glow of a half-burned pillar candle.

Matt eased back in his chair with a lazy grin, raising his glass of tea in a toast. "Oh, and could I have that pie warmed in the microwave for twenty seconds or so, bro? With a double scoop of ice cream?"

A chuckle rumbled from Tess's throat as she hopped up to clear the table, stacking dirty plates with utensils on top. "Good thing I set aside two pieces for the girls before you boys wolf it all down." She pressed a kiss to Jack's sun-streaked hair. "Face it, Son, you're darn lucky it wasn't me or Matt who won against you because we'd keep you busy well beyond midnight."

"Gee, Mom, thanks for the support," Jack said with a mock scowl, rising to attend to Matt's pie.

"Uh, uh, uh ..." Lacey arched a brow in Jack's direction before flashing a bright smile at his mother, her tone as sweet as the glass of peach tea in her hand. "Come on, Tess, sit down, please. Jack'll be happy to collect dishes on his way to the kitchen and even do them after he delivers Matt's pie, right, Jeeves?"

Jack's jaw began to grind. "You're milking this for all it's worth, Carmichael," he said with a threatening tip of his head, his blue eyes searing hers while he relieved his mother of her stack of dishes.

"Oooo ... milk, right!" Lacey tousled Spence's hair. "I'll bet you boys could use a little more chocolate milk too, couldn't you?"

"Yeah!"

Matt slanted back in his chair with a broad grin, hands braced to the back of his neck. "Uh, Lace, hate to impose, but my car could sure use a shine ..."

"I'll give you a shine, Ball," Jack said with bump of Matt's shoulder while he reached for his dirty dishes, "right around the eye." He tilted Matt's plate, plopping an uneaten maraschino cherry into the lap of his cousin's khaki Dockers shorts. "Whoops—need me to toss those shorts in the wash too?" He snickered as he collected dirty utensils and plates. "Although I can't guarantee much since cherry juice stains."

Matt grinned. "No problem, Doc, I got 'em out of your drawer."

"That settles it," Jack groused, rounding the table to stack dishes clear up to his chin, undoubtedly inflicting stains of all kinds on his white T-shirt. "I'm putting a padlock on my bureau tomorrow."

Matt aimed the cherry at Jack, splotching his cousin's nose with pink juice before it plopped on the top plate. "Come on, Jack, you know I can't afford new clothes on a coach's salary, and you're in the big bucks now, so have a heart. Besides, I'm the cousin and near brother you love as well as your best friend, remember?"

Jack's mouth skewed into a wry smile. "I have a heart, Ball, but I'm afraid it's a little bruised by 'friends' like *you*."

Lacey's cheeks steamed with embarrassment, Jack's innocent remark hitting a little too close to home. She glanced at her watch, suddenly anxious to deliver the pie to her father and be on her way. "Goodness, it's well after eight. What time did you say Daddy usually gets home, Tess?"

"Soon, sweetheart, I promise." Tess cocked her head as if to listen. "Wait—I think I heard a car door slam, so that could be him now." She popped up and scurried down the driveway, returning a few moments later with Shannon and Cat in tow. "Nope, just my girls finally home, in time for peach crumble pie and ice cream."

"Did you say peach pie?" Cat's voice carried from around the corner of the house before she entered the patio behind Shannon, whose face lit up at first glimpse of Lacey. With a gravelly chuckle, Cat pushed past her sister, a hungry gleam in her eyes. "Count me—" One foot on the flagstone patio, and her body froze along with her smile, jaw gaping enough to house a colony of mosquitoes.

Tess gripped Cat's shoulder, her firm hold meant to imply a warning, no doubt. "Lacey and her cousin Spence joined us for dinner, girls," she said in an even tone that brooked no argument, "and it was Lacey's grandmother who provided the pie. So grab a seat, and Jack will do the honors of serving it warm with ice cream."

Pie congealed into a hard lump at the pit of Lacey's stomach when Cat flicked her mother's hand away and backed off, her look caustic. "Suddenly I'm not so hungry anymore," she said with a sneer, slipping into the house with a slam of the screen door. "I need a shower."

"Catherine Marie!" Tess called, but Cat disappeared into the house, the sound of another door slamming indicating she had obviously fled to her room. The regret on Jack's mother face was as pronounced as the nausea in Lacey's gut. Bending over, she hooked an arm over Lacey's shoulder, her voice threaded with the same sorrow Lacey felt inside. "She'll come around, sweetheart, just give her time."

Shannon squatted beside Lacey's chair, gentle blue eyes steeped in sympathy. "Mom's right, Lace. Cat tends to bury her hurt behind humor and anger, but she couldn't be this angry if she hadn't loved and missed you as much."

"I know," Lacey whispered, her gaze rising to meet Jack's solemn one.

"What's wrong, Mom?" Davey peered up beneath a crimp of tiny brows.

Matt's chair scraped a flagstone as he stood up. He pushed it back in and gave Lacey's shoulder a quick squeeze while he glanced at the boys. "Who wants to help me dig up some worms for a little night fishing?"

"Me, me, me!" Both boys shot up with a squeal.

Matt's gaze flicked to the patches of sky through the trees, now washed in pink hues of dusk. "Best get moving then, 'cause our light's almost gone. Thanks, Aunt Tess, for supper. Nice to know you and the girls can relax while Jack does the dishes." Sliding Jack a wicked grin, he herded the boys toward the driveway, leaving a chuckle behind. "Keep my pie warm, Jack."

"Make sure they wear life jackets on the dock," Tess called.

"Yes, ma'am." Matt gave a backwards thumbs up before sending Lacey a sober smile over his shoulder. "Pulling for you, Lace, with your dad, so here's to smooth sailing."

"Thanks, Matt," she called, "if I don't drown first."

"You won't." Tess shored her up with a brisk rub of Lacey's back. "Shan and I will be over here throwing you a lifeline with prayer, guaranteed. And if you need anymore pull than that, ol' Jack here can always toss you the string of his pretty apron."

"Cute." Jack plodded toward the kitchen, but not before delivering a wink over a pile of dirty dishes. "Of course, you could always have me take the pie over, Your Majesty, but then he'd probably throw it at me, which would be a waste of a perfectly good pie."

"But so worth it," Lacey muttered, her smile sloping sideways.

A car door slammed, and the blood drained from Lacey's face.

Tess scurried down the driveway a second time to peek through the hedge, then returned in a sprint, darting into the kitchen to retrieve her father's pie and a container of her homemade ice cream. In a squeal of the screen door, she was back, placing both on the table before she slid into the chair next to Lacey and squeezed her hand. "Okay, sweetheart, when he opens the front door—"

"*If* he opens the front door," Lacey corrected.

Tess arched a brow. "Yes, well you just keep pushing that silly haunted-house bell of his until it drives him crazy, you hear? He'll open it fast enough."

Lacey's jaw dropped. "Yes, that's *exactly* what that awful doorbell sounds like!"

"Oh, I remember," Shannon said with a nervous giggle, "it always gave Cat and me the shivers."

One side of Lacey's mouth quirked. "Me too, Shan, not unlike Daddy when he was in one of his moods."

Worry lines crinkled above Tess's nose before her gaze flicked to Shannon. "Shan, why don't you have Jack heat up that pie for you, darling, okay?"

"Sure, Mom." Shannon rose to give Lacey a hug, a hint of understanding in her tone. "Don't be a stranger, Lace—we have a lot of catching up to do, all right?"

Lacey embraced the quiet friend who had always been such a source of strength. "You bet, Shan. Soon, I promise."

The screen door creaked closed when Shannon entered the house, and as soon as she did, Tess spoke, her voice barely a whisper. "Lacey, I hate to ask this, but your dad never ..." A lump bobbed in her throat. "Well, you know ... he never hit you or your mom ... did he?"

Lacey shuddered. "No, but to be honest, Tess, most of the time growing up he was so distant and removed that I almost wished we could evoke more of a response out of him, you know? Of course, that all changed once I showed an interest in boys." She grunted. "Lots of response then, all of it bad."

"Oh, honey ..." Tess gathered her in a tight hug, her comforting hold infusing Lacey with a much-needed strength to face her father. "I think he's changing, I really do. He wouldn't talk to me either until I refused to take no for an answer, and you just have to do the same. Now he doesn't seem to mind so much when I bring him monster cookies or come over for a chat." She pulled away, eyes narrowed in thought. "Of course he did put locks on the gates to keep me out, I suppose ..." Her shoulders lifted in a dismissive shrug as she gave Lacey a smile. "But, oh well—I don't let that bother me, and you shouldn't either. Whenever I hear him out on his patio, I just shimmy through that hole in the hedge at the back of his yard while he's reading the paper."

Lacey couldn't help the twitch of a smile. "And he actually talks to you?"

Tess grinned, eyebrows dancing like the twinkle in her eyes. "Eventually. Kinda hard to ignore a pest with a plate of cookies in her lap and a talent for chatter." She winked. "The poor guy can't say no to sweets to save his soul."

A giggle tripped from Lacey's lips that broke into a sob as she threw herself into Tess's arms. "Oh, Tess, I'm so grateful you were in our lives over the years before everything changed. You were like a second mother to me and such a good friend to my mom." Her expression sobered as a malaise settled in, grief stabbing as always whenever she thought of her mother. "Mom suffered so much guilt over everything that happened, that it seemed to suck the life out of her. I don't think she ever quite forgave herself, nor was ever the same."

Tess patted Lacey's back, her touch helping to soothe the awful ache inside. "I know, honey." Her weary sigh fluttered the hair at the back of Lacey's neck. "I'll admit it took me a while to forgive both Karen and Adam, but through the grace of God, I eventually did. I even wrote her a number of letters telling her so, but she never responded."

"She was too ashamed," Lacey whispered, swiping the wetness from her face.

Tess nodded. "I know." With a brisk buff of Lacey's arms, she offered an encouraging smile, chin elevated with a steely confidence. "Well, it's a new day, young lady, and a new opportunity to heal wounds and bring some joy into your life ... *and* into your father's." She ducked her head to lean in, tone as gentle as her smile. "Just remember, Lacey ..." Her gaze was suddenly somber. "It's not about you, honey, it's about your father. Allowing God to use you and your burgeoning faith to shine His light and love into the dark and desolate world of a man who is so very lost." She blinked several times, dispelling a sheen of moisture as she stroked Lacey's cheek. "And I promise you, darling, with everything in me, that through your hard-won obedience, God will heal you both in the process, unleashing untold blessings that will bring so much joy into your lives." With a gentle pat of Lacey's arms, Tess pulled away. "You're welcome to come back after if you like, but if you decide to go home, I'll expect a full report the next time you come for dinner, understood?"

"Yes, ma'am." Lacey gave a crisp salute as she picked up the ice cream, her grin misty. "Wish me luck?"

Tess's smile was soft. "Oh, honey, you don't need luck if prayer and faith are involved, so go get 'em, Lace, and don't take no for an answer."

With a shaky nod, she drew in a cleansing breath and turned toward the street, hoping to quell the storm of fireflies flitting in her stomach.

"Wait!" Darting past Lacey, Tess ducked into the house for several moments before she reappeared with two pieces of cooked bacon in a baggie. "There—that should do it. Trust me—Beau has a sniffer that will make your father miserable if he doesn't answer the door."

A hoarse chuckle tripped from Lacey's lips. "Thanks, Tess—so much!" Swallowing a knot of nerves, she made an about-face to march down the driveway.

"And make him invite you in," Tess called in a loud whisper, hand to her mouth. "Tell him no visit, no pie—Tess's rules."

"Yes, ma'am." Lacey's return whisper carried a trace of a smile, easing some of her trepidation on her lonely trek to her father's front porch. Skirting the hedge, she wished her confidence loomed as large as her shadow fanning across her father's lawn. Somewhere faraway an owl screeched, and the eerie sound pebbled her skin.

Inching her way up the steps, she braced herself with a hefty dose of oxygen, the smell of marsh, honeysuckle, and peach pie merging to create a new scent that suddenly buoyed her spirits: *hope*. Finger on that obnoxious bell, she suddenly felt it—a surge of peace that assured her that not only could she do this, but she wouldn't do it alone. Away from this house, she was a woman who was successful, witty, and bold, possessing a fun and vibrancy that seemed to draw both students in her class and the people in her life. But the moment she'd crossed that narrow bridge into Isle of Hope, her past had sucked all confidence dry, flinging her back into the abyss of being her father's daughter again.

A disappointment. A failure. A whore.

"No!" she hissed, finger strained white against the bell, "I *will* succeed." A lump shifted in her throat. "Eventually." Squaring her shoulders, she rammed the button again, determined to forge a relationship with her father no matter how long it took.

Bong-Bong-Bong.

The silly thing groaned like a ghoulish death knell, and Lacey steeled her jaw, butting her thumb to the bell and not letting go. *A death knell, indeed.*

For her fear.

CHAPTER TWENTY-ONE

*P*eering into his state-of-the-art fridge, Ben wondered why he even bothered—there was never anything decent to eat unless Tess paid a visit. His stomach growled in rebellion as he surveyed the shelves with a grim press of lips. Week-old Hamburger Helper, a couple of moldy sandwiches from the cafeteria at work, and condiments galore. His mouth zagged sideways. Not exactly fine dining.

He started to grab a bottled water and paused, his gaze zeroing in on the half-empty carton of Blue Moon that Mort had brought over with a pizza a month ago. His salivary glands suddenly kicked in like they used to after Karen had left him, when he'd started drinking more than normal, graduating from beer to the hard stuff in record time. At the point of three highballs before bed, he began waking up with the shakes, the kiss of death for a heart surgeon who needed rock-steady hands.

That had been the day he'd quit alcohol altogether, unwilling to risk the lives of patients or his career to dull the pain of a failed marriage and family. A maniacal exercise regimen at the gym had helped some, as had racquetball games to the death with surface friends. And tournaments with fishing buddies who didn't go deep unless it was to hook a fish at the end of the line. But what had helped the most was steering clear of feeling anything at all, both in the workplace and at home, earning him—as Tess had so rudely pointed out—names such as Dr. Doom and Dr. Snark.

Jaw set in stone, Ben snatched a beer, silently blaming this sudden relapse on none other than Tess O'Bryen, who had so blatantly forced her way into his life. The first time she'd invaded his yard with that stupid package had unnerved him completely, rattling him so much he'd swiped one of Mort's Blue Moons before the evening was through. He'd bolted the sucker so fast he'd gotten a headache. That had been his first beer in years, and his next one had been the night she'd invited him for pizza. The thought of spending time on the patio of the ex-best friend who'd betrayed them both was too much to handle on his own. Since then, he'd popped a Blue Moon the next two times Tess appeared at his door, to get on her teetotaler nerves if not to help take the edge off of a pushy neighbor who refused to leave him alone.

Twisting the top, he took a deep glug, telling himself an occasional lousy beer wouldn't hurt. He wasn't an alcoholic after all—he'd already proven that when he quit cold turkey. Besides, he had no intention of buying anymore when these were all gone, and the thought appeased him as he foraged in the produce drawer for an orange. He grunted when he found only one, shriveled and sporting green and white mold on the lower half. "Figures," he muttered, "even Vitamin C is giving me problems now." He sailed it across his spacious stainless kitchen into the "gourmet's dream" sink, craving Tess's homemade pizza to go along with his beer if he couldn't have a slice of orange. It landed with a loud thump, causing Beau to come up for air from his dinner bowl and bark. Ben raised his beer in a toast to man's best friend and his. "At least one of us is eating well, Big Guy, so bon appétit."

Tucking the newspaper under his arm, he slogged into his den and turned on the TV, caving into his oversized recliner. He glanced up and groaned, noting he'd forgotten to close the shutters after letting Beau back in. His mouth quirked as he took a swig, flicking through the channels. Motorized teak plantation shutters he *used* to keep open before Tess had bulldozed into his life. A faint smile lifted the edges of his mouth as he stared mindlessly at the TV, finally settling on a show with Tim Allen while he put his feet up. He rested his head on the back of his chair and sighed. She was a pushy little thing, he'd give her that, as skilled an angler as he ever met, baiting him with Pollyanna hope and so much energy.

A scowl tainted his tongue as he slugged down more beer. *Too much.* First she'd lured him with cookies and a package, then set the hook with a pizza that was downright criminal. The week after that it was a taco casserole she claimed to have leftovers on, and then last night she reeled him in with brownies so addicting, they should be considered illegal. Apparently she was settling into a cozy routine of tempting him with delicious concoctions, claiming her family was usually busy on Thursdays and she hated to eat dinner or dessert alone. Somehow he suspected she was just plain stubborn in pushing a friendship, so he'd hoped the new padlock on his gate would be subtle enough. But probably not for a woman who'd simply bypass the gate altogether to blaze a trail to his back door via a hole through the hedge, pounding on the glass until he'd finally relent and open the door. And then, despite the annoyance that always twisted his lips, she would waltz in with wonderful smells that hooked him as neatly as a catfish on Velveeta.

He'd been content with his life before she'd started sticking her nose in it. Happy with Beau, his career, and his select group of friends. He didn't have a family, but

he had hundreds of kids whose lives he impacted
through overseas trips for the Save a Child's Heart
Foundation twice a year, not to mention a hoard of little
ones he bonded with weekly through The Children's
Heart Foundation. True, he had no woman to share his
life, but he'd already found out just how dangerous that
could be. He much preferred casual dates with bright
and beautiful doctors, lawyers, and the occasional too-
young pharmaceutical saleswomen just to mix it up.
Setting his beer on the table, he reached to rub Beau's
head after his closest friend had ambled over to collapse
beneath Ben's chair.

No, a ray of sunshine like Tess O'Bryen only made
him realize just how dark and dismal his life really was,
and he didn't like that one lousy bit. Not when after
three straight Thursdays, he was starting to look
forward to her visits like Pavlov's pup with a 20-oz T-
bone. He upended his bottle, chugging way too fast.
Working late on Thursdays was looking better all the
time. His mouth crooked. Or maybe he should just
break his own cardinal rule and invite a date. That way
when Miss Perky bounced over, she'd think twice
before doing so again. Some of the tension eased in his
shoulders as he mulled the idea over in his head. Yeah,
that could work, he decided, a little awkwardness to
keep his neighbor on her side of the fence.

Bong-Bong-Bong.

His eyelids sank closed in a groan even as his pulse
spiked in his veins. *And then, maybe not ...* Nobody
dared violate his self-imposed seclusion except Tess, so
it could be no one else. Even the Girl Scouts and
Jehovah Witnesses didn't bother him anymore, which
was just how he liked it. Relaxed dinners with friends
or peers after work were one thing—he could sparkle
and shine with the best of them on the surface. But once
he crossed the threshold of his inner sanctum, he
wanted to be left alone, he and Beau, immune to

relationships that could wreak havoc with his life. His lips compressed into a thin smile. Which was why it irked him beyond belief that a part of him *wanted* it to be Tess on the other side of that door. Barging into his life—*again*—with something wonderful to feed his empty stomach while her easy banter and sweet spirit fed his empty soul.

Woof, woof, woof! Beau bolted, then pranced in circles in front of the carved double teak doors, obviously more excited than he at the prospect of edible gifts.

"Calm down, Big Guy," he said with an upraised palm, "stay." Feigning a low growl, Ben unlatched the deadbolt and gripped the knob hard. "This late, you darn well better have food ..." he groused in a gruff tease, tempering his smile as he swung open the door.

"Wouldn't dream of coming without, Daddy."

His blood turned to ice water as he stared at his daughter. She stood there on his porch bold as you please, chin high with a dauntless smile despite the hint of caution in her eyes. Lifting a decadent-looking pie in her hands, she rattled a paper bag clutched beneath, the smell of fresh peaches all but cramping his empty stomach. She tilted her head in a playful manner he remembered from when she was a little girl, searing his heart with memories he'd much rather forget. Her voice baited him in a sing-song tease. "Mamaw's homemade peach crumble pie baked fresh this afternoon, Daddy, topped with Tess's homemade vanilla bean ice cream, of course." Her teeth tugged at the edge of her smile. "Oh, and bacon for Beau," she said, obviously waiting for him to invite her in.

Which was the *last* thing he wanted to do. But his stomach was growling and Beau was whining, and he was obviously outvoted two to one, so he opted for the next best thing. "Tell your grandmother and Tess thanks," he said in a clipped tone, extending his hand through a foot-and a half-long crack in the door while he reached for the pie.

Her chin nudged up an inch while she apparently waited for him to open the door.

His eyes narrowed. "What, you taking lessons from Tess now?"

A smile flickered at the edge of her lips. "As a matter of fact, I am, and she said, 'no visit, no pie—Tess's rules.'"

"Tess's rules, my backside—then give *her* the pie." He flung the door closed and turned the lock, temper singed over Tess coaching his daughter. *Women!* Give 'em an inch, they take a mile, and that was one road he had no desire to travel again. "Can it, you big sissy," he said to Beau over his shoulder, who stood whimpering at the door while Ben strode back to his chair. "If I can do without peach pie and ice cream, you can do without bacon."

Bong-Bong-Bong.

Jaw grinding, Ben snatched the remote to turn up the volume, glaring at Tim Allen like it was all his fault. He scowled when he realized what he was watching. *Last Man Standing*, Allen's new TV show. *How appropriate.* Because, so help him, if it took a steel-plated door and a house like a bunker, he'd be the last man standing in this war of wills.

Bong-Bong-Bong.

Woof, woof, woof!

He burrowed deeper in his chair and cranked the volume up.

Bong-Bong-Bong.

Woof, woof, woof!

His mouth pinched along with his patience as he aimed the remote at the TV, thumb knuckle white on the volume till he thought his ears would explode.

Bong-Bong-Bong.

Woof, woof, woof!

A dull ache started to throb beneath the sockets of both eyes, and crushing his thumb to the mute button, he hurled the remote into the sectional. With a hard yank of the recliner handle, his feet bottomed out along with his temper. Jumping up, he stomped to the door, lashing it wide. "What the blazes do you want, Lacey?"

The pie quivered in her hands despite the firm thrust of her chin. "Just to talk, Daddy, nothing more."

His glower could have melted the plastic wrap on top of the bloomin' pie, which taunted with mouthwatering bubbles of peach oozing between chunky crumbs of sugar topping. The gurgle of his stomach merged with Beau's pitiful whining, sealing the deal.

And his doom.

He grunted, the sound more of a growl as he shoved the door open with a crack to the wall. "Looks like I need a hedge all the way around. Put it in the kitchen, and I'll take it from there."

She shot past him faster than Beau after a rabbit, darting down the hall with Benedog Arnold on her heels. His glare could have singed the dog's tail. A shameless turncoat completely corrupted by his pesky neighbor.

"Thanks, Daddy. You go, sit, and I'll serve it up, okay?"

"No, it's not okay," he muttered, slamming the door hard so she knew he was ticked, both at his estranged daughter for pushing her way in and the bossy neighbor who egged her on. It now appeared he would have to get tougher regarding his desire to be left alone, both with Lacey and with Tess. Huffing out his annoyance, he plodded back to his recliner and dropped in with a loud whoosh of leather, quickly changing the channel to an NCIS marathon. Arms cushioned behind his neck, he faked total absorption when she returned with his pie.

"Here you go, Daddy," she said in a perky tone that reminded him of the pretty pest next door. "It's to die for, I promise."

To die for. He issued a silent grunt as he snatched the plate from her hand. Yeah, well his pride had already expired, buried in a pine box six feet under. Grunting his thanks, he swallowed the drool that pooled in his mouth, maintaining a Gibbs-like scowl while he shoveled in the first bite. He fought the urge to moan when Mamaw's pie grazed his tongue, but the cool swirl of Tess's ice cream took him down as it melted in his throat. Against his will, his eyes shuttered closed in a moment of pure ecstasy.

"You want something to drink? Decaf, milk?"

He gave a curt shake of his head, gaze returning to DiNozzo and Ziva sparring over something to which he hadn't a clue.

"Well, then how 'bout you, Mr. Beauregard?" she said in a cheerful tone that got on his nerves. "Would you like some dessert too?" Standing in Ben's line of sight to the left of the TV, Lacey waved two pieces of bacon, causing Beau to leap into the air with the most pitiful noise Ben had ever heard.

NCIS lost him on that when he glared at his daughter, jaw gaping. "For crying out loud, I can't believe she sent bacon too!" He shook his head and scooped another bite in his mouth, his annoyance robbing his pleasure over one of his favorite desserts. "And she calls herself a God-fearing woman. Somebody needs to tell her bribery's a sin."

His daughter chuckled. "I'll be sure to give her the message," she said as she disappeared into the kitchen. To clean up, he assumed.

Wrong. Sporting a large piece of pie and an even larger smile, she moseyed in and made herself comfortable in the center of the white leather sectional, feet tucked under as if she planned to stay.

He scarfed down the rest of his pie and tossed the empty plate and fork onto the end table with a loud clunk, then rested his arms on the chair, gaze glued to the TV. "What do you really want, Lacey?" His jaw hardened to rock, like his tone.

"To talk, Daddy," she said quietly. "To clear the air and heal our relationship."

"We don't have a relationship. That ended the night you cursed me at your mother's funeral, saying you wished it were mine instead, and that I was dead to you.'"

"I didn't mean it," she whispered, "I was angry."

He jerked his head in her direction, the acid in his tone burning as much as the fury in his eyes. "You ignored any attempts I made to salvage whatever pathetic relationship we had."

Tears welled in her eyes, but he fought the emotion that tugged at his heart. Placing her unfinished dessert on the coffee table, she shifted to face him, perched on the edge of the couch with arms clutched to her sides. "I've changed, Daddy, I promise."

"Yeah? Well, I have too." He saw her lip quiver at the coldness of his tone. "I'm through with the grief of so-called family, kiddo, so you can pack up your good intentions and go home."

"I'm here to make amends, not give you grief," she whispered.

He arched a brow. "You're giving me grief right now. I'm tired, I don't want to talk, and I want to be left alone."

She winced before she engaged that familiar lift of her chin. "Fine, we won't talk." Snapping her dessert up from the table, she continued to eat while she watched NCIS, gaze glued to the screen like it was that silly *Gone with the Wind* movie her mother and she used to love. During the commercials she tossed Beau's tattered duck for him, laughing and teasing with him like she used to when he was a pup. The silly mutt promptly deserted him once the show came back on, cozying up to her on the couch like she'd never abandoned them both. His eyes thinned to slits as his mouth went flat. *Traitor.*

When the show ended, she hopped up and gathered their dishes, striding into the kitchen to clean up he supposed, making so much racket he could barely hear Gibb's monotone voice. Not that he was listening …

"I'll take Beau out before I go," she called, and he breathed a sigh of relief when he heard the kitchen door close. *Thank God she's leaving soon.*

A few minutes later, the door squealed open and he immediately shut his eyes, head tipped to the side on the back of the chair. He heard the pantry door open and shut and knew she was giving Beau his treat just like she used to after letting him out. Her footsteps padded across the wooden floor along with the click of Beau's claws, and Ben feigned exhaustion, his breathing quiet and even to mimic the rhythm of sleep.

"I'm leaving, Daddy," she whispered, but he only continued to doze, snorting an exhale he hoped would convince her he was out. His heart seized at the touch of her lips to his brow, but he never moved a muscle, certain she would hear the wild clip of his heart. He couldn't be sure because his eyes were closed, but he could have sworn a hint of a smile colored her tone. "I love you, Daddy, and I'll be back."

He waited till long after her footsteps receded down the hall and the front door closed with a quiet click. Only when he heard the rumble of a car engine did he finally open his eyes, staring at the TV screen without seeing a thing.

"I love you, Daddy, and I'll be back."

He grunted and rose to his feet, not comfortable at all with the unsettled feelings roiling inside, especially the notion that she intended to try this again. He shook his head, an odd mix of annoyance and humor twisting his lips at the thought of her final line, obviously stolen on purpose from one of his favorite movies.

"I'll be back."

He scowled. *The Terminator or his daughter.* Which one would he rather face? He pressed the "system off" button of his remote and tossed it in the chair before heading down the hall, lips in a slant as he cut loose with a yawn.

No contest.

CHAPTER TWENTY-TWO

"*L*acey? Lacey Carmichael?"

Lacey spun around on the weathered dock of Camp Hope, hand shielding her eyes from the sunlight to focus on the tall cowboy at the top of the hill. Her lips instantly curved in a smile brimming with affection at the sight of the camp's seasoned cowboy and all-around coach/handyman, Will Hogan. Nudging his Stetson up, he meandered down the rolling lawn dotted with wildflower gardens and oaks older than the Civil War that once raged all around.

She waved a hand, her grin as wide as Will's. "Why, Will Hogan," she called, hand to mouth, "I thought you'd be long gone by now, rustling cattle on that dream ranch of yours in Wyoming."

His hearty chuckle carried down the lawn and across the freshwater lake where cheers and shrieks sounded behind her from a noisy canoe race on Blue Heron Lake. "What can I say—that woman refuses to let me go," he groused. His good-natured teasing lured a chuckle to Lacey's lips over the longstanding head—— *and* heart——butting relationship between Will and Miss Myra Lee. A relative of Robert E. Lee by marriage, Miss Myra was the camp's spunky director, a widow with a law degree who'd transformed her family's plantation into a camp for orphans with illnesses, disabilities, and other challenges. It had been Will and Miss Myra and a host of employees and volunteers who'd filled Lacey's high school summers with laughter and joy, producing a sharp twinge of homesickness she'd never experienced at home.

Thumbs hooked in the dusty pockets of his jeans, Will halted before her, back-dropped by the lush slope he kept manicured as if it were Wormsloe Plantation rather than a year-long camp for kids. "When in tarnation did you get back, Lacey Lou?" he said, swallowing her up in a hug that smelled fondly of hay and horses and the leather soap he used on every saddle in the stable. "'Cause if it was before yesterday, you got some explaining to do, girl."

She laughed and squeezed back before pulling away. "No comment on the grounds you might make me muck the stables again." Head in a tilt, she smiled up at his commanding six-foot-two stature, his ruggedly handsome air and Tom Selleck moustache always reminding her of the Marlboro Man, no matter his near-sixty age. "I came home to help with my cousin's wedding, but I need something else to do with my summer, so you think you could put a good word in for me with Miss Myra?"

"Ha! You'd get further with that woman on your own merit than mine," he said with a puckish wink, "but I do seem to recall her moaning and groaning about the pitiful lack of volunteers of late, so who knows—I may just get that stable mucked yet."

Lacey held her hands up with a chuckle. "Mucking stables, cleaning cabins, cooking chow—makes no difference to me as long as I can help out."

His brows pinched in thought. "Hear tell you're a teacher now—that true?"

She saluted, shoulders squaring in pride. "Yes, sir, major in communication arts and minor in special education, so I can whip any student into shape bar none, male or female."

He nodded slowly. "Too bad. I was kinda hopin' for the Lacey-Lou touch on those nasty horse stalls, but sounds like Miss Myra might steal you away for more important things." Will glanced toward the lake where hoots and hollers of the older kids echoed across the water when the second leg of the canoe race sped toward the dock. He nodded uphill. "Let's you and me mosey up to the house before the rowdies come ashore, 'cause I'm pretty sure Miss Myra has a job with your name on it, darlin'."

Anticipation coursed through Lacey's veins as they made their way up to the stately plantation house that now served as the gathering rooms, kitchen, and office for Camp Hope as well as Miss Myra's home. On the way, Will filled her in on all the improvements Miss Myra and her board of directors made since Lacey had left—a new log-cabin dorm, volleyball pit, log-cabin rec center, tennis court, bike and hike trails through the woods, fire pit, and a bona fide regulation-size swimming pool. She, in turn, filled him in on the highs and lows of her last eight years, from her master's degree and Nicki's wedding, to her mother's passing and her broken engagement.

Will halted on the first step of the freshly painted white wooden steps that flared down from a pillared wraparound porch, worry lines creasing his stubbled face. "We were sure sorry to hear about your mama, Lace, and riles me but good that some no-count city boy left you at the altar." He hooked an arm over her should to press a fatherly kiss to her head as they continued up to a mammoth black door. "But to be honest, darlin', it don't sound like he's got all that much upstairs, and you sure don't want that in the gene pool, you know?"

She grinned. *Poor Tim—everybody was ready to nail him to the wall when it had been me who changed, not him.* She patted Will's arm as he held open the door, knowing her next statement would make him smile. "Well actually, Will, he was at the top of his law class, but I guess you could say he got spooked when his devil-may-care fiancée got a little too chummy with God."

He paused at the door, hand on the knob as he studied her with a gleam of pride in his eyes. "No kidding? Well it's about time, darlin', 'cause He's been awaitin' on you a long, long while."

Her smile faded to soft. "I know, Will," she whispered, "and I would have never gotten there without the prayers of my grandmother, you, and Miss Myra."

With a stiff nod and a pat of her arm, he opened the door and put two fingers to his teeth, pert near glazing Lacey's eyes with his trademark whistle.

"Mr. Will, Mr. Will—is it time for the trail ride yet?" A flash of lime green blasted out of a door at the back of the hall like a bullet, cross-hairs on Will's denim legs. A tiny girl, surely no older than six, streaked down the polished wood hall in tattered blue jean overalls, dirty T-shirt, and a dusty Atlanta Braves ball cap, her freckled face little more than a blur.

With a gaping smile, Lacey quickly stepped out of the way as the rascal crashed into Will's legs with a slam that jolted both her and Lacey far more than it did Will. He promptly swooped her high in the air, unleashing little-girl squeals that brought a grin to Lacey's face.

"Deborah Lynne Holbrook!" Lips pursed in a mock scowl, Miss Myra Penelope Lee glided down the mahogany staircase like a queen about to hold court, her bisque-colored tailored silk dress flowing in the breeze with every regal step she took. "We do *not* run

in the house like wild Indians, young lady." Barely five foot one, what Miss Myra lacked in height, she made up for with an air of authority that kept a camp full of orphans, several employees, tons of volunteers, and one ornery cowboy in line. "And for the love of civility, Wilson Hodges, when are you going to learn I am not a cocker spaniel to be beckoned by the primitive shriek of a whistle?"

"Uh-ohhhhhh ..." the little imp said with a giggle, clutching tightly to Will's rolled-up chambray shirt as she bounced on his hip.

Will hooked his free arm around Lacey's shoulders, his grin a flash of white in a well-weathered face bronzed by the sun. "Aw, shucks, Miss Myra," he said in a lazy drawl that Lacey knew was mostly for tease, "I was thinking more along the lines of one of those highfalutin' French poodles, you know the testy kind with all that champagne hair in a poof just like yours? What d'ya think, Lacey-Lou?"

The two-inch heels of Miss Myra's buff-colored pumps skidded to a dead stop on the landing of the curved mahogany staircase, both her brown eyes and wispy skirt flaring with the motion. One thin, pale hand fluttered to the single strand of pearls at her throat while her fair cheeks faded even more, a near match to the shoulder-length ash blonde hair always worn up in a classic French twist. "Lacey? Oh, good heavens—is that you?"

Laughing, Lacey rushed to swallow her former boss and mentor up in a hug at the base of the steps, breathing in the calming scent of Chanel No. 5. "Yes, ma'am, it is, alive and well and reporting for duty."

Will cleared his throat. "And toting a teaching degree in communication arts, Your Highness Boss, *with* ..." he said with great drama, giving a wink that shot color right back into Miss Myra's cheeks, "a minor in special ed, no less."

"Hey, who are you anyway?" the ragamuffin demanded with a pert thrust of her chin, brown eyes assessing Lacey in a narrow-eyed squint that implied she wasn't impressed.

"*This*, young lady," Miss Myra said with an arm to Lacey's waist and a lift of her head, "is the ray of sunshine I've been praying for to help fine-tune you and your three classmates in your reading skills." She turned to Lacey, manicured brows arched in question. "That is, if she'll say 'yes' to a job for the summer?"

"*Please* do little Debbie here and me a favor, Lacey-Lou," Will said with a polite tip of his Stetson, giving Miss Myra a lazy smile while he shifted Debbie in his arms. "The woman is so understaffed now, it's like working for a she-bear with a burr in her paw."

Miss Myra arched a pale brow. "Oh, now there's a grizzly calling the cub a crank if ever there was." She reached to tweak Debbie's waist. "He's just mad because I can't spare any of my counselors to muck his silly stalls, right, Debbie?"

"Right!" The little dickens giggled, her squeals bouncing off the magnolia-papered walls when Will retaliated with a monster growl to her neck.

"So, Miss Carmichael ..." Miss Myra faced Lacey again, the professional jut of her chin at odds with the hope in her eyes, "will you consider joining my sparse ranks of volunteers? The pay is great—all meals free and s'mores by firelight whenever you work late."

Will tossed Debbie over his shoulder like a sack of feed. "And trail rides with handsome cowboys and rowdy kids if you dare," he added with a cock of his hip, allowing the wiggly tomboy to possum-hang down his back.

Lacey laughed. "Goodness—what more could a girl ask?"

"Excellent! Then I suppose you and I ought to discuss this further in my office while Will returns to muck the stables and Miss Debbie, to her class."

Will swung Debbie off his shoulder onto the floor with great fanfare while the little monkey giggled and kicked. "Okay, Sweet Pea, you heard the lady—scoot!"

Lacey grinned over Debbie's shenanigans, and then her heart crashed to the floor faster than the little scamp's high-tops, feeling a lot like one of Debbie's kicks had landed right in her gut. The girl's ball cap had apparently dropped while she was draped over Will's shoulder, revealing a head that resembled a baby bald eagle's, round and bare except for a layer of fuzz.

A gulp lodged in Lacey's throat. *Oh, Lord, please— not cancer …*

With a quick snatch of her ball cap, Debbie started to bolt down the hall, but not before Miss Myra hooked the back of her overalls, springing her back like a paddleball on an elastic string. "Excuse me, Miss Holbrook, but what do you have say to your new reading teacher?"

Lips flattened in a scowl, the sprite of a girl studied Lacey through slatted eyes. "I don't like to read," she muttered with a tight fold of arms.

"Deborah Lynne …?" Miss Myra pinched the back of the girl's neck, and the little spitfire hunched her shoulders with an impish grin. "But I'll try, Miss Lacey-Lou, I promise, so it's nice to meet ya."

Smiling, Lacey stooped before her, hands on her knees. "I'll tell you what, Debbie, if you still don't like to read when I'm done with you, I'll jump in the lake fully clothed while I quack like a duck—deal?"

A smile inched across the little girl's face till she was grinning ear-to-ear, the gold fuzz glimmering in the sunlight that streamed from the transom windows over the front door. Without hair, her bald head made her brown eyes all the larger, all the more impish, complementing a tiny upturned nose that gave her a pixie air. She seemed undaunted by her plight, gaze sparkling with the dare of adventure as she tugged on her ball cap and extended a tiny hand. "Deal."

"But ... if you *do* end up liking to read and do well on your test, then I will bring pizza, soda, and your choice of ice cream from Coldstone Creamery for a special movie night just for you and your class, plus choice of a favorite book." She glanced up at Miss Myra. "*If* Miss Myra says it's okay ..."

Debbie's gaze darted to Miss Myra, who dipped her head in a short nod, a smile twitching behind her stern demeanor. "Agreed."

"Thank you, Miss Myra." Lacey held out her hand to Debbie. "So ... double deal?"

The little girl gave Lacey's hand a firm shake. "Double deal!"

"Okay then, young lady," Miss Myra said with a tug of Debbie's hat, prodding her in the direction of the classroom, "go back to your class before Mrs. Bunch sends out a search party, all right?"

"Yes, ma'am." She tore down the hall, only to grind to a halt halfway, whirling around to place sassy hands on her little hips. "S'pose it's best to tell you right here and now, Miss Lacey-Lou." She tossed them a pixie smile, and Lacey swore she saw a bit of the devil in those twinkling brown eyes. "I like butter pecan."

CHAPTER TWENTY-THREE

"*S*o … hear tell you signed up to volunteer at Camp Hope." Resting against the base of one of Mamaw's gnarled oaks, Jack accepted a frosty iced tea from Lacey during a break from building the wedding gazebo. Across the yard, Matt and Nicki bantered with Nate to the ping of hammers and country music from Matt's iPad, ironically blasting Dolly Parton's *I Will Always Love You* while Lacey smiled down. Nodding his thanks, he took a swig, drinking in the heady scent of Coppertone and sawdust along with his lemon-flavored tea. An odd sense of pride warmed him inside that Lacey hadn't lost her passion for a cause near and dear to his family's heart. Swiping sweat from his forehead with the sleeve of his paint-stained T-shirt, he peered up through sun-squinted eyes. "Just to be safe, though, you might want to keep an extra change of clothes in the car." He grinned over the rim of his Dixie cup, remembering all the times Lacey had jumped in the lake fully clothed over a dare or lost bet, delighting the kids to no end.

And him.

Her mouth dropped a full inch as she slacked a leg, hands perched on the hips of her blue jean cutoffs. "Are you clairvoyant or something, O'Bryen? For heaven's sake, I just committed to Miss Myra this morning—how on earth did you find out already?"

Chucking an ice cube into his mouth, he arched a brow. "Besides the fact you're completely predictable?" He crunched on the ice, a grin surfacing while it crushed and crackled against his molars. "Camp Hope is still a top priority for my family, Lace, so we all volunteer during the summer when we can, even Mom." He winked. "I was there after you left today, treating a couple of the kids in sick bay when Miss Myra gave me the good news."

Her gaping mouth edged into a smile while she shook her head, plopping down on the lawn to sit beside him, body butted to the base of the tree just like him. "No kidding? I knew your sisters still volunteered, but I didn't know you were involved too." Knees cocked, she snatched a handful of clover stems from the lawn and started tying them into necklaces like she and his sisters used to do when they were kids. "I ran into Cat and Shan at the archery range while Will gave me the grand tour." Her mouth twisted as she bent to focus on tying a knot in two stems. "Shan gave me a hug, of course, but I swear the temperature dropped twenty degrees from the ice in Cat's eyes." She grunted. "She sliced the bull's-eye clean through, but something tells me she was aiming for a whole 'nother target in her mind."

He chuckled. "Knowing Cat, I'd say that's a pretty safe bet, but she'll come around. Trust me—up to a month ago I would've been taking target practice right beside her."

She peered up in a sideways glance, a cross between a smile and a smirk hovering on her lips. "But not anymore?"

He assessed her for several seconds, suddenly aware that most of the bitterness he'd harbored toward Lacey had somehow ebbed like the tide, leaving behind the rich and fertile ground of a prior friendship he'd treasured. "Nope." He emptied his drink straight up,

then set the cup aside while he propped hands behind
his neck, absently studying the smattering of holes and
stains in his work jeans. "I never thought seeing you
again would be a good thing," he said quietly, "but I
was wrong."

His eyes flicked up to meet hers, and for the first
time he realized that whether it was lover or friend,
Lacey Carmichael was someone who would always
possess a place in his heart. A tomboy little sister with
whom he'd teased and arm-wrestled along with Cat and
Shan before she morphed into the sassy girlfriend with
whom he wrestled in a whole new way. The perfect
antidote to an overly serious egghead, one she'd single-
handedly taught how to laugh and live and love in a
way he had never experienced before. The little brat
had become part of his DNA, it seemed, robbing him of
a part of his soul when she'd left him behind.

Until now. Now having her back in his life—no
matter the capacity—had allowed the tide back in,
slowly filling in some of the gaps in his life. A smile
curved on his lips as he watched her fiddle with the
clover, her very presence helping to ease the quiet ache
in his heart. "I missed you, Lace. Not just 'us' together,
but *you.* Your friendship, your fun, your crazy
perspective on life that helped broaden my own. I
missed having you as part of our family, whether it was
the little pest next door or the girl I used to fish and
laugh with in between kisses down on the dock."

His heart clutched when a film of moisture glazed in
her eyes, and with a swell of affection, he carefully
swept a few silky strands of hair over her shoulder.
"And I know deep down that Cat will feel the same
once you two finally talk."

She expelled a heavy sigh, the motion appearing to
deplete her as she tucked her knees to her chest and
rested her chin on top. "Sure hope it goes better than it

did with my dad," she whispered, a rare malaise weighting her words.

He fought the urge to bundle her in his arms like he used to whenever she and her dad had fought. His jaw hardened at the memory of the high-and-mighty surgeon who had time for everything but his own flesh and blood, and Jack vowed he would never let his practice get in the way of loving family. He gentled his tone. "What happened?" he said quietly, wishing he could give Ben Carmichael a piece of his mind.

And his fist.

She gave a tiny shrug. "Oh, he was cold, as expected, a stone wall higher than that silly hedge between him and the rest of the world."

"Did he talk to you at least?"

Her laugh was harsh. "'Grunted' might be a better word, but he did finally let me in after I wore out his doorbell, so that's something, I guess. Or I should say he let Mamaw's *pie* in." A knot ducked in her throat as she stared aimlessly into the yard, the buzz of a circular saw almost drowning out the low drone of her voice. "He asked me why I was there, and I told him I wanted to heal our relationship. 'We don't have a relationship,' he said in that clinical manner of his, 'that ended the night you cursed me at your mother's funeral, saying you wished it were mine instead, and that I was dead to you.'"

Jack winced, well aware that Lacey's temper and tongue had gotten the best of her at times, triggering Ben Carmichael's well-hidden temper like nobody else could do. *Except maybe me*, he thought with a grimace, *once I started dating his daughter.* Suddenly the calm and collected doctor next door was as cold and belligerent to Jack as he was to his defiant daughter, causing them both a world of heartbreak.

A world of heartbreak. A vile prophecy if ever there was. A shiver chilled his skin as his jaw clamped tight.

Expelling a weary breath, Lacey slumped against the tree, grabbing more clover to add to her necklace. "He's right, of course. I'm the one who turned him out of my life for eight years, so who am I to expect him to welcome me back with open arms?"

Jack's lips took a slant. "Uh, the only flesh-and-blood relative he has?"

Her laugh was bitter. "The only kind of blood Ben Carmichael cares about is the kind he's paid to pump through patients' hearts." She caught her breath and suddenly sat straight up, a smile of wonder dawning on her face as she held up a piece of clover. "Hey, look at this—a four-leaf clover," she said with genuine awe, blinking at him in that wide-eyed, little-girl way that had always melted his heart. "Do you have any idea just how rare that is?"

He studied her with affection, offering a tender smile despite the faint cramp in his chest. "Yeah," he said softly. *As rare as someone who brings sunshine to your soul.*

A giggle popped from her lips as she carefully tied the final two stems of her clover to create a full circle. "Who knows? Maybe my luck has changed." She tilted her head to give him a bright smile with a twinkle of tease. "Or my faith, I should say."

"So ..." he said, anxious to bypass any talk of her newfound faith, "how many days are you volunteering at the camp and what's Miss Myra got you doing this time?"

That was all it took to get her off and running with a glow of excitement. "Well, it's three days a week for now since I've already committed to several of Mamaw's projects, but I'll kick that up to five when I can, at least until I start my new job in Savannah in August. I told her I'd do whatever she needed—counseling, office work, cooking, cleaning or chief bottle-washer, but when she heard I had a degree in communication arts with a minor in special education, that sealed the deal. Seems her current batch of kids has a fair number of dyslectics and slow readers—five or six or so, ages seven through fourteen—so I'll be taking over a small class she's put together to help improve their reading skills." She paused, sobriety dimming the excitement in her face. "Hey, what do you know about a little tyke named Debbie Holbrook?"

"Debbie?" Rifling in his glass, he popped another ice cube in his mouth, his chest both warming and cramping over the little orphan who'd stolen his affections the first day she'd hopped off the bus, skinned knees and all.

All the kids at Camp Hope were wards of the state, orphans or in between foster-care homes at the moment, all short-changed in the realm of home life or health. But few had endured in their short lives what Debbie had. A sigh breezed across his lips as he stared blankly into the yard, his heart melting along with the ice in his mouth. "Well, the good news is she just finished treatment for leukemia last month," he said quietly, gaze fixed on Matt and Nate while they nailed a sheet of lattice to the back of the gazebo, "and I'm happy to say the little sweetheart is now in remission."

He upended the rest of the ice and crunched hard, his smile as stiff as his jaw. "Which is good 'cause she has a host of other problems to deal with, not the least of which are dyslexia and impaired learning." A pop sounded when he fisted the Dixie cup. "All due to a mother who abused both drugs and alcohol, not to mention her daughter."

Lacey's harsh intake of air broke into his thoughts, drawing his gaze to her face, which had paled considerably. "Oh, no ..." she whispered, the raspy croak of her voice telling him eight years may have passed, but it hadn't changed the care and compassion that had always run deep in Lacey's soul.

He swabbed his face with his hand, never more grateful for the medical degree that allowed him to reach out to kids like Debbie. "Apparently she was a mess when she was born according to Doc Miller, Myra's good friend at Atlanta's Children's Shelter, which is where Debbie is from. She's already had surgeries for a cleft foot and lazy eye, but her vision is still pretty poor due to cataracts that need correction. Her mother abandoned her at the age of three when the heart issues cropped up." His lips thinned, voice as bitter as the bile that tainted his tongue. "But not before her boyfriend got his licks in with everything from broken legs to dislocated shoulders."

"Oh, God bless her ..." Pain threaded Lacey's voice.

He slid her a sideways glance, unable to keep his remark free of rancor. "Yeah, well, I guarantee there wasn't a whole lot of that going on."

"What kind of heart problems?" she whispered, obviously ignoring the venom in his tone.

"An atrial septal defect."

Her tan faded to a pasty white. "No ... not a congenital heart defect," she whispered, her voice raspy with pain.

"Afraid so. Just one of the many birthday gifts her mother gave her—a moderate-size hole in the septum between the left and the right atria, which doctors are hoping will close up on its own, but there's no guarantee." He tunneled blunt fingers through damp hair while he expelled a burdensome sigh. "Which means the poor kid might be looking at surgery down the road on top of everything else she's had to contend with."

Lacey nodded, her gaze lapsing into a faraway stare. "You know, for some strange reason, I felt a kinship with her the moment I saw her, and now I know why." The graceful lines of her throat shifted while moisture glazed in her eyes. "She's an orphan with a sick heart that only God can heal, and sometimes I feel the same."

Jack bristled at Lacey's reference to God, wondering if this was how she'd felt years ago whenever he'd pushed the issue of faith. Snatching the crumpled Dixie cup from the grass, he hopped to his feet, not very successful at taming the scowl on his face. "It's been my experience that God's a lot better at breaking hearts than healing them, Lace, but God or man, I'm pulling for you both." He extended a hand to help her up and she took it, her look of sympathy getting on his nerves.

"Not God, Jack," she said quietly, the solemnity of her words giving him pause. "Human beings. God's the One Who picks up the pieces, remember?" A sad smile shadowed her lips. "You were the one who taught me that."

Blood warmed his cheeks at the very notion of his former girlfriend now preaching to him. "Yeah, I did," he said with a wry bent of his mouth. "Too bad I'm not buying it anymore."

"Okay, people, reinforcements are here," Justin called from Mamaw's patio door, arriving late with Sarah after a Home Depot run. He toted a tray of Mamaw's homemade subs while Sarah followed behind with a fresh pitcher of tea. "The food kind, the tool kind, *and* the people kind, who hopefully will do more than just sit around and guzzle tea."

Matt seared Justin with a narrow look from the bottom step of the gazebo, where he sat tipping the last of his drink along with Nicki and Nate, sweat rolling down their faces. "Hey, Dipwad, we've already put in several hours, I'll have you know." His gaze flicked to Jack and Lacey with a crooked smile. "Or at least some of us have. Those two over there have spent the last thirty minutes jawing in the shade."

"I beg your pardon," Lacey said, strolling over to give Matt some grief with hands parked on her hips. "It

was ten minutes, Ball, and Jack had the posts poured and the beams cut before you two masterminds even figured out which hammers to use." She arched a brow. "Not to mention helping me dig the entire trench for the berms on either side of the yard."

"Only because he got here early to impress Mamaw," Matt countered.

Jack hurled the crumpled Dixie cup at Matt. "No, Lazy-Butt, because I was on time and you and Mr. Bottomless Pit there probably stopped at every McDonald's on the way."

Nicki chuckled, ruffling Matt's hair as she passed by on her way to the patio. "He's got you there, babe."

Matt shot to his feet in time to snatch Nicki's hand, spinning her around to capture her in a mock threat. "It's a sad commentary, *woman*, when my cousin's ex-girlfriend supports him more than my future wife supports me."

"That's what you get for marrying a church-going woman, Ball." Jack sauntered over to clamp Lacey's neck, hoping to ease the tension of their prior conversation. "They tend to be a little too honest to suit."

Lacey squealed with a scrunch of shoulders, sliding him a sideways grin. "As I recall, honesty was one of the things you were looking for way back when, Jack O'Bryen."

He slung an arm over her shoulder and grinned, ushering her toward the patio where Mamaw was furling a checkered tablecloth over her wrought-iron table. "Yep. Now the only things I'm looking for are a couple of your grandmother's subs and a tall mug of tea."

"We're not too late, are we?"

Jack glanced up, jaw stiffening along with the arm he'd hooked over Lacey's shoulder. Chase and Kelly stood on the threshold of Mamaw's French doors, the sight of the pretty-boy pastor suddenly spoiling his mood. Sporting a polo that appeared far too snug for a pastor, he hoisted a huge watermelon with one hand, arms sculpted enough to tick Jack off. Beside him, Kelly carried several bags of snacks and chips, her smile lighting up the moment she saw Jack.

"Hey, Chase, I thought you had to work today." Lacey slipped from Jack's hold to give Sarah and Chase a hug, annoying Jack to no end.

"Finished my meeting earlier than expected, so I thought I'd come over to show these yahoos how it's done." He glanced up to grin at Matt and Nate before offering Jack a hand. "Hey, Jack, we've missed that killer serve of yours at volleyball, so it's good to see you again."

Yeah, well, that makes one of us ... He shook Chase's hand and forced a smile. "Just figured you had things well under control, Rev, so I didn't want to cramp your style."

The French doors swooshed open again, and Mamaw stepped out with a gleam of mischief and an oversized pump bottle of Purell, the smell of cinnamon drifting out with her. "All right, young people, warm cookies are in the oven, but not one crumb will be had until these sandwiches are all gone." She plopped the bottle of Purell in the center of the table with a noticeable clunk, chin high. "And not one sandwich is to be had without sanitizing your hands first, is that clear?" Her twinkling gaze landed square on Lacey with a zag of a smile. "There are those who have no qualms about germs, and you know who you are ..."

"Yes, ma'am." Lacey squeezed Mamaw's waist, then quickly complied with an ample squirt of Purell. "Whoops, overkill," she said with a lift of gooey hands.

Chase wasted no time. "Here, I'll help you out." Wearing a grin, he massaged and manhandled her palms so long, Jack was sure the excess Purell had to be bone dry. After twining his fingers with Lacey's, he pulled her into a hug. "Now I'll be germ-free *and* sweet."

Jack fought the urge to roll his eyes while he glanced at his watch, his mind already made up. He wasn't staying around for another episode of the Chase and Lacey Show. "Okay, grunts, I gotta go, so don't botch up my hard work."

Lacey whirled around, eyes wide. "What do you mean you have to go?" The deep ridge in her brow made him happier than it should. "You just told me you were starving."

"That's before I remembered a meeting I have," he lied, giving her ponytail a light tug.

He ducked when Matt pelted one of Mamaw's homemade pretzel nubs his way. "Come on, O'Bryen, you never told me about any meeting." Taking a second shot, Matt missed him again. "You're just trying to bail out of work."

Jack threw Matt off with a lazy shrug before snatching a pretzel to nail him mid-chest. "You have a real talent for the obvious, Ball, but your aim could use some work."

"Come on, Jack." Kelly had that familiar coax in her tone. "These guys need all the help they can get. Besides," she said with a sultry dance of brows, "I was kind of hoping for a glimpse of you without your shirt. You know, all sweaty and laboring in the sun?"

Plate piled high, Justin laughed and draped an arm over Kelly's shoulder. "Don't worry, Goshorn, I'll ditch my shirt if you want."

Jack waved off all protests as he edged toward the door. "Another time, Miss Goshorn. I realize these jokers are poor seconds, but who knows?" He gave her a wink before nodding toward Chase. "Maybe the preacher will comply. So long, everyone." He gave a final salute.

"Wait! At least take lunch with you." Lacey butted the guys out of the way to grab a paper plate and load it with two hoagies and all the fixin's.

"That's okay, Lace, really—" He fisted the knob, anxious to flee.

"Halt!" She froze his hand to the door with a no-nonsense schoolteacher tone, giving him the stink-eye like she used to whenever she wanted her way. A bittersweet grin tugged at his lips when she cocked a stern brow. "Not one more step, O'Bryen, until I get this plate loaded with food and covered with foil, is that understood?"

Nicki confiscated one of Matt's three hoagies and plopped it on her plate instead. "Uh-oh, Jack, she's in teacher mode now, so I suggest you do as she says."

"Yeah, or she may send you to the principal's office," Sarah said with a giggle, bumping her hip to Kelly's. "Or Miss Goshorn's."

"Follow me, please," Lacey ordered, prodding him aside to march into Mamaw's kitchen where the smell of snickerdoodles cooling on the counter watered his mouth. Placing his plate on the island counter, she retrieved foil and another paper plate from the pantry, promptly filling it with cookies before covering both. She stacked and handed them over, then swiped a bottled water from the fridge and plunked it on top. "There." She looked up with a victorious smile. "That should hold you till after your meeting."

"Thank you, Miss Carmichael," he drawled in his best suck-up-to-teacher voice. He chucked her on the chin. "You may be bossy, but I wish all my teachers had been as pretty as you. I'll bet all the boys toe the line in your class, don't they?"

She surprised him with a soft blush. "As a matter of fact, they do, and *you*, Mr. O'Bryen," she said with a sparkle in her eye, "would do well to remember that."

"Yes, ma'am."

Without notice, she stood on tiptoe to brush a gentle kiss to his cheek, and the air heaved still in his throat. "Thanks, Jack, for all of your help," she whispered. "You and Chase are the only ones with construction experience, so the rest of the guys would be lost without you."

Chase.

Figures. "No problem, Lace—glad to do it." He hefted the plates in the air. "Thanks for the eats— they'll be gone before I'm a block away."

"Good." She followed him down the hall and opened the front door. "See you soon, I hope."

"Yeah, unfortunately," he muttered after she closed the door, shoulders in a slump as he made his way to his car. He tossed the plates on the front seat and got in to his convertible, his mood suddenly as hot as his black leather seats in the sun. Something needed to be done about his feelings for Lacey or their friendship wasn't long for this world. He thought about Jasmine and knew she was more than ready to move to the next level, or at least that's what she implied every time they were together. And like he'd mentioned to Sam in his office that day, he'd been leaning that way as well ... *especially* since he'd seen Lacey in that flippin' BP.

He twisted the cap off the water with too much force, splashing his leather console and making a mess. *Just like my life*, he thought before taking a deep swig that seemed to wash away all doubts. It was time, he decided, time to fall in love with somebody else, and although the thought left him as cold as the water chilling his throat, he knew he didn't have much of a choice. There was no way Lacey would have him as is—a man without faith—she'd made that abundantly clear. And there was no way he'd rely on God ever again. So it looked like Jazz would get what she wanted. He pushed the ignition with a grunt. *At least one of us will ...*

"Jack!"

He glanced toward the house where Chase was loping across Mamaw's lawn. Apology etched in his face, he placed palms on the open passenger window. "Sorry to keep you, but do you mind if I ask you a question?"

Jack turned, expression casual despite the uneasy feeling crawling in his gut. "Go ahead."

Chase studied him, his serious expression that of a pastor despite his form-fitting polo. "Are you ... leaving because of me?"

Heat tracked up the back of Jack's neck. "What? No," he lied, taking another glug of his water. "Why would you think that?"

Sober eyes seemed to peer into his very soul, telling him Chase had found his calling. "Because you seem uneasy whenever I'm around, and to be honest, I think you still care for Lacey. So I want you to know that I'll back off if my dating her bothers you at all."

Jack blinked, hardly able to believe any guy would be that accommodating. But then this was a preacher, somebody used to sacrificing his wants for others. Jack suddenly thought of his father. *Until the day they do whatever they freakin' well please.* He took another swallow of water. "No, Rev, don't worry about me. Lacey and I are nothing more than friends, so go for it."

Chase ducked his head, his gaze measuring Jack way too hard. "You're sure?"

"Yeah, I'm sure. Lacey and I were in love as kids, but growing up has a way of changing all that. Besides," he said, tugging a sandwich from beneath the foil with a flash of teeth, "I'm hooked up with a hot blonde right now who's pretty crazy about me."

Chase grinned. "So I noticed. Jasmine, right?"

"Yeah."

"Good to hear." With a tap of palms to the car, Chase stepped back. "Thanks for understanding, man."

"Sure, no problem, Rev. See ya." Putting the car in gear, Jack glanced behind before pulling away from the curb, fingers as taut and hard as the steel beneath his hand.

No problem at all.

"Have a good meeting," Chase called and Jack gunned the engine, jaw grinding along with the gears of his car. *A good meeting.* Not a lie exactly, at least not anymore. He glanced at the clock on the dash. Just a little past noon. Good. Jasmine would be on lunch break soon. Slapping his blinker on, he took the turn to Memorial for his "meeting." A "meeting" of the minds, that is. He shifted into high gear, leaving Isle of Hope in the dust as he shot across Skidaway Narrows bridge with one purpose in mind. To purge any romantic notions for Lacey Carmichael from his brain. A tic pulsed in his cheek as the Z ate up the miles.

And from his heart.

CHAPTER TWENTY-FOUR

*L*acey breathed in deeply, the warm bag of snickerdoodles taking her back to when Mom and she spent days on end baking Christmas cookies for Daddy. "Snickerdoodles are one of your father's favorites," Mom would always say with a secret smile, her teasing tone indicative of just how hard they'd tried to sneak into Daddy's good graces.

Easing the Honda down Bluff Drive, a smile tickled her lips as she passed Jack's house. It broke into a full-fledge grin at the memory of Tess's suggestion of monster cookies or chocolate chip pie as a means of weakening her father's defenses. Yes, monster cookies were good, she supposed, and chocolate chip pie too. But when she was younger, warm snickerdoodles had always earned her a kiss and a smile when she'd met Daddy at the door with a fresh batch, and she was hoping tonight they might work their magic too.

Please, God?

Even so, her stomach churned as much as the batter in the bowl when she'd baked them after dinner, earning her kisses and smiles from Spence and Nicki, if not from her father. Glancing at the dark windows of the house, she put the car in "Park" and turned it off, her hope sputtering as much as the engine when it rumbled and shimmied to a stop.

"The front of the house is always dark," Tess had warned her, "so if he doesn't answer, just keep 'bonging' him to death with that silly doorbell. That usually does the trick for me."

Lacey's mouth took a swerve. *But not for his daughter, I'll bet.*

At least, not *this* time.

Expelling a weary sigh, she made her way to the front door with her bribe in hand, the scent of cinnamon buoying her mood as she pressed the bell with a rush of confidence. Beau's barking commenced on the other side of the door as she waited.

And waited …

And pressed the bell again.

And *again.*

On the fourth try she huffed out a sigh, lips gumming into a flat line. "Okay, Daddy, have it your way," she muttered. She marched to the fence on the side of the house, shaking her head at the sight of a ridiculously large padlock that made it look like Fort Knox. Her smile crooked to the left. "Nice try, Dr. Doom, but keep in mind I inherited my stubborn streak from you …"

Bending over the padlocked gate, she carefully tossed the cookies over and scaled the fence, her spaghetti-strap, baby-doll top billowing up when she hopped to the other side. Without missing a beat, she scooped the bag up and strode to the sliding doors, halting dead in her tracks. Her jaw dropped at the sight of a wall of plantation shutters spanning the length of the family room, closed tighter than a bloomin' bunker. "Gosh, Daddy, you make hermits look social," she mumbled, wondering how the man managed to have any friends at all. Back ramrod straight, she pounded on the glass for a good thirty seconds to no avail while Beau went crazy.

Along with me.

"Really, God?" she said a bit too loudly, her frustration starting to show as she peered up at the dusky sky. "And why am I doing this again?"

"Because it's His way or the highway, remember?" A voice tinged with humor filtered through the hedge.

"Tess?" Lacey moved closer, trying to peek through. "Is that you?"

"Yep. Enjoying a rare moment of silence since Matt and Nicki took Davey and Spence to the drive-in, and Jack and the twins are fishing on the dock." She paused. "Hate to tell you, but I think your dad may be trying to avoid us by juggling his schedule. Normally he takes Beau fishing on Wednesdays. I discovered *that* when I peeked through the hedge while he was banging around in his shed one afternoon, apparently to retrieve his tackle box. But now it appears he's switched to Thursdays, I'm guessing to avoid me since that's when I'd pop over."

Lacey cocked a hip. "Yeah, well if this keeps up, I'm not above making an appointment with his secretary, so he better watch out."

A chuckle floated through the dense branches. "I have a fresh pitcher of peach tea if you care to wait …"

"That actually sounds wonderful," she said slowly, an idea sparking in her brain. *After all, if Daddy isn't home to make amends to, there's always Cat, right?* "But I'd rather not impose on your rare moment of silence—"

"Lacey, stop, you would not—"

"I'd much rather impose on Cat's …" she said in a rush, lips curling at the silence that ensued. Her smile inched into a grin when a low-throated chuckle floated over the hedge. "Now *that* sounds like a capital idea if ever there was."

"I thought you might agree."

"But don't let her give you any guff, you hear? And if she does, send her up to me."

"Oh, I won't have any problem, trust me. I plan to teach her—all over again—that I'm tougher than her."

Tess laughed. "Borrowing a page from Ben Carmichael's playbook, are you?"

Tugging her ponytail holder from her hair, Lacey chuckled as she secured the bag of cookies to the knob of her father's back door. "More like the whole flippin' book. Say one for me, will you?"

An unladylike snort leaked through the privet. "I think I'd rather say one for Cat—she's gonna need it."

"That she is, Mrs. O.," Lacey quipped with a square of shoulders, "that she is."

"And, Lacey …" Tess's tone halted her halfway over the fence. "I'm so proud of you, sweetheart, I could just bust."

Tears took her by surprise when they burned at the back of her lids, this woman's love and respect meaning more than she would ever know. Gulping the emotion that clogged in her throat, she covered with a cavalier air as she jumped to the ground. "Thanks, Mrs. O., but if busting is involved, I'm hoping it's your pride and not Cat's fist."

Tess's laughter infused her with the strength she needed as she sprinted across Bluff Drive and over the lawn to the shoreline that harbored their docks. Pulse thudding, she scurried down the stone pathway where graceful marsh grasses swayed on either side, whispering in the sea breeze as if urging her on. She slowed as she approached the long wooden ramp to their dock, breathing in the scent of summers past with its sea salt and marsh and the tang of fish in the air. A waning sun hovered over the horizon like royalty, resplendent with ribbons of scarlet and gold that bled over the trees before spilling into the water.

A sea gull scooped high overhead with a loud squawk, drawing her gaze to her father's dock, recently power-washed and stained according to Tess, but seldom used. A familiar malaise settled, as cloying as the stickiness in the humid air. Shaking it off, Lacey silently eased her way down the ramp.

The weathered wood vibrated with the motion of Jack and his sisters clowning around, bobbing up and down as much as her stomach. Playful banter and jests ping-ponged back and forth while their laughter echoed over the water, causing a sharp pang of homesickness to cramp in her chest. Oh, how she longed to be a part of them again, to be an O'Bryen, if only in spirit instead of in name. Another sea gull screeched overhead, swooping back into the sky with the glint of a fish in its beak. In a gentle gust of breeze, resolve suddenly surged in Lacey like the air beneath the gull's wings, causing hope to soar as lofty and high as the bird in the sky. *And I will be*, she decided with a stiff set of her jaw, *if it takes all summer to do it*.

With a firm tug of her cut-offs, she tiptoed down the rickety ramp so Jack and his sisters wouldn't hear. Sprawled barefoot in paint-weathered Adirondack chairs spaced ten feet apart, each bobbed corks in the river amidst chatter and laughter and the occasional pelting of shrimp.

"Uh-oh, looks like somebody's going to be washing my car and making my bed for a week," Jack said with a hard jerk of his rod, rising to his feet to reel in what appeared to be a good-sized fish.

The girls groaned and bobbed their lines all the harder while Jack fought with his usual confident swagger when it came to games or sports, his gloating making her grin. *Jack O'Bryen, nice guy, cocky winner.* Net in hand, he squatted over the edge in faded cutoffs that rode up to reveal powerful thighs. "Face it, ladies, I'm the undisputed king, proving once again that men reign supreme in the sport of fishing." Body taut, he braced his battered Sperrys to haul the catch in, calves bulging with the strain.

"Hey, it's not over till sunset," Cat said, jumping up to fish the same corner as Jack, where a saffron sliver of sun still shimmered over the water. "So don't give me any flack, Jack."

Laughter ringing over the river, Jack stood to show off his catch, bare chest gleaming with sweat while he held it high. "No flack, Catfish," he said with a slow turn, "just deep-down pity 'cause check this bab—" He stopped, eyes flaring in surprise as he lowered his fish, a slow smile sliding across his face. "Hey, Lace, what are you doing here? Come to challenge the King of the Dock?"

Cat spun around so fast, Lacey was surprised she didn't fall in the water, although the scowl on her face was as potent as if she had. Her eyes narrowed to slits. "What's she doing here?"

"Knock it off," Jack said in a quiet voice that pinched Cat's lips in a silent glare.

"Good to see you again, Lace!" Shannon was up and hugging her in no time, her warm embrace helping to take the sting out of Cat's rejection.

"Thanks, Shan." Nodding toward her dad's dock, Lacey managed an off-center smile. "I actually came to see Dr. Doom, but he's obviously avoiding me, so I thought I'd come over to give you guys some trouble."

"Too late," Cat muttered. Posture stiff, she strode over to the storage chest Jack made years ago and tossed her rod in, letting the lid slam with a hard crack. "I'm outta here—"

"Oh, no you're not." Jack grabbed her arm on her way past, grip tight. "This feud's been going on way too long, so it ends here and now, Cat. I cleared the air with Lace, and now it's your turn."

Cat jerked free, chin lashing up as she planted stiff hands on her hips. "No freakin' way. She may have batted those stubby lashes to make you forget how she turned on us, Jack, but not me." She seared Lacey with a sneer. "So why don't you run on home, you little backstabber." Eyes wide in mock sympathy, she tipped her head, hands to her cheeks. "Oh, wait ... you can't because even your own father doesn't want anything to do with you."

Cat's nasty remark cut deep, but Lacey was not about to let anger ruin her chances at making amends with her former best friend, not when she'd made such strides with her brother. "Look, Cat, I'm really sorry— for everything—and I'd like to make it up to you if you'd give me a chance."

"You want to make it up to me?" With a fold of her arms, Cat stepped close with a caustic smile. She waved an arm toward the water. "Then why don't you just take a flying leap into the river right now and hold your breath for a while." She leaned in, wildfire in her eyes. "Say, an hour or two."

"Come on, Cat, leave her alone," Shannon said softly, quietly looping a protective arm to Lacey's waist. "Jack's right—it's time to leave all that bitterness behind and move on."

"Sure, I'll leave it behind—right now." Cat shoved Lacey out of the way and stormed past, halfway up the ramp before Jack caught up with her.

He spun her around. "Looks like somebody needs to cool off." Sweeping her up in his arms, he carried her kicking to the edge of the dock, her shrieks ricocheting off the water. "Grab her shoes, Shan."

"Shannon, *nooooo—!*" Panic edged her sister's cry as she pummeled Jack's chest.

Working her lip, Shannon darted forward to slip Cat's Sperrys off, her giggle nervous as she hugged them to her chest. "Sorry, sis."

"Bon voyage, kiddo." Biceps straining, Jack heaved Cat into the air, clothes and all. Her arms and legs flailed wildly before she hit the water with a loud "*ker-ploosh!*"

Hand to her mouth, Lacey couldn't stop the chuckles that rolled from her lips. "Oh, Jack, I can't believe you did that …"

He turned her way, trouble glinting bright in his eyes as one thick brow jutted high. "Oh, you think this is funny, do you?" Ignoring Cat's tirade from the water, he strolled forward with a wicked smile.

Her eyes spanned wide, palm in the air. "Oh, no—don't you dar—"

He scooped her up so fast she barely had time to squeal.

"Jack, no!" Hands grafted to his neck, she curled her toes tight to secure her own shoes while she screamed, digging her fingernails into his hard-muscled back. Her voice was little more than a screech. "These are brand-new deck shoes …"

"Ooops, sorry." Balancing her with his knee, he clamped her to his torso like a vise, free hand sliding the length of her calf till it locked on her shoe. He peeled it off and lobbed it to Shannon with a chuckle.

Lacey bucked like an 800-lb. marlin on 80-lb. test, thrashing against a chest that felt like rock. "Jack, please, I'm sorry for laughing …"

"Tell that to Cat," he said, his devious chuckle reminding her of all the times he'd hurled her and his sisters in the drink, lording it over them as "King of the Dock." Dislodging her other shoe, he kicked it away from the edge, his whisper warm in her ear. "Sink or swim, Lace. This is your chance to make it right—don't blow it." Her heart stopped when his lips grazed her cheek before she went airborne, the heat of Jack's touch doused by a cold blast of brine.

Lacey surfaced in time to see Cat scale the ladder before Jack flung her back into the river, her body flying over the water in a spastic cartwheel. The grim smile on his face confirmed neither of them would see dry land anytime soon until their feud was put to rest.

Lacey bit back a chuckle. Drowned and buried at the bottom of the, dark, cold Skidaway River. She flipped her wet hair back in a spray of seawater.

Just like my past ...

Cat shot back up in a gush of foam, the outrage in her eyes roiling more than the river. "So help me, Jack, I'm gonna tear into you like you've never seen ..."

He grinned, hands perched low on his thighs. "Gotta get out of the water first, and that ain't happening till you two brats either drown your grievances or each other, so have at it."

"I'll have at it, you jerk," Cat spat, slapping through the water with a strained clench of teeth. "My fist, your face ..."

"Ah-ah-ah ..." Jack reached down to haul the ladder up, locking it out of reach. "I'd conserve energy if I were you, Catfish, 'cause between your stubborn streak and temper, you're gonna need it."

Lacey paddled toward Cat while she bit back a smile, thinking that when it came to stubbornness, that was pretty much the buffalo fish calling the carp fishy.

"Shan!" Cat's voice held a definite plea. "Let the ladder down, *please!*"

Brows knit in sympathy, Shannon squatted at the edge of the dock, sporting the squirm of a smile despite the empathy in her tone. "Gosh, Cat, I really wish I could, but you know what a bully Jack can be. Goodness, I'd be as wet as you if I crossed him."

Jack hunkered alongside Shan and looped an arm to her shoulders, a flash of teeth gleaming white in a bronzed face too darn handsome for his own good. *And* Lacey's. "Obviously the smart twin in the family," he said with a wink in Lacey's direction, earning a tsunami-style dousing when Cat hissed and slashed water their way. His laughter bounced over the waves. "Gosh, Shan, I can't tell if she's mad as a wet hen or drowning, can you?"

Shannon chuckled. "A little of both, I think."

A swear word sizzled the air when Cat kicked away from the dock, arms slicing through the water while she swam for the shore.

"Uh, Shan ..." Tone casual, Jack squinted toward the murky waters of the grassy shore. "Where did Matt see that nest of water moccasins last week?"

Cat's arms rippled still in the water, the pink shadows of dusk settling all around.

"Not sure, but somewhere between our dock and that boulder where the stargazer fish stung you last month, remember?"

"Oh, yeah, that was painful as I recall. I wouldn't be caught dead over there again."

"I'll—show—you—dead," Cat rasped, grinding out another questionable word that bordered on breathless.

Lacey took a quick dive to smother another chuckle, afraid she wouldn't be able to stop. When she surged from the water, Cat was heading her way, obviously in an effort to reach the shore on the *other* side of the dock. Limbs taut, she silently paddled in place as Cat approached.

"Get out of my way," Cat hissed, and in one angry swish of water, it all came rushing back with a slow curve of Lacey's lips. The reason that Catherine Marie O'Bryen had been her best friend from the time they were small. When Lacey had first spotted her on their dock, shrieking at the top of her lungs while she barreled into the river, Lacey knew she liked her. A year younger than Lacey, Cat had been fearless and fun and so full of adventure that Lacey had formed an immediate bond with the twins next door, the three of them as tight as the Three Stooges. And almost as crazy. At least Cat and her. Whether hiding Jack's underwear in the freezer and toads in his bed, or drawing magic marker hearts on his basketball with initials of his latest crush, Cat became Lacey's twin as much as Shan's. As fiery and fervent as Shan was sweet and shy, Cat had a passion for life that rivaled Lacey's own, giving them a special connection. But it had been Lacey—older, bolder, more athletic and well-to-do—who had been the leader, quickly winning Cat's respect.

Lacey issued a silent grunt. *But not anymore ...* "Make me," she said with a feisty dare in her eyes, well aware the only way to deal with Cat O'Bryen was to fight fire with fire. *Or dunk with dunk.* She lunged, taking Cat under with a masterful push that sank them both deep beneath the swirling sea, a watery free-fall that erupted in a tangle of arms, legs, and fingers itching for hanks of hair.

They both launched from the water like cannon fire, water sluicing off their bodies as they wrestled, rabid sea nymphs snarling and twisting in a dance to the death, be it feud or friendship. "How-'bout-I-make-you wish-you-never-came-home, you little witch—" Cat dove for a fistful hair that pulled the pin in Lacey's grenade with a bloodcurdling shriek.

With an unnatural burst of power, Lacey twisted free and locked Cat from behind with an arm to her neck, yanking her flush against her heaving body. "Say it!" she rasped.

"Never!" Cat hardly got it out for her wheezing, fingernails gouging into Lacey's arm.

Lacey tightened her hold with a grin as steely as her will. "Definitely the stupid twin," she said with a grunt, her chuckle harsh against Cat's ear. "When you gonna learn, O'Bryen?" With a tenacity forged in purpose and prayer, she slammed a palm to Cat's head and dunked her again, jerking her back up in a gush of water. "Say it, Catfish. I pump iron at the gym, so I can do this all day." She locked her in another chokehold while Cat coughed up water, barking like a seal with croup—one who had obviously swallowed more water than pride.

"You w-win," she wheezed, hoarse and heaving harder than the air pump for her daddy's white-water raft.

Lacey grinned and tightened her hold. "River swear," she said through clenched teeth, resorting to their childhood version of pinky swear, where the Skidaway became the sacred tonic of truth in which no lie could survive. She smiled at the memory. *And* where fibs and falsehoods were threatened with underwear dunks, icy winter dips, or gagging on raw bait.

"River s-swear ..." It was barely a croak, but it cinched Lacey's title of River Queen, securing Cat's allegiance to do whatever the queen asked.

Exhaling her exhaustion, Lacey released her, swimming around to face a stone-faced Cat. Eyes as cold as the night breeze that nipped at their sodden skin, she looked so young and vulnerable, blonde hair plastered to her head except for a lopsided ponytail as bedraggled as she. Lips tipping in a faint smile, Lacey gently pulled a twig from Cat's hair, her tone laced with regret. "Cat, I'm really sorry I got so rough, but your friendship is too important to me to go on this way."

Cat's voice was a hiss. "Yeah, I saw how important it was when you dumped me for Nicki."

Lacey swallowed hard, well aware she could never tell Cat the truth why she'd turned her back on her after Jack went to college, hanging with Nicki senior year instead of her. She expelled a silent breath and shot a glance at the O'Bryen's dock, which was now deserted, Shan obviously back at the house while Jack silently fished the far bank. The ladder was back down, she noted, and nodded toward it. "Can we talk? Please?"

Mouth pinched tight, Cat swam toward the dock, mounting the ladder without a word while Lacey followed behind. Distancing herself, Cat dropped down on the edge, arms stiff on the wood while she dangled her feet in the dusky water, gaze straight ahead.

Lacey sucked in a fortifying breath and joined her, careful to give Cat her space as she hunkered down a few feet away, uttering a silent prayer while she slipped her legs over the side. "I screwed up," she said quietly, the grief in her words as thick as the guilt that coated her throat. "Big time. Nick moved back, and I was so angry at Daddy, I just wanted to get away." She stared at the water, gaze lost in the sluggish roll of the river. "Hanging out at Nicki's helped me to do that," she said with a lick of her lips, her mouth chapped and dry despite the water lapping around their feet. "What can I say?" She peered at Cat out of the corner of her eye, her expression sheepish. "She was older and more experienced, and I was dazzled by the freedom she had after her mom died, especially when Uncle Cam was too busy to notice we were both running wild."

Cat met her gaze, a touch of hurt in her slitted eyes, tempering the fury somewhat. "We were best friends, Lace," she hissed, the bite in her voice indicating her anger ran deep. "From toddlers to teens, we told each other *everything*, did *everything* together. For crying out loud, in some ways I was closer to you than my own sister." She blinked hard several times, as if to thwart the sheen of tears that welled, tone hard. "Then one day your slut of a cousin rolls in, and suddenly I'm not good enough anymore, and neither was Jack, apparently."

"No!" She reached out to touch Cat's hand, an ache convulsing in her throat when Cat jerked away to lock her arms to her chest. "That's not true," Lacey whispered, desperate to make Cat understand that it wasn't her or Jack who weren't good enough. "If anything, you were too good, Cat, both you and your family. You guys were always so happy and close, it got harder and harder to go back home where my parents fought all the time and Daddy railed on me night and day. So when Nicki moved here ..." Lacey grabbed a long twig from the water, methodically breaking it into tiny pieces. "I saw my chance to get away. Only Nicki was pretty wild as you know, and it wasn't long before I started changing too."

"No joke." Cat snatched her own stick from beneath the dock so fast, Lacey thought she might whack her with it, but she only mimicked Lacey, shredding it into fragments of wood as splintered as their friendship. "You stopped coming around unless Jack was home, which made me feel like dirt, and you never once invited me along."

"*Because* you *were* too good, Cat," Lacey said with a crack in her voice. She gripped Cat's shoulder with shaky fingers, relieved when she didn't pull away. "I didn't like myself very much during that time because my bitterness and rebellion toward my dad sucked me into a black hole where I did things I'm too ashamed to talk about. Every single time Nicki and I went out—the places we went, the people we met—I felt like I was spiraling deeper and deeper into a lifestyle I couldn't stop." She squeezed Cat's shoulder, fingers gently skimming down her friend's arm with an affection that caused tears to sting. "But I could stop you," she whispered, "by not coming around except when Jack was home, so that's what I did." She swallowed the emotion in her throat. "Because I loved you too much, Cat, to take you down with me."

Cat peered up, a wet spark of anger glimmering in red-rimmed eyes. "And what about Jack? I suppose you loved him so much that you left him high and dry, without even a goodbye."

"Yes, as a matter of fact, I did," Lacey said in a rush, her voice no more than a rasp, "I … wasn't cut out to be a pastor's wife, Cat, and Jack deserved better."

"Yeah, Lace, he did—better than turning your back on him without saying goodbye."

"I had no choice," she whispered, her words hoarse with regret. "You know Jack—he would have talked me out of it, and I couldn't let that happen."

Cat turned to face her square on. "And why is that exactly?" she snapped. "Because he wasn't good enough for you?"

The hard plane of Cat's face softened through the blur of moisture Lacey tried to blink away. "No, Cat, because I wasn't good enough for him. Or at least that's what my father told me the night he kicked me out of the house."

The tendons in Cat's throat convulsed. "He ... kicked you out? But ... but I thought you just left on your own ... He told my parents you planned to live with your godmother in San Diego, that you wanted to go to school out there."

Lacey nodded. "That much is true, but only because Daddy convinced me that a pastor didn't need a whore as a wife and he was right." She looked away, unable to face the shadow of sympathy she saw in Cat's eyes because she knew she didn't deserve it. The mournful croon of a dove carried over the water as she stared, the mist on the marsh as foggy as the memories she'd tried so hard to forget. "I ... got involved in things I'm not proud of, Cat ... terrible things I never even told Jack, not the least of which were booze and drugs, so I knew my father was right." A harsh laugh broke from her lips. "Jack deserved better than me," she whispered, "and I knew leaving was the only way to make sure that he got it."

She stared across the river, barely seeing the waves of sea grass that whispered in the breeze. "Besides, I wasn't ready to settle down, and Jack was, at least enough to put a ring on my finger. And to be honest, Cat ..." Her eyelids drifted closed, weighted with remorse so deep, it ached to her very soul. "I was so screwed up in my head and my heart that I wasn't even

sure I could honor a commitment like that." She
exhaled loudly, her chest rising and falling like her
dreams had so long ago. Her gaze lifted to meet Cat's,
the saddest of smiles edging her lips. "So I left."

Cat shook her head. "I'll tell you what, Lacey
Carmichael, you are one messed-up chick."

A smile shadowed Lacey's lips. "*Was* one messed-
up chick, Cat ... and *duh!*" She tweaked the back of
Cat's neck, sidling closer until their thighs almost
touched. "You can thank me now if you want."

Cat scrunched her shoulders, her chuckle tumbling
into the misty air. "Yeah, I guess you're right. I could
have been stuck with some whacked-out sister-in-law
who would have screwed up our family even more than
her freakin' mo—" Her lips suddenly gummed tight, as
if she'd just realized she might upset the balance of an
already tenuous truce.

"'Her freakin'mom'— I know," Lacey whispered,
"go ahead and say it." Her heart cramped just speaking
the words, stunned at how much it still hurt, the damage
her family had done. First her, then her mother, and
then her father, in shutting everyone out. She bit her lip
and looked away, tears pooling against her will. "There
are no words, Cat, to express the sorrow I carry inside
over what my mother and I did to your family, and I
just hope and pray ..." She swallowed hard, the taste of
her regret a bitter bile. "That someday you'll be able to
forgive us because God knows the scars are deep—on
both sides."

Cat's heavy sigh floated into the air, mingling with
the mist. "I know," she said quietly, "but the truth is
your mother didn't act alone, Lacey, no matter how
much blame I wanted to lay at her feet. And trust me, I
laid plenty." She hesitated for a brief moment before
she slowly reached to tug Lacey's hand, drawing her
gaze. "But talking to you tonight ... clearing the air,
well, it's suddenly made me realize just how much

better it feels to forgive than to hate." She squeezed
Lacey's palm, affection softening her face for the very
first time. "So, yeah, I forgive you, I guess ..." Smile
lines crinkled at the edge of her eyes. "If you'll forgive
me for being such a bullhead."

Lacey laughed and hooked an arm around her
shoulder. "No, way, Catfish—that's one of the things I
always liked best about you—your spit and fire.
Figuratively, that is, not literally."

"Lace?"

Lacey slid her a sideways smile. "Yeah?"

Cat's shoulders rose and fell with a heavy sigh. "I'm
really sorry about your mom and the part my dad
played in it all." She looked away, her gaze moist as
she stared out over the water. "Somehow it's easier to
forgive you and your mom because you both came from
a pretty dysfunctional household, but Dad ..." Moisture
pooled in her eyes, her face sorrowful in the purple
hues of sunset. "He knew better. The man had it all—a
great wife, a great family, and a church that revered and
respected him, but it wasn't enough." Bitterness edged
her tone like the shadows of dusk edged the night. "*We*
weren't enough, and apparently neither was God, and to
be honest, Lace, I don't know if I'll ever be able to
forgive him for that."

"Yes, you will," Lacey said quietly, the assurance in
her tone as solid as the faith in her heart. She gently
tucked her head against Cat's, the two of them lost in
the lazy loll of the river. "Because if God can change a
train wreck like me to the point where I'm actually
reaching out to a man who not only wants nothing to do
with me, but whom I've bucked and despised most of
my life, then he can change you."

Cat glanced at her, a touch of awe in her tone. "Shut
the front door, you really have changed, haven't you?"

Laughter spilled from Lacey's lips as she pulled Cat
into a side hug. "In my heart, Catfish, not in my

aspirations. I still have a competitive streak a mile long, which is why *I'm* Queen of the River and you're not."

"So … I assume you two are done making amends?" Jack ambled down the ramp with a lazy grin on his face, his cocky air more than evident. He stopped behind them to dangle his prize catches over their heads, the scent of fish and man wrinkling Lacey's nose.

Both Lacey and Cat ducked to the side to avoid the drip of his heavy stringer. "Very impressive, Brye, but I'm not sure who smells worse—you or the fish. I suggest a shower."

He chuckled. "Right after I clean these babies." He strolled over to the cleaning station he'd built and tossed them on top before shuffling back, hands butted low on his hips. "So who won? The loser can help me gut and clean."

The girls exchanged glances. "Deal. But we're not done yet, are we, Cat?"

A slow grin slid across Cat's lips when she obviously spied the devil in Lacey's eyes. "Nope."

Lacey nodded toward the rope swing where she and Cat had settled so many competitions over the years with the farthest drop. "Despite beating her soundly, your very stubborn sister has challenged my supreme authority as queen, so the rope shall decide." Lacey raised her hand and Cat followed suit. "Here, help us up so I can shut her up once and for all."

A husky chuckle rumbled from Jack's throat as he flashed a smile, arms extended. "Cat's had eight years of practice, Lace—you sure you know what you're doing?"

"Oh, yeah," she said with a smug look, clamping onto his hand at the same time as Cat, Jack's muscles taut as he drew them both up.

"Good, because this I gotta—"

Kerplunk! Jack hit the water like a 200-lb. cannonball, Sperrys and all, a thunderous fountain spray dousing the girls and the deck. Adrenaline pumping from their coordinated yank, Lacey and Cat high-fived, their laughter bouncing off the other shore when Jack finally popped back up, a soppy scowl on his face. "You tricked me," he said, spitting water like a rusty spigot.

"We prefer to think of it as helping you to clean up, Jack," Lacey said with a sweet smile.

"Not me." Cat shot a smirk, hip cocked while she folded her arms. "It's called payback, Flack."

"At least I took *your* shoes off," he groused, slamming a wave of water at them with the slash of his hand.

They jumped back with a giggle, turning to head toward the ramp. "Hey, I'm starved," Cat said, finger-combing her hair, "and there was leftover apple cobbler as I recall."

"Ooooo, with ice cream, I hope." Lacey bent over to fluff out her hair.

The ladder groaned with Jack's weight. "Hey—where you guys going? I thought you weren't done."

Halfway to the ramp, Lacey hooked an arm over Cat's shoulder before tossing Jack a cheeky grin. "Nope, we're done," she said, her grin spanning wide at the sorry sight of Jack's sopping Dockers puddling his Sperrys. She couldn't resist a wink. "For *now*."

CHAPTER TWENTY-FIVE

"*F*ine—have it your way." Tess's smile was long gone as she sipped a peach iced tea in the moonlit shadows of her patio, waiting for Ben to get home while darkness shrouded both of their houses. She peeked at her watch, mouth skewed in a dry smile. Almost eleven-thirty—another late night for the doctor, apparently, something that was becoming a habit of late. Which just confirmed what Tess suspected all along.

Dr. Doom is avoiding us.

If he came home at all the night Lacey had brought the cookies, it had been too late for his daughter, who had salvaged the evening nonetheless with reconciliation between her and Cat. But now a week later, on a night he *usually* returned by eight after fishing with Beau, he was nowhere to be found. In fact, she hadn't seen squat of Ben Carmichael for over two weeks now, and after five chats or dinners where she actually *thought* they'd forged some kind of friendship, it kind of ticked her off. So if it took sleeping out on her patio till dawn to tell him what she wanted to tell him, Tess intended to wait him out.

The stakes were too high.

Two down, one to go, she thought with a tight smile, resting her head on the back of her cushy chair. Lacey was on speaking terms with both Jack and Cat now, and the only holdout was her father. Tess's smile went flat. Of course, in order to speak, one has to be present …

A shaft of light suddenly lit up the sky over Ben's hedge like the dawn of a new day, and given the late hour, not too off the mark. The slider door squealed open, and Tess heard Beau whine and bolt toward the back of the yard, most likely in search of a rabbit, before the door closed again. Lumbering up from her chair, she reached for a plastic bag that contained Tupperware with brownies along with two pieces of bacon for Beau. A yawn escaped as she ambled to the back of her yard, recalling the brand-new shiny padlock she discovered on Ben's front gate just last week, denying her usual access.

Real subtle, Carmichael.

"As if a padlock is going to keep me away," she muttered, tying the bag to her belt before inching her body through a small opening she'd discovered on her side, hidden behind a massive lilac bush on Ben's. Wincing from the scrape of the branches, she carefully crawled through, chuckling at Beau's delirious reception. Quivering on his hind legs with a pitiful squeal, he promptly sat. "You are such a cute watchdog," she said, fishing the bacon from the bag to toss it his way, "even if you can be bribed."

With a quick brush of leaves and twigs from her blouse, she marched to Ben's back door and knocked, waiting several moments before she opened the slider and called inside. "Ben? It's me—Tess. Can I come in?"

No answer.

She heard a sound from either down the hallway or in the kitchen and called again, to no avail. Stepping inside, she closed the door and paused in the family room, admiring as always, the sleek white leather sectional against the rich teak floor. "Ben?" she said again, trailing a palm along the smooth surface of the polished stone sofa table, a smile surfacing at how far their friendship had progressed in five weeks. She'd managed to coax him into dinner or dessert on her patio or his several times, where they'd chatted and laughed under the stars on those rare nights the kids were gone. Once she'd even talked him into a game of Scrabble at his kitchen bar, sipping lemonade and sparring like siblings over the ineligibility of certain words.

Untying the bag from her belt, she moved toward the kitchen, assuming that's where he was. She couldn't help smiling when her gaze lighted on the ridiculously overstuffed and totally "guy" recliner that seemed so out of place—the one Ben butted heads over with his designer. *Absolute proof you can take the man out of the cave, but you can't take the cave out of the man.*

She peeked into the kitchen. "Ben?"

"Tess?"

She spun around, hand to her chest while Ben stood in the hallway in tight faded jeans, worn Topsiders, and a polo. His perennial tan and windswept dark hair implied he'd spent the afternoon and evening on his boat. Face in a scrunch, he approached, surprise etched into every pore on his face. "What are you doing here?"

"Sorry to come over so late," she said with a sheepish smile, "but I had something important I needed to ask you ..." She paused to catch her breath before forging on, the pinch of his brow not a good sign. "And I baked double fudge cheese swirl brownies too, so I figured you'd want some."

She removed the container from the bag and held it out, the absence of his smile tightening her gut. "I remember how much you enjoyed them last time," she said in a rush, somewhat unnerved by his lack of response, "so I thought I'd bring you a treat while they're still fresh." Hoping to tempt him, she held the container to his nose while she swiped a glance at her watch. "Of course the statute of limitations may be up on fresh ..."

"A treat," he said flatly, a ghost of a smile flickering on his face as he reached for the brownies. "You mean a bribe, don't you?" He popped one in his mouth and carried the container into the kitchen.

"Maybe," she said, following behind. "I suppose I do have a favor of sorts."

"Of course you do." He set the brownies on the black granite breakfast bar and strolled to the fridge, retrieving a carton of milk followed by two glasses from a sleek ebony cabinet. Easing onto a black leather and chrome barstool, he placed the items on the bar with a wry twist of lips. "But the padlock stays." He pushed one of the glasses toward her with a dry smile. "Milk?"

"Ah, yes, the padlock," she said with an off-center grin, joining him at the bar while he poured her a glass of milk. "Nothing subtle about you, that's for sure." She filched one of his brownies, shimmying onto a stool to face him. "If you wanted me to stay away, Ben, you could have just come out and said so."

"I have," he said with a droll smile, "on a number of occasions as I recall." He watched her while he chewed, that annoyingly tolerant look on his face as if she were one of his patients. "Would it have worked this time?"

She hiked her chin. "No, but it wouldn't have hurt my feelings as much as a padlock."

His face sobered as he shoved the brownie plate away, hazel eyes piercing her straight through. "What do you want, Tess?" he said quietly.

Brushing brownie crumbs off her hands, she avoided his eyes while she drew in a breath to ready for battle, then met his serious gaze with one of her own. Her chin tipped up in challenge. "It'd mean a lot to me if you'd show up for the Camp Hope fundraiser next week."

"Why?" The hazel eyes never blinked, just stared at her in that unnerving way he had.

"Because it means a lot to me." She hesitated. "And … to Lacey," she said quickly, taking advantage of the trace of affection she saw in his eyes. "She's very involved at Camp Hope, you see, and it could be an icebreaker, Ben."

His chest expanded as he kneaded the bridge of his nose, his voice tired. "I'm not looking to break any ice, Tess. My life is fine just as it is."

"That's a lie." Her mouth thinned considerably. "Admit it, Ben, you're a coward. A fearless pioneer in medicine, but a knock-kneed little boy when it comes to opening up and sharing your feelings."

"You know nothing about my feelings," he bit back, all fatigue apparently lost in a sudden spark of anger that ignited a bit of her own.

"Yeah, nobody does—that's the point." Her eyes shuttered closed as she blew out her frustration, reining in her temper with a deep inhale. "Look, I'm sorry," she whispered, "I just worry you'll end up all alone—"

"Excuse me—Ben?" A thirty-something blonde in a bikini stood in the doorway, blue eyes assessing Tess head to toe before they landed on Ben with a sweet smile. "I can't find the shampoo."

"Did you check the linen closet in the master bath?"

"No, but I will," she said with a flash of perfect white teeth. Her glance landed on Tess once again with a curious smile, silence lingering …

Ben gave a gruff clear of his throat. "Uh, Cynthia, this is my neighbor, Tess O'Bryen." Smile stiff, his gaze flicked back to Tess, his unease palpable when his eyes reconnected with hers. "My colleague, Dr. Cynthia Andreyuk."

"Hello." Tone as cool as her body, given the goose bumps that covered more skin than her suit, Dr. Barbie offered the perfunctory nod, her smile as plastic as the doll she favored.

"Hi." Tess lifted a palm, suddenly feeling way overdressed. She tucked a loose strand of hair over her ear in nervous habit before she whisked the brownie container from the counter. "Brownie?"

A shadow of a smile played on the woman's lips. "No, thank you—the shower calls." She did an about face in the skimpiest swimsuit Tess had ever seen, tossing a smile over a beautifully sculpted shoulder. "Nice to meet you, Tess." Her eyes flicked to Ben's and held. "I won't be long."

Tess's jaw sagged as she watched her sashay through the family room and back down the hall, barely able to tear her gaze from the hypnotic sway of the woman's hips. She didn't bother to hide the gape of her mouth when she turned to Ben with a spike of her brow. "Well now, I can see my worries of your loneliness are completely unfounded." She slid off her stool as heat steamed her cheeks. "Enjoy the brownies, Ben." Spinning on her heel, she darted from the room.

"Tess, wait—"

Ignoring Ben's voice, she fisted the handle of the slider and opened the door, allowing a quick scrub of Beau's snout before letting him in and escaping outside. The salty scent of the marsh hit her full force, its distinct sulphur smell sharper than usual. Not too far off, the hoot of an owl carried through the thick, humid night, a distant and eerie call, but probing nonetheless.

Who-who-who ... made a fool of themselves tonight?

"Uh, that would be me," Tess muttered, tromping through Ben's backyard like the obnoxious and nosy neighbor she'd just proven herself to be. "What in the world was I thinking?" She grunted, slapping at the limbs from the hedge hole while she bulldozed through, the sting of the branches hurting a lot less than her pride. "Well, apparently I wasn't."

"Ouch!" She froze on the other side, sucking air through clenched teeth when she felt a sticky wetness slither her arm. "Great, just great!" she hissed, the coppery smell of her own blood making her mad. With a rare show of temper she hauled off and kicked a mole hole, finally stomping on it like a wild woman until she was completely out of breath. A weak moan withered on her lips as she put her hands to her eyes, shoulders hunched and spirits as bleak as the bare spot beneath her feet. "For crying out loud, what is wrong with me?"

You're jealous.

The thought, so utterly absurd, struck with a blow that could have drawn more blood than the stupid hedge. "No," she whispered, shaking her head with almost as much force as when she'd bludgeoned the poor lawn. "That's ridiculous. Ben is nothing more than a neighbor and friend."

Really?

Her eyelids slammed closed, and instantly her chest cramped at the image of an overstuffed bikini on a body ten years younger than hers. "No!" Her eyes popped open to a moonlit yard riddled with as many holes as her good intentions appeared to be. "I'm doing this because it's the right thing to do, for Lacey's family and mine," she whispered, the sound harsh to her own ears, "and to restore a friendship that was once very dear, and that's the *only* reason."

Of course it was.

Until tonight. When one overdeveloped Barbie doll pranced into Ben's kitchen like she owned it.

And him.

A low groan rattled from Tess's throat while she stumbled toward her patio, feeling every single ache of middle age as she sank into the wrought-iron chair. "God, forgive me," she whispered, more ashamed of her feelings than her air-headed behavior. Ben Carmichael was off-limits as a man, and she knew that.

Other than the fact he was nice to look at—if you ignored the scowl—never once had she entertained the thought of anything more. Only friendship.

Or so she thought.

She put her head in hands. *Lord, I am such an idiot, and a blind one at that ...*

The realization that she might suddenly be attracted to him—possessive of him—throbbed more than the gashes in her arm. Sucking in a sharp rush of air, Tess made an iron-clad decision that tightened her jaw along with her resolve. He wanted privacy? Fine. She'd give him all the privacy he and Dr. Barbie could handle, with an emotional padlock of her own. From now on, any communication between Ben Carmichael and her would begin from *his* side of the hedge, while she put up a hedge of her own—through prayer.

Prayer that he and Lacey would reconcile. Prayer that both families would finally be healed. And prayer that she could be the supportive neighbor and friend that Ben Carmichael desperately needed.

And nothing more.

Because despite her deep faith in God, a true passion for prayer, and a belief in the Bible that went beyond bone deep ...

This was one time when "love thy neighbor" was just not going to work.

CHAPTER TWENTY-SIX

"**Y**ou sure you want to do this?"

A ball of nerves dipped in Lacey's throat as she stared straight ahead at the Isle of Hope Marina, gaze fixed on the third cabin cruiser moored on the second dock. "Yes," she said quietly, the tremor in her tone betraying her confidence. "I figure since Daddy has gone to so much trouble to avoid me, the least I can do is go to some trouble to confront him, right?" Nicki's hand grasped hers across the console of her car and squeezed, and Lacey slid her a tentative glance, grateful for the support. "Besides, when I stow away in his cuddy cabin, he won't be able to ignore me, right?"

Nicki chuckled. She offered another press of Lacey's hand before she propped both arms and chin on the steering wheel, peering at Lacey's father's twenty-eight-foot Formula with the cobalt blue bimini. "No, but he can toss your butt over the side, and if it's all the same to you—that's my favorite pair of white capris you're wearing."

Lacey grinned, glancing down at the form-fitting, cropped-ankle capris that were as light as air. She was pretty darn sure she wouldn't be giving them back anytime soon because now they were her favorites too. Somehow the thought and the grin eased the muscles at the back of her neck, allowing her orange crop top to expand in and out in a liberating sigh. She tweaked Nicki's waist, amazed at just how much it meant—and helped—to have her cousin's support. A calm suddenly buoyed her with hope like the colorful flags billowing in the breeze, their tall masts not unlike arms lifted to heaven while the sailboats bobbed and swayed on the water.

"You know, Lace," Nicki continued, eyeing the hodge-podge armada of sailboats, yachts, houseboats, and cabin cruisers, "this may not be the best spot for a truce."

Lacey peered at her cousin. "What do you mean?"

The barest twitch of Nicki's lips defied the sobriety of her tone. "Well, Robert Mitchum and Gregory Peck didn't do too well here in '62, as you recall." She gave Lacey a sassy smile. "What was the name of that movie again?"

Lacey's mouth hooked to the right. "Cape Fear, you little brat, and if you're implying the title is prophetic because the movie was filmed where the marina now stands, you're dead wrong. Because we both know the good guy wins in the end."

"You're right, he does," Nicki whispered, a glaze of moisture glimmering in her eyes. "In case I haven't told you lately, I'm proud of you, Lace. It's not easy to forgive and forget like you're trying to do with your dad."

Heat bruised Lacey's cheeks as she slung the strap of her sack purse over her shoulder and grabbed the container of monster cookies she'd baked per Tess's recipe. "He won't be able to resist them," she'd insisted, but Lacey had her doubts.

"Haven't accomplished anything yet, Nick," she said with a shaky sigh, "because it's Daddy who has to forgive and forget, remember? For me turning my back on him like I did." She opened the passenger door and slid a leg out, unwilling to take any credit for actions fueled only by the grace of God. "So any credit belongs to God, not me, since I'm not even sure I've let my own bitterness go."

"Maybe not, but you will." Nicki turned the key, and her trusty Toyota rattled to life. "You sure you don't need me to pick you up? It's not a problem, you know."

"Nope." Lacey bounced up and leaned in with a smile, hand poised on the door. "I'm taking the optimistic approach and assuming Daddy will drive me home *after* we stuff ourselves with Oreo Overloads to celebrate our new relationship."

Nicki's eyes softened despite the crook of her smile. "Okay, sweetie. Well, you know I got you covered. Bless up, girl!"

"Thanks, Cuz—countin' on it." Lacey closed the car door and tapped her palm twice on the window before Nicki eased out of the parking spot and pulled away. The brief double blip of her horn reminded her that God did, indeed, have her covered. Bolstering her confidence with a deep draw of fishy air, Lacey marched down the ramp to the second dock. Chin high, she made her way to her father's boat, which was all gassed up and ready to go according to Mark, the seventeen-year-old hottie who worked the dock pumps after school. A tiny smile crept across Lacey's lips as she sent him a wave, trying to ignore the heat creeping up her neck over flirting with a kid nine years her junior. The one who promised to let her know the next time her father called to have his boat ready and waiting.

Almost six, she thought with a glance at her watch, and stealing a furtive look at the parking lot, she gingerly stepped over the side of her father's 28-ft. Formula 280 Sun Sport, wasting no time slipping into the cabin below. Complete with dining table, microwave, toilet and sink, the spacious cuddy cabin had everything she needed to stow away, including a porthole to ensure they were far enough out before she revealed her presence.

It wasn't long before she heard the grind of tires on gravel in the paved parking lot, and peeking out the window, she spied her dad's black Range Rover glinting in the sun. Her heart stalled when only he and Beau got out of the car. Sadly, she'd almost hoped he wouldn't be alone—one of his fishing buddies or the rare date—acting as a buffer to guarantee a civil response. A shaky breath wavered from her lips as she pulled the cabin door closed like before, and tucking herself out of sight in a dark corner, she waited.

"Calm down, bud, I'm just as anxious to get on the water as you," her father said with a chuckle, the sound of Beau's excited whimpers followed by a gentle rock of the boat when they boarded. Storage doors opened and closed several times accompanied by the sound of her dad's footsteps above as he untied the boat. The smell of exhaust soon infiltrated the cabin when the engine roared, the hull rumbling so hard it was a contest over who was shaking more—her or the Formula. Eyes closed, she felt the sensation of gliding through the no-wake zone, her stomach tightening when the vessel cleared and picked up speed. Between her nerves and the fumes, nausea began to rise and although she'd planned to wait till they were too far out for her dad to turn around, bile clotted in her throat, making her dizzy.

Peering out the porthole, she saw the O'Bryen's dock zip by and put a hand to her mouth to stifle a heave. "It's now or never," she muttered, and opening the cabin door, she gulped in the sea air to clear the fog from her brain and the fear from her throat. Beau spotted her first, his delighted squeal making her wish she'd brought bacon along with the cookies. With her Tupperware in hand, she crept out slowly, peeking up the galley steps.

Face averted starboard, her father's handsome profile tripled her pulse. Sable hair streaked with silver ruffled in the wind while he stood, body relaxed in casual stance, both hands on the wheel. His loose polo flapped wildly against his broad chest, and all at once Lacey's heart cramped at the image of a nine-year-old girl leaning against that very chest, helping to steer during one of those rare times Daddy acted like he cared.

Beau danced on his hind legs and barked several times, and the second Daddy glanced her way, his face cemented to stone.

She slowly ascended the steps, purse over her shoulder and Tupperware offered in truce. "Hi Daddy." She gave a sheepish shrug. "I brought monster cookies," she said, hoping against hope that the man would at least crack a smile.

He didn't. "What are you doing here?" he said in the same deadly voice he'd used when she was a child. "And who let you on?"

She swallowed hard, not likely to throw sweet Mark under the bus. "I thought we could talk."

His jaw calcified further as he wrenched the wheel to the left, banking the boat so fast, it slammed Lacey against the side. The cookie container went flying, crashing open onto the carpeted fiberglass deck. Before Lacey could even breathe, Beau pounced on the scattered cookies, tail wagging like it was the Purina lottery. Her father swore, and Lacey winced. For all his faults, her father had never been a profane man unless she'd pushed too far. He jerked the throttle back to neutral, and the high plane of the boat crashed back to the water, hull slinking into the river in a slow, ominous glide, as if plunging into quicksand.

Like her hope …

"Beau, no!" With a firm yank of Beau's collar, her father dragged the dog back, pushing past Lacey in an effort to put him into the cabin. He slammed the door closed and turned, the gray pallor of his face not a good sign. "I want every solitary crumb picked up—*now*—before we get back to the marina." Without another word he shoved by, bumping her arm on his way to the wheel.

Few people knew Ben Carmichael had a temper because he always hid it so well. Except with Lacey and her mom, who somehow always managed to ignite it. And true to form, her Dad's temper had always lit hers as well. *Like now*, unleashing a once-familiar spark of rebellion, which was tempered—thank God—by her faith. But it was more than enough to put fire in her eyes and grit in her bones. Snatching the Tupperware, she slammed every cookie and crumb back in, her eyes scorching his. "I'll pick them up," she said while he glared right back, hand poised on the throttle as if waiting till she was through, "but you need to know, Daddy, that I have no intention of leaving this boat until we talk."

"You had your chance to talk." He restarted the engine with a harsh grind before pushing the throttle forward, "when I begged you to return my calls after your mother died, my letters, my emails." Anger chiseled his profile while he stared straight ahead, aiming for the marina. "You made your choice then, kiddo, and I have nothing more to say."

"Yeah? Well, I have plenty to say to you." The temper she'd inherited flashed like a Fourth of July finale before she doused it, forcing it to sizzle away. Gorging her lungs with a deep swell of air, she clutched the cookies to her chest, desperate to contain the emotions that itched to explode. The same rebellious emotions that had once been, for her, as common as air. "Daddy, I'm sorry for whatever I did to make you so angry, but I'm trying to make amends here, to apologize—"

With a sharp jerk of the throttle, he cut the engine and spun to face her, the deadly calm of his voice belied by the clench of his jaw. "I don't *want* your apology, Lacey," he whispered, "I *want* you to leave me alone."

Temper threaded thin, she struggled to contain it, a fragile fiber of faith holding her back. "Daddy, please ..." She moved in close to lay a trembling hand to his arm, "I beg you—give me a chance ..."

"Like you gave me?" His gaze chilled her to the bone despite the warmth of the summer night. Blasting out a noisy exhale, he dislodged her hand when he bowed his head to knead the bridge of his nose. "No, we've done just fine without each other all of these years, and I have no intention of going back to a life where you give me nothing but trouble."

"But I'm not here to give you trouble!" she shouted, "I'm here to give you love!"

His head lashed up. "You're giving me trouble *now*, forcing something that doesn't exist and never did." He angled a brow. "I'm the 'demon father,' remember? The 'spawn of Satan you were going to hate till the day you died.'"

She swallowed hard, the vile sting of her own words condemning her on the spot. "I didn't mean that," she whispered, knowing full well she did at the time.

"Whether you did or not, the fact remains that you and I are too combustible to ever get along, too damaged to heal the scars both of us have inflicted, and I have no stomach to go there again." He turned the ignition and lanced her with a cold stare. "So I'm asking you nicely once and for all, Lacey, to let it go and leave me alone."

She blinked, eyes dry sockets of shock while she stared, hardly able to believe he was rejecting her all over again. Hurt swelled like a river of poison swarming its banks, drowning any reason or restraint. "What kind of monster are you?" she whispered, wanting to wound him like he had wounded her. "A heartless shell of a man who turns his own flesh and blood away!" He seemed to wince before his eyelids briefly closed, as if her own anger had sapped all of his, but she was too far gone to stop. "Why did even you marry my mother, then?" she shouted, her voice as raw as her heart, "only to ruin her life and mine along with it?"

The twitch of his cheek told her she'd struck pay dirt, the mother lode of guilt, apparently, over his failure as a father, a husband, a man. Even so, his gaze remained fixed on the marina a mere mile away as he steered the boat forward.

"Tell me!" she shrieked, shaking his arm. But he ignored her, the tight pinch of his mouth telling her he had no intention of giving her anything at all, not even the courtesy of an answer.

Bitterness buried deep rose like bile while the pain of her past sparked tears in her eyes. Well, he may have gotten away with it for the last twenty-six years, but not anymore. Hurling the container aside, she latched onto his arm like before, only this time she jerked it hard, a rare swear word hissing from her lips. "I want to know why! Why you married my mother if you didn't love her?"

"I *did* love her," he shouted. He flung her hand away before he gripped the wheel again, slamming the throttle wide open.

And then it hit her—as hard and biting as the wind that slapped at her face, paralyzing her with an ache so brutal, the air was sucked from her lungs.

It wasn't Mom. It was me ... She sagged against the wide captain's seat, her eyelids flickering closed from the rawest pain she'd ever known. He didn't just reject her, she'd been a burden he'd never wanted, the poison that had destroyed his marriage. Somewhere a seagull screeched over the rush of the wind and the roar of the

Formula, and a scream of her own rose within. A primal cry from a little girl who only wanted her daddy to love her.

Lids snapping up, she slashed her hair from her face with eyes blazing. "It was me, wasn't it?" She stared, moisture welling against her will. "I was the one you hated, not Mom."

"No!" He jerked the boat to a stop so abruptly, she stumbled against the captain's seat, fingers digging in while both the boat—and her life—tilted off-center. He was breathing hard, gouging his hair like he used to before his temper would snap. Only this time, the anger in his eyes had given way to an anguish she'd never seen in her father before. "I didn't hate you!"

"Well, you sure didn't love me."

"I tried!" he shouted, sweat slick on his brow as he gouged at his temple.

"Yeah? Well, tell me when, Daddy, *please.*" Her tone bled with sarcasm, fists clenched so hard, she thought her knuckles would crack. Leaning in, she took full advantage of the regret she saw in his eyes. "When the O'Bryens were around? Because I sure don't remember unless there were people to impress."

"That's a lie!"

"No, *you* were the lie!" she cried. "Pretending to be a father when you were nothing but a stranger."

"You weren't easy to love."

"How would you know? You never even tried."

"And this is why!" he shouted, the gorge of blood in his cheeks evidence she'd finally tripped his temper. He gouged shaky fingers through his hair as a dangerous tic pulsed at his temple. "From little on, you've been nothing but grief."

"Then why did you even have me?" she shrieked, striking the seat with her fist.

"Because you were a mistake!" Eyes wild, he slammed his hand on the wheel, his scream renting the air as much as her soul. Fury scorched his face scarlet while words she had goaded spewed in a violent hiss, his spittle striking like a blow to her chest. "A med student with a bright future, tricked by a girlfriend who gets knocked up with a kid I wasn't even sure was mine!" He wheeled around, fumbling with the ignition switch, grinding it as savagely as he had just attacked his only daughter.

A daughter who now stood welded to the carpet of the fiberglass floor, too paralyzed to move.

A mistake. That's all she'd ever been. No matter how hard she had tried to please him, she never could. Her ribcage convulsed in pain. Nor ever would.

Heart bleeding, she watched with a glazed stare while he hunched over the wheel with a hand to his eyes. "I'm sorry," he whispered, voice gruff with remorse, "I never meant to say that ..."

No, never meant to say it.

Never meant to marry her mother.

Never meant to forget the biggest mistake of his life.

Her body was numb while dizziness buzzed in her brain and all she wanted to do was flee, to get as far away from Ben Carmichael as she possibly could. Dazed with pain, she absently zipped her purse and moved toward the back of the boat like a sleepwalker, vaguely aware of a voice now edged with fear.

"Lacey, *no!*"

But she didn't listen. Stepping over the gate to the platform, she leapt into the water, the glug of her descent drowning out her father's panicked cry. The Skidaway River swirled around her, enveloping her with warmth like her father's arms never could. *No, not my father. A stranger.* She surfaced in a gush of saltwater with a dull pain in her chest, and ignoring his frantic shouts, she slashed through the waves in a fury, seawater flushing the tears from her eyes. The rumble of his engine and hoarse pleas drew near, but she shut them out as tightly as she planned to shut him out of her life.

"Lacey, wait!"

Wading wildly through the shallows, she stumbled onto the shore, breaking into a dead run. The marshy grass lashed at her legs like needles while her body heaved with breaths as fractured as her heart. Behind her, her father called over and over, panic and pain bleeding into his cries, but she refused to spare even a glance.

"Lacey, come back—*please!*"

But the hurt inside told her she couldn't, wouldn't.

Ever again.

CHAPTER TWENTY-SEVEN

*D*usk was Jack O'Bryen's favorite time of day, especially when he could fish all alone on the dock, his mind free from the clutter of work. He sailed a cast across the rippling water with a quirk of his lips. Not that working with kids at Memorial was "work," but there was a tranquility he craved that came only from the sound of water lapping the shore or the faraway chirp of an osprey sailing overhead. Somehow the indigo glow of the water against a scarlet sky always seemed to calm him like few things ever could, willowy grasses swaying and shushing his problems away with a sea-scented breeze. Sperrys firmly planted on the far edge of their dock, he reeled in and cast again, his slow exhale in quiet rhythm with his line as it gracefully looped over the water.

Problems? What problems? He was a twenty-nine-year-old pediatrician poised on the threshold of a lucrative career in the practice of his choice at a hospital he loved. He was dating the prettiest nurse at Memorial and had the day off. What more could he want?

Lacey Carmichael, maybe?

The thought swallowed his good mood as quickly as a fish swallowed his lure, spitting it out before Jack could even reel him in. Expelling a weighty sigh, he ambled over to sink into one of the Adirondack chairs, freshly sanded and painted per his mother's honey-do list. His toss of the line back into the water was lackluster at best, kind of like his moods tended to be whenever his thoughts strayed to Lacey.

Fishing rod limp in his hand, he leaned back and closed his eyes, succumbing to the temptation to dwell on the woman who had slowly become his best friend all over again, like years ago, before they'd fallen in love. His lips cocked to the right. Yeah, only for him, the falling in love part was still a hazard, buried deep to keep Lacey from running away, obviously petrified she might be leading him on. She'd made it more than clear that friendship was all she wanted, and with Chase in the picture, that pretty much sealed the deal. So, friends it would be.

Because when it came to Lacey Carmichael, he'd take any crumbs he could get.

Mouth clamped, Jack opened his eyes to crank in his line, determined to purge Lacey from his thoughts, at least for the moment, to better enjoy the peace of water and sky. Focusing on fishing, he changed to his favorite bait, rigging his line with shrimp and popping cork before he recast and settled back in his chair. The river seemed almost glasslike, melding into sunset with a hazy layer of fog that slowly rolled over the water, obscuring the faint silhouette of trees on the other shore. The shadows of dusk enveloped him with its familiar peace while the mournful wail of a loon filled the night. A sad smile lighted on his lips as he recalled his mother's explanation when he was small, that the loon was calling for its mate, "I'm here—where are you?" The memory coaxed Jack's eyes closed once again while he listened for the return cry. "I'm far away—come find me."

Far away.

Just like Lacey.

And Jack would give anything to find her again.

He sat up at the ripple of a splash, brows knit when he didn't feel a tug on his line. It sounded again, and he turned to squint through the fog, something sloshing down the shore.

"Jack?" It was no more than a rasp, a voice so out of breath that Jack had no idea who it was until a dark silhouette slowly emerged through the haze.

"Lacey?" He shot to his feet, rod and reel clattering onto the dock as he blinked in shock, finally bolting down the ramp to meet her on the shore. With a tight clasp, he held her at arm's length to make sure she was okay as he took in her sopping clothes and matted hair. "What on earth happened?" he asked, the hitch of air in his chest cracking his voice.

"Oh, J-Jack …" With one violent heave, she fell into his arms and began to sob, her broken words slicing through him as if her pain were his very own. "D-Daddy and I h-had an awful f-fight, so I j-jumped off his b-boat …"

His arms swallowed her up, clutching her so closely her wet clothing bled into his, along with her pain. "Shhh … it's gonna be okay, Lace," he whispered, palm gently massaging her sodden back. He pulled away to rub her arms, ducking to peer into eyes swimming with both tears and sorrow. "Are you cold? Because we can run up to the house if you need to chang—"

She shook her head hard, body shivering in his arms. "No, Jack, please—can we just t-talk on the d-dock … like we used t-to?"

Like we used to.

Love surged in his chest as he pressed a kiss to her hair, his voice and touch tender. "Sure, Lace. Come on—I have an old blanket we can wrap you up in, okay?"

She nodded, and without another word, he swept her up in his arms, finally depositing her in his Adirondack chair, gut churning over what she'd gone through tonight. Squatting to briskly rub both of her arms, he assessed her with a tender smile. "Are you hurt anywhere—scrapes, scratches, anything that needs immediate attention?"

"Just my heart," she whispered, her wobbly smile betrayed by a fresh sheen of tears.

He pressed a soft kiss to her cold nose. "Well, you're in luck, Miss Carmichael, because the doctor is in, and he's all yours for the night." Jumping up, he fetched the old picnic quilt from the storage closet, then grabbed one of the bottled waters he'd brought, suddenly noticing the slight chill in the air. "You sure you don't want to get into some dry clothes first?" He bent to carefully tuck the blanket around her. "It's pretty cool tonight."

Limp strands of her bangs shook along with her head as she looked up, moisture puddling in her eyes. "No ... b-but would you m-mind ..." A muscle convulsed in her throat along with one in his heart. "I mean do you think you c-could ... you know ... h-hold me like you used t-to when D-Daddy and I would f-fight?"

His pulse forgot to beat for several seconds. *Would I mind?*

"You bet," he said, voice gruff as he scooped her up and repositioned her on his lap in the chair, pulse ricocheting out of control. He wrapped the blanket around her before tucking her close, finally resting his head against hers. "So ... what happened tonight?" he whispered, ignoring the aching familiarity of holding her like this once again.

She sniffled, and a faint smile shadowed his lips, remembering all the times he'd cuddled and coddled her, this little girl he so longed to protect. She swiped at her nose with the side of her hand, and he chuckled. "Sorry, Lace, I'm fresh out of Kleenex, but this quilt is due for a wash, so have at it."

A congested giggle escaped, trailing into a broken sob. "He h-hates me, Jack," she whispered, the frail hurt in her tone slashing right through him, "he always has."

His breathing stilled. "Your father? No, Lace, I don't believe that."

"It's t-true," she said in a nasal stutter, clinging so much, her nails dug into his chest. "H-he told me s-so tonight—said I was a m-mistake ..."

"What?" He couldn't help it—he jerked back to look in her eyes. "He said that?"

She heaved and nodded at the same time, the motion so pitiful, he wanted to bust on Ben Carmichael till the man bled raw. "S-said Mom tricked him ... got 'knocked up' as he s-so crudely put it, with a b-baby he wasn't even s-sure was h-his ..." Her voice trailed off into another gut-wrenching sob, and all Jack could do was crush her to his chest, eyelids sinking while he cuddled her close. He kissed her head, nuzzling her damp hair while the scent of peach shampoo took him back to a time when he had a right to hold her like this, pick up the pieces, and then kiss the hurt away ...

"He's just an angry and bitter man, Lace, whose temper has always gotten away from him, especially with you." He gently lifted her chin with his thumb, heart twisting at the liquid grief in her eyes. "As much as I wish you weren't his daughter, a person would have to be deaf, dumb, and blind not to see the resemblance between you two." He slowly caressed her eyebrow, tracing its perfect arch. "You have the same remarkable hazel eyes, flecked with gold in the sunlight that glitter like smoky emeralds whenever you're angry or hurt. Or the oval shape of your jaw," he whispered, her skin like silk beneath the glide of his fingers, "which leads to that same formidable chin as your father's, the one that always promises a challenge." Slipping a damp strand of hair over her ear, he infused a trace of a smile to chase away the sadness he saw. "Hate to say it, Lace, but except for the hair color and monumental grudge on his shoulder, you're your father's daughter no matter what the idiot says."

The faintest glimmer of a smile broke free on her beautiful face, lifting the weight of the world off of his shoulders. A harsh grunt escaped as she swiped her nose with the side of her hand. "Yeah, I know—kind of makes a bald-faced liar out of him, doesn't it?"

He smiled. "Especially when he calls you a mistake, because the only mistake here is his." Jack lifted the quilt to dry the tears on her face and dab at her nose. "Because as God is my witness, Lace, if you were a mistake, then you're the most perfect one I've ever seen."

Her head tipped to the side. "I thought you didn't believe in God so much anymore?"

It was his turn to grunt. "Didn't say I didn't believe in him, just don't have much use for Him." He tugged her back against his chest to deter any further talk of God. "So you really did it? Jumped off his boat? Not when it was running, I hope …"

She settled in, legs tucked and body scrunching close. "The engine was running, but I didn't care. I dove off the back—the same crazy dance of rebellion and anger I was so good at in my teens." A fractured chuckle rumbled against his chest. "What can I say, I'm the Queen of Shock and Awe when it comes to Ben Carmichael, but I'll tell you what, Jack, I would have given anything to see his face."

He grinned. "Me too." He released a heavy sigh, chin propped on top of her head. "But all the hurt and anger aside, Lace, you can't let the past—yours or your dad's—dictate your future, and it will if you let it. Bitterness has a way of making us cold and hard, and I don't want to see that happen to you. Ever. Because as far as I'm concerned that is one way that you are not your father's daughter, Lacey Carmichael, and that on its own has always made me proud."

She issued a grunt. "Can't take much of the credit there—you were the one who always browbeat forgiveness into my head whenever Daddy and I would fight, remember?" She lowered her voice several octaves, mimicking one of the silly platitudes he'd always spouted back then. "'Don't ever forget, Lacey, forgiveness is the greatest gift we can give to ourselves.'"

His fingers nipped at her waist, unleashing that glorious giggle he loved. "'*Browbeat?* As I recall, *Miss Carmichael,* it was always you who came to *me* for advice and comfort, yes?"

Her laughter lit up the night. "Yes, it was, Dr. O'Bryen, and it's a good thing you didn't go into psychiatry, I suppose, or you'd be sending me a hefty bill."

"Nope. I don't charge *friends,*" he said quietly, the very taste of the word bittersweet.

Sitting up, she cradled both hands to his cheeks, her voice the softest of whispers. "Especially best friends, Jack, because that's what we are. And every single day of my life, I thank God He allowed me back into yours."

He palmed her hand with his own, swallowing an awful lump in his throat. "I had no choice, Lace—you own a piece of my heart, and you always will."

"Me too," she whispered, the husky sound drawing his gaze to her mouth, lingering on parted lips he craved to taste.

"I missed our friendship when I was gone, Jack—your love and your comfort, yes, but most of all, your wisdom." Ever so gently, her hand on his cheek twined with his, her touch a tender agony over all they had lost. "'The words of the wise bring healing,'" she said softly, and he immediately recognized *Proverbs 12:18*, pulse stuttering that he remembered any Scripture at all.

"That was always you, Brye, the words of the wise healing my tortured soul, staunching the flow from all the wounds Daddy and I inflicted." More moisture pooled in her eyes as her fingers caressed the curve of his jaw. "Thank you, Jack, for all you've done for me in the past and for all you continue to do. I think I would be lost without you." Nestling back into his hold, she kept her hand warm within his. "No, I *know* I would, because nobody's ever been able to calm me like you."

"Not even Chase?" he asked, his casual tone cloaking the pride that surged in his chest.

"Nope, not even Chase. Although he does have it over you in one area ..." She peeked up with an impish smile, glimmers of the little brat she used to be twinkling in her eyes.

His gaze narrowed. "So help me, Mike, if you say volleyball ..."

Her giggle was pure mischief. "Well, that too, I suppose, but no—I was going to say he prays with me about things like you used to do. Unless, of course, you'd consider—"

"No!" He stood and dropped her on her feet so fast, she wobbled as much as his heart, which suddenly needed a lot more distance. She laughed so hard, the blanket dropped to the dock, revealing a soaked orange crop top plastered to luscious curves and shrunken enough to highlight a tan and toned stomach. Battling a gulp, he turned to retrieve his rod and reel, ticked off at just how easily the woman could simmer his blood.

"Here—I'll let Chase do the prayin', and I'll do the playin', deal?" He thrust his rod and reel into her hands and strode to the storage closet for another, anxious for the smell of shrimp instead of peach-scented hair. "Game on."

"Yes—prepare to die!" The bounce in her step told him he'd succeeded in diverting her attention, both from his former faith and the row with her father. She had the line cast in the water before he could get a shrimp on his hook, and fumbling to hurry, he pricked his finger. The hook immediately drew blood, only the first of many times Lacey Carmichael would make him bleed, no doubt, now that Chase was in her life. She chattered on while she popped the cork in the water like a pro, tripping his pulse with a sexy grin over her shoulder. "Lucky for you, Dr. Jock, that the only fishing Pastor Chase does is at church."

She reeled in and cast again, and his gaze roved white capris that molded to every curve, just like he'd hoped to do once, after Lacey became his wife. Smile thin, he joined her at dock's edge, casting the shrimp— and his regrets—as far away as he could, sinking them both into the bottomless memory of the Skidaway River. "Yeah," he said with a grunt when Lacey squealed over a bite. "Lucky me."

CHAPTER TWENTY-EIGHT

"You're joking, right?" Lacey gaped at Cat and Shan, knife poised over a home-baked cherry pie donated to the Camp Hope anniversary fundraiser going on all weekend. The smell of popcorn and funnel cakes competed with wood smoke and barbecue while a large crowd of orphans and adults milled and mingled on a lawn crowded with booths, games, and carnival rides. Lacey blinked, hardly able to believe she'd heard correctly. "You think *Jasmine's* the bad influence?" Shock shaded her tone while she sliced the pie in eighths before shoveling pieces onto paper plates. "From what Nicki says, Jack has quite the reputation at the hospital—a player every nurse is dying to get her hooks in."

"Well, that much is true," Cat said with an off-center grin, snitching a brownie from the plate Shannon was arranging at the bakery booth where all three had volunteered. All around them, children's giggles and shrieks echoed in the warm night air, the sound as melodious as the circus music that drifted from the carousel down on the shore. "Dr. Romeo is one of his nicknames at Memorial, according to my friend Kathy, because he dates no less than three nurses at a time."

"Or did," Shannon corrected, calmly swatting Cat's hand as she attempted to filch another brownie. "Till Jasmine. And you're on a diet, remember?"

Cat's eyes narrowed to slits of sapphire. "We're in a flippin' bakery booth, Shan—have a heart." Her scowl instantly morphed into a blazing smile as two elderly widows approached, sweet Carol Green and her adorable sister Trixi Oberembt, delivering pies they'd obviously overbaked for the fundraiser, given the charcoal crusts around the edges. "Mmm, blueberry and peach lattice, ladies, two of my favorites, thank you!" Cat sniffed both pies that no doubt smelled like charcoal too, given the sisters' unfortunate reputations for inedible baked goods.

"They're *all* your favorites," Shannon muttered, scooping an arm to her sister's waist. Her smile tipped as she bumped Cat's hip with her own. "You swore me to hold you accountable, remember? 'One-brownie limit on pain of death?'"

A wicked grin slid across Cat's face as she snatched another brownie behind her sister's back. "I wasn't talking about *my* death," she said with a chuckle, promptly popping half in her mouth.

"I swear, Cat, you are the sidetrack queen," Lacey said with a shake of her head, her grin matching that of her friend's. She snapped her fingers in front of Cat's face. "Uh, focus, please? We were talking about Jasmine and Jack?"

A scrunch crinkled Cat's delicate nose, making her look more like ten than twenty-five, especially with brownie crumbs at the edge of her mouth. "Now there's a brownie deterrent if ever there was—talk about loss of appetite."

It was Lacey's turn to wrinkle her nose, eyeing the cherry pie with a rumble of her stomach. "What—you don't like Jasmine?" she asked, downing a swig of her bottled water.

Cat answered with a grunt, tearing off a piece of plastic wrap to cover the newly cut pieces of pie. "The Queen? Oh, she's okay I guess, just not for Jack. She's the daughter of the head doc at Memorial *and* Jack's boss, so Kathy says whatever the Queen wants, she gets, if you get my drift." Her lips swerved sideways. "And Kathy says she wants Jack—in the worst way— so I just worry she'll break him down."

"Break him down?" Lacey halted, water bottle suspended at her lips. She tried to ignore the twinge in her gut that felt too much like jealousy. "You mean marriage?"

Tucking the plastic wrap around a second piece, Cat paused to give Lacey a droll look, her shapely blonde brows arched high. "Uh ... no ... I mean virtue, as in Jack's?"

Lacey began to hack, the water she'd just sipped clogging her throat. Shannon patted her back with firm taps, concern wedging the bridge of her nose. "You all right, Lace?"

Lacey's ponytail bobbed frantically in response while she waited for her airway to open back up, finally emitting a raspy reply. "Yeah—fine, thanks. Went down the wrong pipe." She nailed Cat with a piercing gaze. "Are you trying to tell me that Jack Carmichael— the bachelor catch of Isle of Hope, who's dated scores of women and has a player reputation according to Nick—*that* Jack Carmichael doesn't—" Her throat bobbed as she circled a hand, hoping Cat would get her drift so she wouldn't have to say it aloud. No such luck. Unleashing a silent groan, Lacey dipped her head in question, face flaming brighter, no doubt, than the stupid cherry pie. "You know ... *get around?*"

Cat grinned, obviously pleased she could rattle her best friend. "Nope." She repositioned several wrapped pieces of pie, her perfectionist tendencies in play as she arranged the baked goods into a perfect display. "Kathy says Jack's reputation is all bark and no bite, and she should know." She turned to give Lacey a pointed look. "*She's* the nurse we all liked before Jack dumped her for getting too serious. Kathy claims Jack may play around, but he refuses to sleep around, a fact verified hotly by the nurse he dated before Kathy—Miss Lisa 'Va-Va-Boom' Daus."

Lacey spun to grab a plate of cookies off the back table, more heat broiling her face. She snatched one from beneath the plastic wrap and set the plate on the front counter, completely disrupting Cat's handiwork. "I find that very hard to believe," she mumbled, cheeks chunky with cookie. "A hunky doctor *and* red-blooded American male who's ditched all prior morals and beliefs? In today's world that all but guarantees sexual activity."

"No, *really*, Lace ..." Shannon said with a blink of blue eyes that seemed more intense than usual, as if underscoring a point with more depth than her words could convey. "Jack made a pact with Cat and me that if we kept it 'above board' as he put it, he would too, and I believe him. He always sleeps at home and usually gets in at a pretty decent hour too."

"That's because Mom'd kill him if he didn't," Cat quipped, tossing a loose brownie crumb into her mouth. "But Shan's right, Lace—Jack did make a pact with us a few years back."

Lacey shook her head, sagging against the counter with an open-mouthed smile. "Well, I'll be. Shades of the minister coming back to haunt, I guess." Feeling spunky, she snitched a brownie with a wide grin. "You know, I do believe that's the best news I've heard in a long, long while. Good for Jack!"

"And bad for Jasmine," Cat said with a waggle of brows.

"All right, ladies, your shift is up." Miss Myra marched up to the booth with two volunteers in tow, apparently unruffled by the humidity in her crisp, white peasant top and colored maxi. Her trademark single strand of pearls completed the ensemble. "Go get your dinner."

"Yes!" Cat fist-pumped the air, and Lacey grinned, herding the twins out of the booth toward the picnic tables, corralling Debbie, Davey, and Spence on the way. They found Tess and Mamaw chatting, along with several of Mamaw's card-club friends, all waiting on them to eat barbecue.

Davey darted toward his mother. "Mom, Mom— Lacey dunked Jack a gazillion times!"

Lacey grinned, recalling the highlight of her day, when she and the twins doused Jack and Matt in the dunking booth.

"Did she, now?" Tess gave him a squeeze while her gaze met Lacey's. "Good girl—it's always been my opinion a boy can never have too many baths."

"I hate baths," Davey muttered, shrugging his mother's arms off to run after Spence and Debbie as the twins ushered them to the cotton candy stand nearby.

Tess patted the seat next to her. "Sit down, Lace," she said with a gentle smile, "how are you doing, sweetheart?"

Lacey slipped onto the bench beside Tess, grateful for the woman who was both a mother and a good friend. The night she and her father had fought, Tess had joined her and Jack in the kitchen to finish off the apple pie from dinner. Somehow the woman had tugged the truth of Lacey's awful evening with her dad right out, etching deep concern in Tess's brow. The same concern Lacey now saw behind the tender look on her face.

Lacey released a quiet sigh. "Better," she whispered, grateful Cat and Shan had taken Debbie and the boys to get cotton candy while Nicki was chatting with Mamaw and her friends. She hadn't told anyone else what had happened that night because it was too painful to share, but she knew she needed to soon. Both Nicki and

Mamaw cared too much to keep them in the dark over how deeply her father had wounded her, but she wasn't ready quite yet.

This evening was the first time she'd been able to really laugh all week, other than the night Jack had worked his magic on the dock, deftly removing the initial sting of her father's painful revelation. She'd been in a bit of a malaise since then, but tonight it had finally begun to lift. Maybe with lots of time and prayer, she might be able to consider reaching out to her father again, but one thing she knew for dead sure—it wouldn't be anytime soon.

Tess squeezed her waist. "Good. I've been praying for you." A shadow passed over her eyes as her smile dimmed, reminding Lacey how upset Tess had been over her father's callous remarks. Even now, her lips thinned into the same stubborn look as her son when he was ticked about something, indicating Tess's anger at Ben Carmichael had yet to wane. "*And* for that mule of a father of yours to wake up."

"Hey!" Lacey's voice came out as a high-pitched shriek, the feel of cold water dribbling down her back causing her to jump a mile. She spun halfway on the bench to see Jack standing behind her, wringing his sopping polo over her head with a flash of teeth that provoked laughter around the table.

"So … how's it feel, Carmichael? Because every single drop belongs to you."

Nicki squealed across the table, attempting to fend Matt off after he tugged her onto his wet lap, their tussle making everyone laugh while egging Matt on. Grinning, Lacey scooted away when Jack sat down, wedging his dripping body between his mother and her. He spiked fingers through his wet hair while a puddle of water pooled on the bench, forcing both Tess and Lacey to move further away.

With a twist of his shirt, he flicked the excess water at Lacey. "Hey, since the men gave their lives for the cause, it's only fair the women who took aim serve them BBQ, right, Matt? And I'll even buy for the table." Jack reached in his jeans pocket and tossed a wad of smashed paper tokens down in a soggy splat.

"Hear, hear," Matt said with a pound of his fist on the table. "We almost drowned, so it's the least you girls can do. And since Jack talked me into volunteering for the dunking booth, I'll have double everything."

Lacey chuckled as she hopped up from the table, snatching the stash of pre-paid tickets good for food, booths, or rides. She pinched them by the corner till they dangled limp from her hand. "Gee, you'd think a doctor'd be smart enough to empty his pockets before he goes for a swim." She snapped her fingers in front of Jack's nose. "Ante up, Dr. Romeo, I'm starved, so I doubt this'll be enough. Worked up quite an appetite vindicating every nurse at Memorial."

Jack grinned, hands braced behind his neck to reveal well-defined muscles. "What's the matter, Mike?" he asked with a leisurely drawl. "Jealous?"

"Ha—dream on, Doc." Lacey held her palm out, chin nudging up to deflect the heat broiling her cheeks. "Come on, O'Bryen, buck up—I'm hungry."

"Yeah, Jack." Cat and Shannon nudged in on the bench next to their mom while Davey and Spence sat across the table with Debbie to share a huge cotton candy. "Shan and I had a late meeting at school, so we didn't have lunch."

Chuckling, Jack turned his pockets inside out, tossing a wet tissue onto the table. "Sorry, ladies, clean out except for a very used Kleenex."

"Here, sweetheart." Tess rifled in her purse, calmly removing five twenties from Jack's wallet before handing it back to her son. "Donate whatever's left, all right? Jack's loaded, aren't you, darling?"

"Uh, thanks, Mom, but not anymore, apparently," he said with a dry smile. He glanced up at Lacey with a lazy grin that flash-froze her pulse when it fluttered her stomach. He winked. "Unless, of course, we're talkin' brains and brawn."

"Thanks, T-Tess," Lacey stuttered, whirling around to escape Jack's teasing gaze, blatant quivers of attraction sending shock waves through her body. Her throat parched as dry as the kids' cotton candy. *What on earth is wrong with me?* This was Jack, for heaven's sake—an ex-boyfriend, yes, but one with whom she'd managed to forge a very comfortable friendship. So where were these annoying tingles coming from? Anxious to dodge unwanted attraction, Lacey ambled over to Mamaw. "How 'bout I buy back one of your famous peach crumble pies for the table after I fix you and your friends a plate? Jack's buying."

"Why, that would be lovely, dear," Mamaw said with a twinkle in her eye, the elfin smile on her lips an indication she was enjoying the tease at Jack's expense. She dug her Purell from her purse to hand it to Lacey. "Here, dear, dab a little on before you handle any food, all right? And with so many at our table, perhaps two pies would be better if Jack doesn't mind."

"Sure, why not?" Jack said, tone droll. "And take orders from the next table while you're at it, Lace, why don't you?"

"Oooo no, let me do it …" Cat popped up with Shannon to give Lacey a hand, nabbing Jack's wallet while Shannon diverted him with a massage of his shoulders. She tossed it to Lacey before he could stop her. "Here, Lace—now we can check out the silent-auction table, too."

"Great idea," Lacey said, bobbling the wallet. "There are a couple of iPads over there with our names on them, right, Nick?"

"Oh, you bet." Chuckling, Nicki slung an arm over Lacey's shoulder.

"Hey," Matt said, snitching a piece of the kids' cotton candy, "maybe the kids should go along to bid on some toys."

"Gosh, really? Thanks Mr. Jack!" Debbie scrambled off the bench, the cotton candy all but forgotten as she tugged on Spence's arm. "Come on, guys, I saw lots of cool stuff."

"Thanks a lot, Goof Ball," Jack said, wadding the soggy Kleenex before pelting it at his cousin.

Grateful for the diversion, Lacey slacked a hip in a smart aleck pose, shooting Jack a cocky smile. "You know, Jack, I'm always shocked at just how generous you are with your money—especially given all the splashes you already took for the cause."

Arms folded on the table, Jack glanced up with a half-lidded smile that had no right to loop her stomach like it did. "Yeah, real shocking, Mike. Just wait till you see how generous I am with payback once I get you back on the dock."

Heat zinged up her face like a rash gone awry, the memory of their last time on the dock taking her mind in a totally different direction. He was talking dunks in the water, she was certain, but all that came to mind was cuddling on his lap while he stroked and kissed her hair.

Real shocking? That her romantic feelings for Jack O'Bryen had been rekindled in the span of single night? God help her, nothing could shock her more.

"Uh, excuse me, Lacey?"

"Yes?" She spun around and froze.

That is ... until now.

CHAPTER TWENTY-NINE

*B*en Carmichael stood there, as paralyzed as his daughter, questioning his sanity in even coming here tonight. But Lacey hadn't returned one of his calls, and the guilt was eating him alive. He'd barely slept a wink since that night, at least not well, and wouldn't until he could finally apologize and get on with his life. A slow exhale seeped from his lips as he stared at a sea of faces, gaze locking on only one—that of his daughter's, which appeared as deprived of blood right now as his own. A knot of pride obstructed his air and he swallowed hard to clear it away, hands buried deep in the pockets of his Dockers as he sucked in a deep swallow of humility. "Can we go somewhere and talk?" he asked quietly, quite certain the regret in his tone was no match for the hurt he had caused.

"I thought you didn't want to talk," she snapped, shoulders squaring in that defensive posture she'd had when she'd been a teenager, jaw thrust and mouth compressed.

His temper chafed, itching to flare like always when Lacey challenged him with her rebellious air. Gaze flicking around the table, it converged with Tess's for the briefest of moments before she quickly looked away, clearly telling him he was on his own. *Fine.* With a lift of his jaw, he stared Lacey down, determined to do what he came here to do. "We need to talk—alone."

He could see a storm brewing in her eyes, gaze thin and patience even thinner, the tic in her cheek twittering as hard as his own. "I'm busy right now," she bit out, and it took everything in him not to turn on his heel and bolt like he always had before.

"Is h-he a bad man?" A little girl's voice wavered with fear.

"No, darling." Mamaw rose from her chair, smile soft as she patted the girl's shoulder, her gaze kind as it connected with Ben's. "Just a very unhappy one." She made her way to where Lacey stood at the end of the table with a pool of tears in her eyes. "Go," her grandmother said quietly, slipping an arm around her granddaughter's waist, barely loud enough for him to hear. "This is the moment you've been praying for."

Lacey didn't move. Her body quivered as imperceptibly as marsh grasses in a moonless evening while she stared, a single tear slowly trailing her cheek.

"Go," Mamaw said again.

This time Lacey looked at her, her lip trembling as much as his gut. "For you, and only you."

"No, darling girl." The old woman hugged his daughter, pulling back to give a nod to the sky. "For Him, and only Him."

Offering a jerky nod, Lacey handed a wallet to Nicki. "Get started, Nick. I won't be long." Face set, she rounded the table and brushed past him, stalking down the hill to an empty picnic table by the lake.

He followed silently, figuring he deserved all the disdain she wanted to dish out. He had dealt a mortal blow, one that Karen begged him never to divulge, then added insult to injury by implying she wasn't his daughter. He knew better. Sure, Karen dated a few others in the two months they'd broken up—she made sure he knew about that—but he was the one she'd been crazy about. The one she'd given her all to when he'd pressured her without mercy. And he had—relentlessly. But then he had the gall to blame her when she came up pregnant, accusing her of sleeping with other guys. His gut twisted. What a royal jerk he'd been. When Lacey had come along, she'd favored him right out the gate, but he'd been too selfish to acknowledge it, making Karen pay for *his* mistake. Guilt churned in his gut. She'd deserved better. A heaviness settled as he trailed Lacey down the hill.

And so did her daughter.

She spun around when she reached a lone picnic table on the edge of the lake, eyes blazing in the moonlight. "So ... what do you want, *Dad*—or should I even call you that?"

He winced. "I should have never said that, Lacey—I was wrong."

"And not for the first time—you treated Mom like garbage."

"I know," he whispered, gaze dropping to the grass where he fixated on an apple core. Another piece of garbage, just like him.

Rotten. Tainted. Corrupt.

"Why?"

His eyes shuttered closed, Karen's face haunting him like she did so often in his dreams. "Because I was a selfish, immature rich kid," he said quietly, realizing for the first time just how wrong he had been. "A cocky punk who was angry that his stupid behavior caught up with him."

Her chin lashed up in defiance, but trembling all the same. "So it was my fault, then."

"Mine—not yours," he emphasized, head bent to pierce her gaze with his own. "I wasn't ready for a baby, Lacey, and I took it out on you and your mom, and I'm sorry. In fact, there's no way I can tell you how sorry I am." He expelled a shaky sigh. "But I'd like to try all the same," he whispered, not blaming her one bit if she told him to go jump in the lake. But he had to try. He couldn't live with himself if he didn't.

She folded her arms, the action more defensive than confrontational. "How?"

He slipped his hand in his pocket to pull out the latest iPhone he bought to replace the one he figured she lost when she jumped off his boat. He held it out, Adam's apple bobbing uncomfortably in his throat. "I figured you'd need a new phone."

Her brows lifted. "A phone? You think a phone can make up for all you did?"

"No!" His palm shot up. "No, no I don't." He laid the phone on the picnic table, then slipped his hands back in his pockets as he offered an awkward shrug. "But it's a start, pathetic as it may be."

Lips pursed, she stared at him like he was the devil incarnate. And then—ever so slowly—the corners of her mouth edged up so minimally, he thought he might have imagined it in the shadows. "Pathetic is right," she said softly, a gleam of moisture glimmering in her eyes. "The least you could have come up with is the latest Mac."

He hadn't realized he'd been holding his breath until it leaked out in one arduous exhale, his chest almost aching from relief. Fighting the moisture that burned at the back of his eyes, he picked the iPhone up and held it out. "I'd give anything to take back what I said that night, Lacey," he whispered, muscles convulsing painfully in his throat, "and all that I did to you and your mom."

Answering tears glistened in her eyes as she took the iPhone from his hand. "Anything?" Moonlight glowed in her face like hope.

His gaze locked with hers, features guarded except for the barest trace of a smile. "Almost," he said, nodding behind her to where dark waters lapped against the rocky shore. "Except jump in the lake."

The corners of her mouth flickered just barely, as if a smile were battling to break free. "Good." She strode past him to stop two feet beyond, forcing him to turn.

Her chin snapped back up, but it couldn't daunt the twinkle in her eyes. "I'll bring dinner once a week, either scratch at your house or fast food on the boat— your choice." Her tone was sharp, no-nonsense, and completely matter-of-fact, reminding him so much of himself that a near smile nudged at his lips.

He bowed his head, as if thinking it over, finally responding in a tone that matched hers to a dare. "The house, Tuesdays, six o'clock. We both know the boat's too risky."

A bona fide grin slid across her beautiful face. "Deal. And just for the record?" She turned to leave, but not before tossing a crooked smile over her shoulder. "The way I cook? You haven't seen risky."

CHAPTER THIRTY

"Oh, Debbie—no!" Hands over her eyes, Lacey peeked through two fingers, biting the edge of her lip while Debbie "Wild Child" Holbrook raced toward the Slip 'N Slide in Mamaw's backyard. "Slide—*now!*" Lacey said under her breath, right before the little girl's feet flew up in the air, landing her flat on her back in the first few steps.

"Uh-oh … a little more slip than slide that time," Nicki said, shading her eyes as she watched Spence and Davey help Debbie up, the boys' laughter merging with Debbie's giggles.

"Debbie? Are you okay?" Lacey held her breath, watching with Nicki and Mamaw.

The little dickens glanced over, a grin splitting her face. "Wow, waaaaaaaaaay cool, Miss Lacey, can I do it again?"

Lacey's smile edged to the right. "Uh … sure … but we'll need a little more slide than slip next time, sweetie-pie, so I don't pass out."

Shaking her head, Lacey stretched back on her chaise in her tank top and shorts, soaking up all the sun she could before the nip of fall chased their tanning days away. Closing her eyes, she emitted a contented sigh. "Thanks for letting me bring Debbie over to play with the boys, Mamaw. She had so much fun running around with Spence and Davey at the fundraiser, that she's been hounding me ever since to see them again."

"She's a precious child," Mamaw said, her tone wistful as she watched the children play. "Reminds me of both of you when you were small, squealing and sliding and sunbathing for hours on end."

A bittersweet sense of melancholy shadowed Lacey's mood as she stared into the backyard, now resplendent with a freshly painted gazebo and lush gardens for Nicki's upcoming wedding. "Those were some of the happiest days of my life," she said, voice wistful, "especially when I could come over here when Mom and Daddy weren't getting along." Her tone went dry. "Which was most of the time."

Nicki cocked her head, eyes narrowed in thought. "You know, Lace, you've always said that, but after Uncle Ben showed up at the fundraiser last week, I've been wondering if maybe some of your frustration wasn't just from typical teenage/parent head-butting." She glanced over at Lacey, nose in a scrunch. "Do you think it's possible some of the bad blood between you and your dad was more how it seemed at the time than it actually was?"

"You were a mistake ... a kid I wasn't even sure was mine."

Her father's words pierced all over again, bringing a sudden sheen of tears to her eyes. "I don't think so, Nick, not after what he said to me that night on the boat."

"What exactly *did* he say?" she probed gently, silent questions lingering in the air of things both she and Mamaw had obviously been waiting to ask.

Lacey sucked in a harsh breath and expelled it as thoroughly as if it were the pain she'd carried all of these years. "That I was a mistake," she said quietly, eyelids sagging closed at the weight of the revelation.

"That Mom tricked him into marriage by getting pregnant with a kid he wasn't even sure was his."

She heard Nicki's soft gasp, and lids lifting, her gaze locked with Mamaw's, the glaze in her grandmother's eyes matching hers. "He never wanted me," Lacey whispered, speaking the words out loud for the first time since the night she'd cried in Jack's arms, the very utterance branding her soul. "Which means *I'm* the one who ruined *his* life—and Mom's."

Mamaw grunted, the sound so out of character that Lacey blinked. "Oh, poo! You didn't ruin his life, darling," she said with a jab of a smile, "you saved it." Laying her knitting aside, she leaned forward, hands folded neatly in her lap. "Your father was nothing more than a spoiled rich boy who dug himself into a hole deep enough to bury a donkey. Trust me—your grandfather and I were not happy when he started pursuing Karen, who, I might add, turned him down repeatedly until he wore her down."A frail sigh drifted from her lips while her gaze trailed into a distant stare. "She fell harder for him than any boy she'd ever dated, and why not? He was handsome, wealthy, and lousy with Irish charm." One side of her lip cocked as her eyes reconnected with Lacey's. "Hard to believe right now, I know, but he was, although your grandfather preferred the term 'blarney,' among other less flattering words."

Lacey grinned outright, memories of her crusty and outspoken Grandpa Phillips coming to mind.

The humor in Mamaw's face faded as her smile did the same. "I remember the day Karen told me your father first mentioned marriage. They'd been dating a year, and she was over the moon that he promised to propose, but '*after* medical school,' he said, although I know she was praying for sooner. I had a suspicion he just told her that to pressure her into intimacies. And he was an outrageous flirt as well, so I always wondered if he didn't have other girls in the wings, you know? But your mother was a good Christian girl, Lacey—active in choir and youth group—so she stood her ground for a long time, I know. But like I said—your father was used to getting his way, and he did." Her mouth compressed into a thin smile. "He played, got caught, and then blamed you and your mother for the rest of his life, never taking responsibility for his actions." The edge of her lip quirked, making her look like a silver-haired pixie with a sparkle in her eyes. "*Until* your grandfather paid a visit to his stepfather, Dr. Randall Carmichael."

"Oh, good heavens, Mamaw, what on earth did he say?" Lacey's mouth hung open at the idea of no-nonsense, blue-collar Grandpa Phillips confronting a society physician like Grandfather Carmichael, God rest his soul.

"And more importantly," Nicki said with a grin, "did he have a shotgun when he said it?"

Mamaw laughed. "No shotgun, but a very clear message that informed Dr. Carmichael that his stepson was nothing but—and I quote, 'a playboy with a pedigree'—who would never amount to anything in life if he didn't take responsibility for his actions."

Jaw gaping, Lacey put a hand to her mouth. "Oh my goodness, Mamaw—I had no idea!"

A soft chuckle rolled from Mamaw's lips. "Neither did your father until Randall pulled the plug on his stepson's wild ways, claiming no grandchild of his would ever come into this world illegitimately." Mamaw shielded a hand to her mouth, voice low as if imparting a secret. "Apparently he bore the scourge of illegitimacy himself, which was far more shocking back in the day. So that, along with being at his wit's end with a rebellious stepson who frittered away his time and education on less savory pursuits, your Grandfather Carmichael lowered the boom."

"How?" Lacey was now sitting on the edge of her chaise, rapt with attention.

Mamaw's jaw jutted up. "Clipped his wings, that's how. Told your father in no uncertain terms that if he didn't quit his wild ways and settle down—which meant doing right by Karen and focusing more on his studies—not only would he yank his dreams of med school, but he'd boot him out of the house and the will as well, freezing all funds till he grew up and became a man."

Lacey exchanged a look with Nicki, their open-mouth smiles a stunned reflection of the other. All at once, they both started laughing so loud, the kids in the yard turned to stare. "Poor Daddy," Lacey said between ragged heaves, the tears in her eyes now from laughter, "a player who gets his due." She swiped at the excess moisture and shimmied back into her chaise, studying her grandmother with a curious look. "Why didn't you ever tell me this before?"

Mamaw gave a small shrug. "You had enough grief over your father, darling—I didn't want to add to it."

Shaking her head, Lacey plopped back against the chaise once again, still amazed that the strict, upstanding father who'd berated her on morality had actually been a wild child himself. Another grin slid across her face. "And to think of all the grief he gave me over Jack ..."

Sympathy shone in Mamaw's eyes. "Which probably one of the reasons, sweetheart. Your father didn't know a lot about trust since he wasn't very trustworthy himself back then."

"Well, I wasn't an angel by any stretch of the imagination, but to ride me every chance he got, always accusing me of playing around—with a minister's son, no less—was downright hypocritical. Especially when all along he was no better than me."

"Worse, actually," Mamaw admitted. "After your mom and he were married, she received several angry letters from girls he'd strung along while he and Karen were dating."

"Oh, that dirty dog!" Nicki chuckled. "Who would have thought a bad boy lurked beneath Uncle Ben's straitlaced and professional demeanor?" She shot Lacey a wink. "I certainly hope you intend to use this valuable information if you two ever get on good terms again."

"Count on it!" Lacey said with a throaty laugh.

"Speaking of being on good terms again," Mamaw began, pausing when a sopping wet Spence darted over to drip on her shoes.

"Can we go inside now, Mamaw?" he asked, feet dancing on the hot pavement. "Debbie's hungry."

"Figures." Chuckling, Lacey started to rise.

"No, sit," Nicki said, bouncing up from her chaise. "I'll clean and feed these little grub worms—I need more iced tea anyway." She paused. "Anybody want a refill?"

"No, darling, but thank you." Mamaw offered a grateful smile.

"Yeah, thanks, Nick—you're a sweetheart, no matter what Matt says," Lacey called, earning an answering jest from Nicki when she stuck out her tongue.

"So …" Mamaw picked up her knitting again, peering over her spectacles with a tender smile. "How are the dinners with your father coming? Any progress?"

Lacey scrunched her nose. "Some, I guess, but we've only had two so far, so it's hard to say. At least he opens the door when I ring the bell now, so that's definite progress. And if grunts count, he even occasionally responds to my questions—but only during commercials, of course." Her smile canted. "We eat in the family room with the TV, naturally."

"Oh, God bless him …" Mamaw shook her head, her smile still intact, a clear indication that despite all the trouble Ben Carmichael caused for her daughter and granddaughter, she bore no grudge. *Or* dealt with it long, long ago.

Lacey grunted in the grand fashion of her father. "Yes, well, it's going to take a boatload of blessings to get through to him, I suspect. The man's door may be open now, but his heart's closed tighter than those silly plantation shutters he uses to shut everybody out." She sighed, wondering if she and her father would ever be close.

"He's softening, darling, make no mistake." Mamaw's knitting needles flew faster than mud-slick kids down a Slip 'N Slide.

"I don't know, Mamaw. I thought so when he came to the fundraiser, especially when he almost cracked a smile, but he makes no eye contact, grunts the minimal amount of words, and goes stiffer than those stupid shutters when I even attempt to give him a hug."

"You mark my words, sweetheart, there isn't a person alive who can't be softened by the love of God."

Guilt wrenched a weak groan from Lacey's mouth. "But that's just it, Mamaw, it's *not* the love of God here—just the frail love of a daughter who's been rejected so much, her heart is battered and scarred." Exhaling a noisy sigh, Lacey looked up, meeting her grandmother's gaze with a misty one of her own. "Whenever I leave, I always hug him and tell him I love him, but he just stands there like a granite boulder, arms limp at his sides and mouth sealed, never saying a word." She blinked to ward off the moisture that welled, her voice trembling for the very first time. "And I gotta tell you, Mamaw, every single time, a little piece of me dies all over again."

"Oh, sweetheart." Placing her knitting on the table, Mamaw rose to perch on the edge of Lacey's chaise.

She cupped her granddaughter's hand between her own fragile ones, the tenderness of her manner easing the ache in Lacey's soul. "But in a way, that's a good thing, Lacey, because your broken heart is not capable of loving your father the way he needs to be loved. The Bible says 'the human heart is the most deceitful of all things, and desperately wicked,' which means you can't rely on it *or* yourself to heal your father's heart. Only God's unconditional love is capable of that."

Lacey's gaze wandered into the backyard with a zombie stare, her whisper enmeshed with pain. "Well, God needs to show me how to do that, then, because I'm not sure how many times I can bear Daddy's rejection before my heart becomes as hard as his."

A gnarled hand slowly caressed her cheek, drawing her attention to the beautiful face of her grandmother, delicately etched with both wisdom and love. "Ah, but that's the trick, darling—seventy times seven," she whispered, her countenance aglow with a faith so strong, the power of it melted into Lacey's soul. "God's love is unconditional because if it wasn't, all of us would be lost. So you see, Lacey, it's that same unconditional love that saved you, changed you, ushered you from the dark into His glorious light—that will do the same for your father. Only this time, darling girl, it will be *through* you. Through *your* unconditional love that brings dinners weekly without expecting anything in return but God's joy and approval. Because when one is loved so desperately and so unconditionally as we are loved by God, our hearts long to respond. To love Him back in a way that will not only glorify Him, but bless us as well."

She patted Lacey's hand, the love in her eyes as warm as the gentle touch of her hand. "Which means, you are not doing this for your father on earth, Lacey, but for your Father in heaven, not expecting anything from Ben whatsoever, just from God. And trust me, darling—you can't out-give God."

"But what if I fail?" she whispered, fear nipping at her heels.

Mamaw's chuckle was soft and low, as if failure were not even an option. "Oh, Lacey, don't you know? God's love *never* fails."

In your unfailing love you will lead the people you have redeemed.

Head bent, her grandmother smiled. "So you see, sweetheart, you're not alone in this—God's unfailing love girds your heart with the strength to do what He's called you to do, so failure is not an issue." She reached to give Lacey a firm hug before rising to her feet with a hike of her brow. "The only issue here is—will you obey?"

Lacey's eyelids fluttered closed, a sense of awe overwhelming her until tears burned hot. She used to be just like her dad—hard, cold, bitter, unwilling to give. But in the span of only months, God had opened her eyes to the depth of His love for her personally, giving her a freedom and a hope she had never experienced before. Peace suddenly purled through her body like warm oil, as if anointing her for the task ahead.

Will I? Her silent consent came while liquid joy welled in her eyes. She glanced up, gracing her grandmother with a glorious smile. "Yes, Mamaw—I believe I will."

CHAPTER THIRTY-ONE

"Come on, Big Guy—don't look at me like that. I've had a rough day and it's too blasted hot for fishing." Ben tried to ignore the pathetic look on Beau's face as the little mongrel waited patiently by the front door, posture stiff while he sat on his haunches, still as a statue. How the animal knew it was Wednesday was beyond him, but he always did, as anxious to get out on the boat as Ben usually was.

Fanning fingers through his hair, Ben cocked a hip and vented with a noisy sigh. Except for tonight. Nope, tonight he was restless for some reason. The idea of fishing right now was about as appealing as one of those fancy soirees Cynthia always dragged him to. Making small talk as shallow as the sissy champagne flutes everybody carried around. Give him a highball or beer any day of the week over bubbles and chit-chat. God help him, he hated chit-chat!

God help him?

Ben grunted and turned on his heel. "Hounded" was more like it, badgering Ben at every turn to seek a god as phony as his best friend had been. "Pastor" Adam O'Bryen, friend, neighbor, and all-around good guy, had been the only person Ben had ever opened up to, ever let in. The progress had been slow, but after over twenty years as neighbors and friends, Adam had made inroads that nobody else ever had. A sour taste tainted Ben's tongue.

Especially with my wife.

He lashed the fridge door open, desperate to wash the memories away with a cold beer. His lips twisted along with the cap of the O'Doul's Tess had pestered him to buy after he'd slipped and admitted to a prior problem with alcohol in one of their patio chats.

"As a surgeon, you have no business drinking alcohol of any kind, Ben, especially with a history like that," she'd insisted. She actually had the gall to leave a six-pack of O'Doul's non-alcoholic beer on his back step the next night with a big red bow. At the time he'd been ticked, quite sure God had never created a pushier woman, but in the end, he'd popped one open with a pizza, and it actually tasted pretty good. A smile itched on his lips, but he refused to give in. Because then it ticked him off that she'd been right. Nothing worse than a pushy woman who's right. Especially one who'd blackmailed him with sweets to procure a promise.

"Yes, Mother, I promise to never drink alcohol again," he'd finally pledged, just to get her off his back, figuring it couldn't hurt to be accountable to someone who actually cared. He hadn't imbibed since.

He took a deep draw of the O'Doul's, actually wishing it were a hardcore brew, grunting over the irony that people devoted to God apparently drove him to drink. First his stepfather with his constant hounding about church and God over the years followed by Karen, and then a hypocrite ex-friend who stabbed him in the back. All followed up neatly by a pretty pest from next door who plied God along with her pizza and cookies. He tipped the bottle high, the non-beer going down cold and sharp, helping to take away the bad taste in his mouth from any thought of religion. He slammed the fridge door closed with too much force, the bottles inside rattling along with his nerves. And *now* he had his holy-roller daughter to contend with, who had some cock-eyed notion that Crockpot meals and his favorite desserts would crack the code.

Not a chance.

O'Doul's in hand, Ben snatched a couple of Beggin' Strips and peanuts from the pantry and strolled into his family room to turn on the TV. Setting the beer and peanuts down, he walked to the hall to wave the Beggin' Strips in the air, waiting for Beau to take the bait. The dog only blinked, and Ben's mouth cocked to the right. "Come on, buddy, I know it's not Tess's fried bacon, but have a heart."

Stretching with an impatient squeal, the black lab only laid down at the front door, obviously as stubborn as Ben's neighbor.

Not to mention my daughter.

Lacey. Before he could squelch it, a smile crooked the edge of his lips, and shaking his head, he tossed the Beggin' Strips onto the floor before settling back in his recliner. The kid was a chip off the old block, that was for dead sure. Karen had always been so easy to control and keep in line, it seemed, but not her daughter. Ben took another swig. *My daughter*, he reminded himself, a young woman as pigheaded as he. He stared as Jethro Gibbs slapped DiNozzo upside the head, thinking he should do the same to himself.

For opening the door even a crack.

For allowing Lacey to come over at all.

For secretly liking it when she did.

He pelted peanuts to the back of his mouth, hating to admit the kid was chipping away at his armor, earning his respect, making him smile. His molars ground the peanuts to dust.

Making me care against my will.

His eyes narrowed on the television screen, a million miles away from Ducky's forensics lab where Gibbs' stony demeanor kept people from getting too close, just

like Ben was determined to do. As much as he was
starting to look forward to Lacey's visits, he could
never let her know, never really let her in. He wasn't
going there again—allowing a woman to railroad his
life. Mouth in a slant, he fired more peanuts, well aware
it wouldn't be easy. The kid was like Chinese water
torture—sheer obstinacy cloaked in a smile, wearing
him down with peach pie and perkiness that got on his
nerves.

But only because it weakened his will to be alone,
making him realize just how sterile and lonely his life
really was.

He upended the beer, slamming it back till it was all
gone.

Just like Tess.

The thought caught him off-guard, making him
painfully aware he hadn't seen hide nor hair of Tess for
over three weeks now, other than that cool look she'd
given him at the fundraiser. And this from a perky pest
who'd invaded his space as much as twice a week at
times. He frowned, annoyed at how much he missed
her. Between an overloaded docket of surgeries, weekly
dinners with Lacey, and endless functions with Cynthia,
he'd been too busy and spent to notice. But he was
noticing now, and he didn't like the empty feeling it left
in his gut.

Clicking the remote, he silenced the TV like he
wished he could silence the sudden yearning to hear
Tess's laughter again, to banter over pizza and monster
cookies like before. To revel in that secret thrill of
teasing her till a beautiful blush crept into her beautiful
face.

Ben scowled, tossing the remote on the table. *Calm
down, Carmichael, she's only a neighbor.* He lumbered
up from his chair, the sudden sprint of his pulse making
a liar out of him. Snatching the Beggin' Strips up from
the floor, he strode to the sliding door and waited for

Beau, well aware that the prospect of cornering a baby rabbit was far more enticing than any fake bacon. "I'll be right back, buddy," he called after Beau darted through, his own gaze flitting next door where Tess's kitchen and patio light twinkled through the dense hedge. His lips quirked. *Not unlike my twinkle-toes neighbor.* With a quick inventory of his fridge and freezer, a smile eased across his face when he spotted a half-empty carton of Häagen-Dazs Tiramisu—the secret weapon Cynthia had left once and Tess had devoured. Good. Something to tempt her for a late-night chat on his patio. If she was even home. More than likely she'd be hounding him if she was. Shutting the fridge door, he checked out the hall mirror just in case, wondering why on earth he was worried about how he looked. This was Tess, for Pete's sake, not Cynthia.

Then why are your hands sweating like a kid on a first date?

"Because it's blasted hot outside," he muttered, uncomfortable with the notion that it was anything more. Ducking out the front door, he rounded the hedge, grateful both Jack's and the girls' cars were nowhere to be found. Hands in his pockets, Ben ambled down the drive, stopping short at the sight of Tess sprawled on a chaise, eyes closed and an iPod in her ears. Hurt sliced through him so unexpectedly, he felt a flush rise in his cheeks.

She was home? By herself? And hadn't bothered to come over?

Settle down, boy—you switched your schedule up, remember? She doesn't even know you're home.

Exhaling an unsteady breath, he berated himself for being so touchy over a friend and neighbor. His eyes roved the length of her and suddenly friendship was the furthest thing from his mind. Lush blonde hair usually pulled up in a ponytail spilled wild and free over bare shoulders bronzed by the sun, setting off a red crop top that put a lump in his throat. Sure, he'd always noticed Tess had a cute shape, but stretched out on the chaise in short shorts that revealed shapely legs and a taut stomach, flat-out made his mouth go dry. Swallowing hard, he attempted a casual stance with hands in his pockets and hip to the wall, striving for a calm he didn't quite feel. "You know," he began with a gruff clear of his throat, "anyone would think you're avoiding me."

The woman popped in the air like a firecracker, faintly patriotic with her red crop top, face bleached white, and blue eyes glazed with shock. She gasped with a hand to her chest, her breathing labored. "Holy freakin' cow, Ben—are you trying to give me heart failure?"

He chuckled and strolled forward, pulling a chair from the table to sit down. He made himself comfortable with a stretch of his legs, the soles of his Sperrys casually propped on the edge of her chaise. "Nope, but if I did, then I guess I'm the guy you'd want around."

She didn't smile, inflicting an instant cramp in his gut. "No fishing?" she asked, avoiding his eyes while she attempted to tug her top down to cover her stomach, an action that only provided a deeper view of the cleft at her neckline.

He cleared his throat, forcing his gaze from the swell of her breasts to her face, which now sported a pretty blush. Crossing his ankles on the chaise, he offered an off-handed shrug. "Nope, not in the mood. Too tired. Too hot. Too bored."

Too lonely.

Her eyes finally connected with his, the coolness he saw chilling the sweat on his skin. "Really? I would think 'bored' would be just what the doctor ordered."

He blinked, face screwed in a frown. "Are you … okay?"

"Sure," she said, tone clipped. "Why wouldn't I be?"

"I don't know." His forehead wrinkled with a faint shake of his head. "You just don't seem yourself tonight."

"And what's that, Ben?" she asked with a jag of a brow, "too pushy, too perky, too big a pain in the butt?" She swung her legs to the floor and stood. "Gotta go—I have things to do."

"Wait." He halted her with a hand to her wrist, eyes in a squint. "Are you ... angry about something?"

She flicked his hand away, plunking hers to her hips. "Angry? Now why on earth would I be angry, Ben?" Her eyes sparked hot, as if he'd lit the fuse of that blasted firecracker.

He blinked, completely baffled by her behavior. Frustration swarmed as he countered, the slightest edge to his tone. "I don't know, Tess, maybe you should tell me."

Her arms snapped to her chest in a tight fold. "Oh, come on, Dr. Doom, surely someone bright enough to perform open-heart surgery can figure this out. Or wait," she said, palm splayed to her chest in feigned innocence. Her blue eyes circled wide. "Maybe one doesn't *need* a heart to operate on them." She snatched her iPod up and turned toward the door.

"Hey—" He hooked her arm, grip firm, thoughts tumbling as fast as his heart. "This doesn't have anything to do with Cynthia, does it, having her over?"

She jerked free, blood gorging her cheeks. "I don't give a flip how many women you have over, Dr. Carmichael, as long as one of them is your daughter and you *don't* gun her down with selfish and thoughtless words. Good night, Ben."

She spun around and stalked to the door, the thought of her shutting him out strangling the words in his throat. *No!* His stomach spasmed as he shot to his feet, arm jolting the screen to a stop before it could slam in his face. "Don't do this, Tess," he rasped, heart battering the walls of his chest, "don't shut me out when *you're* the one who opened the door."

Everything stilled when she did—his pulse, his air—emotions suspended in time while his mind did a free fall, spinning at a pace that left him breathless. Her back seemed to sag as her head bowed, and when she finally turned to face him with a glaze of tears in his eyes, all oxygen seized in his lungs.

God help me—I need her.

"Tess ..." His voice was a croak as he reached for her hand, fumbling to twine his fingers through hers. "I'm no good at this, but talk to me, please."

Her eyelids flickered closed as a reedy sigh shivered her body, and before he could stop himself, he gathered her close, tucking her head beneath his. He breathed in the scent of lemon in her hair, reminding him so much of the woman he held in his arms—fresh, clean, with just enough tart to tingle the senses. The faintest of smiles curved on his lips. "You're right, you know. Surgically I can heal a heart better than most, but when it comes to my own, I'm totally clueless."

An adorable grunt muffled against his chest. "Oh, so you actually have one?"

He grinned. "Well, I could tell you, but then I'd have to kill you."

She pulled away, the smile fading from her face. "You already have," she whispered, "every time you turn Lacey away."

A muscle convulsed in his throat as he nodded, gaze on the floor. "I know."

"I'm willing to listen, Ben, but I'll need more than idle talk ..."

His lids lifted halfway, pulse throbbing when his gaze lighted on her lips. *Yeah, me too ...*

"I'll need total honesty, complete candor, and a willingness to change."

So help me, I already have ... His mind traced the curve of her steeled jaw, skimming across those adorable pursed lips, wondering how he could have ever missed that delicate spray of freckles across her perfectly formed nose.

"And you'll need to apologize to Lacey, of course," she continued, "and become the dad that she needs."

Her words doused with a cold chill. "What?"

Ignoring the sudden scowl on his face, she dragged him back to the table and pushed him down in the chair, one beautiful brow hitched high as she scolded with a finger. "So help me, Ben Carmichael, if you want my friendship, there's going to be a high price to pay—"

He couldn't help it—he grinned. "Häagen-Dazs?"

That stopped her cold. Her brows bunched low. "What flavor?"

He rose with a bit of a swagger. "Maybe you need to come over and find out."

She shoved him down, the threatening finger back in play. "Don't you dare sidetrack me, Carmichael—I can*not* be bribed."

"Tiramisu."

A lump bobbed in her throat several times before a rasp broke from her lips. "All right, but you need to know I'm not fooling around here."

Head tipped, he challenged her with a skim of a smile. "Mmm ... maybe you should ..."

She tossed her hands in the air with a huff. "Okay, that's it—you're obviously not serious here—"

He fisted her wrist with a gentle hold, gaze burning hers with a smoldering look. "Oh, but I am," he whispered, stunned at the sudden desire coursing his veins, wondering how feelings could go from friendship to fire in the scorch of a touch. A need—deeper, stronger, more urgent than anything he had felt in a long, long time—seared all reason, obliterating everything but Tess. His gaze dropped to her lips for

CHAPTER THIRTY-TWO

What am I doing here? Tess hooked a strand of hair over her ear, fingers quaking as much as her knees as she stood on Ben Carmichael's front porch.

"I need to leave a note for the kids," she'd told him, "and then I'll be right over." But she stalled writing the note and stalled changing from her crop top and short shorts into *loose* running clothes that covered her head to toe. Her finger hovered precariously over the doorbell. And she was stalling now.

Big time.

She felt all of sixteen again, wavering in the glow of the front porch light he rarely turned on. Her stomach was as queasy as if it were one of those horrific haunted houses the kids always dragged her to on Halloween. Ghosts and goblins and things that go bump in the night.

Heat instantly bruised her cheeks as she tugged down on Jack's old T-shirt, stretching it to cover as much of her full-length yoga pants as she possibly could despite the steamy night. The blatant desire she'd seen in Ben's face tingled her skin with a heat that had little to do with the weather. Her jaw hardened along with her will. Well, there would be no "bumps in the night" tonight or "bumps" in the road either, not if she could help it.

Too many ghosts in our past.

Her eyes shuttered closed, and the memory of Ben's words, his touch, his look, paralyzed her as she braced a hand to the wall, body and mind swaying with indecision. Should she turn around and go home? Or brave the wolf who could very well take a bite out of any resolve she might have. She kneaded a sudden headache at the bridge of her nose. Where on earth had this mutual attraction come from? Out of the blue like this, when her sole desire till now had only been to reconcile Lacey and him.

Sure, Tess, whatever you say ... Sweat beading her brow, she could still feel the fire of his touch even now, the heat in his eyes that confirmed what she'd been unwilling to admit since the night she'd encountered Cynthia in his kitchen. She was attracted to Ben Carmichael. A low groan ached in her throat. And apparently he was attracted to her. Panic seized like a fist, freezing her feet to the floor. *Oh, Lord, I can't do this ...*

The door whooshed open and there he stood in all his glory, muscled body filling out a polo a little too well for a man his age. With a fold of arms, he butted a shoulder to the jamb with that little-boy grin she remembered whenever he'd trounced her, Karen, and Adam in Scrabble. Only back then it made her smile.

Not buckle her knees.

"The ice cream's melting," he said, the husky tease in his tone doing a little melting of its own. "What took you so long?"

Her cheeks pulsed with heat as she bolted into his house, inching sideways to avoid touching his arm. "Had to change after I wrote a note for the kids," she called over her shoulder, all but sprinting down the hall to the back of his house. "Told 'em I was taking a long walk."

Yeah, a long walk.

Off a short pier.

She shuddered at the click of the front door.

Into a sea of attraction that could very well drown us both.

Making a beeline for the far edge of the sofa, she nudged her sneakers off and curled into the corner, feet tucked beneath her legs. She summoned up a sassy smile, desperate to deflect the jitters tumbling inside. "Okay, Doctor Doom, only one scoop or I'll have to run an extra mile in the dark." She glanced around. "Where's Beau?"

With a secret smile, Ben strolled into the family room with a smug look that told her he knew exactly how nervous she was. Those deadly hazel eyes scanned from the top of her messy bun down Jack's mammoth T-shirt to the tips of her painted toes, laughter crinkling at the corners on his way to the sliding door. "Extra mile? I doubt that, Tess. Five minutes in this heat bundled up the way you are should sweat any calories for an entire week." He let Beau in, unleashing a flurry of tail-wagging and whines that made her smile, helping to ease the tension at the back of her neck.

"Hey, Mr. Bodacious," she said when Beau laid his head on her lap, "I've missed you!"

"You do realize how offensive that sounds that you missed my dog instead of me?" Ben slid her a lazy grin before disappearing into the kitchen.

"Kind of hard to miss somebody who shuts you out with padlocks and plantation shutters," she called, ruffling Beau's snout before kissing him on the nose. "Besides, I was mad."

"Was?" She heard cabinets open and close. "Does this mean I'm forgiven?"

She grinned and stretched her legs out, starting to relax as she patted the sofa to lure Beau onto the couch. "Only if I get a gourmet cone with my ice cream, mister."

He reappeared—along with her tension—toting two cones and a Beggin' Strip, which he promptly tossed to Beau before handing her one of the cones. "I may be a lot of things, Tess, but I'm not stupid." Kicking his Sperrys off, he settled in on the other side of Beau, propping his long legs on the teak coffee table with bare feet crossed. "Comfortable?" he asked, tongue swiping the top of his cone as he studied her with a sideways glance. "Or do you need me to sit in the kitchen?"

She chuckled despite the rise of blood in her cheeks, deciding if she hoped to get anywhere regarding Lacey, they needed to address the annoying gorilla—or dangerous doctor—in the room. She wiggled her toe into Beau's fur, giving his backside a mini-massage. "Nope. As long as my trusty guard dog is here and the doctor behaves, we should be good."

"We could be, you know," he said quietly, watching her with a hooded stare while he worked on his cone. "'Good,' that is. There's something's happening between us, Tess, and scary as it may be, you can't tell me you don't feel it too."

She looked away, her voice strained. "I feel it, Ben, but it's not a good thing, and I don't think we should go there."

"Why?" The cone paused at his lips while he assessed her with a serious gaze, as if contemplating the best medical procedure for a surgery.

"Because it's not right—we have too much history." Avoiding his piercing look, she concentrated on cleaning up her melting cone, the subject matter completely robbing the joy of tiramisu. "It would be too weird for everybody—us, our kids, my church—"

"I don't care what anybody thinks, Tess—"

She glanced up. "I know you don't, Ben, but I do."

A flicker of hurt flashed across his face before his jaw tightened. "It's just a blasted attraction I want to explore, not a proposal of marriage."

Temper toasted her cheeks while her chin lashed up. "Yes, well before I 'explore' a relationship with any man, Ben Carmichael, I need something far more important than attraction."

"Really." He scowled, grinding his cone to nothing in several hard crunches. "And what could possibly be more important than attraction?"

She stopped mid-chew, an ache in her chest over the real reason they could never become involved. Her voice softened as all temper faded away. "Faith," she said quietly, "a deep and abiding belief in God that binds two hearts together."

"Yeah?" His eyes snapped, darkening from hazel to deep brown. "And how'd that work for you the last time, Tess?"

The air locked in her throat, his swift jab striking a blow that brought tears to her eyes. The cone trembled in her hand as she scrambled to her feet, discovering first-hand the painful nick of Ben Carmichael's tongue that Lacey had always implied. She started for the kitchen, intending to pitch her cone and leave. "And to think I almost doubted Lacey when she told me the awful things that you said."

"Tess, wait!" He jumped up and circled the coffee table, cutting her off at the door with a grip to her arm. "I'm sorry. Sometimes my temper gets the best of me and I say things I don't really mean."

"Like telling Lacey she was some other man's mistake?"

He had the grace to blush, his hand dropping along with his gaze. "Yeah, like that," he whispered, chafing the back of his neck. "It was a vile thing to say, and I've apologized to Lacey, and now I'm apologizing to you, for sniping at you like I did."

His humble tone doused all fire in her eyes. "Why do you do it, Ben? Why do you hurt the ones who only want to love you?"

His gaze rose to meet hers, eyes somber despite the tiny tug of a smile. "Are you saying you want to love me, Tess?"

"I *care* about you, Ben," she emphasized, "just like I cared about Karen and still care about Lacey, so you can wipe that smirk right off your face." She took a step back, barely aware the cone was dripping down her arm. "So tell me *please*, Ben, because I truly don't understand—*why* do you attack the people who care?"

Without a word he took the melted cone from her hand and disposed of it in the kitchen while she followed, silently dampening a paper towel before wiping the ice cream off her arm. When he was done, he tossed it in the wastebasket and walked out of the room, returning to his spot on the sofa where he perched on the edge with his head in his hands. "I'm no good at this, Tess," he whispered.

"No good at what?" She carefully moved to her side of the sofa, gaze pinned to where he sat with a rare slump of shoulders.

"Opening up. Admitting the truth. Exposing my weaknesses." He leaned back against the sofa, trailing into a glazed stare. "Facing the fact I was a failure as a husband and father."

"You're *still* a father, Ben," she said softly, heart cramping at the look of defeat on his face. "And Lacey's giving you a second chance—"

"No!" His head shot up, the pain in his eyes constricting her throat. "I don't deserve it and I don't want it."

"But why? Love covers a multitude of sins, and that's what Lacey is offering—her love."

His head was shaking before she could even finish the sentence. "I was no good at it before, Tess, there's no reason I'd be good at it now."

"People change—they make mistakes, they learn, they move on."

He grunted. "You bet they, do and I've learned plenty. Which is why I've moved on, and Lacey needs to do the same." He slashed a hand through his hair, disrupting his usually meticulous appearance. "I'm no good at this whole love thing, Tess, and I'm smart enough to admit it."

"And yet you want a romantic relationship with me," she said, her smile dissolving along with her hope. "Not exactly a glowing endorsement Dr. Carmichael."

He glanced up, capturing her gaze with a potent one of his own. "You're different," he whispered. "Don't ask me why, but I trust you." One edge of his mouth tipped up. "Maybe because you've never screwed me over, so there's no grudge to get in the way."

"You had a grudge against Karen?"

He issued another grunt. "More like a full-blown vendetta."

"Why?"

The distant stare returned as he rested his head on the back of the couch, focusing on the ceiling instead of her face. "I felt like she tricked me into marriage. I loved her in my own juvenile way, sure, but made it perfectly clear I didn't intend to get serious until I had an M.D. behind my name. When she came up pregnant, I got mad, accused her of sleeping around …"

"Oh, Ben …"

He glanced over, his guilt almost palpable. "I'm not proud of it, Tess, but back then I was a spoiled punk running away from responsibility, a freewheeling college student more interested in partying than studying." His gaze returned to the ceiling, the burden of regret weighting his tone. "A kid addicted to pleasure and as selfish as they come. I rationalized that if she was sleeping with me, she had to be sleeping with others, so I refused to admit she loved me, refused to admit the baby was mine."

"Ben—Karen loved you, she always did."

A bitter laugh broke from his lips, void of all mirth.
"I know that now, but after my stepfather forced me to
marry her, I just wanted to make her pay for ruining my
life." He continued in a lifeless drone, as if his shame
had sapped all his energy. "I ignored her for the rest of
her life, Tess, and I ignored Lacey too, except when
people were around. A real first-class jerk. By the time
I could finally see that Karen loved me and Lacey was
mine, it was too late."

He stared straight ahead, and she didn't miss the
gleam of moisture in his eyes. "By then, I was so
riddled with guilt that I blamed them all the more, for
making me feel like a failure as a man." His Adam's
apple shifted as his gaze finally met hers. "When all the
time the failure was mine."

"You're a different man today, Ben; you can start
over."

"No, Tess. I didn't deserve Karen's love, and I sure
don't deserve Lacey's. Especially when I still harbor
bitterness over things I refuse to go into here." He
shook his head, jaw tight. "I don't trust myself, and I
won't do that to Lacey. I failed her as a father once, and
I'm not going there again."

Tess sat up, her patience suddenly as thin as her
gaze. "You know what, Ben? You're right—you did
fail her, but newsflash, buster—you got blood in your
veins just like the rest of us mortals, and failure is the
name of the game, so get over it." She jumped up and
marched to where he sat, ignoring the sag of his jaw
when she leaned in, hands on her hips. "You know what
I think? You're a bigger failure now than you ever were
before, and all because you're too freakin' scared to
take a chance. Oh, you cloak it in noble intent, saying
you don't want to hurt Lacey, but that only wounds her
all the more by heaping rejection on top of inane,
selfish, cowardly, too-stupid-to-live, moronic failure.
Two wrongs don't make a right, Dr. Doom, or don't

they teach that in medical school?" She reloaded with a deep breath before unleashing the rest of her fury. "As far as I'm concerned, you're nothing more than an older version of that same spoiled little kid who's simply made a career out of running away."

He stared, mouth hanging open in the faintest of smiles. "Are you done? Because I think I can dig up an old feather pillow and some tar if you're not."

She blinked, a hand flying to her mouth when she realized just how awful she'd sounded, attacking him more harshly than he had attacked her. She sank beside him and put a hand on his arm. "Oh my goodness, I am *so* sorry, Ben—I have no idea where that came from."

His mouth quirked. "I do. The wellspring of bottom-line truth from a woman who calls 'em like she sees 'em. Which is one of the reasons I trust you so much." He gently brushed her hair from her eyes, his facial muscles softening along with his voice. "There's not many people who could get away with that, especially after I opened up to confess deep, dark secrets I've never told anyone before."

Her head tipped. "Not even Karen?"

Melancholy shadowed his smile. "Especially Karen. She was the source of all my anger, all my distrust, and then when she and Adam ..." He looked away, hardness sculpting his features once again. "I shut down completely. Turned my back on everything—God, family, friends." His exhale seemed to go on forever before his gaze settled on hers. "Until you." Affection warmed the smile that flickered at the edges of his mouth. "A blunt, opinionated, annoyingly perky and completely pushy woman who loves people—and '*cares*' for them—" He reached for her hand, feathering her knuckles with the pad of his thumb, his smile as gentle as his touch. "Just the way they are."

Pulse sprinting, she carefully tugged her hand free and moved away to face him head-on, opting for "blunt and opinionated" with a side of "pushy" to drive her point home. "You're right, Ben, I *do* care for you just the way you are—pig-headed, stubborn, and totally clueless in the realm of love. And as a 'completely pushy' woman who cares for you, I believe that the truth spoken in love is not only the best gift I can give, but the most critical as well."

She ducked her head to peer into his face, aching to see this man happy and whole. "I'm begging you, Ben—for your sake and Lacey's—stop running away. Let the bitterness go and start over. It ruined your marriage and it will ruin your life if you don't take a stand against it once and for all."

He stared back for several seconds, face immobile except for the faintest flicker of a muscle in his jaw. "And how do you propose I do that, Tess?" he whispered, gaze guarded.

She sat back, hands on her knees. "Well, it's pretty clear you're not ready to forgive Lacey, Karen, or yourself, nor do I think you're capable of doing so on your own. So I'd say the only place you can start is by getting back on track with God."

"With God," he repeated dully, his tone acidic enough to convey his disdain.

"Yes, with God, Dr. Doom, the only One capable of fixing this sorry mess you've gotten yourself into."

Scowling, he burrowed back into the sofa with a stiff fold of arms, the veneer that settled over his features not boding well for her cause. "I don't believe God exists anymore, Tess, and the only thing sorry about this so-called 'mess' I'm in is that the one woman I'm attracted to and would like to know better is playing hardball."

"Oh, horse hockey," she said with a scowl that rivaled his own. "You do so believe God exists, Dr. Genius, because guess what? You can't *turn* your back on something that doesn't. And as far as getting to know *me* better, the only way to do that is to know God better, so that pretty much nips us in the bud, now doesn't it?"

She fought the twitch of a smile when his jaw began to grind. "Blackmail, Tess? Somehow as a God-fearing woman, I thought you'd be above that."

"Nope." She countered with a crisp fold of arms. "I'm a Christian, Ben, not perfect, something both of us have learned all too well in the past." She bent forward, her jaw as steeled as his. "Get this and get it good, Carmichael." She poked a finger against his chest to make her point. "I will do anything short of highway robbery to bring peace and joy to the people I love."

He gripped her wrist mid-air like a spring-loaded trap, snatching all oxygen from her lungs. "There's that word again," he said softly, his gaze burning as much as his hold. "I wouldn't be tossing it around too casually, Mrs. O'Bryen, or putting your hands on me unless you mean business." He skimmed the inside of her wrist before gliding up to twine his fingers with hers. "Your hand is sticky," he whispered, eyes lingering on her lips while his thumb slowly circled her palm.

"I gotta go!" She shot up faster than one of Davey's bottle rockets, so flustered, she darted into the kitchen instead of out the front door, bolting to the sink to scour her hands. Fingers trembling, she snatched a dishtowel from a stainless steel rack, head bowed and eyes closed to compose herself while she dried off, berating herself for agreeing to come over. "Talk about a lamb in the lion's lair," she muttered, spinning around with a squeal as something tickled her neck. Her body flashed hot when she realized it was Ben's lips.

"Don't go," he whispered, caging her in, the smoky look in his eyes all but welding her to the spot. "I might be willing to negotiate, Tess ..."

Her heart battered her ribs. "Yeah? Well, I'm no—" The gentle brush of his mouth against hers stalled the words in her throat, robbing her of both reason and resistance when his kiss intensified. Liquid fire coursed through her body at the rush of feelings she hadn't felt in such a very long time. She wanted to push him away, but her insides melted into submission, rendering all resolve as limp as her legs.

"So help me, I want you, Tess," he said, his voice hoarse as he cupped her face in his hands. Hungry lips lured her eyelids closed when they locked a moan deep in her throat. Her breathing was as ragged as his when he moved in close, melding his body to hers.

"No!" She shoved him back, every muscle quivering with a painful mix of longing and fear. "I can't do this, Ben—and if you persist, our friendship is over."

He paused, chest heaving and eyes dark with desire. "You don't mean that."

"I do," she said with a thrust of her chin, "as much as I care for you, we can never be anything more than good friends and neighbors, not with the issue of faith in the way." Arms locked to her waist, she stepped out of his reach, the threat in her tone more than real despite the awful tremble in her limbs. "I need your word this won't happen again."

He studied her, his face a stone mask before he finally expelled a weary breath. "All right," he whispered, slipping his fingers through hers to lead her back to the couch. "Put your shoes on, neighbor—you need to go home."

She did as he asked, avoiding his eyes while she tied a double knot in each shoe. Rising, she followed him to his front door, waiting as he opened it wide. Head cocked, she assessed him with a soulful gaze. "Do I have your word, Ben? Because I need to hear it before I go."

Hands plunged in his pockets, he glanced up beneath dark lashes, a melancholy smile shadowing his face along with a day's worth of dark stubble. "You have it," he said quietly, slowly lifting an arm to gently trace a finger along the line of her jaw. "But I can't help but wonder …" The wounded look of affection she saw in his eyes caused her heart to cramp in her chest. "Who's running away now?"

CHAPTER THIRTY-THREE

"*F*or crying out loud, O'Bryen—you're acting just like you did in eighth grade when Kayla Patek dumped you for the lifeguard at the pool." Matt finger-shot a balled-up straw wrapper at Jack, the mini-cannonball ricocheting off of Jack's temple—right next to the throbbing nerve. "I don't think you went within 500 feet of the rec center that year."

Jack scowled and itched the side of his head where the silly straw ball had hit, glaring at Matt while he parked as far away from the door of the church gym as he possibly could. He deserved to get slapped in the head with a real cannonball for letting Matt talk him into volleyball tonight. Somehow he'd managed to miss the last three weeks, coming up with some excuse or other to avoid watching some other guy fawn over the woman he loved.

Loved. A sick feeling settled in his gut as he rammed the stick shift to neutral. Present tense, not past—a slow-motion revelation that had haunted him since he'd held Lacey in his arms on the dock over a month ago. He issued a silent grunt. Diving right back into his carefully guarded heart. He jerked the handbrake up, thumb drilling the ignition button to turn off the car. "I'm not up to watching Preacher Boy drool all over Lacey, so sue me, Ball."

Matt studied his cousin with a sideways stare, his tone suddenly quiet. "Come on, Jack, you act like you still have it bad for Lacey, which doesn't make any sense. You've been seeing Jasmine exclusively for a while now, sometimes three or four nights a week, right?"

The silence in the car was deafening as Jack slumped over the wheel, arms limp in a fold while he squinted aimlessly through the windshield. "Yeah."

"Wait a minute." Jack never moved a muscle when Matt gripped his arm, his voice laced with shock. "You've fallen for Lacey all over again, haven't you?"

"Nope." Exhaling a tenuous breath, Jack hurled his door open and got out, slamming it harder than usual. "Not 'again,' Ball—*still*." He started walking toward the building, forcing his cousin to run and catch up.

Matt halted him. "Jack, look—I'm sorry. I would have never badgered you to come tonight if I'd known."

The edge of Jack's lip curled as he cocked a hip, studying Matt out of the corner of his eye. "Who are you kidding? You're relentless when it comes to pushing me into church, basketball, and coed volleyball."

No smile lit Matt's eyes, only wrinkles of concern etched beside. "No, man, seriously—I'm sick about this. Why didn't you tell me?"

Jack shrugged, hands tucked in the pockets of the Rock and Republic jeans Jasmine gave him for his birthday. "Give me a break—your wedding's next week. You got enough on your mind without worrying about your older and wealthier—*and* better-looking—cousin."

A crook of a smile settled on Matt's lips. "Older by six measly months, and if you're better looking, then why am *I* the one getting married?"

Jack kept walking, rolling his shoulders to get rid of a kink in his back. "I don't know—Nicki's blind, maybe?"

"Or the smartest woman alive." Matt fell in step again. "For the love of Lacey, Jack, when did you figure this out?"

Jack slid him a withering look that was all show. "Cute, Ball."

His cousin stayed him again. "And for crying out loud—does Jasmine know? Because you two have been pretty hot and heavy the last month far as I can tell."

A heavy exhale breezed from Jack's mouth. "No, Jasmine doesn't know, although she's been complaining that I've been distant lately." He tunneled his fingers through his hair with a loud grunt. "Distant, my hindquarter. I've been a million miles away ever since I comforted Lacey on our dock over a month ago, after a fight with her dad."

"Oh, man, just like old times, huh?" Matt buried his hands in the pockets of his Levis, shoulders hunched in sympathy while compassion flickered across his face.

Jack scratched the back of his neck, head bent in resignation. "Yeah, only without the make-out sessions that always followed."

"Look, Jack, you don't have to be here tonight, honest. This changes everything as far as I'm concerned. I'll just cover for you like usual." Matt winced. "Although I'll have to fall on the sword again with Lacey. She always chews me out over my 'snob of a cousin who's too good to hang with the peons.'"

Jack grinned. "Don't worry, Ball—the little brat always saves plenty of grief for me whenever I see her." He took in a deep draw of air, grateful for the reprieve that Matt was tossing his way. "Which, if I have my way, won't be till the rehearsal." He slapped Matt's shoulder. "Thanks, bro, for letting me off the hook. I think I will head out, if that's okay. Nicki'll give you a ride home, then?"

"Sure." Matt cuffed his shoulder. "I'll be praying for you, man. This can't be easy."

"Thanks, Matt." Jack turned to head back to his car, shooting a half-hearted grin over his shoulder. "As ticked off as I am at God right now, I think I may need all the prayers I can get."

"You got 'em, bro."

"Jackson Alexander O'Bryen—*halt!*"

A groan sandpapered Jack's lips as he dropped his head, the sound of Lacey's voice spurring him on at a quicker pace. He pretended he didn't hear, fingers sweating while he closed in on his car, not ten feet away.

"Oh, no you don't." A star of the women's track team in high school, Lacey was apparently still up to snuff as she skidded to a stop beside him, huffing and puffing while she blocked his door. "You are not going anywhere, bucko. We're one player down 'cause Nate has the flu, so you need to man up, O'Bryen."

Jack slacked a leg, arms folded with a patient smile. He tried to ignore how hot she looked in black biker shorts and a deep-gold Nike racer tank, the exact color of her eyes. The little brat actually had the nerve to jut her lower lip. "Come on, Jack, we need you."

He sighed. *Yeah, I know the feeling.*

Prodding his waist from behind, she started bulldozing him toward the gym, obviously no intention of letting him get away. He fought the crack of a smile over this pushy peanut of a girl bullying him toward the door. "Come on, Lace, I don't feel so good."

She paused, moving in front to assess him through narrow eyes. "You look fine to me—what's wrong with you?"

Heartburn, you little brat. He rubbed the center of his chest. *The lovesick kind.* "Uh, I don't know, acid reflux, maybe?"

"Good." She looped her arm through his and continued to drag him toward the building. "I have Pepcid AC in my purse, so we'll fix you right up."

Jack groaned to cover up the chuckle on the tip of his tongue. "Were you this pushy when we were going together, Mike? Because if you were, I must have been a real wuss."

"More," she said, grunting as she opened the door and pushed him through. "And for your information, O'Bryen, you're still a wuss." She wrinkled her nose as if she smelled something bad. "Just ask Jasmine."

"Jack—you're here!" Kelly wasted no time glomming onto him, tighter than Lacey's Spandex pants. "We've missed you, big boy."

"Good to see you again, Jack." Chase flashed a set of perfect teeth as he extended a hand, pumping Jack's arm like he was his long-lost brother. "We could use a little fresh blood," he said, bobbling the volleyball back and forth. He paused to dispense a Gibb's flick to the back of Matt's head, muscles rolling along with the ball in his hands. "Your cousin is a little too close to the wedding to be much good at anything but mooning over Nicki."

"As it should be," Nicki said with a snooty lift of her nose, snaking an arm around her fiancé's waist. She gave Jack a coy wink. "We need some extra manpower on our team tonight since Matt's head is in the clouds, obviously spellbound by his future wife."

"Hey ..." Matt scooped Nicki close to nibble at the lobe of her ear, causing her to squeal. "It's that provocative perfume you dab behind your ears, you little vamp, that weakens my skill at the game, like Samson and Delilah."

Jack chuckled while he loosened his polo from the waist of his jeans, breaking Kelly's hold when he flipped his shirt out for more freedom to move. "You gotta have some skill in the first place, Ball, before it can be weakened." He clasped his hands high overhead, stretching to limber up as he slanted a smile at Lacey. "And don't go counting on me for manpower—somebody just called me a wuss."

Lacey's chin shot up. "That's because you were being a baby, Dr. Jock, whining about heartburn when you know we need your help."

"Mmm ... wuss, baby, whiner?" Chase took his position on the other side of the net along with Justin and Kelly and the rest of their team. "Sounds like a rift on the team that we'll be glad to exploit. Belly up to the net, ladies and gentlemen, and we'll serve up a little crow."

Matt circled an arm over both Lacey's and Jack's shoulders, leading them to their side of the net with an evil grin. "Think you two can kiss and make up long enough to score us a win? Ouch!" He grabbed his side where Jack speared him with an elbow, pretending offense despite the gleam of tease in his eyes. "Hey, man, that's my serving side." He sauntered off to the front of the net, but not before delivering another cocky grin. "Now *that's* the kind of punch we need tonight, O'Bryen, so let's give it all the pent-up fury you've got."

And give it he did, dominating the first two games with powerful serves that even the pretty-boy preacher had trouble sending back his way.

"*Yes!* Perfect kill, Doctor Jock," Lacey shouted, leaping into the air when Jack aced the final point to score the third win of the night. She high-fived Sarah and Nicki while Chase ambled over to shake Jack's hand.

"I forgot just how deadly you could be, O'Bryen," Preacher Boy said with a gleam of white, scuffing the back of his neck.

"And with acid reflux, too." Lacey sashayed over with her hands on her hips.

Chase tossed the ball back and forth with a genuine smile. "Well, that does wonders for my humility, I suppose, so I guess I owe you my thanks."

"We need to celebrate!" Lacey hooked her arm through Jack's. "This calls for pizza at the best—Sweet Melissa's!"

Jack eased his arm free of Lacey's, hoping to placate her with his it's-going-to-be-okay doctor smile he'd perfected in residency. "Sorry, Lace, but I have an early day tomorrow—office meeting at the crack of dawn before the first appointments of the day."

"Oh, poop!" Her brows crashed into a little-girl frown that was so adorable, he was tempted to kiss her forehead and send her home with a lollipop. "But it won't be the same without you, Jack—you're our MVP. And you got by fine in residency with little or no sleep, right?"

He couldn't resist. He tapped her on the nose. "Yes, but I'm also working extra hours since I'm taking off Thursday and Friday for the wedding, remember? Besides, it's more like MBP—most bleary-eyed player, so I really need to go home."

"Double poop," she muttered, sidling over to stand next to Chase with a pouty fold of her arms. "Okay, but Melissa's has always been your favorite, Brye, so I hope you know what you're missing."

Uh, wouldn't worry about that ... He managed a smile. *And we're not talkin' pizza.* Giving her a wink, he shouted his goodbyes to the group and made his way to the door, grateful for the brisk breeze that cooled the sweat at the back of his neck.

"Hey, Jack!"

He glanced over his shoulder, fighting the scowl that itched to break free. Chase caught up with him in an easy sprint, complete with the warm smile he always wore on his perfect Abercrombie face. "I know you have to get going, but can you spare a few minutes?"

Jack paused, the hint of a frown digging deep at the bridge of his nose. "Uh ... I guess so, sure." He turned to walk back to where Chase stood about ten feet away, glancing at his watch for good measure. "What's up?"

"I was wondering if you'd help me lug a few boxes from the church lobby up to the second-floor nursery—new cribs, changing tables, you know, delivered today."

Brows in a scrunch, Jack hesitated, wondering why in the heck the pretty-boy pastor needed him with plenty of able-bodied guys still inside.

As if reading his mind, Chase shifted, hands propped loose on his hips. "Seems like the gang's pretty anxious to head out after tearing down the nets, so I hate to ask them. Besides," he said with a broad grin, "hopin' to pick your brain on a pediatric problem, if you don't mind."

Mind? Jack's jaw locked. *Sure. You've picked the woman I love, so why not pick my brain too?* Obliging with a stiff nod, he directed a hand toward the church vestibule, following Chase to the front door without a word. He waited while Preacher Boy dug a key from his pocket and let them both in, flipping the lights in the vestibule.

Six mammoth boxes sat dead center, and Jack resisted the urge to groan. A few? His mouth went flat. Somebody needed to tell ol' Pastor Chase that bald-faced exaggeration bordered dangerously close to a lie.

"I know it looks like a lot, but they're not too heavy—just awkward."

Tell me about it. Jack hefted one side of a box in blatant silence while Chase lifted the other, thinking he might actually want to chat and get to know this guy if not for Lacey and his mistaken devotion to God. As is, he far preferred "awkward" over too friendly with some Bible-toting pretty-boy trying to win his quota of souls for the month. *Especially* when one of those souls belonged to the girl he had once hoped to marry. Clamping his jaw to stunt all discourse, Jack gave Preacher Boy nothing but grunts, heavy breathing, and one-word responses, no desire to get friendly with the competition.

"Thanks, buddy." Chase slapped Jack on the back after the last box thudded to the nursery floor, and turning out the lights, he led him back down the steps to where they came in. Chase nodded toward the sanctuary. "Mind giving me a few minutes before you leave?"

Yes. Jack glanced at his watch again. "Sure," he said in a clipped tone, trailing Preacher Boy as he slid into one of the last pews, moving in to give Jack plenty of room.

Perched on the edge of the seat, Chase stared straight ahead, elbows on knees and chin resting on clasped hands. His usual warm and out-going air was suddenly as quiet and serious as the large, wooden-beamed church lit by the dimmest of lights. "I appreciate your time, Jack," he said quietly, eyes meeting Jack's for the first time. "I imagine as a doctor, people hit you up all the time for your opinion, so I apologize for doing the same."

One arm over the back of the pew, Jack lifted a shoulder in feigned nonchalance, shades of the caring minister he had once hoped to be rising to the surface. "No more than a pastor, I suppose," he said with a penetrating stare, a strange longing flooding his soul over a career choice that might have been. "What's on your mind?"

Chase exhaled loudly and sat back. "It's my little sister, Chloe—stepsister, really, since my mom remarried after she and my dad divorced." A faint smile tipped his lips as he stared into the sanctuary, as if seeing something other than gray padded pews and a platform with screens and wall sculptures. "She's only five, but man, what a pistol," he whispered, cramping Jack's gut when he glanced over with a sheen of tears in his eyes. "She lives with my mom and her dad in a small town in Missouri, and the local doc—a G.P. with a family practice—is concerned she might have something called retinoblastoma." He paused. "You know what that is, right?"

Jack nodded, the very word like a punch in his gut. "Cancerous tumor of the eye," he said quietly, his mind instantly reverting to medical mode. "What are her symptoms, Chase?"

His chest expanded and contracted with great effort. "She was having trouble seeing in school according to my mom—double vision mostly—right about the same time she started complaining her eyes hurt. The local eye doc fit her for glasses, but that didn't seem to help, but when her eyes started to cross, we all got pretty worried. The doctor apparently consulted with a colleague in San Diego who concurs that Chloe might have this cancer."

A nerve in Chase's jaw flickered as he blinked several times, as if to clear moisture. "He said she needs a full eye exam, including a CT scan or MRI and maybe an ultrasound. The problem is, that kind of medical help is three hours away and they don't have insurance since my stepfather was recently laid off." He straightened then, shoulders squaring along with his jaw, reminding Jack of the Navy Seal Matt said he once used to be. "So I guess I'm asking straight out, Jack—do you know anything I can do to get Chloe the help that she needs?"

Jack pulled his business card out of his wallet and handed it over. "Absolutely, Chase, and the timing is perfect because a rep from the National Cancer Institute was in last week. So shoot me an email and I'll send you information about St. Jude's Research Hospital in St. Louis. It's the only pediatric specialty cancer center the National Cancer Institute funds, so it's totally committed to caring for and supporting children with cancer regardless of a family's financial or healthcare resources. They also provide free lodging to patient families who live more than thirty-five miles from the hospital, so all you need is a doctor's referral, which I can provide, and we'll get the paperwork started. How does that sound?"

The muscles in Chase's throat convulsed several times before he was able to speak. "Like the miracle I've been praying for, Doc," he said in a hoarse voice, extending his hand to shake Jack's with a firm grip that seemed to bond the two men together. "Thank you, Jack. You don't know what this means to me."

Jack rose, any animosity he might have had for Chase Griffin siphoning right out at the look of sheer gratitude on the man's face. "Oh, I think I do. I spent three years in a peds internship and residency, remember? Seeing kids and families get the help that they need is one of the greatest joys I've ever known. Trust me—it's my pleasure."

"Even so, I'd like to pay you back, if I could," he said carefully, probing Jack with an intense look that signaled the tables were turning once again, making Chase the "healer" instead of Jack. He stood to his feet, the gloss of moisture in his eyes suddenly gone, replaced by the calm confidence of a pastor. "And I have a feeling that maybe I can."

Jack waved him away. "No payment necessary, Rev; helping Chloe is payment enough."

Chase dipped his head, eyes in a squint as he studied Jack with more than a little curiosity. "Can I ask you a question?"

"Sure."

Chase scratched behind his ear, as if in deep thought. "I guess I'm wondering why you've stayed away from volleyball this last month. I mean you're clearly *one* of the best on the team," he said with a glint of tease in his eyes, "and it's no secret you're a competitor to the core." He butted against the back of the pew, eyeing Jack with a casual fold of arms. "And I know you're not all that big on church, but volleyball and pizza in a gym hardly qualify for that."

Jack strove for an air of nonchalance despite the uptick of his pulse. "No real reason, just busy I guess."

"Really?" Chase angled to face Jack head-on, one thigh balanced flat on the back of the pew. "'Cause I kind of get the feeling you might be avoiding Lacey and me."

Heat circled Jack's collar like a ring of fire. "Not sure why you would think that."

"Probably since you tend to get moody whenever I'm around her," he said, gaze focused on Jack like a laser. "And if that's true, I think you should know we're only friends."

Jack blinked, Chase's statement catching him off-guard. "What?"

"Yeah, for a couple of weeks now, as a matter of fact." He rubbed his jaw with the back of his hand, as if talking about it didn't set all that well. "She told me she had feelings for some other guy and hoped we could be friends. It wasn't my idea, of course, because frankly I like Lacey a lot and was hoping to pursue something more."

A tic twittered in Jack's cheek against his will.

"Personally," Chase continued in a matter-of-fact tone that seemed at odds with a knowing look in his eyes, "I think she's still in love with you."

Jack's body flashed cold and then hot, sweat slicking both his palms and the back of his neck. His voice came out as a croak. "What?"

"Yeah, she pretty much implied that, in my opinion, so I guess the one thing I want to know is ..." He pierced Jack with a stony look straight out of the Navy Seal handbook. "What are you going to do about it, O'Bryen?"

Jack slowly sank down into the pew, barely aware how he got there, mind racing as fast as his pulse. Lacey was still in love with him? He swallowed hard. The little brat never let on once in the last month she'd hung out with his sisters and him—on the dock, at the camp, at his house for games of basketball and wiffle ball. His eyelids drifted closed, seeing every nuance of her face across the patio table during dinners with his family, hearing the music of her laughter when she'd finger-flick food at him behind his mom's back. The familiar scent of peach in her hair when he'd held her from behind, teaching her how to swing a golf club in his backyard.

Sensing Chase waiting on his answer, Jack expelled a heavy breath, head bowed while he kneaded his temples with forefinger and thumb. "There's nothing I can do about it, Chase. Lacey's made it pretty clear she wants a guy who feels the way she does about God, and the truth is, I don't." He sagged back against the seat, eyes wandering into a distant stare. "At least not anymore." A harsh laugh tumbled from his throat. "The old 'unequally yoked' glitch back to bite me in the butt. God knows how I wrestled with it myself back when Lacey veered off the path her senior year." A sad smile lined his lips as he saw her in his mind's eye, the pixie vamp who'd tease him with kisses and more, tempting him with moonlight skinny-dipping that'd taken every ounce of willpower he had. But he loved her then— body and soul—and he loved her now, enough to be friends, at least, despite the dull ache in his chest.

He looked up at Chase, an unlikely confessor given Jack's aversion to him before. "Kind of ironic to love her like I do, you know? Only to be tripped up by a precept that means absolutely nothing to me anymore. And now everything to her." His chest expanded and depleted with a noisy blast of air. "No, as much as either of us may harbor feelings from the past, it appears we'll have to settle for being only friends."

Lips tight, Chase nodded. "Well, I have to admit— you and she sure carry it off well," he continued, drawing Jack's gaze once again, "but I have a gut feeling you're both pretty miserable with the way that it is. So as an occasionally annoying pastor wired to 'fix' things in people, I'm going to ask you one more time, O'Bryen—what are you going to do about it?"

"I just told you—"

"*No*," he emphasized, cutting him off, "what are you going to do about God, Jack? After all, if He's the obstacle between you and Lacey and you *claim* to love her like you do—"

"I *do* love her," he shot back, prickles of their prior enmity niggling once again.

A trace of humor glinted in Chase's eyes despite the stern set of his jaw. "Then I'd say it's about time you man up, Dr. Jock, and get back in the game."

"Meaning what?" The clip of Jack's tone was as frosty as his eyes.

Chase straightened to his full six-foot-two height before strolling toward the other end of the pew. "Meaning you need to unload that bag of garbage you've been carrying around since your father had an affair."

"He was a frickin' pastor!" Jack shouted, fury scalding his face.

Chase paused in the aisle, hands slung low on his hips. "Yeah, I know. Those sorry excuses for human beings who have blood in their veins just like you."

Shooting to his feet, Jack bolted from the pew. "I don't have to take this garbage."

"Sure you do, Jack," Chase called, a note of levity in his tone while Jack stalked toward the door. "Unless Lacey's not worth it …?"

Jack ground to a stop at the door, sucker-punched by a preacher with a smirk in his voice. He hung his head, nerves screaming to cut loose with a fist. He slammed a palm to the wooden door, the sound echoing through the church like Chase's words in his mind.

"Unless Lacey's not worth it …? "

He spun on his heel, bludgeoning a finger in the air while he glared. "Fifteen freakin' minutes, Preacher Boy, and I'm outta here, ya got that?"

Chase grinned, rankling Jack even more. "Yeah, I got that, Jock Boy." He ambled toward the door as if they had all the time in the world. "So, tell me, Doc, how do you like your coffee?"

"I wouldn't worry about it, Rev, I'm not gonna be here that long."

Chase hesitated with a palm to the door, the grin fading into a solemn smile that somehow stemmed the tide of Jack's temper. "Sure you are," he said softly, too soft for a bruiser of a man who used to kick butt in the Navy. "I'll make it black and strong because something tells me we're gonna need it." He gave the door two sharp taps before offering Jack an understanding smile that completely disarmed the rest of his anger.

"Because between you and me, looks to be a pretty long night."

CHAPTER THIRTY-FOUR

*L*acey did her best not to cry, but once Chase pronounced them man and wife and introduced Mr. and Mrs. Matt and Nicki Ball to the crowd, there was no stopping the waterworks. Nicki looked beautiful, of course, and Lacey couldn't be happier for her and Matt. They both glowed more than the twinkle lights strung around the gazebo in the pink haze of dusk, and there was no question that theirs was a match made in heaven.

Swiping the moisture from her face, she peeked at Jack out of the corner of her eye, standing with the groomsmen on the other side of the gazebo steps. His heart-melting grin caused her stomach to tilt, those blue eyes agleam with quiet laughter over something Nate whispered in his ear. A wistful sigh drifted from Lacey's lips. Talk about eye candy! In black tails and tie, he made her mouth go dry, surging her pulse as much as a year's supply of Lindt truffles.

His gaze converged with hers, and a slow grin eased across lips she'd once kissed more times than she could count. Hair in a messy updo of tangled curls, she was certain everyone could see the blood crawling up her neck at the memory, and when he sent her a wink, she thought she just might faint. Heart thudding, she jerked her gaze to the gazebo where Matt and Nicki were doing some serious kissing of their own, rallying the intimate crowd of one hundred with cheers, catcalls, and deafening applause. Lacey whooped and clapped with the rest of them, her joy genuine despite the tears that slipped from her eyes. A marriage made in heaven, indeed. She forced a bright smile to hide the ache in her heart. Something she and Jack might have had once.

But not anymore.

The string quartet crescendoed into the wedding march, and Nicki and Matt stepped from the gazebo in a spray of bubbles and rice. Face flushed with joy, the bride clung to Matt's arm while he beamed like the sun that was sinking over the Skidaway. Every tree, trellis, and shrub twinkled with little white lights that lent a fairy-tale shimmer against a watercolor sky, while lace and linen tables sparkled with candlelight and china.

"Oh, Nick, I'm so happy for you two!" Lacey flung her arms around her cousin, no stopping the tears as they both laughed and cried together. She pulled away to hold Nicki at arm's length, scanning her cream off-the-shoulder gown. Its clean and simple lines were adorned by a scattering of seed pearls on the fitted bodice while the tulle skirt flowed to a white rayon runner emblazoned with *And the two shall become one.* "Even after crying through the entire ceremony, you still look gorgeous!"

"Thanks, Lace. I couldn't have done this without you, Cuz." She skimmed a finger along the short off-the-shoulder sleeve of Lacey's lavender chiffon dress. "And you look beautiful, too, not only managing to find a dress that looks great on you, but on both Sarah and Kelly too."

Lacey looked around, admiring Sarah and Kelly as they chatted with the groomsmen—or in Kelly's case, flirted with Jack a little too much. "They do look pretty, as do the groomsmen in those tuxes Matt picked out— hubba-hubba!" Her heart did an annoying flip when Jack glanced her way, but she quickly pivoted to scan

Mamaw's yard, its transformation into a romantic and intimate reception nothing short of stunning. Guests meandered and mingled around lace and linen-clad rounds tucked here and there among lush gardens and trees. Off to the right of the gazebo, the string quartet played at the edge of a cozy dance floor surrounded by potted plants and ferns, their lilting dinner music soon to be switched out by a DJ just setting up. "I'll tell you what, Nick, Uncle Cam spared no expense, that's for darn sure."

Nicki glanced at her father—home from his naval commission in time for the wedding—now chatting with Tess, Shannon, and Cat at Mamaw's table while Davey and Spence swooped Power Rangers through the air. Her smile tipped. "Yeah, the poor guy felt so guilty for being gone so long, he insisted on carte blanche, but having him home means more than anything."

"Hey, they're serving the head table, woman, and I'm hungry." Matt slipped his arms around Nicki's waist, making her squeal when he nibbled her neck.

"Me too," Jack said into Lacey's ear, sidling close to drape a hand over her shoulder.

Lacey jolted, the heat of his hand on her bare shoulder and the warmth of his breath against the exposed skin of her throat zinging sparks through her body. Her jaw tightened as Jack ushered her to the head round in the center of the yard, its satin tablecloth shimmering with candlelight and a spray of calla lilies. *Get a grip, Lacey*, she thought as Jack seated her, *this is your best friend, not a date.*

Yeah, that was the problem.

This was Jack. The best friend who'd begun plaguing her dreams, stealing her sleep, invading her thoughts. This wasn't supposed to be happening, she silently groused, outwardly laughing as the guys heckled Matt. Blame it on the magical fairy-tale wedding or the fact that Jack looked like a Dolce and

Gabbana ad in his tux, jaw shadowed with a bare rasp
of beard. Or even the frequency with which she'd been
hanging out at the O'Bryen's of late, fishing on the
dock, dinner with the family, horsing around like she
was just one of the kids.

Only she wasn't.

Tess wasn't her mother, Shannon and Cat weren't
her sisters, and Jack was definitely *not* her brother. Not
the way her heart had begun to race whenever he
entered the room. For whatever the reason, she was
beginning to feel things for Jack again that she had no
right to feel. He was going with Jasmine, after all, and
Lacey had no intention of falling for a man without
faith.

Too late.

"Speech time, so wish me luck, Carmichael, and in
case I haven't mentioned it, you're a knock-out in that
dress."

Halting mid chew, Lacey glanced up with prime rib
bunching her cheeks, not sure if it was the horseradish
sauce or the potent look in Jack's eyes that sent a brain
freeze crackling through her body. Either way, her
hands were sweating and her throat closed up.

Rising, Jack ting-ting-tinged his champagne flute,
drawing everyone's attention as he raised his glass in
Matt and Nicki's direction. "I'd like to propose a toast
to the man who's been both best friend and brother as
well as a cousin … and to the woman who *finally* took
him off our hands." Chuckles tittered through the crowd
as Jack entertained with stories that elicited both
laughter and tears, priming Lacey for her own toast
where she literally broke down and cried.

The evening was a blur, from the flip of the garter—
snagged by Jack in a good-natured scuffle with
Chase—to the toss of the bouquet, handily won by
Kelly after she bludgeoned Lacey's toe. Pictures were
taken and cakes were cut, and when the music started,

Lacey felt ready to drop. Glancing up, she saw Jack laughing with the DJ and was grateful he wasn't around to ask her to dance. Sagging into her satin-covered chair, she eased her heels off and massaged the foot that Kelly had trounced, not inclined to further punishment on the dance floor.

"On your feet, Carmichael—I'm in a tux, which is the only time I'm prone to dance, so take advantage." Tugging her up, Jack didn't even give her a chance to respond, simply dragged her barefoot across the grass to a dance floor already swarming with people. Ignoring her protests, he looped his arms around her waist and studied her in a squint. "Have you always been this much of a shrimp, Mike, or am I getting taller?"

"Only your ego," she quipped, wishing her best friend didn't look so darn sexy, jacket off and shirtsleeves rolled to reveal thick forearms, veined and scattered with hair.

"Hey, blame it on the tux, not me." He gave her a wayward grin that pooled heat in her belly when the music began to play. "Can I help it if girls think doctors in tuxes are hot?"

She looked away, annoyed by the fire flaming her cheeks. "Hotshot, you mean," she countered, just aching to wipe the smirk off his face and not really sure why.

His low laughter rumbled beneath her ear when he tugged her to his chest, the strains of Randy Travis's *Forever and Ever, Amen* finally registering in her brain. *Oh, goodie.* Jack's favorite song to sing during their moonlight floats in his dad's dory. With a confidence and skill that suddenly ticked her off in the face of her own unease, Jack melded them into the music as if he were on *Dancing with the Stars*, his moves fluid and totally in control. "Ah, jealous, are we?"

"Ha! You keep thinking that, Dr. Romeo." A smile shadowed her lips as she closed her eyes, sinking into the warmth of his hold with a quiet sigh. Well, if nothing else, she could enjoy this one dance with a man who spiked her pulse before she shot down anymore slow dances the rest of the night. He started humming the song against her hair, voice husky and low, and her eyelids could do nothing but sink under his spell. The heat of his body and scent of Obsession cologne disarmed her completely, confirming that Jack O'Bryen was quickly becoming an obsession in which she could no longer indulge.

Not as a boyfriend *nor* as a best friend.

His low baritone hushed to a whisper when the familiar lyrics blew warm in her ear, a man pledging his love forever and ever, until the day that he died ...

Against her will, hot tears pricked, and Lacey pushed away from his chest with a plastic smile, determined to break the spell of a "best man" who was anything but "best" for her. "Not too close, O'Bryen. If it's all the same to you, I'd rather not risk Jasmine slashing my tires." The distance she put between them helped to clear the fog from her mind, and lips in a slant, she scanned the backyard. "Speaking of the little missus, what time is she coming tonight?"

"She's not."

Lacey's gaze snapped to his, mouth sagging open. "Are you serious? Why on earth not?" She tried to deflect her shock with a casual air, brushing imaginary lint off his gray satin vest before teasing with a slide of her palm down a shirtsleeve taut with muscle. "Goodness, if I had a boyfriend who looked like you in a tux, Brye, I think I'd be here to protect my interest."

He didn't let go when the song came to an end, his hands all but burning through the chiffon when they firmly anchored to the small of her back. "Because a best man has an obligation to the maid of honor, Miss

Carmichael." The tease in his tone quickly faded to soft when his gaze flicked to her lips and back. "Especially when *his* interests are at stake ..."

Blood shot to her cheeks, all but asphyxiating her as she stumbled back, her knees as weak as her smile. "I need air," she rasped, not sure she knew what he was talking about, but not willing to stay and find out. A gulp wobbled her throat. "And something *really* cold to drink ..."

She whirled around to bolt away, only to bounce against his chest when he tugged her back, locking her in a powerful hold. "There's air all around you, Lace," he whispered, so close she could smell the Godiva chocolate on his breath from the wedding favors strewn on the table. "But a walk to the dock would be nice. I'll grab a couple of waters on the way."

She tried to squirm free as politely as possible, pulse pounding harder than the bass of the Third Day song the DJ was now blasting into the night. "Jack, my feet are killing me, so I'm afraid I need to pass on both walks and dances—"

His sober look stopped her dead in her tracks. "We need to talk, Lace," he said quietly, "and for me, it's pretty serious."

She stared, dread crawling in her stomach at his solemn look. She swallowed hard. "All right—you get the waters, and I'll grab my shoes."

Her mind and her stomach were awhirl as she snatched up her heels at the table, grateful that the wedding party was out on the dance floor and not likely to notice where she and Jack went. What could he possibly want? And what on earth could be wrong? In a slow blink of those deadly blue eyes, it seemed as if he'd morphed into the Jack of old—serious and intense, with that fierce gleam in his gaze that told her he cared way too much. A tremble rippled through her as she put on her shoes, well aware that *that* Jack was far more dangerous to her state of mind than the man about town.

Especially now.

"How are your feet?" he asked as she carefully picked her way through the grass in Mamaw's front yard where a vermillion sun leaked ribbons of gold over the roof of the community dock at the end of the street.

She gave a slight shrug, taking the bottled water he handed her while avoiding his eyes. "Nothing three hours in a hot soak won't cure." Praying she wouldn't trip in her heels, Lacey winced as she limped along toward the dock a block away. Mid-wince, she gasped when Jack halted to swoop her up in his arms, swirling heat in her stomach. "What on earth are you doing, O'Bryen?" she squeaked, grateful it was getting dark so no one would spot her in his arms.

He stopped midway, enough dusky light in his face to see the jut of his brow. "You're going to break your silly neck in those stupid heels, Lace, and frankly, I don't want to ruin Matt's wedding with a trip to the emergency room, all right?"

She squirmed in his arms, attempting to get down. "I'll take them off, then."

"Nope." He continued to stride toward the deserted dock, now washed in shadows of purple and pink. "You're a tenderfoot, remember?"

"Fine." She unleashed a loud bluster of air, not at all comfortable with the tingles from the constant bump of her body against his. Neither spoke while he carried her to the far edge of the dock, the sounds of the night cocooning them in a familiar setting far more magical than any fairy-tale wedding. The strains of music seemed to melt into the background, giving way to the croak of tree frogs and the distant hoot of an owl. Lazy squeaks sounded as the dock shifted on the water, its moonlit shadows appearing to roll along with the river.

An eerie beauty that had always both seduced and soothed.

Especially in Jack's arms.

He carefully set her on a chipped and peeling Adirondack loveseat facing the river as if she were just as fragile, sliding in beside her and tugging her close. They sat side-by-side, silently staring into the moonlit waters while she reluctantly rested her head on his shoulder. The gentle lap of the waves were a welcome tranquilizer for Lacey's ragged nerves. A tranquility that immediately fled at the whisper of his very next words.

"I love you, Alycia Anne."

Her body stiffened against his while her breath seized in her lungs. Swallowing hard, she sat up, gaze pinned to his sculpted profile. "I ... love you, too, Jack," she managed in a casual tone, determined to ignore the intensity in his. "And I thank God He's allowed us to be friends."

Before she could even move, his large palm curled around hers, knitting their fingers together in a tender hold that notched her pulse by several degrees. He turned his head to lock her in a powerful gaze that literally numbed her to the chair. "We're far more than friends, Lace, and we both know it."

No! Fighting his spell, she jerked free and shot to her feet so quickly, she tottered on her heels, the beds of her nails white as her fingers balanced on the arm of the chair. "I can't go there, Jack—"

In a single thud of her heart he rose, facing her with a firm brace of her arms. "And I can't go anywhere else."

His tender look seared both her soul and her body with a rush of desire so potent, she nearly drowned in a sea of want.

"I'm desperately in love with you, Lacey, and the truth is, I've never stopped, even with a mountain of hurt and heartbreak piled on top." His voice lowered to a gravelly whisper while his thumbs coaxed with a slow graze of her arms. "I need you in my life, Lace—as my friend, yes, but also as my wife and lover." Fire licked through her veins when his gaze lowered to her mouth, eyelids sheathing closed as he slowly bent in.

"No!" She shoved him away, breaking his hold. Her breathing was erratic while she held him at bay, the flames of desire igniting her temper as well. "In the name of decency, Jack O'Bryen, what kind of man cheats on his girlfriend?"

The edge of his mouth twitched as if a smile hovered beneath. "I'm not 'cheating' on her, Lace, I'm trying to declare my love for her."

She folded her arms with a huff. "Well, I imagine Jasmine would have a few choice words to say about that."

The smile broke free as he scooped her close again, holding her captive in the circle of his arms. "I imagine she would, but since I broke up with her last night, she doesn't carry much weight, you know?"

Her body went limp. "You b-broke up w-with Jasmine?" Mind racing, she tried to think back over the last few weeks when Jack always seemed to be around whenever she hung out with Shannon and Cat. Her heart stuttered more than her words. "For h-heaven's s-sake, *why?*"

He caressed the edge of her jaw, his eyes as tender as his touch. "Because I'm still in love with my old girlfriend, Mike, the one who was supposed to be my wife."

Her heart seized. "I can't, Jack," she whispered, her voice a rasp as she struggled to break away. Moisture stung in her eyes. "I can't marry a man with no faith."

His palm gently brushed the hair from her face. "I *do* have faith, Lace. Faith in the fact that we were always

meant to be together and that both of us are still in love
with the other."

She shook her head vehemently, desperate to dispel
any notion he might have of getting back together. "I'm
not in love with you, Jack, not that way," she said
loudly, more to convince herself than him. "I do love
you, but as a friend and nothi—"

He paralyzed her with a possessive kiss that
obliterated all protest, any denial utterly lost in a groan
that ached all the way up to her lips, which now
trembled more than her limbs. Breathing shallow, she
just stood there with eyes closed as if in a trance, barely
aware he had pulled away for the chaotic beat of her
pulse and the traitorous thrum of her body.

"Uh, you know, Mike, we're going to have a
definite problem if that's how you kiss all of your
friends ..."

Eyes popping open, she shoved him away, the heat
of his kiss scorching all the way to her cheeks. "Just
what do you think you're doing?" she rasped, shock
overriding all desire as she stared, jaw distended. "That
is *not* proper behavior between friends—"

His silenced her with a kiss to the tip of her nose.
"You are so cute and flustered when you're caught in a
fib, you know that?"

She stomped her foot. "I don't care what you think,
Jack O'Bryen, I am *not* fibbing."

Slacking a leg, he propped his hands low on his hips.
"It's not what I think, Lace, it's what Chase thinks." He
folded his arms with a smile that might have been a
smirk in better light. "Unless you're calling Preacher
Boy a liar?"

Stomach cramping, she whirled to stare out at the
moon-striped water, arms stiffly crossed. All fight
slowly siphoned out over a truth she so desperately
wanted to deny. "No, I'm calling him a big mouth. He
had no right to say anything."

"But he did," he whispered, his strong arms wrapping around her waist from behind. "So what I want to know, Alycia Anne Carmichael, and what I want to hear from the lips of the woman I love is …" Her heart stopped when his mouth skimmed along the nape of her neck with the softest of kisses, unleashing shudders through her body while he slowly feathered her ear. "That you still love and want me too."

Her eyelids drifted closed, the words beating a frenzied drum of consent against her ribcage, just aching to break free. *Yes, Jack, I still love you and yes, I still want you too.*

But I can't …

She slowly turned to face him, her face streaked with tears as she cupped his jaw with a rush of love that almost buckled her at the knees. "It won't work, Jack," she whispered, "no matter what feelings I may have." Her throat convulsed with grief. "I need a man of faith."

A slow grin eased across his lips as he tugged her in close. "Then, lucky for me, I am."

Her heart skidded to a stop. "What do you mean?" she whispered, not daring to breathe.

"I mean …" He cradled her face, taking his time to skim her mouth with a gentle kiss that seemed to take on a life of its own, flaming into a passion that wrenched a moan from his throat. He jerked back, eyes on fire and his breathing as ragged as hers. "God help me, Lace, I'm so crazy about you, I want to marry you right now."

Ignoring the throb of blood in her veins, she fisted his silk vest with both hands and rattled him but good. "Focus, O'Bryen!" she shouted, enunciating each syllable with a harsh whisper that all but spit in his face. "What-did-you-mean?"

His teeth flashed white in the moonlight as he leaned in to nibble at the lobe of her ear. "It means you're out of excuses, Mike, for turning me down," he whispered, his chuckle warm against the goose bumps that popped on her skin. "I made my peace with God."

She froze as if he'd just tossed her into the drink, and with a choked swallow of air, she launched back, hands all but gouging his arms as she gaped in shock. "B-But how? "W-When?" Her heart was stumbling along with her words.

Laughing, he swept her up and settled back in the chair with her on his lap. "You might say I had a 'Come-to-Jesus' meeting with your ex-boyfriend," he said with a quick nuzzle of her neck, "who turned out to be a pretty decent guy." His mouth wandered to her ear, and she squirmed out of his reach, suddenly short on patience as she two-fisted his vest once again. "Details, O'Bryen, not lip service. Not one more kiss, bucko, until I have all the facts, you got it? Now start from the beginning, Jack, and don't leave anything out."

His eyes took on a dangerous gleam. "Ah, but there *will* be kisses," he said with a grin, fingers fondling a loose curl from her hair. "Lots and lots of kisses …" Depositing a kiss to her forehead, he bundled her close and told her about the night Chase cornered him at the church, first to wrangle his help moving boxes, and then for medical advice for his sister.

"He's a smooth one, Lace, I'll give 'em that," he said with a low chuckle, the respect and affection in his tone making her smile as she rested against his chest. "Softening me up with talk of his little sister who has cancer, near breaking my heart. He was so blasted grateful when I told him I could set her up with the St. Jude Foundation, we almost formed a bond, you know? And then he reeled me in like a speckled trout on a shrimp popping cork in high season." His chest rose and fell beneath her head as his voice took on a gruff quality that told her he was battling his emotions. "I owe him my life, Lace," he whispered, "for bringing me back to the God Who saved my sorry soul. Even got me to pray for my dad if you can believe that, drilling it home that forgiveness and prayer is the only way to be set free from the past."

A grin curved on her lips as she stroked his chest with her palm. "Straight out of the Jack O'Bryen handbook, as I recall."

His chuckle rumbled in her ear. "Yeah—dirty pool if I ever saw it." He pressed a kiss to her hair, his scent enveloping her along with his arms. "So I'm free now, Lace. Free to be the man God's called me to be and free to pick up where we left off ... if you'll let me."

"If I'll let you, huh?" Squeezing him in a ferocious hug, she pulled back to study him.

He smiled and tipped his head. "What?"

Her eyes narrowed in tease, but her pulse slowed into a painful thud, heart wavering over a tiny seed of concern. "You're not just doing this to win me over, are you, Jack? I mean, you've recommitted to God for yourself and not just for me, right?"

His grin mellowed into the serious and sensible boy she'd fallen in love with so very long ago. "As much as I love you, Lace ..." He feathered her jaw with the pad of his thumb. "And I do—if Chase hadn't reawakened my passion for God that night, we wouldn't be here right now. Not only because I couldn't do this with a straight face, but because I couldn't do it to you. I love you too much to go against your faith, Mike, and the desire of your heart. But ..." His arms slid to her waist in a loose hold while he placed a gentle kiss to her forehead. "If you'd like to see a little more proof, Carmichael, I'm more than willing to revert to friendship again and put the lip service on hold till you're absolutely sure ..."

Warm shivers fanned through her as she stroked the curve of his jaw, stomach quivering as much as her hand. "Not sure I could handle that after tonight, O'Bryen," she whispered, throat ducking when her gaze drifted to his mouth, "so I may have to resort to faith …"

A slow grin traveled his lips. "What a novel idea."

Fondling a wisp of her hair, he leaned in to nuzzle her mouth in a gentle mating that flooded her with joy like high tide on a warm, summer day. His lips trailed to caress the soft flesh of her ear before he whispered his love. With every glorious word, her heart beat faster and faster until she was sure she might faint.

Jack—*her Jack*—had found his way home! And in doing so—God willing—she would find hers …

In his arms for the rest of her life.

CHAPTER THIRTY-FIVE

"**R**un, Wesley, Run!" Jack grinned as he cheered the towheaded orphan on, the Camp Hope outfield scrambling to retrieve the ball that had sailed over their heads. The tiny legs of the ten-year-old batter pumped as furiously as Jack's heart as he waved the runners from second and third all the way home, puffs of powdered dust billowing in their wake. Before the all-girl outfield could even throw the ball back, Wesley slid in to score feet first, kicking up a storm of dirt that left the catcher—aka his girlfriend, Lacey—in a fog. With a whoop that rivaled the shrieks and cheers of his all-boy team, Jack hoisted the little guy in the air. "Wow, we needed that dinger, slugger, so great job." He tossed a sideways grin to Will Hogan, his co-captain. "Way to put those girls in their place, eh, Will?"

"I'll give you a dinger," Cat called from the pitcher's mound, her eyes as thin as her smile as she slapped the ball back and forth in her glove. "Just step up to the plate, Dr. Jock, and I'll be more than happy to put *you* in your proper place."

"Ah-ah-ah …" Jack hooked an arm around Wes, his grin deliberately diabolical. "Good sportsmanship is the hallmark of great athletes, ladies, along with the win." He gave Lacey a wink as she seared him with a paper-thin glare. "But then I guess you wouldn't know about that."

"That's it." Lacey hurled her catcher's mitt down and stomped to where Jack stood. She thumped his chest so hard, he was tempted to pin the offensive hand behind her back and kiss the scowl off her face. "You are going down in flames, bucko, and trust me—every girl on this team will be basking in the heat."

Jack couldn't resist. He snatched her wrist mid-thump, the burn in those deadly eyes sparking more than a little heat of his own. His voice lowered to husky as he leaned in, locking wits with the little brat who'd stolen his heart. "For your information, Mike, I've already gone down in flames *big time* and trust me, sweetheart—I'm loving every shiver of heat."

The fire in her eyes shot straight to her cheeks, which now sported a healthy sunburn that had nothing to do with the sun. "Yeah? Well, bundle up, Doc, because I hear a cold front's coming through." She spun on her heel, but not before he saw the faintest twitch of a smile on those beautiful lips. Lips that for the last three weeks had laughed, teased, and given him a glimpse into the soul of the woman he hoped to marry. A forever kind of love that had lain dormant till she reignited his hope and set his heart aflame.

Not to mention his body.

"Okay, guys, bottom of the ninth and we're winning 5 to 3, so let's wrap this baby up." Jack rallied his team with a loud clap of hands. "Only one out to go, so we gotta make it count." He grimaced when a gangly boy named Henry stepped up to the plate with several blind swings, because "count" it did—as a third out. "You'll get 'em next time, sport," Jack said with a pat of his back, enjoying these Saturday morning softball games Will Hogan set up for the kids.

The tables turned when the first two batters on the other team put a girl on second and third, and immediately some of Jack's good humor fizzled as their lead slipped away.

"Whoops—looks like your team's putting us in our place again, Jack," Cat called from the sidelines with a definite smirk on her face. "The winner's column!" She high-fived Shannon while Lacey gave a thumbs-up from third base where she was coaching for the next run.

Jack ignored her, focusing on Debbie instead as she shuffled to the plate, her usual spunk lagging behind like the bat she dragged in the dirt. "You okay, sweetheart?" he asked, bending to study her more closely. Concern wedged his brow when he noticed a faint tinge of blue in her lips. He grabbed her little hand, rubbing her knuckles while he eyed the beds of her nails, pulse stuttering over their pale color. No trace of blue, but definitely not pink like they should be. "Have you been chewing blueberry bubble gum?" he asked, relief coursing when she nodded her head. He placed a palm to her flushed face and forehead, noting a slight warmth that could easily be from the heat of the day. "Deb, you're warm, so I think you need to sit this bat out, sweetheart."

"No—*please!*" All spunk was back in play as she stepped away to demonstrate several hard swings, her little chin thrusting high while she pled her case. "I'm the best hitter on the team, Dr. Jack, and if you take me out, it'll be pure cheating."

A smile threatened his solemn doctor manner as he stared her down. "Open your mouth, young lady," he ordered, and fought a grin at her blue tongue and blueberry breath. He heaved a heavy sigh and stood to his feet. "Okay, kiddo, you're cleared for this one bat *only*. No running for the rest of the day, and if I catch you, I'll order a nap. Is that clear?"

"Yes, Dr. Jack," she said in a sweet sing-song voice that made him grin. A twinkle lit her brown eyes as she teased him with a sassy sway of hips. "Miss Lacey said we're gonna make monkeys out of you guys, but you're not gonna make me take a nap if we do, are ya?"

He balled a fist into his catcher's glove as he squatted behind the plate. "Nope, but you gotta win first, you little hooligan, so batter up."

"Okay, sweet stuff," Will bellowed with a flash of teeth, "show me what you got."

Thud. Jack's glove swallowed the ball whole as Wes shouted "steeeee-rike!"

"You can do it, Debbie, eye on the ball," Shannon called from the bench where Cat was biting the nails on both hands like she was nibbling corn on the cob at the fundraiser picnic.

"Come on, Deb—put a little sass in that swing," Jack whispered, earning a gap-tooth grin from the little dickens who'd probably rob him of a win.

"Strike two!" Wes shouted with a squeal, apparently the team's self-appointed umpire.

Debbie dug in, grinding the toes of her Keds into the dirt as she positioned herself just so, her little tush way out in the air. The ball came cruising her way, and Jack held his breath.

Crrrr-rack! The ball went into orbit and so did the bat as Debbie took off like a rocket. She rounded first base to the shrieks of her team before anyone could get a glove on the ball.

"Go, Debbie, go!" Lacey screamed at third, bouncing in the air like she was a cop on a flippin' trampoline, waving the other runners in. Both girls whooshed across home plate, squealing so loud Jack winced at the sound. *And* the score.

The winning run was rounding second, but her pace had slowed considerably, and to Jack, it seemed like Debbie was running in slow motion, the hollers of her teammates fading into the background like a dream. She staggered at third, almost tripping on the bag, and when she labored to make it home, his heart clutched at the gleam of sweat on her face.

"Jack!" Will's shout drew his gaze as the ball flew through the air, slamming into his glove just as Debbie crossed the plate.

Pandemonium exploded, but all Jack could see was the deathly pale little girl who slammed into his legs before she collapsed to the ground.

"Debbie!" Hurling the glove and ball away, Jack dropped to his knees, heart constricting as he pressed his middle and index finger to her throat, the pulse rate as sluggish as Debbie had been before her bat. "Debbie?" He forced his voice to remain calm, hoping to mask the anxiety clawing in his chest, but she remained unconscious. "Lacey—call 911," he shouted. "Cat, Shan—get the kids out of here."

Frenzy swirled around him like the fear in his gut. Focusing on Debbie, he shut out Lacey's shaky voice on the phone, the sobs and whimpers of the kids, and Cat's and Shan's soothing whispers as they herded them all away. His eyelids flickered. "Please Lord, keep her safe …"

"What can I do?" Will asked, desperation threading his tone as he knelt by Jack's side.

"Give me your glove," Jack ordered, bunching it on top of his catcher's mitt to elevate Debbie's feet. He felt for a pulse again, and this time it was barely there. Tilting Debbie's head back, he placed the heel of his hand on her breastbone and gave thirty fast compressions before placing his ear close to her mouth, praying for the slightest sound or feel of blueberry breath.

Nothing.

"God, please," he whispered, pinching Debbie's nose closed as he covered her mouth with his own, giving her two rescue breaths that made her chest rise. Barely aware of Miss Myra and Will hovering, he continued compressions, the wail of a siren coming closer and closer.

It didn't take long for the paramedics to take control, quickly transporting her to the ambulance after her breathing kicked back in. She was still unconscious when they wheeled the gurney away, her body so tiny and frail.

"Jack ... will she be okay?"

He turned at the sound of Lacey's nasal whisper, her face wet and splotched with grief. Hooking her waist, he bundled her in his arms, resting his head on top of hers. "I don't know, Lace," he whispered. "Her history of congenital heart disease complicates things a lot." He pressed a kiss to her hair. "But one thing I do know is God answers prayer, which is what we'll be doing on the way to the hospital." He gave her a quick squeeze. "Let's get moving."

Cat and Shan volunteered to stay behind with the kids while Miss Myra and Will followed Lacey and Jack to Memorial, endless prayers winging high. Upon arrival, Jack left them in the waiting room to race to Peds ER, zeroing in on the whirl of activity around triage.

The nurse looked up when he pushed the curtain aside. "Jack, what are you doing here?"

"She's a patient of mine, Connie, from Camp Hope." His gaze locked on the rise and fall of Debbie's chest, grateful her breathing appeared to be an even rhythm despite her unconscious state. He caressed the girl's clammy forehead to check for fever, her eyelids closed and tinged blue like her lips. "Any signs of cognizance?"

The triage nurse glanced up briefly, continuing to record Debbie's vitals while staff milled in and out. "The paramedics said her eyes flickered open in the ambulance and that she moaned and said a few words before passing back out, but nothing since. Can you give me her history, Jack, and we'll get her registered?"

He nodded, a knot of worry ducking in his throat as he assessed Debbie's limp body. It felt strange being on this side of the stethoscope, watching a little girl he loved hang in the balance. Mind numb, he filled Connie in on Debbie's condition and what happened before she collapsed, finally conferring with the attending physician, Greg Mathews, a buddy of his from med school.

"We'll get an echo stat," Greg said with a solid grip of Jack's shoulder, "and catheterization, if necessary. Let's hope her circulation remains stable to avoid any strain."

Gut twisting, Jack gave a short nod, eyes glazed as his friend returned to Debbie's room to issue orders. *Hope, yes ... and pray.* With a bow of his head, he kneaded the bridge of his nose, more to dispel the moisture that threatened than to ease the headache that was beginning to throb. Almost a month ago, hope would have been the only option he had, and a shallow one at that, at least without God. But now he had an entire arsenal at his disposal—a relationship with the God of Hope Who not only loved him, but every precious curl on Debbie's little matted head.

He turned and strode down the hall, absently slapping the push-button wall switch to go through the double doors that led to the waiting room. The minute Lacey saw him, she leapt up from her chair as if spring-loaded, meeting him halfway with fear in her tear-swollen eyes.

"Her vitals are stable," Jack reassured with a quick skim of her arms, "which is good, although she's still unconscious."

"What does that mean?" Lacey whispered, voice hoarse as Miss Myra and Will flanked her on either side like bookends, worry etched in their brows.

He ushered them back to their seats, taking one himself as he explained Debbie's condition in a low voice, striving for a calm he didn't quite feel. "They're running an echo right now, which is a test that uses sound waves to take a picture of Debbie's heart. It's completely safe and doesn't hurt, but most importantly, it'll tell us how to proceed."

They peppered him with questions, and the physician in him took over, responding to each and every one in a serene and steady manner.

"We've known all along that Debbie's had a congenital heart defect, Jack," Lacey said in a strained voice, "and she's been fine. Why now?"

He covered Lacey's hands with his own, hoping to soothe her worry with a gentle rub of her knuckles. "Many kids with congenital heart defects don't need treatment, Lace, just close follow-up by their physicians, which Debbie has had. But sometimes …" He couldn't thwart the duck of his throat. "Sometimes the defects get worse, and in those cases, doctors may have to repair them with catheter procedures—which is what I'm hoping for. Or …" He gave her hand a tiny squeeze. "Worst-case scenario, open-heart surgery. Either way, she's in good hands, Lace, both with the ER staff and God. But it sure wouldn't hurt if we prayed."

Tears brimmed in Lacey's eyes as her lips began to quiver, and with a weak sob, she launched into his arms, nails digging into his back. "Oh, Jack, I love you so much …"

At the sound of her words, the flicker of hope in his chest blazed bright, inflaming his faith in the God who healed both his heart and his relationship with this woman he loved.

Now may the God of Hope fill you with all joy and peace as you trust in Him, so that you may overflow with hope by the power of the Holy Spirit.

A Scripture once so familiar now flooded peace through his body, and in that exact moment, Jack knew to the core of his being that this "God of Hope" would not disappoint. With a renewed fervor, he buried his face in the crook of Lacey's neck, the moisture stinging his eyes from sheer gratitude instead of from fear. "Me, too, Lace," he whispered, "me too." Taking her hand in his, he quietly led them all in prayer, not as the minister he once aspired to be, but as a doctor healed by the Great Physician, Who he prayed would heal Debbie as well.

"Jack?"

His head jerked up at the call of his name, throat going dry at the serious look on Greg's face. Jumping to his feet, he followed his friend into the ER, both men pausing after the doors sealed shut. "What is it, Greg?"

His friend's solemn face told the story before the words ever left his mouth. "I'm sorry, Jack, but it looks like catheterization won't be an option. She's got an ASD that needs surgery."

The blood iced in his veins. "When?" he said, voice cracking on the question.

"As soon as possible. I've put a call in for Dr. Schmidt—he's the cardiac surgeon on call, and triage is prepping Debbie now."

Jack nodded, his exhale shallow as it slowly parted from his lips. He gripped the physician's shoulder. "Thanks, Greg. Will you let me know when Schmidt gets here?"

"Sure thing, Jack, and I'm sorry, man. It's tough when the patient is someone we know, but we'll do our best for her."

"I know you will. Thanks, buddy." Dazed, Jack pressed the wall switch and made his way down the short hallway to reenter the waiting room, his bleary-eyed gaze immediately connecting with Lacey's. "They're prepping her for surgery now," he said quietly, ushering her back to where Miss Myra and Will watched through somber eyes. "She has an atrial septal defect or ASD, which is a hole in the septum between the heart's two upper chambers." He exhaled slowly, keeping his voice as level as possible. "They've contacted the heart surgeon on call."

"No." Lips strained white, Lacey sat straight up. "If at all possible, I want Daddy to do it," she said, never more sure of anything in her life.

Jack hesitated. "Lace, time is of the essence here, and Dr. Schmidt is on his way."

She shook her head, unable to explain the strong feeling that compelled her to insist, but somehow she knew it was right. She whirled to face Miss Myra, clutching the older woman's hand with a confidence that didn't come from within. "Daddy is one of the best heart surgeons in the country, Miss Myra, and I'd like to call him if it's okay with you."

A ridge in her brow, Miss Myra studied her for several seconds before giving the nod. "Call him, then, my dear, and we'll see what God decides."

Fingers fumbling on her phone, Lacey punched in her father's speed dial and waited, not daring to breathe while the phone rang in her ear. "Come on, Daddy," she whispered, eyelids sinking closed like they were made of lead. Her hand began to sweat against the plastic as she waited, an eternity measured by fractured beats of her heart. Her pulse seized at the sound of his voice.

"Hello?"

"Daddy?" Against her will, tears flooded so fast her gaze blurred into a million lights. "I need you," she whispered, breaking on pitiful sob.

"Lacey?" The panic in his voice rose along with its volume. "What's wrong—are you hurt?"

She shook her head, rivulets of saltwater streaking her cheeks. "No, not me—Debbie. The orphan at Camp Hope that I told you about?"

"Yes …?"

"They're p-prepping her for heart surgery right n-now, Daddy, and another s-surgeon is on h-his way, b-but I was hoping—"

"I'm on my way. Is Jack there?"

"Yes …" She handed the phone over to Jack, hovering close to listen, head tucked to his.

"Dr. Carmichael?" Jack's grip on the phone appeared to be as taut as his tone.

"I'm pulling out of the marina parking lot right now, Jack, but I need you to fill me in."

"Yes, sir, it's an ASD too far gone for a cath, so they've called in Dr. Schmidt as the surgeon on call."

"Good. Do you have a history for me and vitals?"

"Yes, sir." Jack rose and walked to the other side of the waiting room, taking him out of Lacey's earshot, but within seconds he returned, the stress in his face softening to a smile. "He wants to talk to you."

She grabbed the phone, and instantly more saltwater puddled in her eyes. "Daddy?"

"She's going to be all right, Lacey. It's serious, yes, but nothing I haven't handled a hundred times before, so you and Jack need to go to the cafeteria for a coffee or something to eat. The surgery should take anywhere from two to four hours, and complications are rare, so don't dwell on the 'what-ifs,' all right?"

Nodding, she sniffed, swiping the wetness from her face with the back of her hand. "Okay, Daddy," she whispered, craving the warmth of his arms like never before.

"I'm just minutes away from pulling in to the physician's parking lot right now and will head straight up to surgery. But I'll send a nurse down on a regular basis to keep you apprised, and then come down myself as soon as I can, okay?"

"O-Okay," she whispered, a sudden burst of love swelling along with more tears. "And, Daddy?"

"Yes, Lacey?"

Choking back a sob, she shielded her face with a trembling hand. "I love you so much …"

Silence filled the line for several breathless thuds of her heart until she finally heard the gruff clear of a throat. "I know, sweetheart. I love you too."

CHAPTER THIRTY-SIX

*S*tifling a yawn, Tess lay in her chaise on the patio, head back and gaze glued to the pinpricks of light peeking through the hedge from Ben's backyard. Despite the hint of fall in the cool night air, the tin pie plate of freshly baked monster cookies were still warm on her lap, baked the moment she'd heard that distinctive whir of his garage door opening. Now, long after he'd let Beau out—with a grumpy tone that had given her pause—the warmth of the cookies were beginning to wane along with her patience while she waited for him to whistle Beau in. She knew he would be tired after the stressful surgery for Debbie, so she didn't want to talk. A shaky breath drifted out. Just hand him his favorite cookies.

Nice and safe.

Or would have been if he opened the flippin' door.

In the past, she would have just barged in the moment he flicked on the back porch light to let Beau out, marching right over to ring his doorbell or bang on the slider with a portion of whatever she had baked that week. He'd always been miffed at first, but then they'd settled into a comfortable routine of friendship, a grouch and a perky neighbor finally coming to terms, forging a kinship that had chased her loneliness away. A kinship suddenly too close for comfort, relegating them to far fewer visits, and *always* on her side of the hedge.

A wispy sigh feathered her lips. Sweet heavens, how she missed it all.

The laughter, the debates, the companionship.

Him.

Her mouth settled into a firm line. Which was *exactly* why she was waiting over here until he opened that blasted door, no desire whatsoever to play with fire again. An annoying hot flash bolted through her that she almost wished she could blame on menopause. Oh, it had plenty to do with hormones, all right. Her mouth went flat. The wrong kind. The foil pie plate in her lap crinkled as she burrowed into the chair with a stiff fold of arms, determined to avoid late-night chats alone with Ben Carmichael, at least *inside* of his house. All she wanted to do tonight was to thank him for what he did for Lacey and congratulate him on saving a little girl's life.

That's all?

"Yes," she hissed, arguing with the part of her that longed to be in his arms once again.

"I want you, Tess ..."

"Doesn't matter what we want, Ben," she said in a near growl. She swung her legs off the chaise and tossed the foiled tin on the seat beside her as if it had scalded her hands. "I won't have a relationship without faith, it's as simple as that."

At least not *that* kind.

Beau's whines brought her back to reality, a scrunch in her brow when she suddenly realized both she and the dog had been waiting for Ben to open that stupid door for a solid forty-five minutes. Snatching the cookie plate, she hopped up and strode down the driveway with purpose, bent on seeing to it that Beau got inside, even if her cookies did not.

"Okay, Carmichael, open up ..." She rammed a finger against the bell, the deep bongs reverberating on the other side of the door matching those of her pulse. "*You* may have fallen asleep in that easy chair, big boy, but Beau's whining will keep *me* awake." She tapped her toe impatiently on the stone front porch, finally foregoing on the bell to bang on the door.

No answer.

"Well, I know you're home, mister, unless you're dating a really tall woman with a really gruff voice, so you can't shut me out." Spinning on her heel, she tromped down the steps and around the house, Beau's whining as pathetic as hers. Not thrilled about mounting the wooden fence, she glared at the ridiculous padlock. "It's just plain wrong to force a forty-six-year-old woman in flip-flops to scrape through a hedge or scale a fence," she muttered, dropping the cookie plate on the other side with the hope of beating Beau to it.

As luck would have it, she incurred only minimal scratches by scrambling over the slatted fence via a handful of privet hedge, mere seconds before the lab appeared. The poor guy's tail wagged so hard, she felt a stiff breeze. "Yeah, I know, buddy," she said with scrub of his head, lips puckered to create that ridiculously low baritone she always used to soothe her babies and kids. "Your master can be a real twit. Here ..." She slipped a finger beneath the foil to fish out two pieces of bacon before sailing them into the air. "You deserve this for putting up with him."

Beau darted away and pounced on the treat, giving Tess a clear shot to the back door. One hand cupped to the slider window, she frowned as she peered inside the dark family room, lit only by a faint wash of light from the kitchen. *How odd* ... Her heart skipped a beat when she made out Ben's hulk of a form lying in his massive recliner, obviously asleep. The pinch in her brow immediately softened. "Aw, poor baby," she said, heart going out to the hero who had had a very big day. With a quick scratch of Beau's head, Tess quietly opened the door, shushing the lab's anxious whimpers with a finger to her lips. "Shhh, Beauregard, Daddy's asleep."

Ignoring her warning, the black lab darted to where Ben snored like a freight train, hands limp on the arms of his chair. Beau nudged at his legs several times, but the man never moved a muscle, so still Tess might have thought he was dead. Her lip quirked. Except for the chainsaw grinding in his throat.

"Beau," she whispered with a pat to her thigh, "let's see if Sleeping Beauty fed you." Tiptoeing into the kitchen, she scoped out Beau's bowls, noting both appeared pretty dry. The poor dog actually danced on his hind legs in anticipation, but as the mother of four crafty children, she was not easily fooled. "Oh, no you don't, mister, empty bowls don't mean a thing—I've seen you filch bacon faster than a pickpocket, remember?" She peeked into the waste can and wrinkled her nose over the stash of empty Lean Cuisine boxes, finally plucking out an empty can of dog food lying on top. Further investigation revealed a dry and crusty can, fairly safe evidence Ben hadn't yet fed his dog. "Goodness, your dad must have been bone tired when he came home to fall asleep before feeding his best bud," she said after filling both bowls with the appropriate food and water. "Okay, buddy, dig in!"

Tess spent a few moments wiping food-encrusted counters and washing dishes before placing the plate of cookies on the bar just so, leaving a note to let him know she fed Beau. Dimming the light, she ambled back into the family room, pausing in front of Ben's chair on her way out. A melancholy sigh drifted from her lips. Even in bloodstained scrubs in the dark of night with a snore that could wake the dead, the man still fluttered her pulse. "Good night, Dr. Doom," she whispered, thinking the name more appropriate than ever before. Long on attraction, but short on faith, Ben Carmichael spelled nothing but doom for his smitten neighbor, and Tess said a silent prayer they could somehow remain friends.

She turned to go and stopped, her gaze snagging on an open decanter bottle of Crown Royal on his side table. Her breath hitched when the truth struck hard, as if she'd been whopped over the head by that half-empty bottle of booze. She leaned close to his mouth and sniffed just to make sure, jaw dropping open wider than that of the soused Rip Van Winkle. Ben Carmichael— the man who promised he'd never touch alcohol again—was drunk as a skunk and smelled just as bad.

For some reason, fury shot through her like whiskey through Dr. Doom's veins. *How dare he!* One of the country's top heart surgeons, upon whom people's lives depended. One who not only had no business getting stinking drunk, but had lied to her as well.

"Yes, Mother, I promise to never drink alcohol again."

"Yeah, right," she said, stomping around to turn on every lamp in the room. She returned to yank the recliner handle, and his feet plummeted to the floor with a satisfying thud.

A groan parted from his lips as he stirred in the chair, eyelids still pasted shut.

Muttering under her breath, she flipped on the overhead light on the way to the kitchen and made as much racket as she possibly could, opening cabinets and slamming them closed until she had everything she needed to brew a strong pot of coffee. So strong the man would have trouble sleeping for a week, especially after the tongue-lashing she intended to give. She poured him a steaming cup and tasted it just for good measure, quite certain that one potent sip would keep her up as well.

Coffee in one hand and her own tall glass of ice water in the other, she marched right up to Ben's chair and slammed the cup on the table with a loud bang, sloshing a pool of coffee into the saucer. "Rise and whine, Dr. Carmichael, you've got some explaining to do." She kicked his shoe several times, which did absolutely nothing to wake him up *or* slow down the snoring.

"Ben, wake up," she shouted, rattling his arm to no avail. "Okay, mister." Dipping her fingers in her glass, she flicked iced water into his face over and over, earning nothing but a grunt and several sluggish swipes of his hand.

Patience exhausted, Tess held the glass of ice water over his head. "All right, Sleeping Beauty, you asked for it." With a grim press of lips, she poured the entire glass onto his head, mouth quirking when an ice cube bounced off his nose.

The man shot up in the chair like Poseidon on triple espresso, water sluicing down his face till it dribbled off his chin. "What the—?"

Tess blocked out the string of expletives that followed, kind of wishing she had more water to wash his mouth out with soap. She clunked the empty glass on the table and stepped back with a rigid cross of arms. "Sorry, Dr. Doom, but I figured you'd be too soused to take your own shower."

Razor-slit eyes blinked back before a hoarse voice cracked from his throat. "What?" he whispered, brows scrunched so low, wrinkle lines crisscrossed his forehead like a freakin' game of tic-tac-toe.

She cocked a hip, the sarcasm that dripped from her tone keeping up with the ice water. "Hate to break it to you, Ben, but somebody apparently broke into your house and drank half a decanter of your whiskey."

Dimples of confusion popped in his brow. "Huh?"

"My, my, but we are articulate when we're hammered, aren't we?"

He started to rise in the chair and halted midway with a moan so pitiful, she might have felt sorry for him if he didn't reek like a pub on payday. Hand to his head, he peeked through shaky fingers that shielded his eyes, the tic-tac-toe grid on his forehead suddenly convex. "Tess? What are you doing here?" he rasped. Another pucker crinkled the bridge of his nose as his free hand haphazardly patted his clothes. "And why am I all wet?"

"An appropriate term if ever there was," she sniped on her way to the kitchen, returning with a dishtowel she balled and pelted right at his head. "Here—you might want to mop up that fancy leather chair before it becomes as sloppy as you." She slapped two hands on her hips. "And why am I here? Oh, nothing—just letting your dog in from outside, watering him, feeding him, watering you ..."

Somehow awareness seemed to dawn through the fog in his brain, ushered in by a long, aching groan as he sagged back in his chair. "I ... I don't know what happened," he whispered, bloodshot eyes staring straight ahead in a drunken stupor.

"Really?" She shoved the cup of coffee closer to his chair, slopping more liquid into the saucer. "You know, for a heart surgeon, you can be pretty stupid, Doc. Drink the coffee, Carmichael, all of it, *now*," she ordered, standing watch while he slowly sipped at the cup, eyes closed and dark bristle shadowing his jaw.

Still fuming, she stormed to his bathroom to rifle through his medicine chest, her fury mounting when she saw enough women's toiletries to fill a shelf at Wal-Mart. She nabbed a bottle of ibuprofen and palmed two before slamming the medicine chest closed so hard, it rattled the mirror. With a one-handed yank of the spigot, she filled a glass marred with toothpaste residue and stalked back into the family room. Sympathy softened her approach when she found Ben slouched on the edge of his chair, head in his hands.

Tapping him on the shoulder, she grinned outright at the look of horror on his face when he saw the glass of water she held. He actually jerked back in the chair, bloodshot gaze flaring wide for the first time, revealing whites of his eyes spidered with red. "You're not gonna dump that on me, are you?"

Her mouth crooked. "As tempting as that may be, Dr. Carmichael, no, this is for your ibuprofen, which I imagine will be only the first of many you'll be gulping before you're through. Here." She handed him both water and pills, and he took them with a garbled thank you that came out as a rusty croak.

Water glugged down his throat while his eyes locked with hers over the rim. "Thanks, Tess," he whispered, his voice less gravelly as he placed the glass on the table. His frantic gaze darted to the sliding door before relief slackened his features when Beau nudged the side of his leg. "Hey, Big Guy, sorry 'bout that, but it looks like Tess has everything in hand."

"Including another glass of ice water if you don't explain why you broke your promise to me, Ben Carmichael."

Pain flashed across his features she suspected had nothing to do with the booze in his body. He dropped back in his chair with a slow knead of his temple, eyes closed and face steeped in regret. "It's a long story, Tess," he whispered, "and not one to promote sweet dreams."

"Sweet dreams took a hike when I found my neighbor and dear friend comatose next to a bottle of Crown Royal, so you may as well spill it because I'm not leaving till you do."

His eyelids edged up halfway, a faint glimmer of humor swimming around in those red-rimmed eyes.

"That might tempt me if I didn't have this annoying jackhammer in my head."

Mouth agape, she plunked hands back on her hips, unwilling to let him off with a tease and a smile. "Really? You're gonna hit on me with cutesy flirtations when you're not even a man I can trust?" The humor in his eyes died a slow death along with her patience when she snapped up his cup, emptying the flooded saucer back in before spinning on her heel. Lips thin, she halted at the kitchen door. "You want something to eat with your next cup of coffee? You know, to soak up the alcohol?"

"No, I'm fine. Go home, please."

Her hips shifted into a testy stance. "No, Ben, 'fine' is stone sober and *not* smelling like a still." She cut loose with a loud a sigh, expelling some of her anger as well. "Look, how 'bout a couple cookies? I brought a plate over to thank you for what you did for Lacey today."

He peered up beneath hooded eyes. "What kind?"

One edge of her lip jacked up. "Well, I'm sure you'd prefer rum balls, but sorry, Doc, they're only monster cookies." She bit back a smile with a stern fold of arms. "Which given your behavior, seem oddly appropriate."

He stared for several moments while tenderness melted the strain in his face. "I love you, Tess," he said quietly, the sheen of moisture in his eyes prompting the same in hers.

"Get a shower, Ben," she whispered, "and I'll make you breakfast. We need to talk."

He nodded and rose, slowly making his way down the hall. And, given his declaration of love tonight, she thought with a wrench in her heart ...

Out of her life as well.

CHAPTER THIRTY-SEVEN

*H*e should be happy.
He saved a life today.
Ben turned the shower handle all the way to scalding, well aware saunas were not smart with a hangover, but he flat-out didn't care. He deserved it, despite the praises of his daughter.

"Daddy! You're my hero," she'd said the moment he'd come through the waiting room door, rushing to embrace him with undeserved love in her eyes.

Steam from the shower billowed all around him, fogging his body as well as his mind.

Because of him, a precious eight-year-old child would live to see another day. His eyelids groaned shut, the weight of a million regrets forcing them closed.

And because of me, another lies in an early grave.

He slumped against the shower wall, wishing the water was hot enough to scorch the shame from his mind, but he knew better. He could scrub his body raw, but his soul was stained forever, marking him unfit to be a father.

"Daddy, I love you," Lacey had whispered after the surgery, clutching him so tightly he could barely breathe. And what had he done? Stood there like a monument to failure, heart of stone and arms just as cold, useless appendages that refused to embrace her

back. The memory flushed tears from his eyes as guilt and self-loathing rained down.

First Karen. Then Lacey. Now Tess.

Three hearts of flesh battered against one heart of stone.

Dear God, what would it take to chip the guilt and grief away?

"Ben?"

He startled in the shower, Tess's voice laced with concern on the other side of the door.

"You've been in there for over forty-five minutes. Are you ... okay?"

No. "Yeah, sorry," he called, the effort unleashing a sharp ache in his head. He turned off the water, body clean, but his mind still soiled from a past he wished he could wash away. "Just trying to detox. I'll be right out."

Drying off, he was grateful for the haze of mist on the mirror. He didn't want to face himself right now. It was bad enough he had to face Tess. Desperate for potassium and vitamin B, he popped a multivitamin, then brushed his teeth blind, along with his hair. Feeling somewhat better after his shower, he slipped on his Gap blue-and-white plaid pajama bottoms and a clean T-shirt, finally padding down the hall in his bare feet. He paused at the kitchen door, a strange warmth flooding his soul as he watched Tess putter at the sink in his kitchen.

Like she belongs here.

His eyes roved the length of her, from the curve of a tiny waist to the gentle swell of hips in shorts that revealed killer legs free of the yoga pants she'd hidden behind last time. His mouth twitched. Which meant she'd had no intention of coming inside tonight. Half of him wished she hadn't, while the other half was glad she did. The bad half, he realized, gaze glued to a perfect posterior while she bent over to put the frying pan away. He cleared his throat, the smell of bacon rumbling his stomach. "Smells good," he said quietly, smiling when she spun to face him, dropping a dishtowel on the floor.

"Well, that's certainly an improvement." Her eyes did a quick scan that dusted her cheeks with a pretty blush. Whirling around, she quickly retrieved the towel before pulling a plate of bacon and eggs from the oven. "Sit."

He did as he was told, still feeling a bit wobbly when he eased onto a stool. "You joining me, I hope?"

She plopped the plate on the counter with a silent smile, along with two plates, paper-towel napkins, and utensils before pouring them both a fresh cup of coffee. When she slid onto the stool next to him, he automatically reached for her hand to pray like she always did at her house for dinner. For some reason he had this strange longing to thank her for her friendship and this meal by honoring her God. Bowing his head before she could pull away, he forged on with grace, invoking a God who was slowly calling him home via the woman beside him.

At the end of the prayer, he closed his eyes and tightened his hold, exhaling a shuddering breath. "I'd also like to say that I'm sorry for blowing it big time tonight. Mostly because I hurt my neighbor and friend …" He hesitated, suddenly realizing Tess was so much more, making his next words come out husky and hoarse. "Well, the truth is, she's not just a neighbor and friend anymore, but my best friend and a woman I've grown to love, so forgive me for hurting her, and help her to forgive me too." His heart lifted at the gentle press of her hand, giving him the courage to go on. "Especially when she hears what I have to say tonight," he whispered, his mind made up to finally share the grief that he bore. A split-second decision he hadn't intended to make, he continued, shocked to the core when a rare peace settled on his soul. "And thank you for bringing her back into my life. Amen."

"I thought you didn't believe in God," she said with a trace of a smirk, tone obviously flip to deflect the sheen of moisture in her eyes.

He glanced up with a faint smile, placing the paper towel on his lap. "I figure the fact I survived the wrath of Tess O'Bryen is proof enough."

She dove into her eggs with gusto. "You might want to reserve judgment, Dr. Doom, just to make sure I didn't tamper with your eggs."

He grinned, content to devour the meal while she chattered on about silly things like the mole she caught in her yard or the poor crop of tomatoes she'd had this year, well aware she was giving him time and space to enjoy his food. When he finally finished, he wove his fingers through hers, giving her a gentle squeeze. "Thanks, Tess—that was wonderful."

She slipped from the stool to carry the plates to the sink, a noticeable flush creeping up the back of her neck. "Feel better, I hope?"

"Much, although there's a wicked bowling tournament going on in my head."

The lilt of her laugher worked better than any painkiller he could prescribe. She filled his sink with soap and water, apparently to let the dishes soak before lifting the coffee pot in the air. "I'm throwing caution to the wind and going for one last jolt of caffeine—you?"

"Yeah, one more sounds good, thanks."

Strolling over, she refilled both cups, then emptied the pot and washed it out, turning the machine off before finally returning to her stool. She sat and faced him, smile fading into a somber gaze while her thumbs grazed the sides of her cup. "So, what happened tonight, Ben?" she whispered, ridges of concern letting him know she cared. "How can you go from saving a child's life to the bottom of a bottle?"

A fresh wave of guilt assailed him, worse than any hangover he could ever have. Elbows propped on the bar, he tunneled fingers through his wet hair before shielding his eyes, gaze boring into the hi-sheen black granite counter beneath. The one that mirrored the image of a man who turned his back on his own. "Yes, I saved a life today," he said quietly, "but I'm afraid a hundred lives saved wouldn't take away the guilt that I own."

Tess's hand lighted upon his arm. "What do you mean?"

He sagged against the back of his leather stool, fingers gouging the bridge of his nose. "I mean I said 'no' to saving a life when I should have said 'yes.' A friend of Lacey's who had a little girl just like Debbie. She died of congenital heart failure because I wouldn't intervene."

"But why?" A trace of shock clouded her tone as she removed her hand, robbing him of the warmth of her touch.

His gaze absently traced the silver veins in the black granite, avoiding her eyes. "Because she was the illegitimate daughter of a wild friend of Lacey's," he said, his tone as dead as he suddenly felt inside. "You may not know this, but Lacey got involved with the wrong crowd senior year, a fast crowd, several of whom ended up pregnant." Fresh fury arose at the very memory of that year, of the war zone it created in his own home. Shards of bitterness crept into his tone. "This was a girl who fooled around and got caught, so she couldn't go home, which is one of the reasons Lacey and I fought the night she left." His jaw ached. "She wanted me to help her, to allow this girl to stay in our home," he said slowly, feeling the rise of the same bitterness he'd had for Karen after she came up pregnant. "But I didn't. So when her baby was born

with heart problems ..." He swallowed the bile that
tainted his tongue. "I felt this girl should pay."

"I don't understand, Ben, pay how?"

"With pain over the possibility of losing her child,"
he whispered, staring aimlessly ahead, Karen's voice on
the phone that night still haunting his soul. *"Please,
Ben, Lacey and I are begging you to come—the child
needs surgery."* His gaze glazed into a blur as hot tears
all but scalded the sockets of his eyes, jaw clenched so
tight he felt the burn at the base of his skull. "Karen and
I fought, and I was angry ... so I ..." He swallowed the
regret clogging his throat. "Made her wait." A tic
flickered in the hollow of his cheek. "By the time I
finally waltzed into the hospital, the baby was dead. A
botched surgery at the hand of some hack surgeon,
fresh out of residency." His eyes shuttered closed, the
guilt so fresh and raw, he had no control over the water
that dampened his cheeks. "And all because I was too
judgmental, too selfish, too blasted stubborn to consent
to a simple request from my own wife and daughter."

"Oh, Ben ..."

Eyes trailing into a glassy stare, he shut out the
tender compassion he heard in her tone because he
knew he didn't warrant it. His voice lowered to a
soulless whisper. "Did you know congenital heart
defects are the leading cause of infant deaths in the
U.S.?" He turned to stare at her, his facial muscles rigid
with pain. "I did, and yet I did nothing. Thousands of
babies never reach their first birthday, and because of
me, that child never even made it to her first week."

"Ben," she said softly, "you're no longer that man."

"It doesn't matter. Every time I see Lacey, I'm
reminded of the failure I am. As a husband, as a father
..." His voice trailed off to almost nothing. "As a man.
Toxic to my own flesh and blood." He shook his head.
"No, Tess, fatherhood's not for me, not only because

I'm no good at it, but because I don't deserve it after what I've done. I'm not worthy."

She leaned in, capturing his gaze with the intensity in her own. "None of us are, remember? 'For all have sinned and fall short of the glory of God.' Once, someone asked theologian and philosopher G. K. Chesterton what was wrong with the world, and you know what he said?"

He glanced up. "No."

Her chin rose. "He said, 'I am.' Because the truth is until human beings are cleansed by the Blood of Christ and cloaked in *His* righteousness instead of their own— filthy rags, all—one can never be truly 'worthy.'" She rested her hand on his. "Or free."

He looked away, his voice a monotone. "So if the Son sets you free, you're free indeed," he said quietly, surprised that the Scripture came back so easily.

"Exactly. Because no matter what happens, Ben, until you embrace the very One who knit you in your mother's womb ..." She paused, as if giving him time to really hear the words of her heart. "Your soul will ache."

He peered up. "I can do that, Tess, and God may forgive me, and others as well, but I'm not sure I can forgive myself."

Her smile bore all the hope and joy of an angel aglow before the throne of God. "Trust me, Dr. Doom, you can, because His grace makes it far easier than you can ever imagine, and I should know." Melancholy suddenly shadowed the beautiful curve of her lips. "After what happened with Adam, I blamed myself for everything. For failing my family, for missing all the signs of a marriage in trouble, for being the type of wife to drive a minister to cheat ..." Her lip curled the slightest bit. "For wanting to see him stretched out on a rack, swarming with fire ants."

He grinned. "Ouch. Remind me to never cross you again."

One perfect brow jagged high. "I rather hoped the ice water had accomplished that." Expelling a wispy sigh, she lagged into a distant stare. "I spent the first few years of our divorce bitter and depressed, hating who I'd become."

It was his turn to hike a brow. "You?"

"Yeah," she said with a sheepish smile. "Several stages before I hit perky and prying."

He cocked his head, curiosity crimping his forehead. "So, how'd you do it?"

Her nose scrunched in that adorable way he loved whenever she was concentrating especially hard. "Well, I didn't do it, actually—God did—but first I had to acknowledge and embrace several important truths that I seriously hope you will too."

She stalled long enough for him to peer up in a half-lidded smile, back-circling his hand to prompt her on. "And those would be …"

That netted him a sassy grin before the smile tempered into her serious demeanor, the look that always held him captive against his will. "One, that you're a sinner *desperate* for a Savior, Ben Carmichael, and two …" Love shone like the sun in her sky-blue eyes. "You're greatly loved by a God Who is *desperate* for you." She cupped a gentle hand to his grizzled face. "As well as a daughter who desperately longs to be part of your life."

He averted his gaze. "I wish I could believe that, Tess." Pushing off the stool, he gathered their cups and rinsed them off in the sink, another wave of guilt causing his shoulders to slump. His hands braced on the edge, arms as rigid as the stainless steel beneath his palms. "Oh, I believe I'm a sinner all right, and I might even swallow that bit about God loving me." He turned to lean against the counter, arms in a fold as his eyes drilled into hers. "But only because of you, Tess, because of *your* faith and the gift you are in my life." He shook his head. "Nope, faith is one thing, but family?" He kneaded both temples with forefinger and thumb, his headache returning over the very notion of getting close enough to hurt and be hurt all over again. "I'm afraid I do better without."

She rose from her stool so quickly, it screeched against the black slate floor, closing the distance between them with four purposeful strides. "Did you know people without strong relationships are fifty percent more likely to die earlier than those with healthy ones?"

He couldn't help it—he smiled, giving a gentle tug on one of her silky curls. "As a matter of fact I did, Nurse O'Bryen, so I guess it's a good thing I let you barge into my life, huh?"

A wedge of impatience creased above her nose, trumping the ghost of a smile he saw on her face. She slapped his hand away. "I'll have you know we are hardwired for relationships, Ben Carmichael, by the very God Who exists in a relationship Himself—Father, Son, and Holy Ghost." She stepped in to poke a finger in his chest. "A 'family' of three Persons in One, mister, which means, you bullheaded baboon, since God is the bedrock of our existence, our need for relationship is rooted in Him whether you like it or not."

Battling a smile, he gripped her finger, covering her hand with his own to press her palm to his chest. "Calm down, Tess, I finally concur, on both faith and relationship." He lifted her hand to press a kiss to the tips of her fingers, eyes fused to hers. "But with *you*— *not* Lacey."

"For heaven's sake, why?" she snapped, yanking her hand from his. "It's so simple, Ben. Forgive Lacey and forgive yourself so you can move on and become the man God wants you to be." Her voice lowered to a whisper as she took a step back. "And the man I need you to be too."

He stared, wishing more than anything he could be that man for her, but the fear crawling in his gut told him he couldn't. His voice bore the weight of guilt he'd carried most of his life. "You don't understand, Tess, I can't."

She stomped her foot, an action that would have brought a smile to his face if she wasn't singeing him with her eyes. Her volume rose. "For all that is holy, why not? Please—explain it to me, Ben, because I really don't get it."

"I can't," he whispered, "you wouldn't understand."

Her temper sparked like he'd lit it with a blowtorch. "Oh, I understand all right," she said, arms barricaded to her chest. "You're a coward, Ben Carmichael." She mocked him with a snide voice. "Can't forgive yourself, can't forgive Lacey—"

"I *have* forgiven Lacey," he shouted, her temper finally tripping his. "It's Lacey who won't forgive me if she finds out, Tess, and I won't go there again."

"Finds out what?" Her voice lost some of its heat.

He slashed trembling fingers through his hair, so acutely frustrated he wanted to punch a hole in the wall. "That it was me who killed that baby, because I wouldn't come."

Her brows dipped low. "She doesn't know?"

His lids lumbered closed as he shook his head, arms braced to the counter so hard, he thought they might snap. "No, she doesn't. Karen didn't want to add further strain to an already broken relationship, so she told Lacey she couldn't get a hold of me. Told her she'd left a message that I didn't get till too late."

Tess was silent for several seconds. "Lacey will understand, then, and she'll forgive you, I promise."

"No, she *won't*," he said, his voice a volatile hiss as his blood pulsed in his brain. He turned to sag over the sink once again, his words slinking into a whisper. "She'll end up hating me just like before." His voice trailed off, reality slicing through him like a cold blade of steel. "And so will you, Tess. Eventually."

She moved to his side, hand on his arm. "You're wrong, Ben. Lacey and I are both living for God now, and with His help, anyone can forgive anything."

"I wish I could believe that," he whispered.

"You *can!*" she said loudly, jerking him to face her with a hard shake of his arms. "I have with Adam and Lacey has with you, so give me one good reason, Ben Carmichael, why you can't do the same."

He stared, memorizing every freckle on her beautiful face, every silky strand of blonde hair while he wrestled with her plea to become the man she—and God— wanted him to be. Lifting his hand, he skimmed the curve of her face, wishing with all of his heart things could be different. "Because," he whispered, hoping against hope that the truth would actually set him free. "The child I turned my back on that day, Tess, was not only my granddaughter ..." The silence thundered as loud as the violent beats of his heart. "She was yours too."

CHAPTER THIRTY-EIGHT

*J*aw dangling, Lacey slowly slid into a black leather chair at her father's stainless kitchen table. The black granite top was adorned with two black place settings and a tall silver vase with white calla lilies. She expelled a shaky exhale, barely aware she'd been holding her breath. The idea of her father serving a meal to her—at a formal table, no less, instead of his recliner—was as foreign as the sushi and mango fusion chicken he'd ordered from Asian River. "Goodness," she said with a jittery laugh, her fingers all thumbs as she placed a black cloth napkin over her lap, "I would have dressed appropriately if I'd known we were going gourmet."

He glanced over the shoulder of his navy polo, the half smile on his lips the most humor she'd seen in her weekly visits yet. "It's take-out, Lacey, not fine dining," he said with the barest touch of tease, so faint she might have imagined it. Turning back to the counter, he finished dumping cartons of spring rolls and wontons on a plate before carrying them to the table, the barest of twinkles in his eyes more noticeable close up. "Besides, my tux is at the cleaners."

She tempered a grin with a shy chew of her lip, not used to tease and banter, much less dinner without a TV. "This is nice, Daddy," she said softly, snitching a wonton as he retrieved bowls of mango fusion chicken and rice from the oven and a plate of sushi from the fridge.

"Yeah, it is." Setting everything on the table, he exhaled and propped hands low on his hips, his smile tight despite a casual stance. "And long overdue after all the meals you've prepared for me, kiddo." He nodded at her utensils. "I have chopsticks if you want them."

"Heavens, no," she said with a nervous giggle. "I prefer food in my mouth instead of on my lap, thank you very much."

His answering smile was as polite as hers as he strode to the cabinet, tossing a glance over his shoulder at the black lab sprawled at her feet. "I don't, but I'll bet Beau does." Retrieving a wine glass, he promptly filled it with white wine, then grabbed a beer and returned to the table.

Eyeing the wine glass he'd placed before her, Lacey nibbled the edge of her lip. "Uh, Daddy, I don't drink anymore …"

He twisted the cap off his beer and took a quick swig, eyes sparkling over the rim of his bottle. "Neither do I." With a nod at her wine glass, he lifted his beer for a toast. "O'Doul's—the finest nonalcoholic beer known to man and sparkling grape juice—your favorite, no?"

She did everything in her power to fight the instant sting of tears at the back of her lids, but her father's image blurred all the same. Not only had he remembered her favorite holiday drink as a child, but he had quit alcohol himself. The silent surgeon who preferred a nightly highball with the TV to a cup of cocoa with his wife and daughter. Blinking hard to clear the wetness away, she raised her glass and clinked to his, the idea of dining with her dad making her mood sparkle more than the grape juice in her glass.

Wired for sound, she chattered nonstop like always about everything she could, only this time she bolted through food and conversation like she hadn't eaten or spoken in a week, terrified a lull would burst this glorious bubble. But despite the kamikaze butterflies dive-bombing her stomach, she sensed that this dinner might be different. Maybe it was the hint of a smile on her dad's face as he quietly listened, almost as if he really cared. Or maybe it was the familiarity of the kitchen where, despite her father's radical remodel, was the same room in which they'd shared a lifetime of meals. Whatever it was, Lacey felt a kinship with him for the very first time, as if she were actually in his life instead of just in the room, and as bubbly as the fizz of carbonation that tickled her tongue. Giddy. Excited.

Hopeful.

And hope does not disappoint, she reminded herself, right? She took a breather from her monologue to gulp the rest of her juice. *Oh, please make it so ...*

With a clunk of her empty glass on the table, she jumped up to gather dirty dishes, startling Beau. But not as much as her Dad startled her when he halted her with a gentle touch. "No. This is your night off, kiddo. Put your feet up on the sofa and relax while I get dessert."

"No, Daddy, I insist—" They played tug of war with her plate.

"Go—sit," he ordered, the stern jag of his brow *so* déjà vu, her stomach actually jumped, only this time his command was tempered by the faintest of smiles.

She let go of her plate with a duck of her throat. "Okay." Feeling awkward, she slowly moved toward the door, not sure what to say, but anxious to fill the space. "So, what's for dessert?" She paused while he turned at the sink.

"Homemade chocolate chip pie," he said

She blinked, unable to stop the sag of her mouth. *Homemade chocolate chip pie?* The special dessert her mom always made because it was her favorite? She averted her gaze to the family room when emotion filled her throat as quickly as tears filled her eyes. "How did you get it?" she whispered, head bowed while she braced a hand to the wall.

"How do you think?" he said with a tinge of tease. "I Googled it."

She looked back then, completely undone by the gentleness in his eyes. Her voice came out cracked and hoarse, one breath away from a telltale sob. "You … b-baked it yourself?"

He scrubbed at the back of his neck, a totally foreign blush creeping up before he blocked her view by opening the freezer door. "No guarantees, mind you, but I do have Coldstone Oreo Overload to go along, so maybe that'll save the day."

I will not cry, she promised herself, a promise that bit the dust the moment the freezer door shut with a thump, allowing her father's gaze to meet hers.

He gave a gruff clear of his throat and refocused his attention on cutting the pie on the counter. "You might want to save those tears, Lace, in case it tastes really bad, you know?" He shot her a quick glance. "Two scoops and a thirty-sec zap, plus coffee with cream?"

All she could afford was a weepy nod.

"Got it," he said, busying himself with cutting the pie. "Now go curl up on the couch."

So she did, although "collapse" might be a better word given the buckle of her knees, along with Beau who jumped up to lie beside her. In all the time she'd been bringing her dad dinner, he'd barely taken his eyes off the TV to thank her, much less help with the dishes. Yet here he was, not only waiting on her, but refusing to let her help. Her eyelids drifted closed to savor the moment, startling open again at the slam of the freezer door. She wiped the tears away as she peered up at the ceiling with a scrunch of her nose, humor lacing her whisper. "Don't know what You did, but I'm outta here before midnight in case he changes back."

"Come again?" Her dad strode into the family room with her coffee and pie, his curiosity unleashing enough heat in her cheeks to melt the ice cream.

"Uh, just saying a prayer," she blurted, her face flaming even more.

Issuing a grunt, he set coffee and pie on the teak coffee table before her with a crook of a smile. "Because you're thankful or because you hope you live through it?" He disappeared into the kitchen and returned with his own pie and coffee, shocking her when he settled in on the other side of Beau instead of his easy chair.

"Uh, maybe a little bit of both?" She giggled to deflect the fact that her face was on fire before diving into her pie. Tucking one leg beneath her, she shimmied back into the sofa and took another bite, emitting a moan while she scratched Beau's flank with the tip of her toe. "Mmm … this is really good, Daddy. Gosh, who knew you were so talented in the kitchen?"

He grunted again, stabbing his pie. "Well, not me, that's for sure, unless Lean Cuisine and SpaghettiOs count."

Eyes closed, she rolled the next piece around on her tongue, the ice cream and pie melding into one perfect mix of hot and cold, vanilla and chocolate, combining a blend of two that was so much better together than alone. Like father and daughter, she thought, lifting a silent prayer. "Thanks for going to all this trouble," she whispered, suddenly feeling shy. "The dinner, the pie— you have no idea how much it all means to me."

"Oh, I think I do," he said quietly, finishing off his piece in record time before placing his empty plate on the table. He shifted to face her, pose stiff despite an arm casually resting on the back of the sofa. "After all, I know how much it means when you bring me dinner each week, even though I'm just bullheaded enough to not say a word."

She paused mid-bite, muscles dipping in her throat like she'd gulped spoon and all.

"So actually, Lacey," he continued with an awkward clear of this throat, "I wanted to thank you, yes, but also ..." He avoided her eyes while he reached to scratch his sleeping dog behind the ear, like he needed something to do with his hands. "I was hoping to ... you know, talk. And maybe ..." His voice cracked as he focused on massaging Beau's head. "Clear the air."

She bit back a smile at his use of the same phrase she'd said to him upon her return to Isle of Hope. "I'd like that, Daddy. That's what I've hoped for all along."

Launching up from the sofa, he rubbed his palms against his trousers as if his hands were sticky and he wanted to get them clean. "Yes, well, you might want to reserve judgment on that until you hear what I have to say." He started to pace the length of the family room, kneading the back of his neck as he avoided her gaze. She could almost see the thoughts roiling around in his head as awkward seconds stretched into endless unease before he finally spoke, his voice barely a whisper. "There's so many things I need to apologize for, Lacey—how I treated your mother, how I treated you—but there's no way I can change the damage I've done."

"Daddy—it's not the past I'm concerned about anymore, it's the future."

He stopped to stare, ridges of regret lining his face, aging him ten years. "I know, but the past is tied to our future, sweetheart, and as a very wise neighbor once told me ..." He paused to offer a twitch of a smile. "And a very pushy one, I might add—forgiveness is the bridge that spans between the two."

"But I've already forgiven you, Daddy," she said softly, "because my need for you is far greater than any hurt I may have had." Scooting toward the table, she laid her empty dish down, then perched on the edge of the sofa, knees together and hands clasped on top. "And I hope you can forgive me, too, for all the trouble I caused."

His ribcage expanded with a heavy inhale before he loudly expelled it again, shoulders slumping as if he'd spent all the air and energy he had. "I'm working on it, sweetheart, but there are things—truths—that need to be revealed before we can forgive and forge ahead."

"Yep, you've definitely been talking to Tess," she said with a smile.

The edge of his mouth zagged up. "More like she's been talking to me—or maybe 'badgering' is a better word."

She grinned, heart flooding with gratitude for the woman who'd become not only a second mother, but a dear mentor and friend. "She's a pretty amazing lady."

He hesitated, staring at her through a sudden sheen of tears that snatched the air from her lungs. "So was your mother," he whispered, and the raw grief she saw twisted her heart in two. "I was just too stupid and bitter to know it. Too angry to realize the gift she'd given me in you."

There was no way to stop the moisture that brimmed in her eyes. "We can't change the past, Daddy, but we *can* change the future." She swiped at the tears on her face, wanting more than anything to feel the crush of his arms.

He took to pacing again, and her stomach cramped when he refused to look her way. "Unless the past won't let us," he said quietly, ceasing his stride with a bow of his head, the back of his shoulders sagging along with his voice. He finally turned to face her, his body as worn as she'd ever seen. "We need to talk about the baby, Lacey."

Her heart went to stone at a flashback of her father's rage the night he'd found the empty pregnancy kit …

"I won't have the whore of some holy hypocrite living in my house. If he knocks you up, he can quit that fancy seminary and take care of you."

"I'm not pregnant," she'd screamed, the lie spewing from her lips as naturally as the obscenities that spewed from her tongue. "But if I was, I would never stay here."

The vile memories all came rushing back, and Lacey's breathing grew ragged as she rushed in to defend, feeling eighteen all over again. "Daddy, I never meant for that to happen, I swear, and it was only one time, I promise. And it wasn't Jack's fault—it was mine."

He jagged a brow as he propped hands on his hips, a semblance of a smile shading his face. "As far as I know, Lacey, there's only one Immaculate Conception recorded in history."

Heat braised her cheeks. "I just meant that I was the one who egged him on that night—he didn't want to, so I don't want you blaming it on him."

His lips curved into an almost smile, edged with sadness. "The only blame I'm worried about tonight, Lacey, is my own," he said quietly, finally taking his seat at the end of the couch.

Hunched on the edge, he sat stoop-shouldered with elbows on his knees, fingers woven into the hair on either side of his head as he stared at the floor. "When I accidentally found that pregnancy-kit box in the trash, I was enraged, determined that if you and Jack were fooling around, you were going to pay. I said hateful things, I know, even though you swore the kit belonged to that friend who'd been over the night before." He expended a weary sigh. "I didn't know what to believe, but I figured even if it was your girlfriend who was pregnant, I would kick you out anyway, just to scare some sense in you." His eyes slowly lifted to meet hers. "I swear I never intended for you to stay away forever."

He paused for several heartbeats, the scrape of his uneven breathing the only sound in the room. "And then I found out you ran away with a girlfriend to San Diego, and I felt betrayed, angry, wanting you to pay for making me feel like a failure as a father." He glanced her way, his eyelids heavy with regret. "I was a miserable person and a miserable father, Lacey, and I wish I could take it all back. But I'll be honest, when your mother went to visit you in San Diego and then called to tell me you'd had a baby, it was like a sharp blow to the head because that was the first I even knew you were actually pregnant."

Spasms of regret convulsed in Lacey's stomach as she stared at her father, heartsick over the kind of daughter she'd been. "Forgive me, Daddy—I begged Mom not to tell you because I was ashamed. I thought if I gave the baby up and you never knew, I wouldn't risk you hating me anymore than you already did."

"Oh, Lacey, I didn't hate you," he whispered, his voice rough with regret. "I hated myself. And because of that, I was angry at you and your mother for making me feel less than I already did." He turned away to stare straight ahead, his Adam's apple shifting in profile. "So when she called to say the child had heart problems—"

"Daddy, it's okay." She reached across Beau, fingers grazing his shoulder while emotion swelled in her throat. "It's not your fault she died."

A nerve flickered in the stiff line of his jaw as his eyelids lumbered closed. "That's just it," he whispered, the words no more than a rasp. "It *is* my fault. And every single day of my life I live with the torment of not only what I did to my granddaughter, but to you and your mother."

"Oh, Daddy, no …" Lacey jumped up and squatted before him, softly grazing his arm. "It's not your fault Mom couldn't get a hold of you till too late …"

His eyelids lifted to reveal a man haunted by his past, silent seconds ticking away to the deafening thud of her heart. "But she *did* get a hold of me, Lacey. I was just too angry to come."

Her pulse stopped. The room seemed to shift on its foundation as her mind whirled in a slow spin, body dizzy and vision glazed. "B-But you w-were there," she whispered, straining to remember all that had happened, conjuring up memories she'd worked so hard to forget.

"After, yes, but I should have been there *before*— performing that surgery instead of some baby-faced intern barely out of school. And I fully intended to, I swear, but I …" A lump bobbed in his throat as he averted his eyes. "But I … put off coming right away."

She stared, body paralyzed along with her mind. *He put off coming? Put off saving my baby? His own flesh and blood? Just like he'd put off my mother and me all of those years?* Her breathing shallowed as she stared at him in horror. "But why?"

Glazed with sorrow, his gaze found hers. "Because I was selfish and judgmental and wanted to make you and your mother pay." His quivering fingers—those of a surgeon whose life was to heal—grappled through his hair as if he were an old man, disrupting his neat and meticulous cut like he'd just disrupted her life. "I spoke with the attending physician and felt I had time, so I had every intention of coming, Lacey, I swear, but I … wanted to make a point … wanted to make you wait …" Grief shadowed every line in his face as he peered up, a man broken beneath the weight of his own guilt. "I … never expected anything to go wrong before I got there, never dreamed there would be an emergency surgery. So when the baby died—"

"*Hope*, Daddy," she hissed, all the pain of the loss she'd tried to put behind swamping her all over again, dousing all hope. "She had a name, you know—Hope Olivia Carmichael."

Water welled in his eyes as his throat convulsed. "Yes, of course," he whispered, the very sound broken with pain. "So when … Hope died, I did too, shutting down inside as if I were a corpse—dead to Karen, dead to you, and that's when your mother …" His eyes flickered briefly as if weighted down with a guilt too heavy to bear. "Started counseling with Adam."

He looked away to swab a hand to his eyes, his voice laden with grief. "As God is my witness, Lacey, I have never regretted anything more, and I swear if I could trade my life for hers right now, I would—*gladly*." He straightened and swiped his face with the back of his hand, the dregs of wounded pride in the rise of that formidable chin. "Which is why I fought the possibility of any relationship with you at all, because not only did I fear your anger and hurt once you found out, but I don't deserve the joy of being a father." His mouth tamped down, as if he were preparing for the very worst. "And frankly, I wouldn't blame you if you walked out that door right now and never came back."

She could barely breathe, her chest so constricted she thought she might faint. Both her daughter and her mother were dead, and the man before her bore most of the blame. Which, as far as she was concerned, deemed her so-called "father" dead as well. Her jaw hardened along with her heart and without another word, she rose, body shaking as she silently retrieved her purse from the kitchen.

"Lacey, forgive me, please …" Her father's plea followed her as she ran down the hall, too angry to care about the pain she heard in his voice.

All at once her rage boiled to the surface—a forgotten temper inherited from the man who had ruined her life—and with a violent sweep of her arm across a teak table in his hall, she crashed a piece of pottery to the floor. Without a single glance back, she lashed the door open and fled, slamming it so hard, the thunderous sound still rang in her ears when she slid in her car.

Forgive him? "Never," she hissed, grinding the ignition through a hot blur of tears.

Judge not, and you will not be judged.

She froze, hand stiff on the steering wheel before she fisted the dash. "No—he doesn't deserve it! He didn't have compassion on his own granddaughter, much less his wife and daughter."

Condemn not, and you will not be condemned.

A guttural groan rose in her throat, clawing past her lips in a keening so raw, she collapsed over the wheel in a painful sob, aching for all she had lost.

Forgive, and you will be forgiven.

"Oh, God, I c-can't do this," she said with a violent heave, "he's d-destroyed any love I m-might have ever had ..." Fumbling for a Kleenex in her purse, she wept bitterly, heaves ravaging her body while despair ravaged her heart. Time ticked by in painful shudders, and when the tears finally slowed, she was as depleted and torn as the soggy tissue in her hand.

The Lord delights in those who fear him, who put their hope in his unfailing love.

Her limbs stilled, fluid and grief sealing the air in her throat. *Unfailing love.* The kind God had given to her. Unconditional, unmerited, full of hope and forgiveness she didn't deserve.

Just like her father.

The very thought wrestled in her mind, wringing anguish from her soul and more tears from her eyes. "God help me," she whispered, "I have no power to do this."

Out of nowhere, like a feather on a breeze, a still small voice drifted in her mind …

May the God of Hope fill you with all joy and peace as you trust in Him, so that you may overflow with hope by the power of the Holy Spirit.

Her breath caught in her throat. *The power of the Holy Spirit.*

His, not hers.

Fingers trembling, she pushed the hair from her face. Her eyelids fluttered closed as *His* Word—those of the very God who *created* hope—settled over her like a cocoon of peace and calm, slowing her tears and racing her pulse.

Hope.

Lost through a baby.

Restored through a Savior.

Her head jerked up and she stared at the sky, awed by a million stars that seemed to blur into the glittering promises of God, the 'Bright Morning Star.' Swiping her eyes in wonder, she breathed in the cool night air, drinking in deeply of His joy and peace.

And His hope—oxygen to her soul.

Tears pricked. And to her father's.

"Oh, God, forgive me," she whispered, voice broken and hoarse. Frantically rifling through her purse for more Kleenex, she blew her nose and patted her face, overcome by a sudden rush of love that chased all of her anger away. With a violent surge of her lungs, she flung the car door wide, not even bothering to close it as she sprinted to her father's front porch. Her blood pulsed wildly in her ears as she rammed her finger to the bell, the boom of her heart louder than those silly bongs echoing inside.

Eons ticked away like ragged heartbeats until the door slowly creaked open, revealing the haggard form of her father.

"Oh, Daddy," she whispered, and with a broken sob, she flung her arms around his waist, not even minding that he stood rigid and still. "I forgive you, I do!" Heaves racked her body as she clung with all of her might, the emotion swelling in her throat nearly choking her words. "And I will love you forever, no matter what."

Quietly, hesitantly, movement inched around her, so slowly, she almost missed it.

And then, for the first time in her life, in one hushed moment of awe …

She wept in the arms of her father.

CHAPTER THIRTY-NINE

"*H*ey, where is everybody?" Lacey bounced into Tess's kitchen, making a beeline to where Tess was pulling fresh-baked cookies from the oven.

Glancing over her shoulder with potholders in hand, Tess did her best to force a bright smile. "The girls took Davey and Spence to a movie, and Jack's down on the dock waiting for you."

"Ah, yes, the surprise moonlight picnic—you sure raised a true romantic, Mrs. O."

Tess paused with a hot cookie tin, jaw gaping. "You are not supposed to know about that, young lady," she said with a teasing lift of brows, "thus the surprise?"

"Yes, well next time, keep Davey out of the loop if you want your secret secure." She bent close to the cookie sheet Tess had just placed on the counter and sniffed. "But don't worry, I taught drama in my last teaching gig, so the man will never know." She groaned in pleasure after another sniff, peeking up with an impish grin. "Mmm … dessert, I hope?"

Opening the oven door to put in more cookies, Tess felt the blast of heat—both in the kitchen and in her face—over a subject she needed to broach with Ben's daughter. "Monster cookies," she informed her, a girl she loved like a daughter despite the ache in her heart over the secret Lacey had never shared. Her smile grew taut as she slammed the oven door and turned, dabbing at her forehead with the back of her arm. "For your father," she said with a dry smile, "who *still* hasn't connected the significance of said cookies for the neighborhood 'monster.'"

Lacey's laughter filled the kitchen with song, in stark contrast to Tess's sobs several weeks ago, which had filled Ben's with her unfathomable grief when he'd told her about their grandchild. A confession that had nearly ended their friendship.

Ponytail bouncing as much as she, Lacey grinned, hand poised to steal a cookie while her hazel eyes peeked up with a pixie twinkle. "Well, the 'monster' just *may* have to relinquish that reputation after the headway he and I made last night." She nodded to the cookies. "May I?"

"Yes, of course, sweetheart—help yourself." Tess feigned ignorance with a curious tilt of her head as Lacey shimmied into a chair with her cookie, her voice almost giddy as she relayed the surface details of her breakthrough with her dad. Of course, Tess was already fully aware of all that had transpired between Ben and his daughter because he'd called her after Lacey had left, humbled and awed over the healing God had wrought.

But it hadn't come easy. The night he'd dropped the bomb about their mutual granddaughter, Tess had fled in tears, outrage spewing forth from a wellspring of hurt buried so deep, she hadn't even known it was there. Outrage at Ben for his selfishness, at Lacey for her silent deception, at Karen for never letting her know, and at Adam for destroying their family. Texting her children she wouldn't be home until late, she had walked for hours that night, finally ending up weeping in a chair on her dock. Her fury had depleted her faith like low tide depleted the marsh all around, leaving nothing but the foul scent of sulphur and death.

And bitterness. Oh, *lots* and *lots* of bitterness.

She'd made up her mind right then and there, in the midst of her anger, that she wanted nothing to do with Ben Carmichael for a long, long while, too steeped in venom over a man who could so readily turn his back on his own.

Let he without sin cast the first stone.

Her breath had stilled along with the sea breeze at the whisper of a still small voice while the moon crept behind a billow of clouds as dark as her soul. She'd closed her eyes then, her anger greatly impaired by the conviction piercing within. Yes, Ben had turned his back on his own, but hadn't Tess done much the same? Turned her back on Adam when he'd begged her to quit nursing for a season so she could be the wife and mother he wanted her to be? They hadn't needed the money, but as an overachiever, *she* had needed the success, opting to rise in the ranks rather than accompany her husband on countless conferences and trips. She'd sensed the growing strain in their relationship and the silent anger that simmered beneath, but she thought it would end when the children got older.

Only her marriage ended instead.

Guilt as sinister as Ben's slithered into her mind, reminding her she had not only turned her back on her husband and marriage, but her children as well. Adam had pleaded for reconciliation a year later, but Tess had been too bitter to take him back, severing all ties except those he maintained with the children. It wasn't until she'd sobbed on the dock the night of Ben's confession that she suddenly realized she had robbed her children of both a father and stable home life as surely as Ben had robbed Lacey of the chance to save her daughter's life.

And so, eyes rimmed raw from tears, she had gone back and banged on Ben's door long after midnight, not surprised when he'd answered looking haggard and hopeless like a man who'd just lost his soul. But it was his soul and hers that had been healed that night, and from that moment on, it was as if tragedy had bonded them together, both emotionally and spiritually. A bonding that had paved the way not only for her to truly forgive both Adam and him, but to introduce Ben to an intimate relationship with God. That night Ben Carmichael not only became a new creature in Christ, but a man she could now love to the depth of her soul. And God help her, she was well on her way!

Since then, they'd secretly spent a part of every evening together, whether discussing theology, their past, praying for their families, or just basking in the glow of all of God's blessings. Somehow they'd managed impromptu dinners when her children were gone or in bed, stolen moments on the dock, or long late-night walks along the shore. So naturally the moment Lacey left after their amazing breakthrough last night, Ben had called Tess immediately, overcome with gratitude over what God had done in his life. But no more so than her, when they'd celebrated with iced tea and stale monster cookies down on his dock.

"You're the reason everything has turned around, Tess," he'd whispered, "and I don't want to waste another minute without you firmly fixed in my life." His lips had punctuated each phrase with a caress of her eyelids and nose, finally straying to nuzzle the lobe of her ear. "I want to see you on a regular basis," he whispered, his mouth fondling hers with such tenderness, she all but melted into his arms. "And I want to be *way* more than neighbors, Miss Perky ..."

So did she. But both of them agreed they would take it slow. Or at least *she'd* agreed. Ben hadn't been so inclined, but Tess needed more time. Time for her and her family to slowly adjust to having Ben in their life. Time to get to know him better, good points and bad.

And time to make sure his newfound faith was truly based on his need for God, and not just his need for Tess. A wispy sigh feathered her lips.

"Tess?" Lacey's voice broke through her reverie, bringing her back to the kitchen. "Are you all right?" She half ducked to study Tess's face, two tiny wedges bridging her brows.

"Yes, of course, although ..." She swallowed hard. "I do think we need to talk."

"Uh-oh ..." Cheeks bulging with cookie, Lacey paused before gulping it down, a crooked smile offsetting the flecks of concern in her eyes. "Am I in trouble?"

Tess didn't smile. "You tell me," she said quietly, taking her own seat beside her. Drawing a deep breath for strength, she took Lacey's hand in hers, her gaze tender but direct. "Honey, were you ever planning to tell us about the baby?"

Blood leeched from Lacey's face, sagging both her mouth and her shoulders. Her hand slowly sank to the table along with the half-eaten cookie, voice weak and eclipsed by shock. "W-What?"

"Your dad told me last week, honey," she said quietly, determined to fight the sting of tears that threatened. "Everything—from kicking you out of the house to the hateful things he said about you ruining Jack's dreams of seminary." She blinked hard to dispel the persistent moisture that lined the inside of her lids, her words fading to an aching whisper. "Right up to his prideful delay in providing a surgery that just might have saved our girl." Swallowing her grief, she lifted her chin in an effort to go on. "But as tragic as it was for me to hear, it bonded us in a way that allowed me to talk to him about God. Which is why *he* finally confessed his guilt to you last night at dinner." Her eyes softened. "He's given his life to Christ, Lacey, and that's largely because of you and your faithfulness in forgiving him and seeking restoration."

A river of regret, and perhaps reverence and awe, flowed down Lacey's face, but when she collapsed onto the table in a broken sob, Tess could no more stop from swallowing her up in a ferocious hug than she could stem the flow of her own tears. "Aw, honey, I forgive you for not telling me," she whispered as she knelt by her side, "but were you ever planning to?"

Tess felt Lacey's shaky nod against her chest, her voice thick with nasal fluid and grief. "Eventually, y-yes, b-but not in the b-beginning," she began, her violent shudders causing her words to stutter. "I'd p-planned to give the b-baby up. But when she was b-born sick, I ... I j-just couldn't let her g-go, so I decided to k-keep her. And I would have t-told you eventually, I swear. But then s-she d-died ..." Lacey collapsed against Tess's shoulder, her heaves racking both of their bodies.

"Shhh, sweetheart, it's behind us now," Tess whispered, gently rocking Lacey as if she were her very own. "And our precious little girl will greet us someday in heaven."

Lacey jerked away, her swollen eyes a tortured plea. "I planned to t-tell you soon, Tess, I promise, b-both you and Jack, b-but I was s-so scared you would h-hate me." She swiped at the tears on her face while Tess rose to hand her a paper napkin from the caddy in the center of the table. Tugging a chair close to Lacey's, she perched on the edge while Lacey blew her nose.

"I w-wanted to re-establish our relationship first, b-before I d-did." Lacey hiccupped loudly, the sound bringing a trace of a smile to Tess's lips. "B-but now that Jack and I are b-back together, I'm s-so afraid it will ruin what we have." More moisture pooled in her eyes as she clung to Tess like a lost little girl. "Oh, Tess, I'm so afraid he'll h-hate m-me ..."

"Sweetheart, Jack loves you—always has, and although he's likely to be shocked and upset and yes, even angry for a time like his mother ..." She pulled away to cradle Lacey's face in her hands, tender affection warming her gaze. "He'll get over it, just like I did when I realized how God has brought beauty from ashes when we put our hope in Him."

Lacey slapped the tears from her eyes with the back of her hand, giving an angry sniff. "But it shouldn't have been like this," she hissed with a slam of her fist to the table. "If I hadn't tempted Jack beyond his control that night, and if Daddy hadn't begrudged Mom and me from the beginning, Jack and I might be married now with a sweet little girl named Hope Olivia and heaven knows how many others."

She gouged fingers into her hair on either side of her head with a painful groan that revealed her intense frustration. "It's just not fair! Because of me and my stupid, selfish sin, I triggered a chain reaction of death—first in my relationship with Jack, Cat, and my father, then in the death of my baby, death of your marriage and that of my parents', and finally the death of my mother." She stared at Tess, wild-eyed. "The wages of sin is death, Tess, and boy oh boy, I earned a killer paycheck on this one."

Tess grabbed Lacey's hands. "Stop it," she whispered, an urgency in her tone. "You are not responsible for other people's sins, do you hear? And you are certainly not responsible for the death of your child." She clutched Lacey's arms, stilling her with the intensity of her gaze, the caress of her thumbs. "Life is messy, darling, because human beings are fallible and prone to sin, all of us. Our sins are webs we weave that lock us in, trap us into the sticky and sinister world of guilt and shame." Her chin lifted despite the barest trace of a quiver. "But our God has set us free."

More tears slipped from Lacey's eyes. "I know," she whispered, her nasal words trailing into pain, "but it's not fair that everybody has to suffer because I messed up ..."

Tess enveloped her in a tender hold, stroking her hair with the soothing touch of a mother. "Unfortunately, darling, sin is never fair, but it *is* redeemable." She deposited a kiss to Lacey's hair and gently lifted her chin, smiling into her soggy eyes. "In a sinless world, Lacey, God's perfect will would always prevail, which is what eternity is all about, but in a fallen world like ours where He's given us free will?" She caressed the side of Lacey's face with the tips of her fingers. "His permissive will takes over for each of us, allowing good and bad through the choices we make. Like it or not, people are attached to our obedience and our sin, and whether we choose life or death, blessing or curse, God's way or the world's— there is redemption and hope in *His* Name." She tugged on Lacey's ponytail with a smile. "Not to mention untold blessings that have a way of sneaking in the back door."

Lacey sniffed and wiped her nose with the back of her wrist. She hopped up to wash her hands and snatch a Kleenex from Tess's window shelf, then trudged back to plop into her chair, face and eyes all puffy. "Such as?"

"Well ..." Tess rose to fetch them both a tall glass of peach iced tea, smiling over her shoulder as she pulled the pitcher from the fridge. "For one thing, God redeemed your soul and then your life when He led you back to Isle of Hope—where, I might add ..." She washed a fresh peach from a bowl on the counter and sliced a thick wedge, slitting and sliding it onto the rim of Lacey's glass. "You get to enjoy, and I quote, 'the nectar of the gods, bar none.'"

That coaxed a misty grin from Lacey's lips. "Definitely."

"And," Tess continued, delivering both of their teas to the table, "He not only restored and deepened my son's faith through you—a prayer of mine for years now ..." Her lips trembled as she fought the rise of more saltwater, "but He also used you to redeem your father's soul, Lacey, setting him on the path to be the man and father God always intended him to be."

Lacey's face crumpled as more moisture dribbled down her cheeks.

"Oh, honey ..." Tess put her tea down to sweep Lacey into her arms again, her chuckle low against the young woman's hair. "And you know what's the biggest blessing of all?"

Tess grinned when Lacey shook her head with a little-girl sniff. She kissed her wet nose, swiping away two giant crocodile tears. "*You*, sweetheart—a beautiful blessing to me, my family, my son, and your father. And all because our God redeemed a wrong choice your mom and dad made when they were not much younger than you and my son." She caressed the damp jaw of this beautiful woman who would, hopefully, one day be a daughter in name as well as in heart. "Because you see, Lacey, not only does our God redeem and restore human beings, He redeems and restores the mistakes they make as well, turning tears of mourning into tears of joy."

Lacey lunged into her arms, luring another chuckle to Tess's lips. "Oh, Tess, I love you so much, and I thank God every day for the blessing of you in my life."

Tess squeezed her tightly, pressing a kiss to her head before pulling back to smile with deep affection. "And I thank God every day for the blessing of *you* in my family, sweetheart, because I have a feeling that this time, it's really going to happen."

The hazel eyes dimmed as Lacey gnawed at her lip. "I pray you're right, but I can't help but worry that once Jack hears the truth about the baby, it might ruin everything we have."

Tess's chest cramped as water swam in her eyes. "Oh, honey …" Her lip trembled, a mixture of joy, hope, and confidence swelling in her chest. "When guided by love, the truth never ruins hope, darling," she whispered, "it only sets it free."

CHAPTER FORTY

*J*ack's lure sailed through the air for the zillionth time, soundlessly slicing into the moonlit water, definitely more of a mindless twitch than a skilled cast. The last time he was this nervous was when he took his final boards, his hope for the future shimmering brighter than the diamond ring in his pocket. "Thank you," he whispered, gaze scanning the starry sky with more hope and joy than he ever believed possible, "for healing my heart of bitterness—first with Lacey and then with You." His jawbone tensed almost imperceptibly. "And someday, God willing—with my father."

His phone vibrated inside his back jean pocket, and switching the rod to his other hand, he fished it out, almost fumbling it into the water when he read his mother's text.

She's on her way.

The air in his lungs instantly clotted, as thick and humid as the sweltering summer night, in total contrast to the sudden sprint of his pulse. "For crying out loud, O'Bryen," he muttered, ramming the phone back in his pocket before tossing the rod and reel onto the dock. "This isn't the M-CAT here, so chill." Grabbing the lighter sitting on top of the linen-clad table, he lit the staggered candlesticks in the center, his stomach jumping more than the flames that flickered in the summer breeze. He assessed the table with a critical eye—the gleaming china, polished silverware, and envelope-fold napkin his mother had devised, tucked with a Lindt truffle that Lacey loved—and deemed it perfect. He pulled an extra truffle from his pocket and slipped it into the fold with a satisfied smile.

And one special one with a ring inside.

"Oh my, Dr. O'Bryen ... judging from the trappings of one the most elegant picnics I've seen since I was eighteen, am I correct in assuming you have ulterior motives?" Lacey strolled onto the ramp with a fold of her toned arms, looking luscious enough in a white strapless sundress to set off a whole new set of ulterior motives. His gaze slid from bronzed shoulders kissed by loose strands of silky gold, down a petite but curvy figure that had always driven him wild. A sudden breeze billowed her short flared skirt, showcasing some of the prettiest legs he'd ever seen on a woman.

"Oh, you bet," he said, voice husky as he hooked her close to nibble her ear, the scent of peaches kicking his hormones into overdrive. She squealed when he dove for her neck. "But first—we eat."

"Uh, that's what I'm afraid of ..." Chuckling, she squirmed away, palms flat to his chest, looking so adorable with that warning lift of her chin and schoolmarm smile that he wanted to forego dinner altogether and go right for dessert. Which was *exactly* why he'd decided he wasn't waiting any longer to ask Lacey to marry him ... not the second time around. He'd been in love with her for years, dated her for two, and was promised to her for one before he'd lost her the first time. As far as he was concerned, he wanted to get on with his life. A sudden swell of waves crashed onto the shore, as if in protest.

Correction: *their* life.

Beginning with a *very* short engagement.

He kissed her nose and pulled out her chair. "Don't worry, Mike—you're not on the menu," he said, nudging her into her seat before he scooted the chair in. He opened the sparkling grape juice from an ice bucket on the table while he gave her a smoky look that toasted her cheeks. "Although there are no guarantees for later." A jittery laugh slipped from her lips, and for the first time he homed in on her off-kilter smile and skittish look, noting the red rim of her eyes while tiny beads of sweat glazed her brow. He set the bottle down and squatted to face her, features pinched in concern. "You okay, Lace?"

"I'm fine, Jack," she said, a trace of nasal hoarseness in a voice that sounded anything but, "just a little warm and very, very hungry, mister."

He gently brushed strands of her hair over her shoulder. "Good, because I have all your favorites, babe—chicken salad on croissants, sour cream ripple chips, and—"

"Oreo Overload?" The tension in her eyes gave way to a little-girl excitement that never failed to melt him into a puddle.

His low chuckle merged with the sound of water lapping against the dock and crickets crooning on the shore. "Come on, Mike ..." he whispered, eyes sheathing closed as he gently swayed his lips against hers. "I graduated med school—what do you think?" He nodded over his shoulder at the cooler stowed next to the storage chest.

Her lip started to quiver. "Oh, Jack ..." Lunging into his arms, she almost took them both down. "I love you so much," she whispered, the raspy quality back in force while she clung as if she would never let go.

He bent his head to hers, a tiny seed of concern sprouting over her rare melancholy mood. "Me too, babe." Pressing a kiss to her hair, he pulled away, smile softening at the glimmer of tears in her eyes. "Okay, are we going to have to start with a pre-dessert to cheer you up?" With a teasing shake of his head, he nudged the envelope napkin forward, his heart suddenly pounding harder than the breakers on the shore.

With a swipe at her eyes, a tiny grin peeked through. "Pre-dessert?"

Jack grinned. "Maybe."

She fished her fingers into the napkin pocket and immediately squealed. "Truffles—you remembered!"

His brows slashed low in a mock scowl. "For crying out loud, Carmichael, give me a little credit, will you?"

She peeled the paper from the copper-colored ball first like he knew she would—peanut butter, her favorite—then popped it in her mouth with a sassy smile. "You keep this pampering up, O'Bryen, and I'll be giving you way more than credit …"

Jack fought a gulp, his throat going bone dry.

"Mmm …" Her lids flickered closed, a low moan escaping as she savored the chocolate while Jack savored her. The glazed look she gave him when she opened her eyes made him grin. "Oh, yum, Jack, I forgot how much I loved these things—haven't had one in years."

He squinted. "Seriously? Why? You used to love 'em."

"Yeah, a little too much as I recall." Her smile turned dreamy. "Along with the boy who first gave them to me," she said softly, more moisture glimmering in her eyes.

"Well, then, you have some catching up to do, so one more now and the rest after dinner—atop an Oreo Overload, okay?"

Her watery gaze twinkled as she scooped up the second truffle. "Deal. Mmm … white chocolate, my second favorite …" Fingers deft, she wasted no time untwisting the cellophane outside wrapper while Jack jumped up, pretending preoccupation with pouring the grape juice. Tongue tucked into the corner of her mouth, she started to peel the gold foil while he held his breath. All at once, her brows dipped. Slowly rotating the chocolate ball with her fingers, she examined it like a specimen under a scope, confusion puckering her features. "What the heck ...?" She sniffed, obviously noticing the hairline split, then rolled it and sniffed again, finally parting the fissure ever so carefully. The whites of her eyes expanded in slow motion as something clunked on the table, covered with white-chocolate goo. When moisture brimmed in her eyes, he knew it had clicked, everything falling perfectly in place.

Just like their new life.

Hand trembling, she picked up the tiny bag to gently finger it, water streaming her cheeks. "Oh, Jack ..."

"No, babe ..." He rose from his chair and moved to her side of the table, immediately dropping to one knee. "The proper response, Alycia Anne Carmichael," he whispered, removing the ring from the bag and holding it aloft, "is 'yes, Jack.'"

She hesitated too long for comfort, the tears in her eyes flowing too freely now for a woman about to say yes. Only she didn't. Instead she clutched quivering arms to her waist, while his ring—and his heart—remained suspended in air. She lowered her head. "Oh, Jack ..."

Not the reaction he was looking for.

"Lace?" Ring in one hand, he lifted her chin with the other, heart rate careening into an irregular beat. "Babe, what's wrong? You do want to ..." He swallowed the fear in his throat while he gently kneaded her arm, Adam's apple ducking hard. "Marry me, don't you?"

The look she gave him was more of a woman in pain than a woman in love, and for several ragged beats of his pulse, his world dangled as precariously as the ring.

She peered up beneath lids weighted with grief. "More than anything in this world," she whispered, her voice shrinking into a mournful sigh. "But first, I need to tell you something."

A brain freeze swallowed him whole, as if the clench in his chest was privy to some vile news he didn't want to know. Placing the ring on her plate, he stood without a word and reclaimed his seat, carefully leaning back in his chair with a tight brace of arms. "Whatever it is, it won't affect our relationship." His words sounded a whole lot more confident than he.

"I hope not," she said quietly, the quiver in her voice icing his skin. She avoided his eyes while she traced the ring with the tip of a shaky finger. "Or at least I pray not."

The muscles in his gut constricted. He was not a man prone to anger. Not unless something posed a threat.

To the woman he loved.

To family.

To friends.

To a child.

"For crying out loud, Lacey, spit it out," he said too sharply, rattling the dishes when he slammed a fist on the table in an uncommon show of temper. One of his mother's wine glasses goosed in the air before it rolled off the table and crashed on the dock, breaking into several jagged pieces.

Her body jumped, hand recoiling like the ring had singed her finger. Palm to her chest, she stuttered, words tumbling forth as if the crash of his fist had jolted them loose. "Okay, J-Jack, then, h-here it is—I d-didn't leave eight years ago because I d-didn't love you enough …" She sucked in air as if gorging all the strength she would need, "I left because I loved you too much."

He blinked, confusion fogging his mind. "I don't understand. What do you mean?"

She stared at him for several seconds while sorrow swam in her eyes. "I mean I left to have a baby, Jack," she whispered, "our baby."

She may as well gashed him with a jagged piece of that broken glass—he was bleeding all the same. Shards of shock slashed through his brain with such deadly ease that, at first, he didn't feel a thing. And then like a fingertip neatly sliced with the sharpest of blades, pain began to throb beneath a scarlet pool of blood, making him fully aware.

Our baby. Lacey's and his. A child meant to be the first of many.

"It happened that night in the dory, Jack," she continued in a hoarse voice, resurrecting memories of when he'd diverted her from skinny-dipping with a moonlight sail instead. "My cycles have always been so screwy, I never even suspected until long after you left for seminary. And then Daddy found the pregnancy kit—"

"Girl or boy," he whispered, voice cracking with pain.

She paused, a muscle in her cheek flickering as she reached to graze his hand. "A little girl—I named her Hope Olivia."

At her touch, he jerked away, lids sinking closed. "*You* named her ..." he said, an accusation rather than a statement.

"Jack, I was young and stupid, and I didn't want to hurt your career—"

"My career?" His voice was little more than a hiss, bleeding with pain as his eyes widened in shock, hardly able to believe the woman he loved had so callously pitted their child against a mere job. "Where is she?" It came out a broken rasp.

Hand to her mouth, Lacey blinked, heaves convulsing her body. "She was b-born with a c-congenital heart d-defect," she said on a sob, "and d-died in surgery three d-days later."

His eyelids dropped like a curtain of despair, questions pummeling his mind while pain pummeled his heart. *When was her birthday? How much did she weigh? Brown hair or blonde?* Breathing shallow, he rose and walked to the edge of the dock, head bowed as he propped hands to his hips, limbs as numb as his mind. "When was she born?" His whisper seemed to hang in the humid air, hovering like a ghost on the water.

"April 17, 2007." She sniffled, voice nasal.

He stared at the moonlit river, stomach roiling more than the water swirling in a sudden gust of breeze. *My daughter died on April 20.*

Her chair scraped against weathered wood, and he stiffened at her approach. "Jack, I know it seems selfish—"

"Selfish?" He spun around, eyes blazing. "No, I think this goes well beyond selfish, Lace, all the way to brutally cruel." Ramming a thumb to his chest, he stepped forward, practically spitting in her face. "That was my baby you so carelessly made decisions about, my flesh and blood you abandoned right after you abandoned me."

"No, Jack, I swear," she said with a violent shake of her head, "I didn't abandon Hope Olivia—"

"No?" He jutted a brow, tone harsh. "So let me get this straight—you ran away from a fiancé who adored you because you planned to raise *his* baby on your own?"

"*No* ... n-not at f-first," she said, her hesitancy all but declaring her guilt, "but after she was born, I just knew I couldn't give her up. So we begged Daddy to come, but by the time he arrived, it was too late—"

"Too late?" Jack whispered, shock adding insult to injury that his daughter's grandfather—one of the country's top heart surgeons—never even made it to her side.

Lacey reached to touch him, but he pulled away, too angry to care about the wince of pain that flashed across her face. "Jack, I'm so sorry. I never meant for any of this to happen, I swear, but I ran scared." She buffed her arms, a nervous habit he recognized whenever she was frightened or nervous ...

Or guilty.

Her gaze skittered away. "I ... I didn't think I was ready to be a mom," she whispered, her fractured words confirming her disgrace, "so when Daddy kicked me out, I saw it as fate. He ... said awful things, like a pastor didn't need a whore for a wife, and that I would ruin your career, and he was right." She gently grazed his arm with her fingers, removing them before he could do it himself. "I knew you'd quit seminary as soon as you heard, Jack, and I didn't want that, so you have to believe me—the largest part of me did it for you."

"For me." His voice sounded cold and flat—like his feelings for Lacey at the moment. He held up his forefinger and thumb right in front of her nose, barely a hair apart. "As far as I'm concerned, what you did is this close to kidnapping, and I'm not sure I can ever forgive you."

He heard the catch of her breath, right before more tears spilled from her eyes. "Don't say that, Jack, please—I love you, and I want to spend the rest of my life with you."

Heart thundering, he studied her, some of his anger abating when he realized *this* was the person with whom he longed to spend the rest of his life as well, the girlfriend he cherished and adored up till five minutes ago. The key to a family of his own with the only woman he ever really wanted.

The mother of his child.

And the ones yet to come.

He turned away, head bowed as he gouged his temple with the pads of his fingers, fighting the sting of his own tears. When he finally spoke, his words came out hoarse and halting. "I love you, Lacey, I do, but this ..." He listlessly waved a leaden hand. "Is so ... hard to get past. You not only broke my heart, you broke my trust ... *and* my dream." He turned to face her, his expression a mirror reflection of the agony he saw in her own. "I only hope that someday I'll be able to forgive and forget."

She nodded slowly, and then, as if imbued with grace from on high, serenity settled over her like the sudden shaft of moonlight that broke through a cluster of clouds, taming the tragedy in her face. With a subtle square of shoulders, she studied him, her look of tenderness gilded with the peace and strength he'd seen since she'd returned to Isle of Hope, trademarks of the Lacey who now lived for God instead of herself. "Oh, Jack," she whispered, eyes shining with the same steadfast assurance he'd once espoused himself, "you should know better than anyone—there is no hope without forgiveness."

He stared, the truth slamming so hard, it paralyzed both his mind and his body.

Forgive us our trespasses as we forgive those who trespass against us.

His eyes lumbered closed when he realized Lacey was right. God's forgiveness had not only saved his sorry life—healing his hardened heart of bitterness and despair—but it could also save his future.

If he let it.

For I know the plans I have for you, plans for a hope and a future.

Their hope.

Their future.

A cramp squeezed in his gut. All dangling by a tenuous thread called forgiveness.

Suddenly, the weight of his sorrow and guilt was too much to bear, and turning away, he crumpled onto the edge of the dock, body shuddering with silent heaves as he sat with his head in his hands. "God, forgive me," he whispered, "and please—help me to forgive."

Lost in his remorse, he didn't hear or see Lacey's approach, but he felt the tentative slide of her arm to his waist when she sat down beside him. The steady thump of her pulse as she laid her head on his shoulder, voice frail with regret. "Jack, my heart aches for all the pain I've caused and I hope someday you'll be able to forgive me. Because despite the tragic path that I took, you always have been and always will be the love of my life. And whether you ask me to stay or you ask me to go, I will. But first ..." Her voice cracked on a heave. "Will you—can we—grieve the loss of our daughter?" Her fingers dug in as a fractured sob escaped from her throat. "As one?"

His body stilled, the thud of his heart slowing to beat in time with hers.

And the two shall become one flesh; no longer two, but one ...

One flesh. One family. One burden borne by two.

Somewhere deep inside, his bitterness broke, like the end of a raging fever meant to destroy, cooling both his temper and his hurt. Wrenching Lacey close, he buried his head in her hair to weep, to forgive, and to heal.

And in mourning the precious Hope they had lost, another arose, shining brighter and fuller than the harvest moon above.

CHAPTER FORTY-ONE

"*I* doubt it!"

Laughter erupted around Tess's patio table where a rowdy card game was going on after Lacey and Jack's engagement dinner.

Ben couldn't help a contented sigh, stomach full of BBQ while his heart was full of joy. He smiled as Tess squealed and whooped when she won the noisy card game called "I doubt it," and he seriously "doubted it" that his life had ever been better. Certainly not in high school or college where he drank, caroused, and defied his stepfather ad nauseam, nor in his marriage where he foolishly begrudged first his wife and then his daughter. Tess's chuckles rose above all the others and all at once her smiling face morphed into Karen's tearstained one, producing an immediate stab of guilt. Sipping his iced tea, he closed his eyes to battle a familiar malaise with a Scripture Tess pounded into his brain on a daily basis.

As far as the east is from the west, so far hath He removed our transgressions from us.

His lids popped open, and he grinned when Tess took a bow. Now *that* was the kind of geography he could live with. His gaze all but caressed the woman responsible for his change of direction, and his heart stuttered when she gave him a secret smile.

Talk about something he could live with!

"Okay, we have Mamaw's peach crumble pie and homemade ice cream for dessert." Her blue eyes scanned two patio tables—hers and his on loan—both clad in white plastic tablecloths to accommodate her children and his, with Nicki, Matt, Mamaw, and Spence. "Anybody hungry?"

"Ravenous," he said with a look that had little to do with pie, grinning outright when a touch of color stole into her cheeks. He sighed inwardly, shocked that a heart once as cold as his could now burn with so much love. His gaze happily stole from the off-kilter ponytail and tempting crop top down the tiny waist and trim jeans before trailing back up to a beautiful face that now sported a full-fledged blush. *Yep, definitely looking to share more than tables.*

"Need some help, Tess?" Lacey and the girls jumped up while Mamaw rose as well, ready to abandon her game of crazy eights with Spence and Davey.

"Nope—*sit*—all of you!" Tess ordered, gently prodding Mamaw back into her chair. "I'll just bring everything out to divvy up here, so I think I can handle it." She pushed in her chair with a wiggle of brows. "After all, I just fleeced the whole lot of you in a card game, remember?" Winking at Lacey, she patted Jack's shoulder while he dealt the cards for another game. "Make me proud, Son, although I doubt anything can top your ring on Lacey's finger." Ponytail swishing, Tess slid Ben a private wink on her way to the kitchen.

Taking advantage of everyone's preoccupation with card games, he upended his tea and rose to follow, grateful for a few minutes alone with the woman he loved. Easing the screen door open with nary a sound, he quietly closed it again, unable to fight a grin over her off-key singing. Unaware he had entered the kitchen, she stood on tiptoe while tugging paper plates from a high shelf of the pantry, belting out *Let it Go* so loudly, he was able to sneak up from behind.

"My thoughts exactly," he whispered in her ear, making her squeal and drop the paper plates when he slipped his arms around her waist. He burrowed his lips into the nape of her neck, the scent of lemons—compliments of her Herbal Essence Citrus shampoo—driving him crazy. "Let it go, Tess," he breathed in her ear, "your obstinate rationale for putting me off."

With a nervous giggle, she spun in his arms, gaze darting to the screen door before she warded him off with two firm palms to his chest. "Benjamin Carmichael, stop!" she scolded in a near whisper, a trace of a grin sneaking through, "the kids think we're friends and nothing else, rememb—"

He muzzled her with a kiss aching to be set free from the moment he saw her this afternoon, smudges of BBQ sauce on her upper lip just begging to be licked away. But the boys had been playing in the backyard and her girls were setting the tables, so he'd put the urge on hold.

Till now. The perfect moment when nobody could see them through the kitchen window that overlooked the yard rather than the patio.

The engagement BBQ had been her idea, so she'd insisted on grilling herself, determined he'd come as a guest to help himself to "the best barbecue over the bridge" without lifting a finger. And "help himself" he would, he'd decided, but the only finger he wanted to lift was hers, in order to slide a ring on her hand, something she'd been fighting him on for weeks now.

"I'm forty-six, Tess," he'd told her one moonlit night on the dock last week, pinning her with a serious gaze rimmed by trace of humor. "And I've spent almost eight years virtually alone until some pesky neighbor barged into my life and made me love her. For almost four months now, you've bribed my dog, battered my defenses, breached my house—

"Fortress, you mean ..." she'd interjected with a jut of her chin.

His smile had faded to soft. "Prison, if we're squabbling over semantics." He'd gently brushed the hair from her eyes, placing the mere breath of a kiss to her forehead. "I love you, Tess, heart and soul, and I want you in every possible way." Mischief laced his tone as he leaned in to nuzzle her neck, his breath warm in her ear. "I'm not a teenager anymore, woman, and don't have the time to wait, nor am I so inclined, so you have no choice but to say yes ..."

The sound of the kids' squeals and laughter out on the porch broke into his thoughts, and taking advantage, he devoured her with a lip lock so deep, a low groan rumbled in his throat. "Marry me, Tess, and I'll take the padlock off the side gate, I swear."

Eyes tender, she pulled back to cradle his cheek. "You know we can't do that, Ben," she said softly, the glow of love in her eyes more intoxicating than all the liquor he'd once consumed. "This is Jack and Lacey's time to shine, and I don't want to risk upstaging it *or* possibly upsetting one of the happiest times for both of our families." She perched on tiptoe to plant a kiss to his nose. "Besides, we agreed to ease in slowly and get to know each other a little better so we're sure it's what we really want to do, yes?" She arched a brow, her smile tipping in tease. "Honestly, Dr. Doom, I had no idea you could be so pushy."

He dove for her neck with a half growl, making her giggle and squirm when he tugged on her lobe with his teeth. "*You* agreed, not me, Tess, and I *know* I want you, which is good enough for me. And as far as being pushy, you taught me everything I know."

"Uh-oh, I've created a monster," she said with a giggle that was more of a gasp, jerking away with a glazed look that made him want to kiss her all over again. She warded him off with two stiff arms, cheeks flushed and lips swollen, a clear indication she was experiencing the same desire as he. "I need ice cream," she croaked, attempting to wiggle free.

"Tess," he whispered, locking her close, "just say yes, *please*, and we can set the date later ..."

She stared, the rise and fall of her chest in rhythm with his own shallow breathing as their gazes fused with a heat that threatened to burst into another firestorm of passion. Shuddering with a shiver that merged with a sigh, she gently stroked his sandpaper jaw. "Let's just say it's a definite maybe, all right?" she said softly, eyes smiling before they settled into serious. "But keep in mind that when it comes to marriage, Dr. Carmichael, neither of us are experts, so I think we need to give it the test of time and prayer, don't you?" The edge of her lip tipped. "*Especially* given the chemistry. We've already seen how attraction can skew an outcome the wrong way."

She was right, of course, but that didn't mean he had to like it. "How long?" he groused, tunneling his fingers into her hair with a scowl. "Another month? Three months? Six?"

Her mouth crooked. "Six months, starting today."

He groaned and butted her to the counter to kiss her hard, not giving a whit that her mussed-up ponytail veered even more off-center.

"*With* good behavior, Dr. Doom," she rasped, voice breathless.

He couldn't help it—he grinned. *God help me, I'm crazy about this woman!* Reality suddenly struck, and he expelled a strained quiver of air, the task ahead sobering him considerably. And God's help would be a must to ensure good behavior till he put a gold band on her hand. "Agreed," he said softly while he leaned to nuzzle her mouth with his own. "But keep in mind, Mrs. O'Bryen, that a long engagement won't be doing either of us any favors."

The squeal of the kitchen screen door registered too late, and with a slam of his heart, Tess jerked violently from his arms as if he had thrust her away, the whites of her eyes circled in shock while she stared at her daughter.

"Uh, Mom?" Shannon stood on the threshold, the fire in her face a perfect match to her mother's. "Hate to interrupt, but there's something you need to know." Her somber gaze flicked to Ben and back as she held the screen open, the blush in her cheeks slowly bleaching to chalk. When she finally spoke again her voice faded so low, Ben could barely hear it over the ragged beat of his pulse. With a hard swallow, Shannon blinked at her mother while a lump bobbed several times in her throat. "Daddy's home."

CHAPTER FORTY-TWO

*T*he screen door quietly thudded closed, and it wasn't until several erratic heartbeats later, that Tess even remembered to breathe. Steadying herself with a hand braced to the counter, she slowly met Ben's gaze, which appeared as catatonic as her own.

"What's he doing here?" he hissed, his caustic tone clear-cut evidence that Ben had a ways to go in the forgiveness department.

"I have no idea," she whispered, body trembling as she tugged on her crop top and smoothed back her hair. She and Adam seldom connected anymore after he left for Zambia several years back. Since then his communication via phone and letter had been mostly limited to the children per Tess's request. Ingesting a deep draw of air, she suddenly realized that when it came to complete forgiveness, maybe Ben wasn't alone. With a brush of sweaty hands down the sides of her jeans, she took a timid step toward the door. "I haven't seen him for two years and only talked to him once since then." She placed a gentle hand on Ben's arm, an apology in her tone. "If you'd rather not stay, Ben, I'll understand. You can leave through the front door, and I'll call you when he's gone."

A nerve twittered in his jaw. "No—he's the outsider here now, not me."

She paused, face crimped in concern. "Are you sure you'll be … okay?"

He gave a short nod and prodded her toward the door, his palm warm at the small of her back.

Exhaling a weary breath, Tess stepped out on the patio with Ben close behind, the sounds of Davey's excited chatter dominating the table where Adam now sat in Ben's place. Well beyond dusk, a tiki torch flickered shadows across his handsome face, giving him an ethereal look that made the whole thing seem like a dream.

Or a nightmare.

"Mom, look—Daddy's home!" Davey shouted, and Tess's stomach bottomed out when Adam's gaze connected with hers.

"Hello, Tess," he said quietly, rising with that faint half-smile that had always reminded her of a young Dennis Quaid. His gaze flicked to the man behind her and he nodded, his smile intact despite the barest stiffening of his jaw. "Ben."

"What are you doing here, Adam?" Tess said, too flustered for niceties. She clutched her arms to her waist. "I thought you were in Zambia."

"I was, just got back." He directed another quick glance at Ben before offering a conciliatory smile to Tess. "Look, if I'm interrupting, I can always come back later …"

"No, Daddy—you're not!" The plea in Shannon's voice, soundly echoed by Davey, matched the one in her eyes. "Is he, Mom?"

"No, of course not," Tess said in a rush, cheeks warming at her appalling lack of manners. "We were just about to have dessert in honor of Jack and Lacey's engagement, so you're welcome to join us if you like."

"No kidding?" Adam turned to where Jack and Lacey sat at the end of the table, Lacey's bright smile in blatant contrast to the scowl on Jack's face. "Well,

congratulations, Son, and you too, Lacey—I always
thought you two were a perfect match."

"Thanks, Mr. O'Bryen," she said with a proud grin,
giving Jack a squeeze. "I think so."

"Daddy, where are you staying?" Davey asked with
a tug of his father's polo, which Tess suddenly noticed
hung on a frame much thinner than she remembered.

"I'm booked at Lovett's Low-Country Motel,
buddy, and if your mom says it's okay, you can come
stay with me for a night or two after I settle in."

"Wow, really?" Davey's eyes all but bugged out of
his head as he whirled toward Tess. "Can I, Mom,
please, please?"

"Of course, sweetheart." Her smile returned to
Adam, a hair tauter than before. "So, how long are you
in town?"

Hands in his pockets, he gave a faint shrug. "For a
while—a leave of six months or so."

Tess caught her breath. *Six months?*

"Why?" Jack's voice held an edge that Tess seldom
heard.

His father glanced his way, and Tess noticed the
stoop of Adam's shoulders and the shot of silver at his
temples, giving him a humble air that had never been
there before. "To spend time with my family, Jack," he
said quietly, "if you'll let me."

"Of course we'll let you," Shannon said in a firm
tone that sounded far more like her sister than her,
giving Jack a pointed look that challenged the frown on
his face. She bumped Cat's arm with her elbow. "Won't
we, Cat?"

Not a staunch defender of her father in the past, Cat
had always been the one Tess had to prod to join
Shannon and Davey on their parental visits, her
relationship with Adam as rocky as Shannon's and
Davey's were smooth. Sitting hunched at the table, she

now stared at a water bottle in her hands, her voice barely audible. "Sure."

"Good." Adam's chest expanded and contracted as if he'd been holding his breath, and pushing his chair in, he faced Tess once again. "Then I'll leave you all to your celebration and check back tomorrow."

"No, stay, please—for dessert at least," Tess said, shocked at the words that so easily rolled off of her tongue.

"*Mom.*" Jack's eyes almost singed as he stared her down, tension crackling in the air at his obvious displeasure.

Mamaw was on her feet in a heartbeat. "Tess, would you mind terribly if I had Nicki and Matt drive Spence and me home before dessert? It's been a lovely afternoon and evening, but I'm feeling the effects of my age, I'm afraid, and ready for an early night."

"Oh, Mildred, no—not before dessert!" Tess tucked an arm to Mamaw's waist. "I just need to brew a pot of coffee, then it won't take but a few minutes to bring everything out."

Mamaw patted her hand, sympathy shadowing her smile as she glanced Adam's way. Her head lowered along with her voice. "I think your family may need some private time, dear."

"But what about Spence's pie and ice cream?" Davey asked, a pinch of alarm in his face at the prospect of his best friend going home.

Mamaw smoothed Spence's hair. "Don't worry about Spence, Davey—I have another pie in my pantry, along with cinnamon ice cream in the freezer." She winked at Nicki. "Only one of the many ploys I use to lure Nicki and Matt over to see their old granny."

"Mamaw!" Nicki feigned offense, the semblance of a smile forming on her lips. "I would come over without pie and you know it."

"But not as quickly," Matt said, slinging an arm over her shoulder, "right?" She elbowed him, and he pretended to double over in pain, sliding Jack a sideways grin. "You sure you know what you're doing, Jack? Marriage can be a dangerous proposition."

"Trust me, I know," Jack said, cinching Lacey closer while he shot his father a cool look.

"I'll show you 'dangerous.'" Nicki bent to give Lacey a hug before looping Mamaw's arm and ushering her toward the driveway. "Thanks, Tess, for a wonderful dinner. Bye, all!"

Goodbyes echoed down the driveway as Davey climbed into Adam's lap, his daddy's arms slipping around to hold him tight.

"Tess, I think I'll head home too."

She spun around at the sound of Ben's voice, stomach cramping at the hard cut of his jaw. "I'm so sorry," she mouthed, then raised her voice. "Let me wrap up some pie."

"No, I'm not hungry." He stood there, ill at ease, and she ached to touch him, hug him.

Lacey started to get up. "Daddy, I'll come with you—"

"No." The faint smile on Ben's face clashed with the sharpness of his tone. "This is your engagement celebration, Lacey—you stay with Jack."

She slid back in her chair, and Jack hooked her close.

Tess couldn't help it. She gently touched Ben's arm. "I'll save you a piece."

He nodded, his eyes piercing hers before he turned to go with a half-hearted wave. "Good night, everyone."

Goodbyes rang out as Tess watched Ben disappear down the driveway, and whirling around, she pressed her palms together with a smile that felt way too forced. "Well, okay ... who wants coffee with their pie?"

"I don't want pie, I want the truth," Jack said to his father with a menacing glare. "We've gotten along just fine all these years without you, so why are even you here?"

"Jack!" Tess's shocked response collided with Lacey's, both with mouths agape.

Adam held up a hand as if to calm their responses. "No, Tess, it's a fair question, and one I'd like to answer." Despite the rancor of Jack's look, his father merely offered a sad smile, his voice kind, but tinged with regret. For the first time, Tess noticed the dark circles under his eyes. "I came home to spend time with my family, Jack, and to try and make up for some of the damage I've done."

"Too late," Jack bit out, then seemed to calm somewhat when Lacey stroked his arm.

"No, Son, it's not," he whispered, a strange aura of peace surrounding this man who'd once pulsed with so much passion and life. He pressed a kiss to Davey's head while he snuggled him closer, his eyes never straying from Jack's. "But someday it will be, and I can't live with myself if I don't at least try."

Tess's lungs closed in, the tenor of his tone weakening her limbs. She slowly sank into her chair, painfully aware that his face was pale to the point of ashen, a total departure for the outdoorsman with the perennial tan. "What do you mean?" she whispered, praying it was her imagination that made him appear almost sickly. His eyes rose to meet hers, and in one violent beat of her heart, she knew. Her voice came out fast and clipped. "Davey, it's time to get ready for bed, sweetheart."

"But Daddy's here—"

"He'll be here when you get done," she said quickly, gaze fused to Adam's. "Go brush your teeth and get your jammies on, then Daddy'll be in to read a story and say your prayers, all right?"

Davey heaved a sigh as he slid off his father's lap. "Okaaaay," he said, dragging the word out as he slowly trudged inside.

As soon as the screen door closed, Tess leaned in, palms pressed to the table while she stared Adam down. "I want the truth, Adam—are you sick?"

She saw a glimpse of that secret smile she once loved as he lowered his head. He ruffled the back of his hair with the flat of his hand like he used to whenever he was figuring out what he wanted to say. When he finally glanced up, the smile he wore was so boyishly sweet that she remembered just why she'd fallen in love the first time. "Come on now, Tess," he said with a glint of the tease that had once fluttered her stomach, "did I really look this bad when I wasn't?"

"Daddy!" Shannon jumped up and rounded the table, crouching beside him to caress a hand to his back. "This isn't funny. What's wrong with you?"

He scooped her into a side hold, ducking his head to hers. "No, I don't think it's funny, Shan, but sometimes it's easier to tease than to cry." His eyes shuttered closed while he pressed a kiss to her hair. "Like now."

"Are you going to tell us or not?" Cat demanded, thumping a fist on the table. "Give us the truth *now*, Daddy, and don't sugarcoat it."

Arm braced around Shannon's shoulders, he looked up, his sorrowful gaze traveling from Jack to Cat before lighting on Tess. "I have stage-four pancreatic cancer," he said quietly, "and they tell me there's nothing more they can do."

"No!" Shannon's voice broke on a sob, and she clutched him all the tighter while Cat just sat there frozen in shock.

"How long have they … ?" Jack's voice cracked, sounding nothing like before.

Adam looked up at his son, tenderness swimming in his eyes. "Six months or less, Jack," he whispered, pausing to grace each of them with a wistful smile. "So I was hoping—well, praying, really—that maybe I could spend my last Christmas with my family."

"Oh, Adam ... " Tess jumped up, a heave swallowing his name as she flew to his side, clinging while she wept on his chest. In a heartbeat, Cat was beside them, the four of them in a huddle of mourning while Jack sat paralyzed at the end of the table, a hollow look on his face.

"Okay, Dad, I'm ready!" The screen door slammed as Davey dashed out, skidding to a halt at the sight of everyone's tears. "What's wrong?" he asked, blinking at his family as if they'd all lost their minds.

Arms around Tess and his daughters, Adam laughed despite the tears in his eyes, giving each of them a squeeze before he stood to his feet. "Aw, everybody's just happy to see me, bud, that's all. Hey, you still have those Power Ranger books I gave you for Christmas last year?"

"Yes!" Vaulting into the air in his Power Ranger pajamas, Davey gave a fist punch.

"Good, then let's go tuck you in and do some reading." With a press of Tess's hand, he deposited a kiss to each of his daughter's cheeks before turning to face Jack. "It's good to see you again, Son," he said, "I've missed you."

Mouth compressed in a scowl, Jack gave a curt nod instantly betrayed by a glaze of moisture in his eyes.

"For Pete's sake, everybody, enough with the crying—we have books to read." Adam chuckled as he pulled away, swiping at his face with a grin that transformed him into the husband and father they'd all known and loved. "And since Power Rangers don't cry, that includes me too." Despite his thinner stature, he promptly swooped Davey up and tossed him over his shoulder. "Come on, Mack, let's go fight some evil before I head on home."

Tess watched him lumber toward the door, and with a wrench of her heart, she knew what she had to do. "No," she called loudly before Adam could even enter the house.

He turned at the door, a gouge in his brow while Davey continued to wiggle. "What?"

Squaring her shoulders, she took a step forward with a stern cross of arms, the seeds of a smile squirming as much as Davey over Adam's shoulder. "I'll not stand by and watch you subsist on vending machines and fast food at a motel, not when we have a perfectly good bed that Matt no longer uses."

He blinked. "Here? You want me to stay here?"

"Yes, yes, yes!" Davey shouted, rocking poor Adam so much, he had to hold on to the jamb of the door.

She cocked her head. "Well, yes of course—unless you're partial to the turndown service at Lovett's, because there's definitely no maid service here."

It was a tossup over which spread faster—the moisture in his eyes or the grin on his face. "I can be a slob, Tess, or have you forgotten?"

Her lip quirked. "A wise woman does not forget the vices of an ex-husband, Adam."

The smile faltered on his lips as his gaze swept past her to Jack and the girls. "And it's all right with the kids?"

"Absolutely," Shannon shouted, hooking her arm through her sister's. "Right, Cat?"

Cat shrugged her shoulders before sending her father an evil grin. "Sure—one more person to take a week of dishes sounds pretty good to me."

Adam flashed some teeth before his smiled dimmed. "And, Jack? You okay with this? Because that means we're bunkmates, so if you're not, there's no way I'm staying."

"No, I want Daddy to stay in my room," Davey insisted, eyes round in appeal.

Tess glanced from Davey to Jack, well aware that with Jack and Lacey's whirlwind wedding just three weeks away, Jack would be moving out. They could certainly move Matt's twin bed into Davey's room till then. "Well, maybe just till Jack leaves, Davey, then Daddy will need his own room, okay?" She studied the frown on Jack's face, praying he would understand.

All eyes homed in on a stone-faced Jack, arm draped over Lacey's shoulder. Even from a distance, Tess could see the almost imperceptible grind of his jaw. Lacey peered up at him, and Tess suspected she'd given Jack's leg a squeeze under the table because he finally answered, his voice little more than a croak. "Sure. Majority rules."

"Yay!" Davey bucked and kicked in joy over Adam's shoulder while Shannon bolted for the door, hugging her dad before scooting past. "I'll go put some fresh sheets on Matt's bed."

"I guess I'll go make room in the bathroom closet," Cat said with a heavy sigh that Tess knew was all for show. Her mouth crooked as she eased by her dad and Davey with a dry smile. "I got Matt's shelf when we unloaded him, but I suppose you can have it till we kick Jack out."

Adam grinned, his gaze of gratitude locking with Tess's with such force that her heart buckled in her chest. "Thank you," he whispered before making his way inside.

Expelling a wavering sigh, Tess turned to see Jack and Lacey rise from the table. "You're certain you're okay with this, Jack?" she asked, not quite sure what she'd do if he said no.

He pushed his chair in and drew Lacey close, shooting her a tight smile. "It's your house, Mom, and I'm gone in three weeks anyway, so I'll adjust." His shoulders lifted in a slight shrug. "Besides," he said, a glint of moisture marring his gaze, "it'll do our family good to be whole again for a while—" His voice cracked and he tugged Lacey toward the driveway, shooting Tess a broken look over his shoulder. "We'll be on the dock, Mom."

"Okay, sweetheart," she called, rubbing her arms from a sudden chill that had nothing to do with the cool night air. Beau barked, and her head whirled toward Ben's yard, the slide of his back door prompting more moisture in her eyes. The light through the hedge suddenly blurred into a million haloed stars, as foggy and out of focus as she.

Oh, Ben, what are we going to do?

But she already knew. She sensed it in her bones and could feel it deep in her heart. As much as she ached inside at the very thought, the burgeoning love between Ben and her would have to wait for God's timing, if ever. Because the truth was, her children were too important … and so was the man who'd given them life. The same man she'd vowed to love for better or worse, in sickness and in health … No, not romantically anymore, although traces of the man who'd once stolen her heart were still there—in his mischievous smile, in that little-boy twinkle, in the subtle tease of a tone that had never failed to coax her out of a bad mood. She loved him as the father of her children and as a man who despite the excruciating pain he had caused, was still a part of her life.

Heart and hands trembling, she hurried into the kitchen to wrap pie for Ben, the sound of laughter from upstairs—Adam's husky chuckles mingling with her children's giggles—so surreal. She plunged the knife into the pie, the slice of the blade into the sweet not unlike what was going on in her heart—the sweetness of reconciliation marred by the bitter stab of what this meant for her and Ben.

Pausing to make sure that the kids and Adam were still occupied upstairs, she slipped out the back door and hurried down the drive with the wrapped pie in hand. Her pulse boomed louder than the deep bongs of Ben's doorbell as she shivered on his porch.

The door swung wide, and her heart leapt in her chest at his sober expression, reminding her how painful this would be for this man that she loved ... and for her.

"I brought you p-pie," she whispered, unable to stop the quiver of her lips or the swell of saltwater in her eyes.

Without a word, he pulled her inside and shut the door, taking the pie from her hands and placing it on the foyer table before he swallowed her up in his arms, crushing her close. "Whatever it is, Tess, we'll get through it."

"Oh, B-Ben," she whispered through a broken heave, "I'm so sorry ..."

Sweeping her up in his arms, he carried her into the family room and placed her on the sofa before sitting beside her, taking her hands in his. "He's sick, isn't he?" he whispered, and she nodded, not surprised that as a physician, he'd deduced that far quicker than she. "Cancer?" His voice was low, calm, but even on lips so practiced at conveying bad news, the very sound of the word left a terrible pall in the air.

She could only nod once again, the swipe of her fingers unable to keep up with her trickle of tears. He reached behind to snatch several Kleenex from his recliner table, gently kneading her shoulder as he prodded the tissues into her hand. "What's the prognosis?" he asked quietly.

Swabbing her face, she stopped to blow her nose before she answered in a feeble voice congested with grief. "The d-doctors say he's terminal, no more than six months to live, but I refuse to believe that, Ben." She stared at him through raw eyes that throbbed with a headache. "God can heal, Ben, we both know that He can."

He tucked her close to his chest, the warmth of his body against hers a cocoon of comfort she never wanted to leave. "Of course He can, Tess," he said quietly, massaging her back with a tenderness she'd come to expect from this man who seldom revealed his soft side to others. "And that's how we'll pray."

She hesitated, loathe to utter the next words for the damage they might do. "I ... I asked him to stay," she whispered, "with us instead of at a motel."

His hand paused, so briefly she wondered if she'd only imagined it before the warmth of his palm returned, coaxing the tension from her shoulders. "Of course you did—it's one of the things I love most about you, Tess—your tender heart." There was no mistaking the pause now. "So where does that leave us?" he asked softly.

Her eyelids lumbered closed. "He's my husband, Ben ..."

"*Was* your husband, Tess ..."

She pulled away with liquid pain in her eyes, her stomach in spasms over the wounded look on his face. Stroking his jaw with impassioned tenderness, she leaned to gently brush her lips to his cheek. "I love you, Ben Carmichael—deeply—and someday I hope to become your wife. But for now—Adam's home, and for his sake, my family's, and even myself—I need to distance myself from you and focus on him. At least until he's well enough to get past this or until ..." She swallowed hard, unable to go on. The thought of a man as strong and virile as Adam used to be facing death was too much to bear. Her fingers shook as she gouged them through her hair. "I ... I just can't think beyond that right now, and I'm hoping you'll understand."

"I do," he whispered, skimming his thumb over her knuckles before lifting them to his mouth to do the same with his lips. "I've never loved anyone like I love you, Tess," he said quietly, "and I will wait forever, if that's what it takes."

She blinked, then launched into his arms with a sob, clinging with a ferocity as fierce as the love that she bore. "I love you with everything in me, Ben, and my prayers will be with you every single day, even if I can't be."

He pressed a lingering kiss to her hair before pulling away to gently buff her arms. "You need to go," he whispered, tugging her to her feet.

She nodded and rose, arms crossed and clutched to her waist. "Will you pray for me?"

The edge of his lip canted as he led her down the hall. "You don't really think I'd leave something this important to chance, do you?"

Head bowed, she opened the door and peered up, brows tented in sorrow. "And you'll pray for Adam too? That God will bless him and heal him?"

Hip to the jamb, he folded his arms with the faintest slant of a smile. "You don't make this easy, do you?"

"There's nothing easy about this," she whispered, her voice trembling as much as she.

Eyes closed, he kneaded the bridge of his nose while his chest rose and fell in a cumbersome sigh. When he finally glanced up, his gaze fused to hers with an intensity that conveyed the depth of love that they shared. "Yes, Tess, I'll pray for Adam."

Nodding, she stepped out on the porch, pivoting to face him. "And you'll work on forgiving him, too?" she asked softly, heart lurching when his lips slashed into a scowl.

"For crying out loud, you can't shoot for the moon," he said with an edge to his voice, broad shoulders obviously slumping along with his mood.

She tried to memorize every angle of his hard-sculpted face, every generous curve of the mouth that had brought her so much passion and joy. A soft smile lighted upon her lips despite the grief in her heart. "Oh, sure you can, Ben," she said with a caress of his stubbled jaw, eyes misty with a love she never dreamed she'd have again. "How do you think I got you?"

CHAPTER FORTY-THREE

*H*ands tented to the window, Lacey peeked in the back slider door. Her lips curved in a tender smile as she made out the form of her father in his recliner with eyes closed and Beau on his lap. Light from the TV flickered on his face in an otherwise dark room, and Lacey's heart squeezed at the thought that the gloom of darkness may have crept into his mind as well.

With a gentle tap on the glass, Beau barked and vaulted from the chair. Her father stirred with a blink of wide eyes that bore the faintest flash of hope before they dimmed into a tired smile, confirming the suspicions she and Jack had down on the dock. He was obviously crushed over Mr. O'Bryen's return, and although Tess worked hard not to show it, Lacey surmised Jack's mother secreted the same pain. Both Jack and she had suspected their parents had fallen in love, although neither had given any blatant indication to the fact. But the night she and Daddy had finally reconciled, she'd seen a glimpse of something in his eyes at the mention of Tess, a tenderness in his tone that had escaped her before. Since then, she'd been watching the interplay between the two, and once she'd confided in Jack, he'd seen the signs too.

Without question, her father was in love with Jack's mother.

Easing the slider open, Lacey promptly scrubbed Beau's snout, bending down to nuzzle his head before she quietly closed the door. "Hey, I was wondering if you wanted some company for the latest NCIS?" She sauntered over to her father's chair and leaned to kiss his cheek, giving him a quick hug in the process.

Which he returned, she noted with a rush of joy.

But his smile couldn't mask the sadness shadowing his eyes. "Already watched it," he said with a half-hearted stretch, "but I'm game for your choice of movie if you want, although I draw the line at romance."

Of course you do, she thought with an ache in her heart. She scrunched her nose. "Nope, I'm thinking something more fast-paced and gutsy like one of the Bourne movies—your choice."

"Great—I have all the DVDs, so go for it." He handed her the remote and punched the release button on his recliner, dropping the footrest so he could rise and head for the kitchen. "I'll make popcorn, and there's plenty of Diet Dr. Pepper this time unless you want grape juice."

She forced a bright tone, her words catching on the lump of emotion in her throat. "DP sounds good," she called, queuing up the movie. The smell of popcorn drifted in to rumble her stomach when he returned with two cans of Diet DP. "Thanks, Daddy, you rock!"

His smile shifted off-center. "I'm guessing that's more apt if referencing the Stone Age rather than me being 'cool,' but I'll take it." He shuffled back in the room with two bowls of popcorn and napkins, Beau hot on his heels. "I also have some of Mamaw's peach pie with a little bit of Häagen-Dazs left if you want it." He handed her a bowl and napkin before settling back in his chair and tossing a handful of popcorn to Beau.

Mamaw's peach pie. She secretly winced as she burrowed into the corner of the sofa, feet tucked beneath. *The prelude to disaster.*

"Nope, popcorn is just the ticket, thanks." She absently clicked the remote, and the *Jaws*-like thump of the music for *Bourne Ultimatum* filled the family room with its intense beat, echoing the racing thud of her pulse. Jason Bourne appeared, trudging through the snow in Moscow, wounded and running scared.

Just like my father.

She studied her dad's strong and handsome profile out of the corner of her eye and was so glad she'd come. All of her life she'd needed him and never even known it. Her heart swelled with a staggering love molded and gifted by God.

And now he needed her.

Unleashing a silent sigh, Lacey refocused on the TV where Jason Bourne ducked into a Moscow subway to escape the Soviet police. "Gosh, Daddy, wouldn't it be awful to have to run for your life?" she said casually, not expecting an answer.

"Yeah. But I think I'm about to find out." His mumbled response stopped her cold, muttered so low, she knew he hadn't meant her to hear.

Fixed on his profile, she felt her heart pound in time with the staccato beat of the music. "Daddy?"

He glanced over, fatigue shaping his features. "Yeah, Lace?"

"Can I ... I mean, would it be okay ..." She hesitated with a chew of her lip, so very afraid he might say no.

One edge of his mouth inched up. "Spit it out, Lace. You're sitting here with a lonely old man watching a movie you've already seen when you could be spooning with Jack. It's not likely I'll say 'no.'"

She couldn't help it—she grinned. "*Spooning*? What, are you from the turn of the last century?"

His chuckle warmed her heart. "Nope, but I sure feel like it at times," he said with a weary fan of fingers through his hair. Tenderness eased the strain in his face.

"What do you want, Lace? It's yours, up to half my kingdom."

She fiddled with a piece of popcorn while she peeked up at him with a shy look. "Could I ... spend the night? You know, in the guest bedroom?"

His smile crooked. "You mean *your* old bedroom? Sure, the sheets should be clean although I can't vouch there's no dust." He popped a piece of popcorn in his mouth and chewed for several seconds before his gaze locked on hers. "Why?"

She rolled her lips inward with a timidity and awe that her father had always fostered. "Because I ... want to be close to you," she said softly, "especially tonight."

He stared at her, popcorn paused at his lips, and she wasn't prepared for the sheen of tears that sprang to his eyes. Mouth compressed as if to contain his emotion, he gave a jerky nod and turned away, a muscle quivering in his jaw while he stared at the screen. The blare of horns and police sirens ricocheted off the family room walls as Bourne lunged from a subway train into dangerous territory. Much as Lacey was about to do.

She paused the movie. "Daddy?"

This time he continued to stare straight ahead. "Yeah, Lace?"

"I'm so sorry about tonight," she whispered, her heart wobbling as much as her voice. "For both you and Tess."

He bowed his head, the faintest of smiles curving on his lips. "So all our stealth and secrecy was for naught, eh?"

"Only with Jack and me—everybody else thinks you're just friends and neighbors."

Nodding slowly, he issued a grunt. "Yeah, well, they would be right."

"What are you going to do?" she said quietly, fiddling with a piece of popcorn until it disintegrated between her fingers.

Dropping his palms flat on the arms of the chair, he exhaled a heavy sigh and leaned back, head resting while he stared at the ceiling. "Not much I can do but abide by her request to put distance between us for now." His eyelids sank along with his volume. "May as well ask me not to breathe ..."

The threat of tears stung in her nose. "Oh, Daddy—you love her, don't you?"

Ever so slowly, he turned to face her then, and the vulnerability she saw in this once self-sufficient and untouchable man pierced her to the core. "More than I ever dreamed possible, Lacey, and far more than I ever deserved."

Her hand stilled in the bowl. "I'm so sorry—I'm heartsick for you."

He smiled, although the glaze was back in his eyes. "Me too, kiddo." Placing his bowl on the table, he lowered the footrest and angled her way, shoulders hunched and hands clasped while they rested over his knees. "But now that we're on the subject, I do have a favor to ask."

"Anything," she said with such passion that he actually grinned.

"Calm down, Lace—I'm not asking for a kidney here." He scratched the back of his head, nose pinched while he stared at the floor as if afraid of her reaction. "Although it's pretty close." His chest expanded and contracted with a noisy breath before his gaze met hers. "I was wondering if you and Jack would consider dog- and house-sitting for me after you get married."

She shimmied to the edge of the couch, clutching her bowl in excitement. "Are you kidding?" She wiggled her brows in tease. "I've been wanting to get Jack alone in my bedroom since I was sixteen."

He slid her a droll smile. "Yeah, I know, which is why I watched you like a rabid hawk."

"So, when? And for how long?" She tossed a popped kernel high in the air, snapping it with her teeth.

He peered up beneath dark lashes. "Right after the honeymoon ... for about six months."

Hacking uncontrollably, she watched him through watering eyes as he jumped up and stood close, obviously poised to perform the Heimlich if needed. She waved him off and snatched the can of DP he shoved in her face, glugging it till her pulse began to slow.

"You okay?" He hovered over her like he used to hover over the scotch and whiskeys he always guzzled before dinner.

"Yeah, I'm fine," she rasped, hand to her chest while her gaze glommed to his. "Did you say *six months*?"

His smile was sheepish. "Yeah, I did. One of my oldest friends is affiliated with the International Children's Heart Foundation, and he's been hounding me for years now to sign up for their medical mission trips, so I plan to contact him." He absently scratched his neck, smile suddenly flat. "The ICHF provides life-saving surgeries for babies born with congenital heart defects all over the world, and I'm ashamed to say I've been putting him off. Oh, I've done a number of little overseas junkets here and there for the Save a Child's Heart Foundation, but something tells me this is the right time to donate more of my time and skills." He glanced up. "Not to mention the right reason." He cuffed the back of his head again. "Besides, I know you and Jack want to get into a house as soon as possible, so this would be a way to save rent while you take your time looking, right?"

Her mouth curved into an easy smile. "Are you kidding? It's a win-win all around. Between work, the wedding, and the time we'll be spending with Jack's family right now because of his father, both of us are swamped. Neither of us really has the time to find an apartment we actually like, much less decorate one. And we've been butting heads over renting vs. buying because he wants a house right away, and I think we should save a while, so this is a no-brainer as far as I'm concerned."

"You think Jack will agree?" Her father peered up, the slightest kink in his brows.

She tilted her head in a squint, reflecting on Jack's conversation on the dock. Although he was still angry with his father, he felt compelled to spend time with his family as a unit for their sake, and maybe even for himself, hopefully to dispel the bitterness and hurt he still harbored. Living next door to the O'Bryen's for the next six months would certainly accomplish that, and the very thought tipped her lips into a smile. "I think Jack will thank you, Daddy, because the timing is right—for everyone." As soon as the words left her tongue, a sense of awe settled at just how right this suddenly felt, and she smiled at her dad through misty eyes, voice lowered to a hush. "But then God's timing usually is."

Her father nodded slowly, as if everything had clicked into place for him too. When his gaze finally met hers once again, she sensed a peace that hadn't been there before. "Thanks, Lacey," he whispered, "for loving me despite my many faults."

"Oh, Daddy ..." She lunged into a hug that was quickly returned. "Like *father*, like daughter," she whispered, gratitude surging for all that God had done. "*Both* of you ..."

ISLE OF HOPE   471

CHAPTER FORTY-FOUR

*S*hrieks and giggles echoed down the hall into Tess's kitchen from the front of the house where her family—including Jack—all watched *Shrek* with their father. Punching in the appropriate time for popcorn, she closed her eyes and leaned against the microwave door, the sound of Adam's laughter taking her back to better times.

It had been only a week since he had reentered their lives, and yet to Tess, at times, it almost seemed as if he'd never left. In a matter of only days, her family had circled the wagons, protecting him, enjoying him ... *loving* him. Like one, long, glorious pajama party with no end. Their weekends and evenings were filled with favorite movies, games, and memories past, bonding them together as cohesively as the epoxy Adam used on Davey's model airplane.

She moved to a pot on the stove where a stick of butter slowly melted away, not unlike the hurt and bitterness that had once stifled their family. Even Cat, so guarded in the beginning appeared to be warming up more and more, spending as much time with Adam as Davey and Shan. Jack, of course, was slower on the thaw, his manner considerably stiffer with his dad. But considering his prior red-hot anger over Adam's betrayal, Tess considered it progress.

During the day when Jack and the girls were at work and Davey at school, Tess and Adam would talk and pray over coffee before she left to make her rounds, a habit they'd once enjoyed so many years ago. Then when she'd leave for her hospice calls, Adam would leave for the Salvation Army Homeless Shelter in Savannah, volunteering as many hours as his diminishing energy would allow. "As long as I can drive, I can minister," he'd argue when Tess begged him to stay home and rest, always refusing "her coddling" with a wink and a smile. But she knew the effort took its toll when she'd find him collapsed on his bed in the afternoon, desperate to recharge in order to spend evenings with family. She sighed, the sound melancholy as she stirred the butter with a wooden spoon. *Who would have thought that cancer could heal?*

Removing the pot from the burner, she poured half of it over small bowls of popcorn before toting them in on a tray. Passing them out, she handed the last one to Davey, who sat happily on his daddy's lap while her daughters cuddled close on either side with Jack on the far end. Legs crossed on the coffee table, Adam glanced up with a tired smile, nodding toward the big-screen TV. "Thanks, Tess, but you better hurry—you're missing the best part."

She glanced at the screen where Dragon was stalking Donkey, then back at the sofa, and couldn't help the misty grin that inched across her face. No, *this* was the best part, she decided—the sight of her family crowded side-by-side on their oversized sectional like a package of marshmallow peeps. Not unlike the ones they were presently devouring, frozen since Easter. Shaking her head, she hurried back to the kitchen to prepare the final refill bowl, humming to herself until she heard the sound of Beau's bark through the open screen door. Followed, of course, by the slider when Ben let him in.

Ben.

Hand poised on the microwave door, she froze at the memory of the pain she'd caused the man that she loved. More laughter filtered in from the living room, and Tess was suddenly heartsick over the path each family had traveled. Sagging against the microwave, she put a hand to her eyes, lids sinking closed over the way sin had devastated their lives.

If only Ben hadn't turned his back on his wife and daughter. If only Lacey hadn't run away to cover up her sin. If only Adam hadn't cheated. If only she'd forgiven him sooner and given a second chance. If only Jack hadn't left the faith. Things might have been different and so much pain and hurt may have been spared. Moisture pricked. "Oh, God, if only we could blot out all the mistakes that we made …"

As far as the east is from the west, so far hath He removed our transgressions from us.

A tear slithered into the crook of her smile at the Scripture she'd give Ben every time guilt would rear its ugly head in his mind. Because no matter her failings or those of her family and loved ones, God's mercies *were* new every single morning, redeeming each of their lives on a daily basis. Not His perfect will, maybe, but His permissive one, girded all the same with His unfailing love and infinite mercy.

The steadfast love of the Lord never ceases; His mercies never come to an end; they are new every morning ...

"Tess, are you … all right?"

She spun around, embarrassed for Adam to see the tears glazing her cheeks. "Yes, yes, of course," she said quickly, swiping at her eyes before she opened the microwave door. Retrieving the last bag of popcorn, she tore it open and poured it into a backup bowl, avoiding his gaze as she streuseled the remaining butter. "Almost done."

"You're crying," he said quietly, a hint of alarm in his tone as he moved in close. "What's wrong?" He gently touched her arm, voice thick with that same tender care that had made him so good as a pastor ... a husband ... a father. Head bent, he studied her with a crease in his brow. "Is this too much for you, Tess? Me living here?"

"Oh, no, truly!" She patted his hand and squeezed, whirling quickly to wash her hands in an effort to deflect the sheen in her eyes. "I was just thinking how wonderful it is having you here. You know, spending time with the kids just like ..." Against her will, her voice cracked, and with an unwelcome swell of tears, she doubled over when a sob broke from her throat.

"Just like it used to be before I blew it," he whispered, voice gruff with remorse. "Like nothing had ever happened to destroy all the joy that we had."

Mouth clamped to ward off another sob, she nodded, unprepared for the floodgates that opened when he gently tugged her into his arms. "Forgive me for all the hurt that I've caused."

She nodded dumbly against his chest, his once-familiar scent wringing more water from her eyes. Tucking his head to hers, he gently stroked her hair while she wept for all they had lost.

"I've asked your forgiveness, Tess, for all the mistakes I've made, and God's as well, but the truth is, I don't know if I can ever forgive myself." Emotion all but crippled his words. "It s-seems the closer I draw to God, the d-deeper my sorrow grows over the pain that I caused." Pulling back, he lightly brushed a strand of hair from her face, studying her with grief that clearly matched her own. "Sin may be done in secret, but its pain travels well beyond. And believe me when I say, cancer is *nothing* compared to the ache of hurting you and my family." He stroked the curve of her face, his red-rimmed eyes piercing hers with an agony she understood all too well. "Please forgive me, Tess—I was such a fool, and a cocky one at that."

Her lips trembled into a smile. "Of course I forgive you," she said softly, her words hoarse and nasal like his. "But I share in the blame, Adam, because if I'd just quit my job—"

He chuckled, rubbing her arms with a gleam of affection. "You may as well concede, Tess, in a contest of blame, you don't stand a chance." He rubbed his temple with the pads of his fingers. "You know, I always thought I was stronger than most." A weak grunt parted from his lips as he eased himself down in a chair, his color suddenly pale. "Clearly a case of 'pride goeth before the fall.' And then I fell and learned just how very weak I was." His gaze lagged into a faraway stare, face haggard as if he were wrestling with demons from his past. He continued in a monotone, his words as dull and listless as his expression. "As if that weren't bad enough, I ran away, too proud to admit I was wrong, too selfish and cowardly to stay."

A tremor traveled his body. "When you and I went through that rough patch, Tess, over my insistence that a pastor's wife shouldn't work, my pride got the best of me. Then Karen came to me for counseling, and I told myself she needed me and you didn't, because you were always so very strong …" He looked at her then, torment carved into every feature. "I've thought a lot about it over the years, wondering how I could have fallen so far, but the truth is, like Satan, I was blinded by pride. Convinced I knew best for Karen and me, and guilty enough to want to sanction it all with divorce and remarriage." He shuddered and shielded a hand to his eyes. "It didn't take long to figure out that unrepentant sin does not a marriage make, and by the time we both realized that, it was too late …"

Her body shuddered along with his. "I'm not condoning what you did, Adam, because you were wrong, but I should have forgiven you sooner. I should have given you another chance when you finally came back, but I was so hurt ..."

"I know," he whispered, "and no one can ever blame you for that, Tess."

She looked up, sorrow cramping her face. "I do." The muscles shifted in her throat. "The truth is both of us put ourselves first before God and our children, Adam ..." His face blurred as her lips began to tremble. "And I truly couldn't live with myself, or even stand, if not for God's grace and strength shoring me up."

The faintest of smiles shadowed his lips. "I know." He reached for her hand, giving it a gentle press. "How well I know. It took cancer for me to finally embrace my own weakness, to fully understand that when coupled with faith, it's the key to God's strength in my life."

A fractured giggle tripped from her lips as she swiped at her face. "Goodness, then I must be a virtual powerhouse."

His smile turned tender. "Good to hear," he said softly, "because I'm counting on it."

"Hey, guys, the movie's almost over, and there's talk of a game of spoons." Jack sauntered into the kitchen with his empty glass and bowl, tossing the kernels in the waste can before putting both in the dishwasher. Avoiding his father's gaze, he smiled at Tess on the way to the back door. "I think I'll spare myself some gouging by wetting a line on the dock instead."

"You don't want to play?" Tess asked, knowing full well movies at a safe distance were one thing, but cozy card games with contact were a different story when it came to his father.

He paused at the door, his smile losing its luster when he glanced Adam's way. "Naw—if I'm gonna wrestle something, it's gonna be a monster striped bass on the new lure I bought." He managed a grin aimed solely at Tess. "But I'll try to get back in time to patch any wounds."

The door slammed behind him, and Adam's weary sigh carried across the kitchen. "I don't blame him, you know. I revered my own father. If he'd done to me what I've done to Jack, I'm not sure I'd be so quick to forgive either."

"He'll come around, Adam. It's just a matter of time."

He smiled, the effect almost sad despite the glint of tease in his eyes. "Yeah, I know, but unfortunately, that's one thing I don't have a lot of, so I'm not looking to waste what I have." He lumbered to his feet, seeming to age in the course of a few minutes. "Tell the kids to start without me, will you? I've got a hankering to do a little fishing of my own, with a bait that will make Jack's lure look like child's play."

Tess cocked her head, giving him a squint of a smile. "Yeah? Well, your son's not a gracious loser when someone out-fishes him. Not sure if reeling in the big one is the best way to win the boy over."

Adam made his way to the door, the sudden square of his shoulders reminding her just where her oldest son had gotten his keen sense of competition. Like Jack, he halted with a hand on the door, flashing that cocky grin he'd always employed in the past before he walked away with the win. "Wanna bet?" He delivered a sly grin that couldn't help but make her smile, right before he gave her a wink. "It is if the 'big one' is him."

CHAPTER FORTY-FIVE

*J*ack sat on the edge of the dock, fishing rod limp in his hands as he stared aimlessly into the water, landing a fish the last thing on his mind. Somewhere down the bank an owl hooted, the melancholy sound in perfect sync with his somber mood. A splash caught his attention twenty feet out, and the silvery shadow of a dolphin flipped in the moonlight, chasing some of his gloom away. It sliced into the deep with a whisper *whoosh* that rippled the waves, soothing his soul like few things could.

Especially tonight, when his father's presence in the house churned his stomach as much as the tugs and barges roiled the Skidaway River. Sure, he wanted to make Lacey and his family happy by clearing the air with his dad, but there was a *lot* of air to clear before any of them could breathe easily. He grunted. Who was he kidding? This was an "Adam" bomb ready to blow, tainting the air—and his life—with deadly radiation. Still, he'd made an attempt—for the people he loved— at getting along with the one he didn't.

All week his comments to his father had been rare but civil, allowing him to hover on the perimeter of his family's closeness without ever getting too close to the man who had damaged his respect beyond repair. And yet, deep down in his gut, he couldn't deny he still hoped and prayed for a miracle. A miracle to restore his father's life ... as well as Jack's respect.

"You should know better than anyone—there is no hope without forgiveness."

Expelling a weary sigh, he kneaded his temple with the pad of his fingers, a silent anger seething beneath the surface of his mind. He scowled at the moon. Of course Lacey was right, but it didn't mean it would be easy.

Or imminent.

Lashing his line out of the water, he recast with a clamp of his jaw, wishing she had come over tonight instead of hanging out with Nicki. He could certainly use some of the calming effect she always provided since his father arrived. Her tender touch. Her soothing words. Her powerful prayer. He sucked in a deep draw of marshy air, expanding his lungs with the peace and joy of knowing Lacey would soon be his, a tranquility in and of itself.

The dock creaked behind him, and his heart jumped, praying that his thoughts had just conjured up the woman he loved. "Lace?"

"No, Bud, it's Dad."

Dad.

Jack's body calcified to the dock like barnacles on the hull of a boat, his next cast as stiff as the rod in his hand. "You looking to fish?" he asked, not bothering to turn around.

"In a manner of speaking." One of the Adirondack chairs squeaked with age as his father apparently settled in. "I was kind of hoping we could talk."

Eyelids slamming shut, Jack stifled a groan. "About what?"

As if he didn't know.

"About the mistake I made," his dad said quietly, the gentle lap of the water against the dock in stark contrast to the pounding of Jack's pulse.

Rod whipping back to arc his line, Jack's mouth skewed. "Which one?"

He waited in strained silence, fully expecting the lengthy pause. What he didn't expect was the humility. "We don't have that long, Son," his father finally said with a hint of humor, "and neither do I."

Realty crashed like whitecaps onto the shore, sinking both his eyelids and his hope. His father was dying. The awful truth strangled his emotions for the hundredth time that week.

"So let's focus on the biggest mistake of my life, shall we?" His tone was matter-of-fact, somehow coming off both humble and strong.

Jack's fury swelled. Because he wasn't strong. He was weak, a pillar of faith with clay feet. Nothing more than a fool who built his house on the sand, toppling everything he loved for a moment of lust. Slamming his rod down beside him, Jack sprang to his feet, fists tight as he glared at his father. "Yeah, let's. Why don't you begin by admitting what a self-serving hypocrite you were, espousing piety and purity while you did whatever you freakin' well pleased?"

His father never even blinked, a strange mix of stark regret and potent love emanating from kind eyes that totally disarmed, quelling Jack with a peace that defied the turmoil in his gut. "You forgot stupid, cocky, shallow, cowardly, and blind, not to mention diabolical for destroying people's faith." A nerve flickered in his father's jaw. "Especially my own son's, which I assure you, is something I will take to my grave as one of my deepest regrets."

Jack's jaw felt like rock as he stared, blinking rapidly to fight the sting of emotion. "Why'd you do it then?" His voice cracked. "Why'd you destroy our family?"

A slow, reedy breath escaped his father's lips that underscored the fatigue Jack saw in his face. "Because

I'm a weak man, Jack, and there's nothing more dangerous than a weak man who thinks he's strong." His chest expanded as his gaze trailed out to the water, voice lagging into a low drone laden with pain. "A charming go-getter from the slums who rose to the top of his class in seminary. You know, the pastor most likely to succeed? And I did."

Head bowed, he kneaded the bridge of his nose, lashes spiked with moisture as he closed his eyes. "Wasn't long before I climbed the ranks, snagging head pastor at Isle of Hope Assembly after your grandpa died and we moved in here with Tess's mom. So there I was—a cocky poor kid on high-brow Bluff Drive with a beautiful wife, a smart son, two brand-new baby girls, and one of the most enviable pulpits on the East Coast. Speaking engagements rolled in as fast as pledges and tithes, and Mercer University even courted me for a professorship at McAffe School of Theology." He sighed, the sound fractured by shame. "It seemed I could do no wrong." His eyes slowly rose to meet Jack's. "Until I did."

He hunched on the edge of his chair, elbows draped over his knees and gaze glued to the weathered boards beneath his feet. "You wouldn't know this because you were mostly away at college, but your mom and I started having problems. Little things at first— arguments over the amount of time I gave to the church for travel, counseling, you name it, basically leaving the burden of home life to her. My answer was for her to quit her job, so the little I was home, I badgered her nonstop, which only deepened the divide. In my mind, I was right and she was wrong, and I made no bones about it."

He looked up again, but this time his stare wandered over the water as if he were locked in the past. "I don't think I fully realized it at the time, but looking back, I can see I was slowly losing your mom's respect as a pastor …" A muscle twitched in his cheek. "And as a man." He chafed the back of head. "And because I could do no wrong in my own mind, it was just easier to blame it all on her, to tell myself she was the problem, not me."

He lowered his head, as if he couldn't bear to face Jack's disdain, a shaky hand obscuring his eyes. "So when Karen approached me about counseling … I didn't see any harm. As a high-profile pastor, I'd had plenty of women tempt me in the past, but I was wise to seduction, at least the sexual kind, so I'd never had any problem saying no. An inflated state of mind that only fed my pride, apparently, setting me up for the fall. I told myself Karen wasn't a seductress, but a good friend and neighbor that I cared about, a troubled woman who needed my help."

He grunted, the sound laced with disgust. "The invincible Pastor O'Bryen, straining at a gnat, but swallowing a camel. Adept at reading 'come-hither' looks in women, but totally unprepared for the seduction of respect and admiration in Karen's eyes— the exact opposite I saw in your mother's. Hero worship in the most sinister form, luring me like a lamb to slaughter …"

His body quivered with a depleting sigh before he rose and walked to the far edge of the dock, hands buried in his pockets while he stared at the river. "Once it happened," he whispered, "I swore it would never happen again, but of course it did, brick-walling my pride more and more just to keep out the guilt. Until everything came crashing down …" He turned toward Jack with a slump of shoulders and a glimmer of pain. "I lost my wife, my family, my friends, and my church. The only way my pride could cope, Jack, was to cling to the lie that Karen and I belonged together, to believe that I was the one to deliver her from her troubled marriage and she from mine." He inhaled sharply, releasing it again in a slow, tenuous breath. "So we left."

"You mean ran away with your tail between your legs." Jack's words hissed in the air.

"Yes," his father said calmly, "I ran away like the coward I was." The aura of peace and calm Jack had sensed before settled over his father's shoulders again like the mantle of moonlight that broke through the clouds. "It took losing everything, Son, including my life, to finally understand what I was too blind to see. *Everything* to liberate me from the same pride that lost Lucifer his soul. And that is—God alone is the Alpha and the Omega. *He* is the beat of my pulse. *He* is the strength in my bones. *He* is my beginning and my end, and there is no hope in anything—" His father took a step forward, an almost ethereal glow of faith in his eyes like nothing Jack had ever seen, "*anything* ... except Him."

Unable to speak, Jack couldn't move a muscle, eyes locked on the father he'd considered shallow and weak. The same man who now radiated a strength and peace that seemed to envelop Jack as well. His father gave an awkward shrug as he approached, hands deep in his pockets and smile sheepish. "Sorry—I get a little carried away at the magnitude of Who He is, Jack, and just how much He loves us. Enough to allow us the freedom to choose. And enough to allow those choices to strip us of everything that stands in the way of our ultimate happiness—Him."

His smile faded into sobriety while his gaze bonded to Jack's. "I don't deserve your forgiveness, Son," he said quietly, "anymore than I deserve God's, but I'm asking for it all the same." He peered up at the sky, as if drawing strength from the shaft of light that split the billow of dark clouds overhead. "I don't deserve it, Son, but you do. I don't want to see you make the mistake I made, choosing pride over God. I learned the hard way

that pride is man's greatest weakness. It felled Lucifer
at the beginning of time and it will do the same for
anyone who relies on his or her own strength rather
than God's. It will rob them of God's blessings and
steal their hope and their future." He studied Jack's face
in a silent plea. *"And* it will rob us of the ability to
forgive if we let it, so I'm asking you, Jack, *please*—"
He paused, grasping Jack's shoulder in a firm hold.
"Don't. For your sake as well as your mother's."

Eons passed, it seemed, as Jack stared, feeling the
battle within to forgive or to turn him away. This was
the man he'd loved and revered most of his life. The
man of God who'd inspired him. The father who'd
taught him to fish and swing a bat. The parent who'd
nurtured and encouraged him. His eyelids lumbered
closed. *And* the hero who'd disappointed him, falling
from his sky like Lucifer, flinging his family into the
abyss.

And yet, here he stood, a man on the precipice of
eternity, giving the greatest gift of all.

The truth.

Moisture stung beneath his lids like a flash flood.
Mind in a freefall, he struggled to breathe against the
anger and bitterness that choked the air from his throat.
And then with a violent heave, he gripped his father as
if he were a lifeline, clinging as fiercely as the summer
his dad had saved his life, a small boy determined to
brave the currents of a flooded river. Then, like now,
he'd been drowning in the deep, struggling with the
swirling emotions that longed to take him down. His
father's hold tightened, and with a shuddering heave,
Jack wept against his neck, clutching so hard, his
fingers dug into his back. Like a thundercloud heavy
with rain, years of grief streamed from his eyes,
washing the pain away to nourish a new beginning.

"I love you, Son," his father rasped, "and if there were anything in the world I could do to make it up to you, I would."

Eyes burning, Jack pulled away, hands braced to his father's arms as he searched his face, finally seeing a glimmer of the hero he'd lost through a haze of healing that he knew—in time—would restore what his bitterness had stolen away. He swallowed hard, dislodging the last of his hurt. "There is," he said, throat thick with emotion. "Will you marry Lacey and me?"

His father stared, his startled look containing a flicker of hope despite the spike of his brows. "I thought Tess said your pastor friend Chase was going to marry you."

"He was," Jack said, "but he'll understand."

Jaw twitching, his father blinked several times before he gave a short nod. "It would be one of the greatest honors of my life, Jack," he said, his words gruff and low. He sucked in a deep breath before grinning outright. "Although given my past, I'm not sure I'm the best one to sanction your marriage." He sifted a trembling hand through his hair, his embarrassment evident in a flustered shrug. "As a man of God, I don't exactly have the best track record, you know."

Flashing a gleam of teeth that matched his dad's, Jack draped an arm over his shoulder. "That's okay, Dad—neither do I."

CHAPTER FORTY-SIX

*B*en was a nervous wreck and it wasn't even his wedding. Hands sweating on the wheel of his Range Rover, he slid a peek at Lacey out of the corner of his eye and held his breath for the umpteenth time. She was a fairy-tale princess in ivory chiffon, sparkling head to toe with glittering beads on her bodice that winked along with those on her heels and upswept hair. His chest expanded with both pride and with love. *My* princess.

And ... soon to be Jack's.

He blinked several times as he turned into the lushly landscaped church parking lot, clearing the emotion from his throat before flashing her a brilliant smile. "You sure you don't want to change your mind? I've gotten used to you being underfoot, so you can always join me in the Dominican Republic or Haiti if you're looking to maintain your tan."

She grinned, eyes twinkling as much as the beads on her dress. "Very tempting, Daddy, but then who would take care of Beau and the house?"

Chuckling, he eased up to the brick-columned church portico to drop her off, grateful the parking lot was mostly empty. "Well, we could always ask Tess," he said casually, his smile dimming at the thought of the woman he was leaving behind. "After all, Beau already likes her better than me since she bribes him with bacon."

Lacey's smile ebbed as she laid a hand on her father's arm. "Have you told her yet?" she asked quietly, her tender concern soothing him somewhat.

He placed his hand over hers, giving it a squeeze. "Not yet, but I will." Glancing at the clock on the dash, he gave her a pat. "You better scoot, kiddo." He leaned to kiss her on the cheek. "I'm so proud of you, sweetheart, and I wish your mom could see you today." Eyes tender, he chucked her chin to ward off more emotion. "You're a beautiful woman, Lacey Carmichael, just like her. Inside and out."

"Oh, Daddy, I can't thank you enough for everything ..." She clutched him so tightly and so long, he worried he just might break down and cry. Pressing a kiss to her fingers, she traced them along his clean-shaven jaw before straightening his tie, obviously less successful than he at stemming the saltwater. "To have you here on my wedding day ..." A lump wobbled in her throat as she splayed a palm to her chest. "And here for the rest of my life, is a dream come true, and I love you more than I can say."

Nodding, he gave a gruff clear of his throat, not about to say one single word lest he cry like a girl.

With a final peck to his cheek, she hopped out of the car and slammed the door, revealing a pair of well-worn Nikes while she unceremoniously hiked her dress to bolt inside. Target bag with shoes and makeup in one hand, she opened the massive mahogany and stained-glass door with the other, butting her hip to keep it ajar while she blew him a kiss. Against his will, the blasted tears bullied their way to his eyes.

My little tomboy playing dress-up for life ...

Swiping his face with the back of his suit sleeve, he parked and made his way into the church vestibule where he'd only been one other time—when he walked

Lacey down the aisle for dress rehearsal the night
before. He grunted and strode down the polished
mahogany hallway with a tug of his cuff-linked sleeves,
wishing he had a dress rehearsal for the rest of his life
so he knew what was going to happen. Sure, Tess had
implied she'd marry him before Adam had arrived, but
the ring he'd bought her still loomed on his bureau like
a blasted block of kryptonite, making him weak every
time he saw it. He bit back a scowl, his mood darkening
despite the stained-glass windows that brightened the
hall. It should be on her finger now instead of in his
blasted bedroom, where in the near future, she should
have been too, sleeping in his bed with a gold band on
her hand.

If not for Adam.

He made his way to the groom's room, heels
pounding the hardwood floor like his heart pounded
against his chest, the scent of lemon oil and flowers
assailing him with thoughts of Tess. He planned on
telling her he was leaving at the end of the reception,
but suddenly he itched to get it over and done so he
could just enjoy the evening. *Yeah, right, I'll have a
blast.* Knowing he wouldn't see her or Lacey for the
next six months. He stifled a groan. Maybe he'd send
her a postcard instead ... His hand hovered over the
brass knob of the groom's door while he blew out a
tired sigh. "Buck up, Carmichael, you gotta tell her
sooner or later—"

The door whirled open and Tess gasped as it
slammed into his shoulder.

All righty then, sooner it is ...

"Oh! I am so sorry ..." She blinked, one hand to her
chest and the other pinched on the knob, cheeks
blooming with color as she stared at him wide-eyed.
"Are you all right?"

"Sure." He gave her a crooked smile while he rubbed the shoulder of his charcoal suit. "Well, my shoulder anyway ..."

Her blush deepened as she chewed at the edge of her smile. "You clean up pretty good, Dr. Doom," she said softly, the stark love in her eyes lifting his mood higher than the brick-and-glass steeple on top of the church.

He devoured her visually, no more able to tame the rove of his gaze down her silky sea-foam dress than he could the thundering of his pulse. Leaning in, he restrained himself with a polite hug, drinking in the scent of lemons while he whispered in her ear. "Have you always been this stunning, Teresa O'Bryen, or am I just crazy in love?" He stepped away, grinning broadly at the whoosh of blood up her neck, all the more noticeable with her blonde hair piled high.

"Well, 'crazy' anyway ..." she teased, mimicking him.

"Hey, Dr. Carmichael, you're a credit to our profession in that suit, sir." Jack grinned in the mirror, adjusting the teal tie of his own dark gray suit as Matt and the other groomsmen looked on.

Peeking past Tess while she held the door, Ben shot a quirk of a smile. "Thanks, Jack, but I'm guessing it's time you call me Ben since we're going to be related. And you boys don't look too shabby either."

"Does that include me, I hope?" Adam called from the other side of the room, his grin unable to deflect a look of fatigue in spite of a spiffy dark suit and green paisley tie.

"Sure." For Jack's and Tess's sake, Ben forced a smile he didn't feel, wishing he'd listened when Tess suggested he reconnect with Adam before today. Maybe it wouldn't be so awkward. His jaw ground tight before he could stop it. Who was he kidding? "Awkward" was the only thing it could be with a best friend who'd slept with his wife. Before Adam could say anything else, Ben tossed a smile Jack's way. "I'll be right back—forgot something," he said, ushering Tess out the door.

"Ben?" Her voice was a whispered squeal as he steered her down the hall and around a corner. "What are you doing?"

He'd had *no* intention of kissing her whatsoever, but his body apparently had a mind of its own. The moment they were alone, he found himself pulling her close, lips nuzzling hers in a tender kiss that quickly erupted into passion. The thought of not seeing her for half a year completely shattered all restraint. "So help me, Tess," he said, nudging her to the wall with an agony that shocked him to the core. "I am so in love with you ..."

Her answering moan melted into his mouth before she gently pushed him away, the same torment in her face that he felt in his own. "Ben, I'm in love with you too—*desperately*—but this is not the time nor place."

He swallowed hard and nodded, stepping away with arms limp at his sides. "I know," he said gruffly. "Forgive me, please. I swear I had no intention of doing this." Venting with a shaky sigh, he angled away, fingers gouging through his neatly groomed hair. "It's just that—"

"I know," she whispered, gently brushing the tips of his hand with her own. Inhaling deeply, she distanced herself several feet while she hugged her arms to her waist. "This is so hard, Ben, but I know it's what I'm supposed to do. Every day that Adam gets a little weaker, it seems as if our family gets stronger." Water welled in her eyes, and it took everything in him not to hold her and comfort her. Her chest expanded before she expelled a tremulous breath. "And though it's bittersweet, I can't tell you just how much joy it gives me to see my family together again. Clean slates, clean hearts ... while all the time the bond between us continues to grow."

A cramp twisted in his gut. "You and Adam aren't ..." He licked his dry lips, throat parched at the very thought. "Falling in love again, are you?"

She glanced up, facial muscles slack with surprise. "Oh, Ben, no," she whispered, her touch gentle on his arm. "I love Adam, I do—as the father of my children and a dear friend. But we've been apart for years now, and both of us have moved on with our lives."

Plunging his hands in his pockets, Ben felt like a lovesick teen, petrified his girlfriend would break up with him. He absently scuffed at the wood grain in the floor. "But it could happen, Tess," he said quietly, his breathing suddenly shallow. "Living in the same house again." His gaze rose to meet hers. "'What God has joined together, let no man separate.'"

A slow smile curved on her beautiful lips as she softly caressed his jaw. "You're adorable, you know that? Quoting Scripture like you are?" Sobriety quickly stole her humor. "And, yes, I believe that. But God also knows our frailties, Ben, as evident from Matthew 19:9—'anyone who divorces, *except* for sexual immorality, commits adultery if they remarry.'"

He cupped his hand over hers on his jaw, turning to softly kiss her palm. "I love you, Tess, with ever fiber of my being, but I want you to know that if you and Adam decide to remarry by the time I get back, I'll quietly step away if that's what you want."

She slowly withdrew her hand, brows in a scrunch. "What do you mean 'by the time you get back'?"

Inhaling deeply, he forged on, determined to get it over with. "I've signed up for an extended medical leave with the International Children's Heart Foundation, so I'll be gone for the next six months." He exhaled slowly. "I leave for Haiti tomorrow."

She gasped, face bleaching white. "You're l-leaving? *T-Tomorrow?*"

"A friend of mine has been after me for a long time now, to 'get off my duff,' as he calls it, and give something back to the world, but I've never felt the time was right until now."

A knot ducked in her throat as she nodded, arms barricaded to her waist once again. "Well, I'd say it's perfect timing, then," she said, her voice more than a bit hoarse. "Will you be taking Beau with you?"

"No, that's the good news in all of this." His smile was half-hearted at best. "I asked Lacey and Jack to house- and dog-sit for me, so you'll have everybody you love close by whenever you need them."

Water glittered in her eyes. "Not all of them," she whispered.

"Aw, Tess ..." Without another thought, he tugged her into his arms, head tucked to hers as he massaged her back with the whole of his hand. "I'll write—I promise."

She sniffled against his chest, tone nasal while she made a poor attempt at humor. "You b-better, 'Dr. Doom' ... or you'll m-meet yours ..."

His heavy sigh breezed against her ear. "I already have," he whispered, pressing a kiss to her hair, vaguely aware of the echo of footfalls down the hall. "I'm leaving, remember?"

"Oh ... sorry ... didn't realize ..." Both whirled to see Adam standing stiff at the corner, his normally pale cheeks actually ruddy for once. "Somebody said the men's room was this way, but I must have taken a wrong turn."

Tess pushed away from Ben so hard, he actually teetered. "Yes, it is, Adam, t-two d-doors d-down," she stuttered, obviously as flustered as her ex-husband. She peeked up at Ben with an apology in her eyes. "Thanks for the shoulder to cry on, Ben—we're going to miss you." She patted his arm in a platonic manner before hurrying past, cheeks burnished with a pink glow.

"Goodness, Lacey will think I fell in. See you in the sanctuary."

Ben watched her flee around the corner and heaved a weighty sigh.

"You're leaving?" Adam's approach was casual, but the concern etched in his face betrayed his usual calm.

"Yeah, tomorrow," Ben said too sharply, "for a six-month medical leave to Haiti." He forced a polite smile, jaw aching from the effort. "Lacey and Jack have agreed to stay at my house and take care of Beau, so they'll be close by, which should make Tess happy."

Tranquil gray eyes studied him with an affection Ben had once enjoyed. "But not you, I suspect."

Ben squinted through narrow eyes. "What's that supposed to mean?"

Head cocked, Adam peered up with the faintest of smiles. "Come on, Ben, you were always the brains between us, but I had the street smarts, remember?" In a relaxed manner that had always been his hallmark, Adam slipped both hands in his pockets, his tranquil expression getting on Ben's last nerve. "You're in love with Tess and she's in love with you."

Heat gorged Ben's face. "Did she tell you that?"

Adam shrugged, his smile crooking off-center. "Didn't have to, Doc. My vision's 20/20 even if my pancreas is riddled with cancer. I saw the way she looked at you the night I arrived, Ben, and you, her. And I swear the poor thing jumps every time she hears Beau bark."

Ben's teeth ground tight behind his mask of indifference. Without another word, he started past him.

Adam stayed him with a hand. "Tess deserves a good man like you, my friend. I'm happy for you both."

Frustration boiling over, Ben spun around, jerking his arm from Adam's hold. "Get this now, O'Bryen, and get it good," he hissed, anger and bitterness almost choking his air, "you never have been nor ever will be 'my friend,' so you can just pack up your phony pastor act and get out of my way."

With a strength that belied his poor health, Adam's grip locked him in place, his look of compassion stopping Ben cold. "I can't," he said quietly, the force of his calm carrying the weight of a command. "I've hurt you and Tess before, Ben—I won't do it again, and that's exactly what will happen if you walk away, bitter and angry."

Ben slung his hand away. "I have a right to be bitter and angry," he ground out, all but spitting the words in Adam's face.

"*Yes*, you *do* have a right." Adam's grasp tightened, the intensity in his tone matching the fire in his eyes. For the very first time, his calm appeared shaken, replaced by an urgency that stilled the breath in Ben's lungs. He stared, swallowing hard. "What I did was inexcusable and unforgivable, but I'm not asking you to forgive for my sake, Ben, I'm asking you to do it for Tess and for you."

Ben couldn't move, his body rooted to the floor while his pulse slowed to a crawl.

With a harsh draw of air, Adam quietly released his hold, his gaze fused to Ben's. "Tess deserves a marriage without baggage, a clean start, and so do you. If you take your anger and bitterness toward me into your relationship, it will deny you the fullness of God's blessing as surely as cancer has denied me my health. Take it from the worst of fools who lost it all— unforgiveness is a cancer you cannot afford. And pride only metastasizes it, spreading the poison throughout the entire body." He expelled a fractured sigh that seemed to siphon all of his energy except for a resilient spark of hope, which now glowed with that same strength and passion that had once drawn Ben to God. "I know you may not believe this, Ben, but I love Tess and you deeply, far more than I was ever capable of before. So I'm asking—from the depth of my soul—will you forgive me?" He slowly extended his hand, his gaze glossy with regret. "Please?"

Emotion thickened in Ben's throat until it all but suffocated him, his body teetering on the precipice of decision like his refusal teetered on the tip of his tongue. This was the "best friend" who had stabbed him in the back. He'd robbed Ben of his friendship, his marriage, and his faith. And now he was robbing him of Tess as well. Ben stared at Adam's hand, trembling the slightest bit while the man who offered it stood steady and strong, his humble gaze unflinching.

Deep down in the recesses of his mind, Ben's memory told him that Adam O'Bryen didn't deserve his forgiveness anymore than he'd deserved Ben's friendship years ago. A stir in his gut told him he had a right to hate him, a right to walk away and never speak to him again.

Who, though He was God, did not demand and cling to His rights as God, but laid aside His mighty power and glory ... and humbled Himself ... to actually die a criminal's death on a cross.

Ben's body went cold as his eyelids sealed shut, a heart-wrenching ache in his conscience unlike anything he'd ever experienced before. Jesus Christ laid down His right to be God to die for others. How could Ben not lay down his right to hold a grudge against Adam?

Conviction pierced like a lance through the breast of his Savior, and exhaling a quivering breath, Ben knew he had to let go. Not just his bitterness toward Adam, but the hate and bitterness that had imprisoned him all of his life.

Toward his father, toward Karen, toward Adam.

And toward himself.

Body shaking, Ben opened his eyes, his gaze alighting on the hand before him, which now trembled like his own as he finally reached to take it. Adam's grip was strong and sure, unleashing a peace that calmed Ben's racing pulse. Glancing up, he caught his breath at the depth of caring he saw in Adam's eyes. Not human love—fallible, conditional, imperfect—but the love of Christ shining like a beacon of hope in a lost world that had no earthly clue Jesus Christ was the God of Hope.

The God of Healing.

The God Whose love never fails.

"I guess this means we're friends again," Adam said with a measured smile. "And I suppose now you'll be wanting that twenty I owe you from Super Bowl 2006?"

Humor twitched at the edges of Ben's mouth as he seared him with a half-lidded gaze. "I suppose it does," he said, adjusting his sleeves with a cool look. "With interest." And turning on his heel, he strode down the hall without another word, a smile hovering all the way.

CHAPTER FORTY-SEVEN

"*I* do believe this is my lucky night, Mrs. O'Bryen," Jack whispered in Lacey's ear on the dance floor, nipping at her earlobe to the strains of *You Belong to Me*. Warm shivers skated her spine straight into her stomach, unleashing a loop-the-loop of heat that thinned the oxygen in her lungs. Sparkles of light winked like stars in the canopy roof of the tent Daddy had rented for his backyard, Lacey's stomach fluttering like the shimmer of canvas in the breeze. Jack molded her close while a galaxy of delicate Japanese lanterns swayed overhead, tissue-paper moons in an alabaster sky. "Yes, ma'am, lucky indeed." The tease in his eyes twinkled more than the ficus trees edging the open-air tent. "I don't believe you've stepped on my toes once tonight."

Her eyelids flickered closed when his mouth strayed to nuzzle the nape of her neck, and her breathing instantly ramped up along with her pulse. "Well, I've had time to practice since prom, Dr. O'Bryen," she said in a ragged voice, arms curling snugly around his waist. She gave him a squeeze, fingers fondling the ties at the back of his pinstripe vest.

"And practice makes perfect." His chuckle teased hot against her skin as the music came to an end, along with a balmy breeze, compliments of an unseasonably warm evening. "And not just for dancing," he whispered, his husky words feathering her ear.

"Lacey! Jack!"

She glanced up while Jack hooked an arm over her shoulder, the sight of her new mother-in-law bounding across the white slate dance floor bringing a smile to her face. "Adam's worn out," Tess said, "so I'm taking him and Davey home, but I wanted to make sure ten o'clock is not too early for brunch and presents tomorrow before you head for the airport."

"No, ten's perfect." Lacey's cheeks warmed as she embraced Tess, a bit embarrassed at the implication that she and Jack might want to sleep in.

"Is Dad okay?" Jack's nervous gaze flicked to where Adam appeared deep in conversation with Ben at their families' table.

"Yes, Jack, he's fine," Tess reassured, cupping her son's face. "He said it's been the best day of his life, so no need to worry."

Jack's jaw tightened as he gripped his mother in a tight hug. "I love you, Mom," he whispered, "and I am so glad we're going to be right next door for the next six months."

"Me too, sweetheart." She curled an arm to Lacey's waist. "Especially since I have a new daughter to dote on." She glanced at her watch. "Oops! Almost ten. Better run, but I'll be back shortly." She paused, gaze flitting from Jack to Lacey and back. "You will still be here when I come back, won't you?"

"Yes, of cour—" Lacey halted, glancing up in surprise when Jack pinched her arm.

"Actually, Mom," he interrupted, "I think Lace and I will head out too." He rubbed the back of his neck while he managed a yawn. "We're both pretty beat."

A gleam lit Tess's eyes as she patted Jack's cheek. "Sure you are. Well, come say goodnight to your dad and the others first, then I'll see you both tomorrow."

She darted off, and Lacey peered up at Jack, head tipped in question. "We're leaving our own reception early?"

A boyish grin eased across his face as he ushered her off the floor, fielding comments and congrats from guests on the way. "Yeah, if that's okay. There's something I want to do."

"Uh-huh … I'll just bet there is," Lacey teased, the wayward bent of Jack's smile warming her cheeks.

After dispensing hugs and goodbyes to their families, they made their way to the head table where Matt and Nicki were just getting up to dance. "Hey, you're not leaving yet, are you?" Matt asked, brows in a pinch. "The DJ's just warming up."

"Sorry, bro, you and Nicki'll have to hold down the fort—Mrs. O'Bryen and I are tired."

"Well, not too, I hope." Nicki bumped Lacey's hip with a sly grin before she crushed her in a hug. "Oh, Lace, I'm so happy for you both."

"Thanks, Nick—for everything. The shower, helping me to set up a wedding in record time, and for being my maid of honor." Lacey fought the onslaught of tears as she squeezed her back. "And for being the best sister I never had."

"Oh, poo! You did the same for me, Lace, and we may not be actual sisters, but we're blood, which is close enough for me."

Jack plucked his jacket off the back of his chair. "Since you're so good at grabbing the limelight, Ball, can you keep everybody busy while Lace and I duck out?"

Matt slapped Jack on the shoulder with a wide grin. "Sure thing, bro." He glanced over his shoulder at the DJ "Just let me get my hands on a mic, and I'll wow 'em with karaoke."

"Oh, sure—it'll be the highlight of the night," Nicki said with an affectionate roll of eyes as Matt strolled over to the mic. She turned to give Lacey a final hug. "Have fun tonight, Lace, and get some sleep." Her smile slid off-center as she turned on her heel and gave Jack a wink over her shoulder. "You too, Jack."

He grinned as he drew Lacey close. "Fun and sleep don't exactly go together, Nick, but then you already know about that. The man snores like a buzz saw."

"Ladies and gentlemen—may I have your attention, please?"

All eyes homed in on Matt, grinning on the dance floor with a microphone in his hands.

Jack tugged Lacey toward the gate. "That's our cue ..."

"The newlyweds think they're going to sneak out without a farewell, but we're not going to let 'em, are we?"

"*Noooooo!*" The intimate crowd in the tent exploded in agreement, surging from their seats armed with bottles of bubbles and packets of rice tied in hobo bags of ribbon and netting.

Jack groaned in her ear. "Ball is so dead ..."

"I think it's sweet," Lacey said, grinning as the group formed an aisle per Matt's instructions, right as the DJ began to play *Forever and Ever, Amen.* The sound of her and Jack's "song" brought a chuckle to her lips, and shaking her head, she blew a kiss in Nicki's direction. Her cousin waved along with Matt, who stood grinning ear-to-ear with his arm draped over his wife's shoulder. Turning back to Jack, Lacey planted a kiss on his cheek. "So just buck up, bucko—we have a gauntlet to run."

Jack heaved a heavy sigh, shooting Matt the evil eye before scooping her close. "Okay, then, Mrs. O'Bryen—ready, set, go!" Heads ducked close, the two of them tore through the bubble and rice tunnel with shrieks and laughter, completely out of breath by the time they reached Jack's car in front of his house.

Washed and waxed by Matt himself, Jack's beloved BMW sported a "Finally Married" sign propped in the back window with bobbers, flip-flops, and tin cans trailing off the bumper.

"Almost home free," he said with a chuckle, slamming Lacey's door and slipping into the driver's side while well-wishers followed behind. The car roared to life with a touch of a button, and Jack left the crowd in a snowstorm of bubbles, grinning at Lacey while he gunned down Bluff Drive. A block away, he eased the car to the curb and parked, silencing the engine with a wayward grin. "Alone at last," he whispered, leaning across the console to tip her mouth to his. His smile melted into a look of awe as he skimmed the curve of her jaw, voice husky with love. "You're everything I've ever wanted, Lacey O'Bryen, and I will spend the rest of my days thanking God and loving you."

"Oh, Jack!" Emotion welled in her eyes as she pressed her hand over his. "Me too."

Leaning close, his lips fondled hers gently, slowly, before he pulled away with a glint in his eye. "But first—there's something we need to do." He snatched the "Finally Married" sign from the back window, then popped the trunk and got out of the car, opening her door before he bent to untie the shoes and cans from the bumper.

"What are we doing?" she asked, brow crinkled as she watched him retrieve a duffle from the trunk where their two small suitcases were also stashed for the evening.

He slammed the trunk and rounded the car. "Payback, Mrs. O'Bryen." The look in his face spelled trouble before his gaze flicked to her lips and back. "And retribution long, long overdue ..." He tossed a pair of flip-flops at her from the duffel. "Here—put these on."

"What in the world ...?" Giggling, Lacey slipped her heels off and wiggled her toes into the flip-flops while Jack tossed her shoes back into the car. Hooking her arm, he marched her back down the street toward his house. Finger to his lips, he tugged her along the lawn to the stone pathway that led to the water. "Wait!" She stopped him when they reached the ramp, and hiking her gown up in one hand, she placed her other back in his before silently tiptoeing the rest of the way to his dock, which was now bathed in the soft light of a harvest moon. "Somehow, Jack O'Bryen," she said while he tossed the duffel on an Adirondack chair, "fishing never entered my mind for my wedding night."

The sparkle in his eyes matched the stars overhead. "Mine either." He reeled her in with an achingly slow kiss that sped up her pulse. "But *this* did." Stepping away, he fixed her with a wicked smile while he slid his jacket off his broad shoulders, causing the lump in her throat to duck several times.

"What are you doing?" Her voice trailed into a squeak when he slowly undid the buttons of his vest.

"A do-over, Lace, to set the record straight."

Her eyes grew when he draped the vest over the chair, and then his shirt, his perfectly chiseled arms and chest making her mouth go dry. Stomach fluttering, her frantic gaze flicked across the street to where the reception was still going strong. "B-But ... but, J-Jack ... there are a hundred of our closest family and friends right across the street—what are you *doing*?"

He grinned and stepped out of his trousers to reveal dark swimming trunks before he sauntered to the edge and dove in. The flash of his cocky smile was embedded in her brain as she stared at the inky water. "Jack!" She rushed forward to peer into the river, hands to her eyes while she muttered under her breath. "So, help me, Brye, when I get my hands on you ..."

He shot up out of the water like a Greek god, water sluicing down sculpted arms. "Come on, Lace, I dare you," he called, moonlight teasing in his eyes, "let's make a memory to keep us warm before we get to the hotel."

"*Jack!*" She stamped her foot on the dock and folded her arms. "In case it's escaped your notice, O'Bryen, I am in a wedding dress here."

His teeth gleamed white in the night. "So ... take it off, Mrs. O'Bryen ... and put on the swimsuit I brought in the duffle."

She tossed a jumpy glance over her shoulder, goose bumps pebbling her skin. "The water's too cold," she whispered, desperate to sway him toward common sense like he'd tried to do so many years ago on that fateful night. "And there's a yard full of people up that hill, for crying out loud."

He tipped his head, grin in place before he swished onto his back, stomach taut as he braced hands to the back of his neck. "Trust me, Mike—you'll never even feel the cold ..."

"Give me one good reason why I should, Jack O'Bryen," she demanded, slamming her hands to her hips.

With the slosh of a kick, he disappeared for several seconds before breaking the surface in a spray of seawater on the far side of the dock. He crossed his arms on the platform, biceps slick in the moonlight. "Because it's a do-over, Lace," he said softly with a crook of his finger. "Come here."

Huffing out a sigh, she marched to the edge of the dock. "Jack, this is craz—*oh!*" She blinked, the sight of his father's dory forming a lump in her throat. Tied to the side of the dock, it bobbed in the water, complete with air mattress and blanket like that night so long ago. Only this time there was also a basket with beach towels, bottled grape juice, and chocolate truffles.

He peered up, gaze intense as he slowly traced a finger on the top of her foot. "So, what do you say, Mrs. O'Bryen?" he whispered softly, "will you sail away with me under the stars?"

A heave caught in her throat as she nodded, unable to thwart the sting of tears in her eyes.

His smile was tender. "I know this sounds silly, Lace, and I can't really explain it, but I just thought since this is the first night of our life together …" He cocked his head, the shadowed look on his face both teasing and tentative. "Maybe we bring it full circle, you know? A way to right the past and celebrate our future …"

His voice trailed off, and she found herself staring in awe at the man with whom she became one in these very waters so long ago, a man who'd come "full circle," just like her. Without another word, she kicked her flip-flops off and glanced up the hill before unzipping her dress with trembling fingers, heart soaring at the look of love in her husband's eyes.

As if sensing her shyness, Jack dove in the water, surfacing at the back of the dory to heist himself up. He clambered over its trolling motor and anchor into the stern just as her dress plopped into a puddle at her feet. With a kiss of a warm sea breeze, she carefully stepped out of it and laid it over the chair, ducking behind the shed with the duffle to change into her suit. She heard a soft gurgle of water from the purr of the trolling motor, and sucking in a deep breath, she tiptoed to the edge of the dock. "Okay, O'Bryen," she whispered loudly, "ready or not, here I come …"

"Oh, I'm ready," he chuckled. His eyes all but devoured her as he slowly lifted her into the boat, her body tingling against his all the way down. "For the rest of my life, Alycia Anne."

"Me, too, Brye," she whispered, her sigh of contentment lost in his mouth with the sweet taste of his kiss.

Forever and ever, amen ...

A NOTE FROM THE AUTHOR

Although this is largely a work of fiction, two things are very real.

First, Isle of Hope, Georgia is not only a real place, it's one of the most beautiful and historical locales in the United States. Located fifteen minutes from Savannah on a peninsula that becomes an island at high tide, Isle of Hope possesses a unique low-country charm along with a rich and vibrant history.

Almost a world apart from the continental U.S., Isle of Hope is a sleepy tidal island with a strong sense of community where picture-perfect cottages reside side-by-side with lush waterside manors and the historic Wormsloe Plantation. Dating back to the early 1700s, Wormsloe Plantation is the oldest of Georgia's tidewater estates and has served as a military stronghold, plantation, country residence, farm, tourist attraction, and historic site.

With a unique Southern charm all its own, Isle of Hope's seaside beauty and low-country allure has drawn movie makers and photographers to its shores for years, boasting such films as the Oscar-winning *Glory*, the original *Cape Fear*, *The Last of the Belles*, *Forrest Gump*, and *The Last Song*. And, with a name like "Isle of Hope," it was—for me—the perfect setting for a story of hope restored.

The second "real" thing about this novel is the estranged relationship between heroine Lacey Carmichael and her father, which purposely mirrors my own relationship with my dad. Although Lacey's circumstances and mine are totally different, the bitterness and unforgiveness is much the same, as is the road to restoration for both Lacey and me, miraculously wrought through the unfailing love of Jesus Christ, truly a God of hope and healing.

I hope you enjoy Jack and Lacey's story and that of the Carmichaels and O'Bryens, two families who had to learn—as I did—that the true "Isle of Hope" resides in the heart of a Savior Whose love never fails.

Hugs,
Julie Lessman

ACKNOWLEDGEMENTS

To Keith Lessman, the man who is the ultimate fulfillment of my greatest hope—babe, I am forever in awe of the joy you bring into my life.

To my dear friend, Bonnie Roof, whose love, prayers, and support are an integral part of this book—thank you for your precious friendship, absolute proof of God doing exceedingly abundantly above all that we ask or think.

To Mildred "Mamaw" Phillips, one of the sweetest and most resilient women I have ever been blessed to know—you bring joy to so many who know and love you, Mamaw, and now to my readers as well.

And finally, to the God of Hope, without Whom I wouldn't survive a single day—I passionately echo the words of Adam O'Bryen from this book: "God alone is the Alpha and the Omega. *He* is the beat of my pulse. *He* is the strength in my bones. *He* is my beginning and my end, and there is no hope in anything—*anything*—except Him."

AUTHOR BIO

Julie Lessman is an award-winning author whose tagline of "Passion With a Purpose" underscores her intense passion for both God and romance. A lover of all things Irish, she enjoys writing close-knit Irish family sagas as well as religious and inspirational romance that evolves into 3-D love stories: the hero, the heroine, and the God that brings them together. Author of The Daughters of Boston, Winds of Change, and Heart of San Francisco series with Revell Publishing, Julie was named American Christian Fiction Writers 2009 Debut Author of the Year and has garnered 17 Romance Writers of America and other awards. Voted #1 Romance Author of the year in *Family Fiction* magazine's 2012 and 2011 Readers Choice Awards, Julie was also named on *Booklist*'s 2010 Top 10 Inspirational Fiction and Borders Best Fiction list. Her last novel, *Surprised by Love*, appeared on *Family Fiction* magazine's list of Top Ten Novels of 2014, and her independent novel *A Light in the Window* is an International Digital Awards winner, a 2013 Readers' Crown Award winner, and a 2013 Book Buyers Best Award winner. Julie has also written a self-help workbook for writers entitled *Romance-ology 101: Writing Romantic Tension for the Sweet and Inspirational Markets.*

You can contact Julie and read excerpts from her books at www.julielessman.com, or through Facebook, Twitter, Google Plus, or Pinterest, as well as sign up for her newsletter. Check out Julie's group blog, The Seekers, *Writers Digest* 2013, 2014, and 2015 "Best 101 Websites for Writers," and Julie's own personal blog, Journal Jots, voted blog of the month in the Readers' Choice poll of *Book Fun Magazine*.

OTHER BOOKS BY
JULIE LESSMAN

Following is a listing of Julie's books, available in both paperback and e-book except for the novellas, which are e-book only. **NOTE:** The links below are Amazon, but most of the following books (except the novellas, *A Light in the Window*, and *Romance-ology 101*) are also available on Barnes & Noble, Berean Christian Stores, Books-a-Million, CBD, Deeper Shopping Christian Bookstore, Family Christian Stores, Indiebound, and Lifeway.

The Daughters of Boston Series
Book 1: *A Passion Most Pure*
Book 2: *A Passion Redeemed*
Book 3: *A Passion Denied*

The Winds of Change Series
Book 1: *A Hope Undaunted*
Book 2: *A Heart Revealed*
Book 3: *A Love Surrendered*

Prequel to The Daughters of Boston and Winds of Change Series
A Light in the Window: An Irish Love Story

The Heart of San Francisco Series
Book 1: *Love at Any Cost*
Book 2: *Dare to Love Again*
Book 3: *Surprised by Love*

Novellas
Hope for the Holidays Historical Collection
With This Kiss Historical Collection

Home for Christmas Historical Christian Romance Collection

Writer's Workbook
Romance-ology 101: Writing Romantic Tension for the Inspirational and Sweet Markets